Centerville

A Novel
By
Kenneth Mattern

Published by Elegant Solutions Software and Publishing Company, LLC.
Copyright © 2022 – 2024
All Rights Reserved

ISBN 979-8985-6640-10

Second printing – revised edition
10 9 8 7 6 5 4 3 2

Dedicated to all the friends of my youth in the village
that is now Centerville

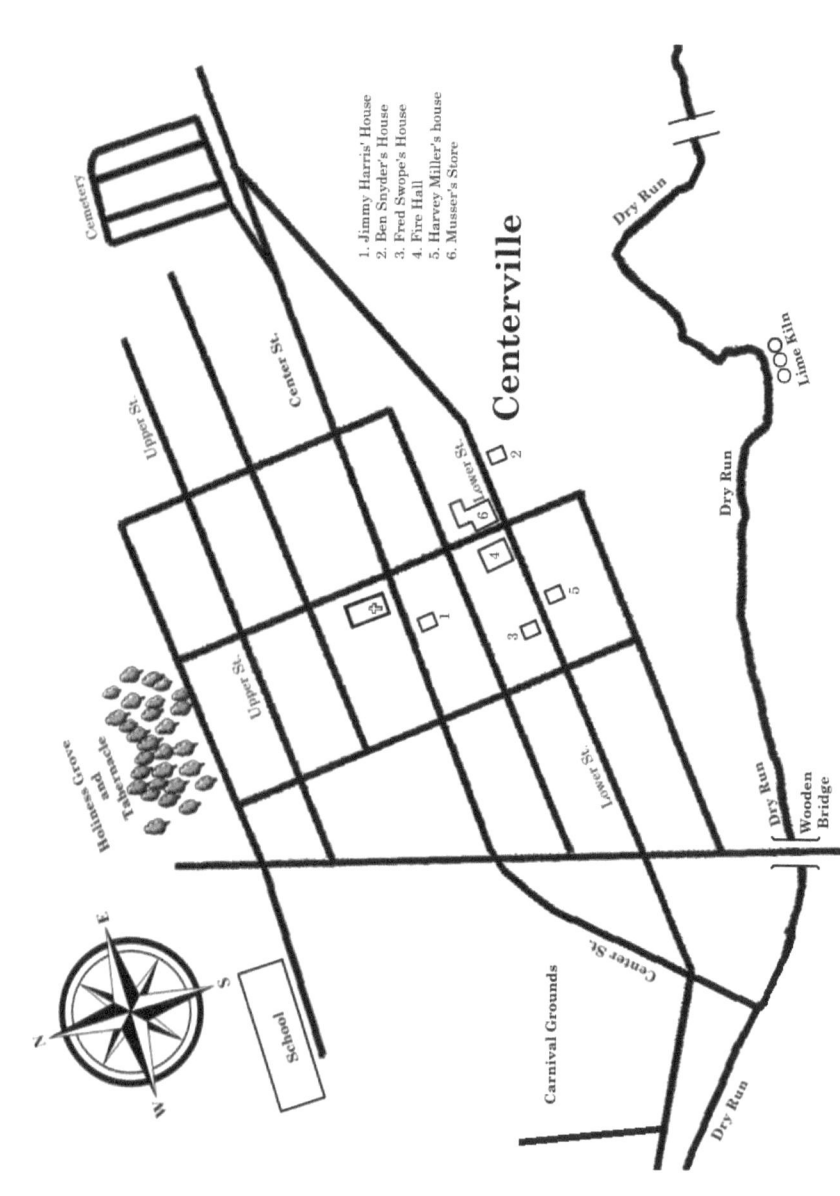

Centerville

1. Jimmy Harris' House
2. Ben Snyder's House
3. Fred Swope's House
4. Fire Hall
5. Harvey Miller's house
6. Musser's Store

Cemetery

Center St.

Upper St.

Upper St.

Lower St.

Lower St.

Center St.

Holiness Grove and Tabernacle

School

Carnival Grounds

Dry Run

Dry Run

Dry Run

Dry Run

Lime Kiln

Wooden Bridge

Centerville

Prologue

Nestled in the hills of central Pennsylvania and platted neatly between two larger towns; Middlebury and Port Mifflin, lays the village of Centerville. Centerville was laid out in 1806 by Colonel George Weirich and the village was originally known as Weirichstadt. The original town had two churches, two stores, a hotel and two schools. The population was about one hundred.

The village had three generally east-west running streets and four north-south streets. They had no official names. The main street through the town was known by the locals as Center Street, thus making the other two streets the Upper and Lower Streets. This main street had been originally laid out to become Market Street. At the eastern end the houses were set back from the street in anticipation of a town square that never materialized. The north-south streets had no names for the first hundred years of the village's existence. Later they were known mostly by the last name of the most prominent family living on the intersection with Center Street. Hence the other streets were called, west to east, Loss, Kuhns, Zimmerman and Bowersox streets. But nobody used those names. There were east-west running alleys between Center Street and the Upper and Lower Streets, as well as one to the south of the Lower Street. The alleys were never paved or named.

Of the two churches the most prominent was the Reformed church which sat on the corner of Center and Kuhns. The Methodist church was located on the Lower Street as were the two stores and the hotel.

For the first hundred forty years of the village's existence, nothing much happened.

Book I
Watermelons

Chapter 1
The Quest (Part 1)

The hot July sun beat down without mercy as Jimmy and Ben lay beneath the cherry tree behind the house. "I wish old Barnyard would come around. I have a dime and one of his little watermelons would be really good right about now."

"Yeah," replied Jimmy. "He hasn't been around in a while. I have fifteen cents so I could get one too." As they lay there talking the clouds flowed overhead while down at the run someone drove over the wooden bridge. You could always tell because the plank deck rumbled like distant thunder whenever a car crossed it. Jimmy and Ben sometimes talked about climbing up the girders and walking across the bridge on the steel frame. Jimmy knew that he could never do it because he was afraid of heights and the twenty feet to the shallow streambed below looked like a mile to him. He knew that if he fell he would die on the rocky streambed. The day would come when Ben would try it and succeed but not this day.

Ben broke the long silence that was growing as long as the grass they lay on. "I have an idea! Why don't we walk out to Barnyard's. His old lady will be there, or maybe Marvin. They keep the melons down in the spring house. We could each buy one and they would be cold. What'yda say?"

"It's a long walk but it'll be worth it. Let's do it! I hafta go inside to get my money. Be right back." Jimmy jumped to his feet and raced into the house. He went up the stairs and to the left to his bedroom. His room was two steps lower than the rest of the rooms on the second floor and so he naturally jumped down into the room. At the rear of the room where the ceiling was low, a half-height door was set into the wall that led into the back attic. It was there where he kept his treasures. No cigar box for him, no, he had a real wooden treasure chest, with straps and hinges on the lid and everything. He actually had almost two dollars in the box. It was hidden behind the remnants of an old brick chimney. The air was hot, dry and had a dusty aroma as he pulled out his box and carefully counted out fifteen cents; three nickels. He returned the box and went back outside to the waiting Ben.

Side by side the boys walked down the sloping back yard to the alley and turned right to walk on the dark cinders. The alley ended just two doors down but ran behind them a long three blocks to what they considered the bad end of town. It was probably the longest alley in the town and extended nearly fifteen hundred feet. By the last block it was so narrow and unpaved that it was almost like a dirt track in the wilderness. To Jimmy it was almost spooky. But at *this* end of the alley they turned left and continued downhill to the Lower Street.

Even in this day, Centerville was tiny. With a population of fewer than three hundred it classified only as a village. There was no police force, just a constable, Oppie Fenster, who lived up the valley road. The village did have a slap happy, totally untrained volunteer fire department. They had regular meetings and drank up their membership dues afterwards. The firetruck hailed from the thirties and was almost as ramshackle as the shed it was parked in. The most the fire department was good for was to freeze Kuhns street in the winter for sled riding. Or to flood the field next to the Reformed Church for ice skating.

There were only four streetlights in the town, simple bulbs protected by metal shades; strung from corner to corner on Center street. Jimmy had been

Centerville

tempted more than once to take a shot with his BB gun at the one closest to his house. Fear of getting caught was the only restraining force that stopped him.

As they crossed Lower Street they passed the Methodist Church on the right and cattycorner was the post office. The post office was in what was once the living room and sun porch of old lady Lauver's house. Jimmy's dad, Eldred Harris, was the postmaster. Most people called him Ned. As far as Jimmy could tell all his dad actually did was read history books and talk to people. It seemed like a pretty good job.

Next to the post office was Martin's Restaurant. It was a real sit down place with three tables, a pinball machine and a jukebox. There was a counter with stools and a candy counter. Downstairs was the whitewashed pool room. There was barely enough room for a pool table but all the "rough" boys could be found there on summer evenings, cigarettes dripping from their mouths as they shot eight ball for ten cents a game. Sometimes they had beer, hidden behind the empty soft drink crates along the back wall.

Directly down the road from the post office was the wooden bridge. At this point the road ceased to be properly paved but instead was tarred every summer and coated with what was called cracker dust; finely crushed stone. After a couple of passes with a steam roller it would pass for macadam.

The bridge itself was not built of wood but, instead was a steel truss bridge. But the deck was laid with thick wooden planks. Every time a car drove across the planks rattled and rumbled. If the car was moving fast enough it could be heard all over town. And it *did* sound like thunder. The steel truss was painted with something resembling tarry silver. There was almost no rust on it. The bridge crossed the Dry Run, which it was mostly. A quarter mile downstream from the bridge half the stream disappeared into the ground. It was believed that there was a large cave into which the stream drained. It was also a good place to fish for sunfish, rock bass and suckers.

On this day, as the boys crossed, they encountered Bart Tuttle, the village, if not the whole township, drunk; as he was today. Snoozing on the bank of the run he looked like a stuffed scarecrow that had been casually thrown from the bridge at the end of the season. They only way the boys knew he was alive were from the voluminous snores emanating from the sleeping rag doll. Jimmy and Ben imagined that they could even smell old Bart as they passed.

"We ought to piss on him, just to see what happens," said Ben.

"He might think its beer and might want more from us. I don't know if I like that," Jimmy laughed. Being smart enough to imagine the consequences, both good and bad, they decided that bad won out and so left the sleeping drunk in his perpetual repose.

"Sure is hot," Jimmy complained. "I shoulda took a drink before we left."

"Yeah," Ben agreed. "But when we get there maybe we can get a drink from the spring. That'll be nice and cold." And so the two boys journeyed on.

As they walked up the shallow hill they began to pass the Patterson home. They were good friends with Richie Patterson. The three boys often waded and fished the Dry Run, played Army in the fields and generally had a good time. But this week Richie was away at the Methodist church camp. Richie always had good stories about church camp and both Jimmy and Ben wished that they could go. But Jimmy went to the Reformed Church and Ben didn't go anywhere, so not being among the saved, they couldn't go with Richie.

Kicking a stone to the side of the road Ben said, "Maybe later we can go down to the lime kill and dig around. Maybe we'll find something."

Jimmy thought that was an excellent idea. "Yeah, and maybe we can take a swim too." It wouldn't really be a swim because the water was only waist deep, but it was wet and cool, just the thing on a hot July day.

The boys ruminated on this topic for the next couple of minutes until a groundhog ran across the road in front of them. Immediately they were off, running after it as though they could actually catch it. Like a dog catching a car, had they actually been able to capture the beast they wouldn't have known what to do with it. They scrambled up the bank and soon discovered the groundhog's burrow high on the bank next to the road. As they sat there waiting to see if it would stick its nose out they could hear the grasshoppers singing in the field behind them. They watched them flit from stalk to stalk in the bronzed air, not having a care in the world. Then in a flash a red winged black bird swooped down from nowhere and caught a grasshopper in mid-flight. It then flew up to the singing telephone line to eat its prize.

"That was neat!" opined Ben. Jimmy agreed with a nod of his head. They sat there for a few moments scuffing the shale bank with their shoe heels before finally scrambling back down to the road to resume their trek in search of watermelon. By now they both sported a fine sheen of sweat and their tee shirts were darkening. They still had a good half mile to go but to young boys in the heat of summer it seemed like miles.

They were heading to Bernard Miller's farm, though all the kids called him Barnyard. He sold fresh milk to families in the neighborhood and butchered hogs in the fall which he also sold locally. His main claim to fame, at least for the young folks, was his watermelons and huge pumpkins at Halloween. Bernard sold produce from the back of his pickup from the time strawberries were ripe in June through October when he picked potatoes. His truck was always filled with fresh produce in the summer months and he made a good living from it.

String beans, limas, sweet corn, onions, potatoes, watermelons, cantaloupe, straw-berries in season and much more, his pickup was like a cornucopia on wheels. In Centerville he would stop on every block and sometimes had to go back to the farm to reload his truck; two or three times on a good day. In the late fall and winter, he would sell smoked hams and was especially busy around Christmas. Once in a while he would sell live chickens but did that only when he had a surplus because many families in the village kept chickens themselves, for the eggs and the fresh meat.

His front yard, and all around the house, was a menagerie of chickens, Guinea fowl, ducks and a couple of geese. The dogs roamed the farm and the cows lined the fence in the afternoon waiting to be let back into the barn. The rest of the time they lazed in the field or slept in the shade down by the stream. At one time the barn was red but now was the color of faded red going to grey barn wood. Miller hired older youth to pick produce when the fields ripened.

Cats dozed on the porch rails and in the shade of the lilac bushes in the yard, once in a while venturing out on a mousing trip to the hay mow on the upper floor of the bank barn. There must have been at least twenty or thirty of them. Miller and his family tripped over them twice a day when they milked the cows. Cats were considered an asset because they kept the mouse and rat populations to a low and manageable level.

Centerville

The heat from the road soaked into their feet as they continued on their journey. The air was still, not even a whiff of a breeze. Behind them they heard the rumble of a car crossing the bridge. They hustled to the left side of the road so they would be as far from the car as possible. It sounded like it was coming fast. Ben looked over his shoulder and saw the grey Ford coup barreling down on them.

"Holy jeezum crow!" he shouted as the car roared past them. "That's Opp Fenster! What's he doing out here today?" The car careened around a curve and disappeared in a cloud of dust as its rear tires skidded off the road. "The way he's driving you'd think that somebody was dead."

"Yeah, I wonder where he's going," Jimmy replied. The boys discussed this excitement as they continued on their quest. Moments later, however, a blue and grey state police car sped past them and not long after that a sheriff's car.

"Must be something big!" shouted Ben. "Hope it isn't too far away. I wanna see what's going on." Ben could barely contain his excitement. He hadn't seen this much action since the firemen's parade last year. They had a real elephant in the parade. It was from a circus that was over at Middlebury. When the firemen started the siren on the ancient firetruck which was right behind the elephant it went crazy and nearly stampeded the small crowd. Of course the guys from the local National Guard unit, who were in the parade, had to chase the elephant with their tank and jeep. Jimmy thought they were going to shoot the beast but thankfully they didn't have any ammunition for the tank's big gun. The tusker ended up down in the field behind town near the lime kiln. There the local "mad" bull took it upon itself to protect its turf and attack the elephant. Of course the bull lost. The elephant charged back and butted the bull into the run. The bull was a lot tamer after that. It must have taken a hundred people to catch the elephant and calm it down. Finally it was led to a circus truck and hauled back to Middlebury. But boy it was fun!

Both boys began running. As they passed through the curve they could see all three cars parked beside the road next to Bruce Walter's house. It was only about three hundred yards away. The boys broke into double time as they raced to get to the scene.

Panting and out of breath Jimmy beat Ben by only a few feet. They skidded to a stop behind the state police car and watched to see what was going on. But they couldn't see very much and could hear even less. Nobody was around but they could faintly hear voices coming from behind the house. They crept around the cars and skirted the house, staying as close to it as they could. Instinctively they knew they didn't want to be seen because they would be chased away.

At the back of the house the crouched next to the sloping cellar doors. There they could see Oppie, the statey and the deputy. They were talking to Bruce Walter himself. Bruce seemed pretty excited and they were trying to calm him down.

"I can't hear," whispered Jimmy, "let's get closer. We can get behind the wood pile." The boys kept as low as possible and made their way to the large wood pile which was only a few feet from the men.

"I knew something wasn't right but I didn't know what it was. The water was smelling kind of funny and I thought that maybe a groundhog fell in and drownded." Bruce waved his hands as he spoke. It was a habit that he had for as long as anyone could remember. Much of the time he looked like he was conducting some kind of unseen orchestra while he talked.

Centerville

"So today I pulled off the cover and shown a light down and that's what I saw!"

The state policeman pointed his flashlight down into the well and said, "Yep, it's a body all right. Been there a while though." He turned to the deputy, "You had better call an ambulance from Middlebury. We're gonna need it. Call the coroner too."

"Think we ought to fish it out?" asked Oppie. "You got a hook there, Bruce?"

Bruce said that he did over in the shed that he called a barn but really wasn't a barn at all. It wasn't much more than an old rickety tractor shed built into the side of the hill, facing west, not south. It was missing a good quarter of its wood siding and the tin roof was more absent than not.

While Bruce hurried to the shed the deputy called for the ambulance and coroner on his radio. The statey and Oppie crouched over the well, looking down into it with their flashlights. The boys could hear them talking but their voices were so low they couldn't understand anything they were saying. Just about then Rufus Ott pulled up in his dilapidated old Chevy truck. It had to be Rufus. Nothing happened without him showing up at the scene. He seemed to have a special facility for sniffing out trouble or interesting events anywhere in the area. It was a known fact. So much so that Jimmy's dad said that it was Rufus' big nose that could smell trouble ten miles away.

Indeed it was Rufus who was first on the scene when the two Bateman kids fell through the ice when they were sledding on the creek the winter before last. And it was Rufus who pulled little Paul out of the frigid water and carried his dead limp body to the shore. In all Rufus was a good man. He just knew how and where to

13

find trouble spots. And here he was so quickly making himself a part of the process, uninvited though he was.

By then Bruce Walter had retrieved a hay hook with a rope. The state policeman supervised while Rufus and Bruce tried to hook the body down in the well. The boys could hear the cop directing the hook, "more to the left...no left! Now down, you hit it. Over... over now down and back, OK come up gently. Be careful...careful, don't jerk it. You got it. Now pull it up carefully. We don't want it to tear off. None of us wants to have to climb down there if we don't have to."

Ben and then Jimmy crouched their way as close to the well as they dared. The men totally ignored them to the point they could have looked into the well and not have been seen.

"Almost there. Only about five feet to go. Keep pulling it straight up." The state policeman directed. "Almost there."

Wide eyed the boys watched as Rufus and Bruce pulled the body up and over the stone lip of the well and dropped it to the ground.

"Looks like a kid!" exclaimed Bruce.

"It *is* a kid!" exclaimed Oppie. "It's that Marks boy that disappeared last month."

Jimmy and Ben saw the blue shirted body at the same time and both recognized the shirt and the high top sneakers.

"It's Patsy!" they both shouted at once. At that the men turned to see the boys for the first time.

"What are you doing here!" exclaimed Oppie as he stepped towards them. Then, as if in a moment of divine revelation, he turned back to the body and said, "Well I'll be goddamned. Look at his pants."

Patsy Marks had disappeared the last day of school back at the end of May. There had been a huge manhunt for him. Police dogs and search parties combed the village, woods and fields for miles around looking for Patsy. Nothing had come of it. The search had petered out to nothing after a couple of weeks. It was assumed that Patsy had run away as there was no trace of him.

At Oppie's exclamation the state policeman turned to Bruce Walter and said, "What do you know about this Mr. Walter?"

Bruce began stammering and then conducting as he said, "Nuh nuh nothing! All I know is that the water started getting funny. God! I've been drinking that! My family has been drinking that." He turned away and began to retch.

Patsy's body lay there, wet and glimmering in the sun. Its long bath in Bruce's well hadn't done it any favors. Like Oppie, Jimmy noted that Patsy's pants were on backwards.

Later the coroner reported that Patsy had drowned.

Chapter 2
Fred and Patsy

Fred loved to fish and suckers liked the cold springtime water. Fred would take anyone he could get to go fishing with him. He was somewhat of a bully to the smaller boys but for the bigger boys, at the same time, he could be fun. He wasn't too much into baseball but fishing, hunting or trapping was something he loved. There was a pool table in the upstairs of his mom's barn and the neighborhood boys often gathered there to shoot pool. It was the table that gave him his popularity, such as it was.

Even though he had been held back in the second grade, Fred was only now just out of the sixth grade. Older than his classmates he was also large for his age. He had his own .22 rifle. He ran a trap line along the Dry Run in the winter and got his fair share of muskrats. The banks along the lime kiln were a good spot for trapping. Another good spot was the log jam above the old farm bridge about one hundred yards downstream.

One of Fred's favorite tricks was to take an unsuspecting kid down through the field to the run and trick them into touching the electric fence. He loved to see them get shocked and maybe even cry. Back in May he and Jimmy had gone down to the field to shoot bow and arrow. Fred had a homemade bow carved from a fresh green sapling while Jimmy had an official store bought Roy Rogers bow. As they were walking along the fence Fred said, "Touch that with your bow."

Jimmy obligingly did so. He rubbed his dry wooden bow along the fence wire and nothing happened. He looked questioningly at Fred, "So?"

"That's funny…" said Fred as he touched his green bow to the fence. There was a bright snapping sound. The green wood immediately conducted the electric charge to Fred's hand and he nearly threw the bow to the ground. He shouted and then heavily sat on the ground and cried.

"Don't you never say nothing about this." He warned Jimmy.

Inwardly grinning, Jimmy promised he wouldn't and somehow the day continued without further incident.

Things were not so lucky for Patsy.

It began innocently enough back just before Memorial Day. It was the last day of school and a half day at that. Patsy, a newly minted sixth grader, lived down the bridge road, next to Bruce Walter's place. He liked to play along the stream that ran behind his home and emptied into the Dry run. He would build little dams there and try to catch and corral crayfish in the miniature lakes he had made.

Early that afternoon, after school had ended, Patsy was playing by the stream. It was a very warm and clear day. A slight breeze flitted though the trees growing over the stream behind his house. Today he was building small rafts and floating them in the water. He was building a canal when he heard thrashing along the stream back towards the village. At first he thought it might be a neighboring dog, there were plenty of them, or even a deer. But to his surprise it was Fred who came barreling through the brush and up to Patsy.

Without a word Fred squatted next to Patsy and began watching what the smaller boy was doing. He didn't attempt to help, just silently watched.

Out of nowhere he asked Patsy, "Do you know what a cog is?"

Patsy, almost in a questioning voice answered yes. He didn't know what Fred was getting at. But he was familiar with his father's machine shop and knew that a cog was just another word for a gearwheel. Patsy didn't know why Fred was asking him about cogs or anything related to gears.

"I'll show you my cog if you'll show me yours."

Patsy suddenly realized that Fred wasn't talking about anything even remotely related to gears, or even machines. In fact Patsy began to get scared. What Fred was suggesting sounded dirty. And if his mother found out she would spank Patsy. For him the world suddenly became still and silent. Nothing seemed to move. Even the trickle of the stream seemed to stop.

Patsy froze while Fred rose and began to unzip his pants. In stone-like fascination Patsy watched as Fred slowly pulled down his pants and stepped out of them. Then he did the same with his undershorts and soon both were on the ground. Patsy could see a dark fuzz of hair growing above Fred's penis. It was large and swollen. It looked like a worm, a big worm, with one eye that was closed.

"Your turn."

Patsy, frozen in fear, stammered.

"You seen mine, now I want to see yours. I'll bet it's tiny and you don't have any hair but I want to see it. Now!" Despite being half naked Fred was a towering and terrifying figure to the smaller Patsy.

As if mesmerized by a snake Patsy slowly stood and fumbled with the button of his fly. It seemed to take forever but his shaking hands finally opened the button and unzipped.

"I can't." He whimpered.

Fred made a fist, "Do it!" he said in a low and menacing voice. "Do it or else!"

Patsy fumbled with his pants and somehow found them around his ankles. He stepped out of them.

"Now the rest. Do it."

Centerville

Zombie like Patsy pushed his underpants down slowly exposing his privates. His shriveled penis a tiny speck between his legs.

Fred stepped forward and cupped Patsy's balls in his hand and squeezed. Not hard but a squeeze none the less. Then he grabbed Patsy's hand and pulled it to his own penis and rubbed it back and forth. Patsy was unable to move, terror and adrenalin flooding his veins. He felt cold, tiny and helpless.

"You like it, don't you. Admit that you like touching my cog. You like it so much that you want to suck it. Get on your knees and suck it! You'll love it. Suck it, I say!"

"No," whimpered Patsy as Fred put his hands on Patsy's head and pushed him to the ground.

But Fred was relentless. Soon Patsy was on his knees, his face pushed against Fred's crotch.

"Open your mouth. Put it in. Suck it!" he shouted. "Suck it." And he forced himself into Patsy's mouth.

In pure abject terror Patsy began to flail and beat at Fred's legs as Fred pushed Patsy's head against himself. Fred felt himself fill Patsy's mouth and in a moment he ejaculated as Patsy coughed and choked.

"I told you you'd like it," Fred growled. Almost satisfied, he knew that there was more that had to be done, more that he wanted to do. He pushed Patsy away and to the ground. He stood menacingly over the smaller boy, fists clenched at his side.

Patsy lay there curled in a fetal ball. Wiping his mouth and still choking Patsy whispered, "Don't hurt me. I won't tell anyone. Nobody has to know. I won't say a thing. Please, please don't hurt me."

"I won't hurt you," Fred growled. 'No, I'll kill you,' he thought. He felt so full of rage so blinded by it that he wanted to hurt Patsy, to kill. He didn't understand why but the rage he felt was overpowering, more than he ever had strangling a cat or shooting a dog. Looking around he spotted a large enough rock to do the deed. He bent and pulled up his pants. "Get dressed," he said.

As Patsy stood and fumbled with his underwear, which had pulled completely off when Fred forced him down to his knees. Fred stepped behind Patsy, grabbed the rock and swung it with all his might into Patsy's head.

Patsy dropped like a stone; blood ran from his head, bright and red in the dappled sunlight. A Jay cursed overhead and flew over Patsy's half naked body.

Suddenly in both a moment of unfathomable satisfaction and near panic Fred realized what he had done and what he had to do. He threw the rock into the stream. Struggling he tried to pull Patsy's underpants onto his limp and unhelpful legs. He finally got them up around his waist. Next the pants. He pulled them on with nervous and shaking hands. Fear began to grip him but still a part of his mind remained calm, thinking and planning. He never realized, even as he was zipping them closed that Patsy's pants were on backwards.

Even though only just past the sixth grade, Fred knew the area better than anybody. He knew all the streams and caves within a couple of square miles. Being fatherless and with a mother in a wheelchair he did what he wanted when he wanted to do it. He was rarely at home but spent his time wandering the fields, hills and woods. He even knew that Bruce Walter had a nice deep well and it was only a couple of hundred feet away.

He never knew that dragging a body, even one as small as Patsy's, could be so difficult. Patsy's arms seemed to catch on every branch, shrub or bush along the way. Not only that but it made a path along the stream that Fred knew he would have to erase. Still he worked on, pulling Patsy's body through everything to get to Bruce's well.

Finally he let go of the feet and crept up Walter's back yard, reconnoitering the area to ensure that he would not be seen. There was a large and long woodpile running parallel to the house and it was not far from the well. Fred pulled the body behind the wood pile and as close to the well as he could get without being seen. It was still mid-afternoon and nobody should be home. But he was careful none the less. He crawled to the well and pushed and tugged at the cover until it was moved far enough to drop the body into the well.

Crawling back he grabbed Patsy's limp body under the arms and pulled it to the side of the well. Struggling to lift it he managed to push the body over the stone parapet. He heard it splash into the water a moment later. Getting the cover back into place was just as hard and by the time he finished he was winded.

Going back to the scene he got a dead tree branch and, just as he had seen in a recent episode of the Lone Ranger, he used it like a broom to erase as best he could the path he had made dragging the body along the stream bank.

Ants were already crowding around the puddle of blood on the ground. Fred hastily kicked loose earth over the drying puddle and then fled back to his home.

That night it rained, erasing all evidence of his deed.

Centerville

Chapter 3
The Quest (Part 2)

The state policeman turned to Jimmy and Ben. "What are you doing here? You shouldn't be here, seeing this."

"He's our friend, or was!" Ben shouted.

Just then the ambulance pulled up, along with a couple of other cars; people curious to know what was going. They gathered like that wherever bad things happened. It was just human nature.

The coroner was in the ambulance. He got out with his doctor's bag and walked over to the body. He bent over it and began his examination. "Body's not as bad as I expected. Water must be cold."

Jimmy watched as the coroner turned Patsy's head from side to side and he saw water run from Patsy's mouth as the coroner rolled him over on his side.

"Get out of here before I take you both in," the statey threatened. Jimmy was pretty certain that they couldn't be taken in but he and Ben knew when they were beaten. Besides the shock of seeing Patsy was enough to make them want to get away from there. They slowly walked back to the road.

"Do you still want to get that watermelon?"

"We've come this far, we might as well. Besides I'm hot and really thirsty."

The boys walked in silence for a while. Then Jimmy spoke, "Did you see that?

"See what?"

"Patsy's pants were on backwards. Why were they backwards? He wasn't that dumb. Something happened to him."

"What happened to him? He fell down the well and he drowned. What else could it be?"

Centerville

"I don't know but I do know that it's more than that. Patsy didn't have his pants on backwards at school. Why would he have them on that way now? I mean, how often do *you* put *your* pants on backwards?" Ben shrugged, Jimmy had a point there. They were both a bit numb by what they had just witnessed. It wasn't like the murder and suicide that happened last year. Jimmy had actually seen those bodies too, but they looked like they were asleep. Not like Patsy who was obviously dead.

Back on the road, they could feel the heat of the baked pavement being sucked through the rubber of their sneakers and against the soles of their feet. Perspiration was beginning to flow more freely now in the breathless sun drenched afternoon. Jimmy began to wonder whether the trip to Barnyard's farm was worth it. What with seeing Patsy's dead body and all. He didn't have the appetite he had half an hour earlier. Still the feeling to see this walk through was more compelling than he understood.

Ben, catching up to Jimmy's quicker thought process finally realized that there was a definite problem with Patsy's backwards pants.

"So what do you mean? Don't you think he fell into the well?"

"Why would he even pull the well cover open? It's heavy. Could he even move it and if he did, why? There's no way that Patsy would do something like that. And why would he climb into the well? None of it sounds right. I'm no Sherlock Holmes but it just isn't right. There is something that we don't know."

Ben knew that there was a lot they didn't know but he wasn't as sharp as Jimmy and didn't know how to articulate what was going through *his* mind. He knew that Jimmy was the kind of person who would look for deep and strange things while he, Ben, on the other hand would look for the more logical reason something happened. Granted, Jimmy was usually right, but not always.

"So do we have a mystery to solve, or what?" Ben asked.

After a long pause Jimmy responded, "I don't know. I guess that seeing Patsy's pants like that is just so wrong I don't know where to begin."

The horror of seeing Patsy was already receding as the boys walked on, each deep in his own thoughts about what they had just witnessed. Youth has a funny way of not being able to keep anything, even something like this, uppermost for long. Time is too short in young life to contemplate the nightmares and fears we all encounter, especially in daylight on hot July afternoons when the world is filled with promise and adventure. These things do not pass but the bubble of the ever present now pulls the young like gravity pulls us all to earth. And so it was with Jimmy and Ben. Neither forgetting what they had just witnessed, nor blithely letting it pass but now more intent on the cold watermelon that the hot afternoon and long walk promised.

In this rural area death, like the balance of their hardscrabble life, was just a part of the fabric. Both boys had already seen their fair share of life and death, admittedly it was the butchering of hogs in the fall and deer and other game in hunting season. But both families kept chickens and beheaded them regularly. Ben had buried his dog at the foot of the garden last winter; digging the grave in the half frozen earth. Life was like that.

And just then flashing past them like red lightening went Trudy Park in her brand new Cadillac convertible. She waved as she flew down the road, her hot

Centerville

breeze blowing against the boys, pushing them ever so gently towards the side of the road.

"Do you know she paid almost five thousand dollars for that car?" Ben said in awe. "She must be really rich to pay that much for a car!"

"That's because her old man makes so much money over at Swinton," replied Jimmy. Everyone knew that Trudy's husband, Paul, made a lot of money running the Swinton bank. "Have you seen their house? It's huge, they even have a swimming pool. Can you imagine that? They don't have to go to the creek to swim! Must be nice. My dad and mom took me over there a couple of weeks ago for a party and I got to swim in the pool. It was really keen!" Jimmy had some small understanding that because his father, Eldred, was the postmaster that he was a part of the "upper crust society" of the village. It still had little meaning for him now, though. He was still just a kid growing up in a small place with little future.

As the car passed into the distance Ben looked to his right and saw another groundhog. "Look there," he said. "There's another one and it's a good size too. My mom could make a nice meal from that."

Ben, like many of his friends from the village ate whatever could be gotten off the land and groundhog was no exception. Fancier society might look down on eating something like this but Ben, and Jimmy as well, knew that this was something good to eat, and in the summer months was a staple as well. Neither understood that they, as was the rest of the town, were too poor to have fresh meat from the store on a regular basis. They thought that everyone ate groundhog in the summer, along with fish caught in the river nearby. They didn't understand that most people didn't live on rabbit, squirrel, grouse and pheasant in the fall and winter. Venison was something special if their fathers were lucky during deer season. And, of course, a number of families kept pigs in sties or pens behind their houses. Jimmy's neighbor kept pigs and his dad helped butcher every fall for a ham or some bacon.

In fact last week Ben's dad had called him from play and said, "Come on. Let's go get supper."

It was early afternoon and Ben had been playing with his younger brother in the back yard. They had been hitting whiffle balls, pretending that they were the Philadelphia Phillies and the St. Louis Cardinals. Whoever was pitching was the one who called the play by play action. Ben, as the pitcher, was calling the plays pretending to be the Phillie's radio announcer Gene Kelly; not the dancer as Ben well knew.

Ben, being the older, always got to be the Phillies while his brother Tom had the opportunity to pick any team that he wished, no matter the league. So some days it would be the Pirates and other days it might be the Orioles. But today it was the Cards.

Bob Miller was pitching for the Phillies on this day.

"It's the top of the fourth and Red Schoendienst is on deck and right now Stan Musial is oh and two. And here's the wind up and the pitch," called Ben in his radio voice. He studied the teams, the leagues and the baseball cards. He listened to games at night in bed when he was supposed to be sleeping and knew the statistics for every player and team. When it came to baseball he was a walking encyclopedia. He paused and threw the whiffle ball hoping for a curve. But the ball went right over the plate and Tom, with a mighty swing, hit the ball over Ben's head which happened to be the single marker.

Every stadium in Centerville was different. But they all followed the same rules, except for Darren's barn. Before domes existed Darren had the only indoor stadium in existence. There was no hay mow anymore, so the roof was a good thirty feet from the dirt floor. Whenever it rained they played in his barn. The grand prize in his stadium that nobody else had was the twenty run homer. To achieve that the whiffle ball had to be hit through the fur de lies cut into the front wall a good twenty feet above the double wide door that led to the street. Needless to say nobody ever made one.

In Ben and Tom's park the pitcher and wash line poles demarked the hits and runs. The small barn behind home plate served as the backstop. A ball hit over the pitcher resulted in a single. Over the first wash line pole, about twenty feet from home plate was a double, the second pole a triple and the hitting fence was a home run. Over the fence, regardless of men on base, was a grand slam but no whiffle ball could possibly be hit the seventy five feet for that feat!

As Musial ran to first Ben's dad called, "Come on. Let's go get supper." So by mutual agreement the game was called on account of rain, which was how most games were called if not completed, even those played in the rain.

Tom lost.

Ben dashed off to meet his dad on the Lower Street in front of the house. He hopped into the front seat of the car and off they went. It was early afternoon. His dad, also named Ben, worked as a delivery man and so usually was home by noon. They sped down the street and out into the "countryside" a short mile from town.

"Now watch Ben. Look up along the road at the hill. If you see a pile of fresh dirt you know that there is a groundhog burrow. We'll stop and see if we can get one."

Not long after that Ben spied a mound and pointed it out to his dad. Of course his dad already knew it was there. He stopped the car and said, "Don't slam the door. Close it as quiet as you can."

Then he pulled his single shot .22 rifle from the back seat and put a bullet into the chamber. Ben got from the car and with exaggeration and closed the front door. Ben senior leaned across the roof of the car and whistled through his teeth. The whistle was loud and shrill. In a moment a groundhog rose on his hind feet to see what the noise was all about. Ben's dad pulled the trigger and the groundhog disappeared.

"Run up and get him."

Ben tore up over the shallow bank and through the field of alfalfa to where he had last seen the groundhog. And there it lay. He picked it up by rear foot and carried it back to the car. Halfway he had to switch hands because it was heavy.

When they got home his dad skinned and cleaned the groundhog and put it in water and salt. Later his mom would cut it up and drag it through flour and fry it. Ben thought it was the best food ever. He never suspected that it was not actually a delicacy. He simply thought that everyone ate like that.

Back on the road Ben and Jimmy continued walking. The groundhog ambled along with them for a few feet and then turned downhill towards the stream. Looking for a cool place above ground, it would lay by a pool and doze the afternoon. At its size it had few natural predators and it was even too large for eating. The big old ones got tough, so this groundhog would probably die of old age if it wasn't hit by a car.

By now the boys had rounded the last curve and were only a few hundred feet from Bernard Millers farm and the promise of cool watermelon. Of course the boys wouldn't eat them until they got back to Jimmy's house. By then they might not be as cool but would still be good.

Centerville

As they passed a honey locust tree Jimmy jumped to slap at the seed pods hanging from the branches. Like most kids he called the trees bean trees. But he knew that the beans were not edible. Still, when he was younger, the pods served very well as make believe string beans or peas when they played house. But he was far too old for that now. Ben didn't know what the trees were and didn't care.

"Wow! Do you hear that?" Jimmy asked. In the far distance they suddenly heard a train whistle. The nearest train tracks ran through Port Mifflin, a good five miles away. Yet they could hear it as clear as a bell. "The air has to be just right for sound to travel that far."

Jimmy could hear train whistles in the quiet summer night when he lay in bed. Watching heat lightening over the mountain through his open window he would wonder where the trains were going and about the people in them.

"That sounds like a steam engine," Jimmy said. "A diesel horn sounds different." There weren't too many steam locomotives left but once in a while one would come thundering through Port Mifflin.

A few clouds drifted overhead as the boys neared their destination.

"What if they're out?" asked Ben.

"What do you mean?"

"What if they don't have any watermelons and we walked all the way out here for nothing. We still have to go back empty handed."

"You could buy a tomato," Jimmy laughed. "They'll have some of those. Or a cantaloupe." He knew that Ben hated cantaloupe.

"Ugh! I'd rather starve."

By then they were nearing the front yard. A large dog rushed out to greet them. In another time or place the boys might have been frightened by this beast but they knew almost all of the dogs in the area and this one was a friend to everybody. The dog came to them and licked their hands and whuffled as they patted his head. The dog walked between the boys as though escorting them to the Miller house.

They passed the house, which was sided with asphalt shingles made to look like bricks, and turned left up the dirt driveway next to it. They climbed the steps to the side porch and knocked on the screen door. The kitchen door was open to let the breeze, if any, through to help cool the house. All the blinds were drawn and the inside of the house was dark. All the better in hot weather like this.

The porch was carpeted by cats, all dozing in the shade.

In a moment Mrs. Miller came to the screen door. "What can I do for your boys? How's your mother, Jimmy?"

"She's fine, Mrs. Miller. We want to know if you have any little watermelons in your spring house. We walked all the way out from town to get a couple."

"All that way?" she smiled. "What would you do if we were all out?"

"Buy a tomato?" Ben asked.

She laughed a most melodious laugh, "Why Ben I don't think you want to buy a tomato. Yes, we have some. You boys go down and pick out a couple. You know how big they can be for what you can afford. Go on now. And make sure you close the spring house door when you leave." She shooed them off the porch and went back to her work.

The boys scrambled down the steps and round the back of the house to the spring house a few feet away. They went down the steps and opened the door. The inside of the springhouse was whitewashed. There was a small open window near the ceiling and it let in enough light to clearly see. To the left was a pool of clear cool water. On a hook by the door was a tin cup. Jimmy immediately grabbed the cup, he bent and dipped it into the water, filling it to the brim. He stepped back and demolished the contents in a single gulp.

"Ahh, that was good," he said as he filled the cup a second time. This time he drank slower but enjoyed it more. When he finished he shook out the last few drops onto the floor and hung the cup back on its hook.

As their eyes adjusted to the light they gazed at the shelf in front of them. On the shelf were lined at least a dozen watermelons of all sizes. There were cantaloupes too as well as a peck basket of pole beans and other vegetables. Scanning the watermelons they each picked a likely one. Ben with a serious mien knocked on his and solemnly pronounced it good. Jimmy knew that Ben had no idea what he was doing.

"I think these look good," said Ben. "Now I want some water too, before we start back." He stooped and filled the cup and drank deeply. "That *was* good!" he exclaimed. "Let's go."

Carefully closing and latching the door behind them the boys walked back to the house and up on to the porch. Ben knocked on the screen door and a moment later Mrs. Miller came out of the dim recesses of the kitchen to see what they had picked.

"Those look like good ones," she said. "I think a quarter each should do." She winked. The boys looked crestfallen as she laughed. "You know I'm teasing. A dime a piece is enough for those."

The boys handed over their money.

"Did you hear?" Jimmy asked.

"Hear what," she asked.

Centerville

"They found Patsy Marks body. It was down Bruce Walter's well. We saw it ourselves on the way over here. They said he must have fallen in and drownded." Ben said almost stumbling over his words.

"Oh that's awful! That poor boy; and his mother. This will just kill her. That's such sad news." She was surprised by this news, like others she had assumed that Patsy had run away, though there was no reason for anyone to think that would be the case. They just couldn't imagine the boy dying. Just then her telephone rang, the news was already spreading. As she turned to go she tried to put on a happy face and said, "Now don't drop those watermelons on the way home. We don't give refunds."

"Don't worry Mrs. Miller, we won't." Jimmy replied. I hope, he thought. In fact just two weeks in his future Jimmy, his younger brother Pete and Ben would walk out to Millers and buy watermelons. Jimmy would drop his on the road and it would crack, oozing watermelon juice. When they got home Jimmy and Pete put their melons in the refrigerator to cool for dessert. Jimmy stole Pete's melon. When Pete discovered the theft he went crying to his mother. Jimmy had to apologize and buy Pete a new melon the next day. In the meantime Pete ate the cracked one. He was even smarter than Jimmy.

Cradling their prizes the boys turned towards home for the long half mile back to town. The melons were light enough now but their weight would exponentially grow the closer they got to home. By the time they reached Jimmy's house they would probably weigh a good twenty pounds apiece, or so the boys would think. But on this day they got lucky.

They hadn't walked more than a couple of hundred feet when Ben's dad pulled up next to them, heading for town.

Centerville

"You boys heading back home?" he called through the passenger window. "Hop in, I'll take you."

"We're going back to Jimmy's place to eat our melons." Said Ben as the boys climbed into the car.

Ben's dad pulled away. In a couple of minutes they had to slow because of crowd at Bruce Walter's place.

"Wonder what happened there? There's an ambulance, a statey and more."

"They found Patsy down in the well," shouted Jimmy. "He's dead."

"How do you know that?"

"We saw them pull him out. And something's not right. Water came out of his mouth and his pants were on backwards!" Jimmy stumbled over his words in the rush to get them all out.

"Slow down. What do you mean his pants were on backwards?" Ben's dad asked.

"They were, I saw it too," said Ben.

"You boys mean backwards? Like the zipper was in the back instead of the front."

"Yes, that's what we mean," said Jimmy. "Something's not right. The men there were talking about Patsy falling down the well but I don't think so."

"You don't? Do you know something more about it? Do you know something you aren't telling?"

"No," moaned Jimmy. "I just know there is something more. I heard Mr. Walter say that he pushed open the well cover to look in. If Patsy went into the well by himself, how did he close the cover? And it looks heavy. I don't know if Patsy could have opened it by himself."

"But," Ben's dad began, "Maybe the cover was already open and Patsy fell in while he was looking down. Maybe later Mr. Walter saw it was open and closed it and didn't know that Patsy was down there."

Centerville

"That might be right," Jimmy agreed, "but what about his pants?"

"That's a good one. I can't answer that. Maybe he was just playing around, or something." A few minutes later he pulled in front of Jimmy's house and the boys jumped out of the car, cold watermelons in their hands.

"I'll see you boys later. I'm going down to the mill to see Jeb Bowersox. He has some arrow heads that he wants me to look at. Don't ruin your supper by eating all of those melons, save some for dessert." With that Ben senior drove off.

The boys turned and went into Jimmy's house to get plates and a knife. The watermelons were calling their names.

Centerville

Chapter 4
The Funeral

A few days later, after supper, Jimmy's dad took him aside and said, "Let's talk for a few minutes."

'Oh no, what did I do?' Jimmy thought as he followed his father into the living room. But try as he might he couldn't think of anything he had done, so he hoped for the best. They sat on the couch.

"I know that Patsy was your friend. They're having his funeral tomorrow. I haven't heard you say anything about going to it. Do you want to go? You don't have to if you don't want. Your mom and I are going and you can go with us."

"Ben and I were talking about that, about whether we were allowed to go. I've never been to a funeral before and don't know what I should do or say. But I think I would like to go."

"Don't worry," his dad said, "You don't have to do or say anything. The coroner released Patsy's body yesterday so they could have the funeral. He said that Patsy must have hit his head when he fell into the well and then he drowned." His father shook his head. "What a shame."

"But what about his pants? Did the coroner say anything about Patsy's pants?"

"Not that I'm aware. But what do you mean? What about his pants?"

"Dad, his pants were on backwards! Ben and I both saw it. They were on backwards. Why? That's what I want to know, why were they like that? It doesn't make any sense."

"I haven't heard anything about that. Are you sure? Someone should have noticed and said something."

Centerville

"Don't believe the kid!" Jimmy exclaimed. "Like I said both Ben and I saw it. Even Oppie saw it, he even said the G word. I saw it, his pants had the zipper in the back and the zipper was in the back because his pants were on backwards. It's just not right."

"Ok, ok. I hear you and I believe you. Maybe he was horsing around earlier. Who knows?" Jimmy's dad actually sighed. "Anyway the funeral is at 2:00 tomorrow afternoon. It's just across the street in our church. But you have to take a bath and wear your suit. And just so you know, his coffin will be closed, so you won't see him. But if you want you can go up and say your final goodbyes. I know you were friends so it would be a good thing for you to do. After the funeral we'll go out to the cemetery to bury him and then come back to the church for a little lunch."

"Lunch? You eat lunch after a funeral?" Jimmy couldn't believe what he heard.

"Yes, Jim, it is what people do. It's a time for people to pay their respects to the family and to gather to remember the person who died. It's what we do. It's not for the dead, it's for the living. I suspect a good number of your friends will be there. You won't be alone."

Later that evening as he lay in bed Jimmy watched the heat lightening over the mountain he finally realized the loss of his friend. He and Patsy had played whiffle ball in the back yard, built forts in the woods by the stream behind Patsy's house and explored the area. They hadn't been as close as Jimmy and Ben were but they had been good friends.

As he rolled over to sleep he heard a lonely train whistle in the night. Hearing it he remembered, dreamlike, a couple of years ago when he lived in Middlebury right next to the railroad yard. He saw steam engines every day and heard their whistles day and

Centerville

night, as well as the chuff of steam as they moved through the yard. Back then he wanted to be an engineer.

One time he and his father were standing by the tracks watching a locomotive take on water. The engineer and Jimmy's dad were talking. Then the engineer said, "Do you boys want to take a short ride? I have to go down there and switch to another track and back up to couple onto those cars over there."

Jimmy's dad jumped at the chance and before they knew it, Jimmy was lifted into the cab and his dad climbed up as well. His dad held him while the engineer moved levers and turned knobs. With a hiss of escaping steam the engine slowly moved forward, pulling the tender behind. Never going more than five miles per hour, the train moved down the tracks for a few hundred feet and then stopped. The conductor, who had been walking beside the locomotive, threw a switch and waved his lantern. With another hiss the locomotive lurched backwards down to where they had started but on a different track.

"Hang on," the engineer shouted, "there may be a little bump when we couple up to the rest of the train." Jimmy's dad held onto a pole that was behind the engineer as the fireman grinned. But there was no bump or clang for that matter. Just a hiss of steam as the locomotive slowly came to a stop.

"That was smooth," said the fireman in a loud voice. The ride over, Jimmy's dad handed him down to the conductor and then climbed down from the engine himself. Jimmy saw the fireman begin to shovel coal into the fiery maw of the locomotive as they walked away. It was a ride he would never forget.

He drifted off to sleep with the memory and the sound of train whistles in the distance.

Centerville

The next day was sunny and bright. The air was clear and the temperature threatened to rise well into the nineties. Jimmy dreaded having to wear his suit in the hot church and at the cemetery. Time seemed to slow as his mother bustled about the house. She was preparing a dish for the funeral luncheon. Jimmy's dad was at the post office and would close it right before the funeral. He would have only enough time to change into his suit before they left for the church.

Time dragged by as Jimmy hung around the house. After lunch he took his bath and an hour later he had to put on his suit. He hated the neck tie. He knew that it would choke him all day. Then his father came home and minutes later they all walked across Center Street to the Reformed Church.

Earlier Jimmy had watched from his bedroom window as the church parking lot filled. First came the long black hearse. Then he saw the preacher, Rev. Paul Hummel, greet the undertaker. After that he watched them take the small white coffin out of the vehicle and carry it into the church. And then the organist arrived. From then on people began to trickle into the church, then Jimmy, his mother and father crossed the street and up the steps into the sanctuary. Sunlight played brightly with the stained glass windows, a stark contrast with somber mood of the people in the pews.

The organ was playing softly and there on a platform in the front of the sanctuary was Patsy's coffin. It was surrounded by flowers. A large spray covered the lid.

Jimmy's mother turned to enter the fellowship hall with her casserole. "Do you want to go up and say goodbye? I'll go with you so you won't be alone," his father whispered. Jimmy mutely nodded and he and his father walked slowly down the center aisle and stopped in front of the casket. Sweat was beginning to run down between Jimmy's shoulder blades. He itched all over.

They stood there for what seemed to be an eternity. Jimmy didn't know what to do. Should he say a prayer? Then, without knowing why, he simply reached out to touch the coffin and said quietly. "I'll see you Patsy. Be good." As they turned to find their seats Jimmy's eyes filled with tears and his nose stopped up. He cried silently for his dead friend as they sat near the front of the church. Until this moment he had not experienced any sense of loss or sadness, not even when he saw the body come out of the well.

People kept streaming in and stopping at the casket until Patsy's parents were led into the church. The organ music got quieter as they stopped in front of the coffin. Patsy's mother was weeping and his father looked stiff as he tried to hold in his emotions. His mother reached out and put a single rose on top of the casket and then they turned and were led to sit in the front pew.

And now, in almost complete silence the preacher came down the center aisle. He too stopped in front of the coffin. He reached out and touched it. He traced the sign of the cross with his fingers and bowed his head. Then he turned to the congregation and raised his arms calling them to stand. The room rustled as over a hundred people came to their feet.

"The Lord gives and the Lord takes away. Blessed be the name of the Lord. Let us pray. Oh Lord God, in your infinite mercy you give us life and in your infinite wisdom you take it away. But in doing so you promise us eternal life in your kingdom which has no end. We gather here today, dear Lord, to remember and celebrate the life of Patrick Eugene Marks."

The preacher droned on and Jimmy's mind began to wander. He never could concentrate for long in church and by now he was sweating profusely. He could feel his shirt stick to his back under his coat. He wondered why they would want to celebrate. Patsy was dead. What was there to celebrate in that? His reverie was interrupted by a hymn and then one of the ladies sang.

Reverend Hummel preached a short sermon and they sang another hymn. By then there was a good amount of weeping and Patsy's mother almost collapsed. Earlier Jimmy had heard his mother say something about Mrs. Marks being sedated by the doctor. Jimmy knew enough to understand that she was drugged so she wouldn't go crazy during the funeral.

And then the preacher said the benediction and it was all over. As they left the church Jimmy could see a number of his friends including Ben. He didn't see Fred, who was not there, but he wasn't looking for him.

They crossed the street and got into their car. Jimmy sat between his parents in the front seat sweating even more in the hot car. He could see that even his ever cool mother had beads of perspiration on her forehead. His dad started the car and turned on the headlights. Oppie Fenster directed the little traffic there was on to a detour down to the Lower Street so the funeral procession could drive to the cemetery without interruption. Jimmy's dad pulled out into the street and took his place in this silent parade, all following the hearse the short mile to the cemetery at the edge of the village.

At the cemetery they snaked single file through the tree shaded lanes until they came to a stop. Then they walked to the grave site with all the other people. Again the coffin was on a platform under a big tent. There were earth mounds to the side along with the grave diggers leaning on their shovels, waiting to fill the hole after the service. Jimmy thought he would die of itching and began to try to relieve it by hunching and relaxing his shoulders. His mother shushed him and his actions did little good.

As they stood at the open grave Jimmy looked around. He nodded to Ben and a couple of his other friends. As he scanned the graveyard he saw Fred back at the tree line about a hundred feet away. He watched as Fred walked back and forth, finally fading into the trees.

The graveside service was brief and they lowered the casket into the earth. The air was still with only the cicadas singing a final hymn of praise. At last, with the casket in the ground, Patsy's father stood by the open hole and shook as he wept for his son. There was no celebration of life here. This, Jimmy knew, was a place for the dead.

The funeral luncheon was a somber affair. Jimmy and most of his friends played quietly in the yard behind the church. There he and Ben talked.

"Did you see Fred there, at the graveyard? He was down by the row of trees. I wonder what he was doing there?" Jimmy asked.

"I don't know. Maybe he wanted to come but his mom wouldn't let him." replied Ben.

"Could be but somehow 1 doubt it. You know I haven't seen Fred much in the past couple of weeks. Have you?"

"Come to think of it, no. He usually wants me to go fishing with him down to the lime kill but not lately." Ben said.

Later that day, as the heat came to a climax and as the sun set, thunder storms came. They shattered the late afternoon calm. The wind blew as though driven by banshees mourning the death of Patsy Marks. Lightening actually struck a tree not far from the fresh grave and wind uprooted trees throughout the village. Rain poured

Centerville

as though from buckets to the hot and parched earth. The storms seemed to last all night.

The next day some said that there had been tornadoes. The Dry Run overflowed and flooded the field behind the village. When that happened the rushing water flooded and scrubbed bare Fred's hiding place near the lime kiln. A cat's collar, the skull of a squirrel, one of the little boats that Patsy made and other things; trophy's he had been keeping were lost forever. It was probably a good thing.

Centerville

Chapter 5
Fire in the Woods

A few days later Jimmy, Ben, Darryl and Richard were playing basketball on the playground next to the elementary school. The macadam courts had lines and goals at each end. It was the closest thing to a real basketball court for six miles around. Jimmy was a terrible basketball player. He couldn't hit the net and could never quite understand the rules. He played only when there were an odd number of players, like today. Ben talked him into joining the game.

The one thing Jimmy could do was to pass the ball. He had a pretty good bounce pass and was accurate throwing the ball. He just couldn't make a basket no matter how hard he tried. Right now, Ben had the ball and was dribbling towards the net when Richard blocked him. He passed it to Jimmy who took off down court, trying to dribble as best he could.

"Walking!" Richard shouted. "Ya can't take that many steps without dribbling the ball. You took three steps. We get the ball."

Bewildered Jimmy relinquished the ball and in his misery moved away from the action and hoped Ben could handle the play by himself. Richard passed the ball to Darryl who shot and scored. Jimmy raced after the ball as it bounced and rolled into the grass next to the court. As he rose he saw Fred walking in the street nearby. He shouted Fred's name and waved for him to come over. He knew that Fred was a pretty good basketball player and maybe he would relieve Jimmy. But Fred looked briefly at him and then turned into the woods on the other side of the road. Reluctantly Jimmy returned to the game.

The game continued in a desultory fashion, neither team really interested in playing. It was hot and the boys were sweating. If they had anything better to do they would have quit the game in a heartbeat but on this late July day they had made their decision to play basketball and so they did.

After Jimmy fouled again, hitting Darryl's arm accidently, the boys began to get into an argument.

"You hit me on purpose!"

"No I didn't. It was an accident and it wasn't even hard. I just bumped into you."

"Yeah, but I was getting ready to shoot." Darryl shouted. As they began to argue a thin stream of smoke rose through the trees in the woods where Fred had recently disappeared. It thickened quickly until Richard noticed it.

"Look at that!" he pointed. "There's a fire in the Holiness Grove. Wonder what's burning?"

The Holiness Grove was a large grove of trees; most people called it a woods. There a number of small cabins had been built near a large open air church which the Holiness folks called the Tabernacle. Every summer they had a camp meeting there for a week in early August. There had been a bit of activity there this very week as workmen cleared out the underbrush and swept between the pews of the Tabernacle in preparation for Camp Meeting. That was only a week or so away.

What a time *that* was. Centerville's population tripled and on Friday and Saturday nights there would be nearly a thousand people shouting and jumping around in religious ecstasy while preachers preached fire and brimstone to the sweating congregation.

Last year Jimmy and his friends had gathered near the Tabernacle to watch the spectacle. It was amazing, exciting and totally unbelievable. Older boys were there too and swept up a few of the swooning girls

Centerville

in the heat of their own religious fervor. Or maybe the girls took the opportunity to swoon for only the right boy.

The week was long and rowdy. In bed late into the nights Jimmy could hear preaching and singing through his open bedroom window. It was an amazing thing to behold. Heat lightening played over the mountain showing the wrath of God while hymns of praise and glory filled the nighttime sky from below. The singing, when it reached its peak, could be heard all over town and it was a beautiful and awful thing to behold. Camp Meeting was almost as good as the firemen's carnival. Almost.

The smoke grew thicker and the boys lost interest in the basketball game and the foul as they saw it billow up through and above the trees.

"It has to be big. Let's go see!" And the race was on. Darryl dropped the basketball. It bounced across the court as the boys thundered across the field and into the woods. As they approached they heard the village fire siren go off. Its pitch rose and then lowered in long, almost painful sounding groans. Dogs barked and howled all over town as though there were banshees on their tails. They did this every Saturday at noon when the siren was tested. But this was no test. This was the real thing.

The boys hurried through the woods and soon saw that the eastern end of the Tabernacle was in flames. This was the end where the altar and marble baptism pool were on display. The orange tongues of fire licked the whitewashed wood with hunger. The flames flowed like upside down waterfalls, streaming up the walls and licking the eaves and ceiling.

Finally the village firetruck's siren could be heard wailing as it chugged up the hill and into the grove. Three men rode on it and two more followed soon after in their own cars. There were no fire hydrants here, or anywhere in the village, for that matter, so the firemen had to hook up to the tank in the truck and get the pump going. But none of them knew how. They were firemen in name only.

Two of them, Pete Spence and Bill Moyer hooked up the hose and stretched it out, aiming the nozzle at the fire.

"Give us water!" Bill shouted.

"I'm trying!" shouted back Stan Yager as he worked frantically at the pumper controls. But nothing flowed. He tried turning a knob and the pump gave a shudder.

"You got water now?" he shouted over the roar of the fire.

Water tickled from the hose nozzle but nothing more. "No" Pete shouted. "Did you open the tank valve?"

Stan worked the valves and pounded on the gauges to no avail. Water would not flow. By then two more men had arrived and all three were arguing with each other about how to run the pumper.

The flames blazed merrily. Jimmy wondered whether there was even water in the tank.

Meanwhile the boys had a grandstand seat to watch the destruction. Jimmy asked out loud whether there was water *in* the tank. That was too good to keep to himself. It was then that Jimmy saw Fred on the other side of the Tabernacle. He was running away from the fire. Jimmy wondered why anyone would run away from a perfectly good fire. Especially one with the keystone firemen in the lead.

Shortly after that the green and white Middlebury firetruck arrived and in moments they were pouring water on the conflagration. Men shouted and soon had two hoses playing on the flames. But the flames were winning.

Centerville

The Centerville firemen were still arguing and shouting at each other about how to get water out of the truck and onto the fire. This was their fire and they should be putting it out!

By the time Middlebury was well deployed the Port Mifflin crew arrived and pulled their truck up along the north side of the burning Tabernacle. In moments they too had water flooding over the flaming roof, steam hissing high into the air.

The boys were having a ball. They had never seen this much excitement in their lives but at the same time they were a bit frightened at the ferocity of the towering flames. The trees writhed in the rising heat and almost looked like they were trying to fly away to escape the heat and flames.

While the village firemen struggled the team from Low Point pulled in with their truck and took on the south end of the fire. The four men soon had water flowing, washing down what remained of the walls and spewing over the blazing pews. Though the fire was nearly surrounded, it was winning. Jimmy was amazed at how fast the open air building was consumed.

Someone shouted, "Get back, she's gonna collapse" and moments later the building did exactly that. As all watched it slowly leaned to the north and then the weight of the roof became too much and the whole thing fell into its own pyre. Smoke, embers and ashes billowed high into the sky as the fire settled in on the pews and endeavored to consume everything right down to the concrete slab of a floor.

Finally the Centerville volunteer firemen got water to flow. A pitiful stream, flowing on the embers and hot spots of what was left of the Holiness Grove Tabernacle. They ultimately endured a shame that lasted for years. It was at least a decade before they were invited

Centerville

to roll in a firemen's parade instead of being held on standby, just in case a real fire broke out somewhere in the county. A strange trust. Oddly enough all the local volunteer fire companies brought their equipment to the Centerville firemen's parade. Just to show off their shiny trucks while Centerville struggled with a truck that was ancient by at least twenty years and multiple owners.

The Tabernacle fire was the talk of the town for weeks to come. Firemen hung their heads as they gained the reputation of not knowing how to operate their own equipment. A few years later a local man had a chimney fire and called the Middlebury fire department who came an extinguished the fire promptly. When asked why he didn't call the village department he replied that he wasn't sure they knew which end of the hose to point at the fire. It took a new firehouse and truck before the community would fully trust them again.

But in this time the embers smoldered for a couple of days. The smoke of the fire could be smelled all over town for the better part of a week. The boys poked around the ashes for a day or so but discovering nothing worth shouting about gave up the hopes of lost treasure.

Jimmy ran into Fred later in the week and noticed that he favored his right arm. When he asked if Fred had burned it trying to put the fire out Fred said that he had. But the furtive look he had made Jimmy wonder whether Fred knew more than he was letting on. Jimmy remembered seeing Fred run from the scene and began to get suspicious. Later he shared his thoughts with Ben.

"Did you see Fred at the fire?" he asked.

Ben thought for a few moments and then replied, "Yeah. I saw him running away. Why?"

"I don't know," Jimmy hesitated, "But I think he had something to do with it."

"Why?"

Centerville

"I think he burned his arm. He was holding it when I saw him running away from the fire. If he didn't have anything to do with it you'd think he would stay and watch. Don't you?"

"You do have a point there. If he hurt his arm it may be because he may have been trying to put the fire out." Ben replied.

"That's what he said but I don't think so." Jimmy said. "I think he started it."

He became even more certain two weeks later when the fire marshal reported that the cause of the Tabernacle fire was arson. He reported that kerosene had been used to set a fire at the altar end of the building. A lot of kerosene. And he had found the burned remains of a dog on the altar where the fire had started.

Chapter 6
River Camping

Summer seemed never ending but at the same time there were only so many things a boy could do on his own. Sometimes he needed friends or family to do different things. Cave Creek, so called because it sourced from a large water cavern thirty miles away, was only a mile from town but might as well have been a hundred for Jimmy and his friends. The river was out of bounds for Jimmy and his friends without an adult present. So it was a great treat when Jimmy's father announced the camping trip.

"How would you like to go on a weekend camping trip down to Cave Creek. You and Pete, your mom and me?"

"Yes! Can I bring Ben? Are we gonna fish?" Jimmy was excited and already planning on what he would take and what they would do. He loved camping and this was the real kind. Old Army pup tents, cook everything over an open campfire. Fish, swim and climb the mountain by day and tell ghost stories by night. This was the best and he couldn't wait.

"Sure if Ben's dad and mom let him. We'll leave on Friday in the morning around eleven and come home Sunday afternoon."

At that Jimmy ran off to find Ben to ask him to go along on the trip. They only got to go camping one or two times in the summer and it was always to be made the most of. It was Tuesday and hot, as usual. Jimmy roamed the streets but couldn't find his friend.

He had started on the upper street, where Ben sometimes played ball at the school but found no one. Being a boy Jimmy detoured through to the remains of the Tabernacle. The area hadn't been cleared, so all the rubble was still there. The smell of burned wood and wet ashes still lingered in the air. The Altar area had been dug through and worked over. Even Jimmy could tell that the area had been searched. He didn't know yet about the kerosene, or burned dog.

Not finding Ben he began to head down to Center Street but he knew Ben wouldn't be there. Though Jimmy lived on Center Street he was one of the few boys who did. Most lived on the Upper or Lower Streets. Walking down the hill and past the Reformed Church he decided that he would probably find Ben near the lime kiln. In fact he could see the remains of the old kiln from where he stood on the sloping street. He could also see someone by the stream there. That's probably Ben, he thought and so he headed down the hill.

Near the bottom of the hill where the streets intersected were the fire hall, formerly a hotel and beer hall, on one side and Musser's store on the left. The barn where the infamous fire truck was parked looked like it was ready to collapse. More than once Jimmy and Ben had squeezed through the permanently half open door and played on the fire truck in the near darkness.

One time Jimmy and Ben had been prowling around the building and had discovered that the cellar door was unlocked. This door consisted of a pair of sloped doors covering a stairway leading down to the dirt cellar beneath the building. Most homes in the town had similar arrangements. They lifted one of the doors and crept down the musty steps into the cobwebby cellar. They explored their way to the stairs leading to the first floor and nervously climbed the steps. Crouching they opened the door and found themselves behind the bar. They were hidden from the street. It was an early midday afternoon and the village snoozed in the sun. The room was quiet and had the dusty aroma of stale beer. Motes danced in the sunlight streaming through the less than clean windows. A dog barked across the street.

Jimmy and Ben crawled along the back of the bar and came to a door. They had been in the fire hall many times but did not know where this door led. Opening it they discovered a stairway leading up into the gloom and the second floor. Urging each other they tiptoed up the steps, wincing at every creaking sound the treads made until they arrived at the summit.

Turning they found themselves in a long hall with windows at either end. The hall was lined with doors. They carefully opened the first they came to. Inside the room was a dust covered wooden chair an empty beer bottle and nothing else. Disappointed they explored some of the other rooms. Most rooms were empty and dusty but one had a bed, chairs, a dresser and mirror. This room was not dusty but surprisingly clean. The boys didn't know that here was where the firemen frequently brought their girlfriends; never their wives.

Downstairs they continued their exploration. Finding nothing of interest they finally left the way they had come. No one was the wiser to their little excursion. Both left thinking that it would be an excellent place to hide out if ever the need arose.

Today Jimmy never glanced at the building but continued across Lower Street and down the hill to the end of the road. There the street ended at the edge of a farm pasture. This was the home of the formerly fierce bull. Now Jimmy wasn't afraid to cross the field, so he crawled under the barbed wire fence and into the tall grass. He could see Ben quickly crossing the field a few hundred feet away. He raised his arm to wave but Ben didn't respond.

Centerville

The boys met at the halfway point. Ben had a fishing rod and tin can for worms.

"Catch anything?" Jimmy asked.

Ben shrugged his shoulders and said nothing. He didn't even smile in greeting. He looked around and then pushed past Jimmy towards the fence.

Jimmy turned and walked along in silence. When they got to it they both crawled under the fence. As he rose on the other side he looked across the field and thought he saw Fred in the distance. "Were you and Fred fishing?"

"I don't want to talk about it." Was Ben's only response.

"You ok? You don't look so good."

Ben's face hardened and he looked at the ground. They walked towards Ben's house in silence. The hot summer day suddenly seemed oppressive. Jimmy didn't know whether he should say anything about the camping trip or not. When they got to Ben's house and Ben turned to go inside Jimmy finally, rushing his words, said, "We're going camping this Friday. I want you to come along. It's down at the river, you know where."

Ben considered for a moment and then murmured, "I'll think about it." And he entered the house.

Troubled, Jimmy slowly walked home alone.

Youth is resilient and the next day it was as though nothing had happened. Ben came to Jimmy's house and they climbed into the treehouse. It rested partially in the cherry tree and partially on the roof of the work shop. It was a good place to sit and watch the world go by.

"Yeah, I'd like to go camping. When are we leaving?" Ben said as though Jimmy had just asked the question.

"Dad says Friday morning around eleven and we'll come back Sunday. Will your mom and dad let you go?"

"Sure. They won't mind."

"Great! I hope we catch some good fish to eat." And so it was set. The rest of the day they planned on what to take and do.

The next two days whizzed by and then it was Friday. Jimmy was up early and after breakfast he pulled Pete's wagon down to Ben's house. There he and Ben put into it blankets, a pillow, Ben's small tackle box and all the odds and ends that a boy needs for a weekend camping trip.

And they were off.

Not long after that they all packed into Jimmy's dad's car, the trunk packed full with his mom's supervision and in the back seat each one holding something on their lap. Jimmy's Army knapsack was at his feet. It was too small to actually carry on his back but it was perfect for carrying sodas and fishing gear on a camping trip or fishing expedition. He could strap it to his belt and it fit perfectly. It was a long five miles to where they could park. A friendly farmer let them park near his barn and from there they had a short walk across a field to the river. Then they would wade the hundred yards across the stream to their camp site. For Jimmy and Ben the water came up to their waists. Each carried as much as he could, as did everyone else, even Pete. Still it took three good trips before everything was carried across.

The boys wanted to go fishing immediately but were told to help get the camp set up first. "The fish will wait." Jimmy's dad said. And so they cleaned the debris from the camp site and helped put up the pup tents. Jimmy and Ben searched for rocks to line the fire pit and Jimmy's dad cleaned out the ground cellar. They had camped here for years; the ground cellar was a hole that had been dug and lined with flat stones a few years back. A larger stone covered the opening. It did a remarkable job of keeping things cool and safe from marauding animals. But it, like everything else, had to be cleaned up and prepared for camping.

Not far from the camp site was a spring. They cleaned fallen leaves and the like from the clear cool water and soon had it flowing quickly. The water was clean and pure. The next task was to gather firewood, which everyone helped to do. After that while the boys finally prepared their fishing rods Jimmy's dad finished off the fire pit with a grill top. When not in use the grill was carefully lodged in the branches of a tree for safe keeping. Now there was enough room to grill hamburgers and hot dogs with enough left over for a frying pan.

Whooping the boys ran downstream to a good spot where they hoped to catch a bass or at least some sunnys or rock bass. Jimmy's dad would clean them and his mom would prepare them for frying. Not long after they had settled in Jimmy's father came along with his own fishing equipment. The fish were hungry today and before long they had pulled in a nice bass and a number of sun fish. When they had enough Jimmy's dad made them throw everything else they caught back into the water. "Let them grow up," he said.

Later that afternoon they had fish and fried potatoes. Jimmy's mom dredged the fish in egg and flour and his dad fried them in a pan while the potatoes were fried with a little bacon and onion in another. A campground feast, the fish were sweet and flaky while the potatoes were brown and salty. Coupled with a bottle of soda it couldn't get any better than that.

After supper they all helped clean the dishes and pans and then lounged around the camp fire. As the twilight gathered, the crickets and other nocturnal insects began to tune up for their nightly concert. By dark they were all in their tents asleep for the night.

The next morning everyone in camp was up early and ready for a great day. Jimmy and Ben planned on visiting the abandoned cabin and then hiking up to Lookout Rock. Pete and his parents decided to walk upstream to a wide and shallow swimming hole. There Pete could swim while his parents swam, or lounged on the pebbly beach. Jimmy's dad always had a book and so did his mom.

"I'm going to pack a lunch, boys, so after your hike come to the beach to eat." Jimmy's mother said as they prepared to march down to the cabin.

"Will do." replied Jimmy. By 9:30 Jimmy and Ben were off on their adventure. The abandoned cabin was not far away. It had been empty as long as they could remember. By this point the front steps and porch had been pretty much gnawed down by porcupines. Quills were scattered all around the building.

As they approached they could hear water spilling over a stone dam that local fishermen had made to raise the level of the river a small amount. It made for good fishing both above and below the dam. Shrouded in pine trees the cabin looked gloomy and a bit haunted. The boys approached with a small amount of caution. They didn't want to encounter a porcupine. They both still believed the old tale that the animals could shoot their quills at their enemies. They didn't know or care that porcupines are nocturnal.

The cabin, itself, was small with two floors and only four rooms. A porch swept around three sides with the front facing the river which was only about one hundred feet away. It had been painted grey which had faded to near invisibility while the shutters, or what

Centerville

remained of them, were painted dark green. A couple of those on the second floor hung at crazy angles. Behind the cabin was a well that had been filled in years ago. The chimney had crumbled to the roof line and bricks were scattered on the porch roof and the ground next to the house. The roof was covered in moss.

The boys gingerly climbed the three steps of the front porch and into the cabin through the missing front door. As they had done in the past they explored the cabin but found nothing new. The real adventure was climbing the stairs to the second floor. There were dark red stains on the plaster of the stairway. They imagined that it was blood spatter from a murder or suicide, even though they had never heard of such events happening.

They toured the upstairs and Ben found a shotgun shell on the floor of the one bedroom. "Wonder how this got here?" he asked out loud.

"Probably someone was squirrel hunting from here. Probably shot through the window. Either that or he killed someone on the stairs. Yeah, probably that. You saw the blood didn't you?" Jimmy said.

"I saw it all right but there wasn't any on the floor or the steps. I bet it was a hunter. There's nothing new here, let's go up to the lookout."

It was a long and steep climb to Lookout Rock. And they were hot and thirsty by the time they arrived. They were at the crest of the mountain and the rock was an overhang that became part of a cliff. The drop to the valley below was steep.

"I bet it's a thousand feet down to the river," Ben said.

"It sure looks it. Dad would probably know. We should ask when we get down to the beach." Jimmy pulled two Cokes from his Army surplus knapsack along with a bottle opener. He opened a bottle and passed it to

Centerville

Ben. Then he took the other and opened it for himself. They clinked the bottles together and drank.

They sat in silence while they gazed out over the valley sipping their drinks. The mountains on the other side of the valley looked distant in the hazy summer air. A slight breeze blew and a couple of vultures circled as they rose and sank in the thermals rising from the valley below. The cicadas sang unseen in the trees.

"I could sit here and look out there forever." Jimmy sighed. He loved places like this.

"So could I," said Ben. After a pause he continued. "Listen, I gotta tell you something but it's a secret. Cross your heart and hope to die you'll keep it?"

"You know I will. You're my best friend. I won't say a word."

Ben looked directly into Jimmy's eyes and then out over the valley. He said, "I know you're wondering what happened the other day down by the lime kill. I know you saw Fred when you met me in the field."

"Yes, I did. And I knew there was something wrong. I was afraid that Fred hurt you. Did he?"

"No," Ben replied, "but I wanted to hurt him.

"We were fishing at the lime kill and I said something about the fire. He said he didn't have anything to do with it. But I never asked him if he did. Then I remembered you talking about his arm and I did notice that he didn't do much with his right arm. He acted like it was stiff or something. He even fished with his left hand. Then he said he saw a dog run into the fire. And that didn't make any sense to me. Why would a dog run into a fire and not away from it? I thought he was lying but I don't know why. But now I think that he definitely did have something to do with it. In fact I think he might have started it.

Centerville

"But then it gets worse. We fished for a while and we worked our way down to the cut. And while we were down in it he said the strangest thing. He asked me if I knew what a cog was. I didn't know what he was talking about but it kind of scared me. I don't know how to describe it but his eyes got, I don't know, kind of empty, like nobody was there. You know what I mean?"

Jimmy nodded even though he wasn't sure at all what Ben meant.

"And then it got really creepy and scary. He stood up and started to take off his pants! Right in front of me and it wasn't like he was going to go swimming. It's not deep enough there anyway. He took them completely off! And he looked really scary!"

"What did you do?" Jimmy breathlessly asked.

"I dropped my rod and picked up a rock and told him that if he took a step closer to me I'd bash his brains in. And I would have done it. I was that scared. I thought he wanted to kill me. Then I grabbed my rod and ran up the bank and started over the field. And then you showed up. I was still scared and didn't know what to do or say. But I felt better seeing you, I'll tell you that."

"What do you think he meant by a cog?"

"I didn't know at right away. First, I thought of gears and motors and stuff like that, but when he took off his pants, I figured that he was talking about his peter."

Jimmy said, "Why would he do something strange like that? Taking off his pants? He must be crazy. But Fred sure has been acting strange lately. And I think he did have something to do with the fire." He paused, his mind suddenly racing. Ideas flicked in and out so fast he could hardly understand what he was thinking. Then he breathlessly asked, "Do you think that he had anything to do with Patsy?"

"What makes you ask that?" asked Ben.

"I don't know but something made me think... Oh my god!" he gasped.

"What is it?" Ben demanded.

"Patsy's pants were on backwards. Do you think that Fred could have been at Patsy's? Could he have done the same thing that he did to you? Do you think he could have made Patsy undress? Do you think he killed him? Do you?" Jimmy, stumbling over the rush of words and thoughts, was almost shouting.

"That's crazy. Fred wouldn't kill anyone. Sure, he can get mean and he did scare the crap out of me but I don't think he could do something like that."

"I don't know," Jimmy said. "Maybe you're right but for a minute it all kind of made sense in my head. But it couldn't have happened that way."

"Yeah," replied Ben. "Let's get out of here and go swimming. Don't tell anybody about this."

"Ben, don't tell anyone about *any* of this, including about Patsy. My thoughts just got mixed up, that's all." But Jimmy couldn't convince himself that his thoughts *were* that mixed up.

The boys climbed back off the ledge and started down to the beach to swim and laze in the Cave Creek.

That night around the campfire Pete said, "Dad, tell us a ghost story. Please?"

"Well, I'll tell you one and then it's off to bed. I don't want you getting nightmares. Hmmm, let me think. Ok boys; listen up because this is a true story.

"Many years back over in Millheim there was a man named Musser. This was in the late eighteen hundreds. The story was that Musser was a murderer and was found guilty in court. He was sentenced to hang. When the time came the hangman asked him if he had any last words. And he said, 'I'm innocent. If I'm guilty the murder weapon will appear on my tomb stone.' And then they hanged him, dead.

"People were superstitious back in those days and I guess he figured that when nothing appeared on his gravestone that they would think he was not guilty and would feel sorry for what they had done. But it didn't work out that way. They buried him in the cemetery there, right by route 45, across from Harvey's gas station. It was a big stone; it must stand six or eight feet high. Yes, boys, it's still there and you can see it when you drive by. I've seen it many times. I think Jim has seen it too.

"Any way it wasn't long after he was buried that a red stain appeared on the stone and it looked like blood. The people would wash it away but it kept coming back. They scrubbed and scrubbed the stone but the blood always came back. They even replaced the stone but it didn't work, after a couple of months the blood was there again."

Even though Jimmy had heard the story before and *had* actually seen the tombstone he shivered a little in the dark. Ben was silent and Pete huddled up to his mother's side, eyes as large as saucers.

"But this time it was different. This time it was like the blood etched the shape of a dagger right into the stone! Everyone saw it. If they scrubbed off the blood the dagger could be clearly seen. Someone hired a stone cutter who polished the surface of the stone until it was shiny and smooth once again but," He paused dramatically.

"It came back! And the dagger too!" He whispered. "Finally the people in the town got a metal plaque and put it over the stain and the dagger. And to this day you can see the plaque on the gravestone, and if you look carefully around the edges, you can see the red stain that the blood made on Musser's tomb."

Centerville

The fire crackled as they sat in silence. An owl hooted somewhere on the mountainside. The boys rose and crawled into their tent. Pete went into his mom's tent and his dad slept outside on the ground.

Between Ben's story and his dad's tale of blood it took Jimmy a long time to fall asleep. Ben, on the other hand, went out like a light.

Book II
Carnival

Chapter 7
Parade

The hot afternoon air was still. Not a breeze stirred the chestnut and maple trees lining Center Street. Other than a vulture or two circling a distant ridge there wasn't a bird to be seen. Even the dogs were quiet. For Jimmy the air felt heavy much like it felt shortly before a late summer thunderstorm; those moments when the whole world stood still as though holding its breath waiting for something to happen.

Today something *was* going to happen. Today was the start of the Firemen's Carnival and, as always, there was a parade to kick it off. Crowds lined Center Street for its entire length. The villagers and parade watchers from nearby communities excitedly waited as though President Eisenhower himself would be the grand marshal. Children ran out on the empty street while traffic was detoured to the Lower Street. Families had picked their spots with care. Those who lived on the parade route had the prime seats. Many of them moved their porch chairs to the curb so they could sit there while watching the parade. Most, however, stood while children sat on the curb or stood clutching their paper bags, hoping to fill them with candy thrown from the firetrucks and floats in the parade. Here and there a younger child perched atop a father's shoulder, perhaps pounding a drumbeat on his head. Occasionally a man would sip from a bottle of Schlitz or Black Label as they stood in the hot afternoon sun.

Up from the carnival ground floated the melodic warmup of the bands as they prepared for their march. Once in a while the call of a single trumpet, the beat from the bass drum or the tattoo of a snare could be heard distantly as individual band members anxiously waited for the parade to start.

Centerville

Jimmy, Ben and Pete sat in front of Jimmy's house; his mom and dad sitting behind them on the sidewalk, on porch chairs. Each boy had his own paper bag in hand; waiting for the copious treats to be thrown from the firetrucks and floats. Once it started the children would scramble, sometimes far too close to the parade vehicles, to gather as much candy from the street as possible.

The wail of a firetruck siren rose and fell in the distance and a few moments later the village fire siren sounded. This was the signal that the parade was to begin. Soon afterward a band could be heard and everyone knew that the parade was on.

And then, for the wait. Just because it had started didn't mean a thing to Jimmy and Ben. It would be at least a good ten minutes or more before the parade actually began to pass them at his home across from the Reformed Church.

For Jimmy the tension mounted. He didn't know why but parades always excited him. His heart beat in time with the drums and his blood pulsed in rhythm to the bands. By this time he felt as though he were ready to explode. He turned to his left to look down the street hoping to see something but knowing that it was still too early. For him the wait was intolerable and interminable.

Ben nudged him with his elbow. "You going down tonight?"

"What kind of question is that? Of course I'm going down. I wouldn't miss opening night for anything, besides I want to play the penny pitch and some of the other games."

Ben nodded, "Yeah, I want to play the penny pitch too. Last year I won about fifty cents and I only started with ten. I want to hit that dollar box in the center."

"You know it's the smallest box on the board, don't you?" Jimmy said.

"Yep, I know it for sure but you never know. A penny could roll right in. I want it to be mine."

"You'll have better luck with the ring toss," retorted Jimmy, changing the subject. "We're going to eat there tonight. Mom is working in the Ladies Aid stand so we'll get hamburgers and hot dogs. I can't wait."

Usually hamburger meat was cooked in meatloaf or in a casserole in Jimmy's house. Only on special occasions, such as camping trips, was it actually eaten in a bun with ketchup and onion. Jimmy didn't like mustard. Hotdogs were fairly common though.

Then far to his left someone shouted, "Here it comes!" Turning, Jimmy could see the color guard slowly marching around the curve in the street; leading the parade. There were four soldiers in the vanguard and a sergeant leading the procession. One soldier carried the stars and stripes and one carried the state flag. They were flanked by two infantry riflemen. Walking at a stiff attention they matched the four step cadence that the sergeant softly called.

"**Hut**, two, three, four, **hut**, two, three, four." The sergeant called the cadence, then a silence for a few beats followed by a single "hut." Their boots struck the macadam in unison making a single stepping sound in the quiet afternoon. No band was playing at the moment and Jimmy thought he could almost hear the soldiers breathe as they passed. Everyone rose as the flag passed. Men took off their caps and hats and both men and boys put their hands on their hearts in silent tribute while veterans, standing at attention, saluted.

Close behind the color guard were a pair of Army jeeps and a couple of military trucks following along. There were two soldiers in each jeep and the back of the

Centerville

trucks were filled with sitting soldiers, rifles in hand as though they were slowly off to invade a foreign country, or the graveyard where the parade would end. If there was a tank this year it would be farther back in the parade, leading the tractors and other farm equipment. Nobody knew why the farm equipment needed a military escort.

Pretty girls, in white short skirted uniforms, came next. They were carrying the Middlebury High School banner, the cleats on their marching boots flashing in the sunlight and snapping on the hot pavement while perspiration beaded their foreheads.

Following the banner was the high school drill squad; boys and girls carrying white wooden rifles. As they marched they twirled the guns, stamped the gun butts on the road and shouldered them all in perfect unison; never missing a step or a beat. Watchers clapped their hands as the drill squad passed. They were followed by the baton team; girls spinning batons and themselves on their heels. The girl's legs flashing in the sun. They threw the batons high in the air and paused as the batons, whirling and glittering in the sun, fell back to their waiting hands. And they marched on. This whole precession took place in complete silence. Not a band was playing.

And finally the high school band came round the curve on Center Street. Lead by the drum major they high stepped down the road to the cadence of a single snare drum. At last the drum major raised his baton and the band began to play. *"Stars and Stripes Forever"* seemed to be their perennial favorite and it was no different this year. As they marched the brass section turned their heads back and forth as though to ensure that nobody had the chance to miss their music. The

Centerville

drum major pranced and high stepped down the street while the crowd applauded and cheered.

As the band passed the floats came into view. The floats were the high point for the children because the candy materialized from them. Leading off were the Future Farmers of America. High school boys and girls wearing blue jeans or skirts and their blue denim FFA emblemed jackets waved and smiled as they tossed candy to the children. Riding on a flat wagon pulled by a green tractor they sat on straw bales. Their banner hung from the side of the wagon, their motto printed in gold with a blue background, *"Learning to Do, Doing to Learn, Earning to Live, Living to Serve."*

Following the FFA was the Farmer's Cooperative float. Its theme included a large basket overflowing with all sorts of locally grown produce. Women were dressed old fashioned costumes and pretended to churn butter. Teenagers, similarly garbed, tossed more candy, lollypops and Tootsie Rolls, to the crowds of children along the route.

The forest service sponsored the Smokey the Bear float. Smokey waved to the watching crowd while children dressed as little bear cubs pretended to fight a small fire. The fire was ingeniously generated by a fan blowing upwards its breeze streaming red and orange crepe paper ribbons into the air. Red light bulbs flickered at the base of the fire. More candy flowed from this flaming cornucopia much to the children's delight.

It seemed that each float that passed provided sweets from a bottomless well of candy. Neco Wafers, Sweet-Tarts, Tootsie Rolls and more. As each passed the children scrambled, sometimes too close to the tractor or wagon trying to beat their brothers, sisters and neighbors to the last piece to fall. After the parade not a single piece of candy could be found on the parade route. From one

Centerville

float, however, came fly swatters with the name of the hardware store sponsoring the float printed on the attached paper tag.

At long last came the firetrucks. Centerville's old truck newly washed and polished, led the way down Center Street. Its siren sang with a deep throaty roar, rising and sinking in pitch as it passed. Not to be outdone the other trucks, from all the surrounding communities, added their wails to the cacophony. Each truck, trying to outdo the others, not to mention the high school marching bands. In fact the band following the trucks gave up trying to play anything and simply marched in step to the big bass drum which managed, somehow, to be heard, or felt, under the roar of the sirens. Children held their ears as the phalanx of trucks passed, only removing them to run to gather candy the firemen threw from the cabs. Some fire companies had come as far as twenty miles or more to participate and they let everyone know they were there.

As all this was happening, a furtive figure crept behind the Reformed Church and pulled open the slanted cellar door and snuck down into it. It couldn't be called a basement because it was simply a rough dirt depression beneath the sanctuary. Barely deep enough to contain the huge old coal furnace, it's ducts crawling across the ceiling like a monstrous spider; cobwebs covered everything in imitation of the furnace spider's web.

Fred slowly moved through the cellar, around the furnace to the short stairway that led to the first floor. Pushing up the trapdoor he climbed into the coat room next to the vestibule. Mounted permanently there on the wall was a ladder that led to another trapdoor and then to the church attic. He climbed upwards, pushing up the second trapdoor and entered the dusty, hot attic. There was little of interest here. Only a few boxes of old

69

hymnals and some pieces of slate that had been used in ages past to shingle the roof. Dim light filtered through the end of the room barely lighting it.

Another ladder, or a continuation of the first, continued up into the belfry. This ladder was different in that it switched from one wall to another and finally spanned the width of the belfry. Fred continued to climb, pushing the bell rope to the side as he climbed. Finally hot and sweaty he pushed open the third trapdoor and climbed into the belfry itself. More than once he had climbed here to survey his domain.

Had anyone bothered to look they would have seen him there, kneeling beneath the large iron bell a good fifty feet above the street. Fred watched the parade from this vantage point and from here he could see much of the parade route and could have spit on the marchers. Instead he kept still, knowing that if he was seen he would be in deep trouble. He knelt there until the parade had completely passed and regular traffic was once again moving below. Then he silently opened the trap door and descended the ladder to the church below and out through the cellar doors at the rear of the building. On his way he made an offering.

But while the parade flowed down the street, unaware of Fred's presence, the last high school band, the one immediately behind the firetrucks marched silently by, grim faced they clutched their instruments to their chests as though afraid the blast of sirens would rip them from their hands and blow them spiraling into the sky. The parade watchers politely applauded.

And finally, at long last, the Army tanks. By now the firetrucks were far enough ahead to allow normal hearing to return. What always surprised Jimmy was how quiet the tanks were. He always expected to hear the treads clank and their engines roar. But instead they passed in near silence. Whenever the parade stopped, as they always did for whatever reason, the tank turrets would turn and the gun barrels would rise to point at the sky.

Perhaps, Jimmy thought, they were looking for a stray elephant.

Following the tanks, this year, were the antique cars. Old Fords, Model Ts and Model As, Packards, Buicks, an ancient Hupmobile and others. These too moved silently but when the driver advanced the throttles of the older cars they would spit and roar for a few seconds before settling back down. Occasionally one would backfire making the older folks and the children jump. Ben would laugh. Following all was a steam driven car; so silent that it moved as though by magic.

Near the end of the parade was a wagon pulled by a tractor. On the wagon was a local country western band. The banner said they were the Shade Mountain Boys. A quartet composed of a guitar, banjo, fiddle and accordion. Dressed in cowboy outfits, boots and white hats they were previewing the music they would be playing that evening. At the moment they were wailing out "Your Cheating Heart" with a verve that far exceeded their talent.

Of course farmers were not forgotten. Local farmers washed their tractors and drove them in the parade. Some showing off the kind of equipment they could afford much to their neighbor's dismay. Some pulled wagons of produce that they would sell over the next few days at the carnival ground. Most were just showing off their green or red equipment. They would be back with them over the weekend for the tractor pulling contest.

Rounding up the rear were the Sunday School children from the two village churches, the Methodist and the Reformed. Dressed in their Sunday best, sweating, wilted and bedraggled, they listlessly waved as they sang "I'll be a Sunbeam for Him." They didn't throw candy.

And then it was over. The world came back into focus and life resumed. The breeze blew once again and birds could be seen on high. All in all Jimmy thought it was an excellent parade. His bag held a fair amount of candy and a fly swatter. He didn't know what he was going to do with *that*.

Regular traffic began to flow along Center Street as people turned to their homes or to their cars to go home or down to the carnival itself.

Jimmy rushed to his dad and asked, "Now can I go?"

His father replied that he could but to be careful. Then he gave him three dollars for his supper. "Don't spend it all on junk or at the penny pitch. And only one Coke!" Jimmy promised that he wouldn't do any of that, already thirsting for the second Coca Cola. He had saved up his own money for the penny pitch and so could afford to ignore his father. And then he and Ben raced down the street to join the crowds at the carnival ground.

Late that afternoon Reverend Hummel passed through the sanctuary as he did every day. He enjoyed the quiet solitude and the way the lowering sun played with the stained glass windows and barred its rays across the room. It was such a peaceful place. Often he paused to meditate in the front pew or say a silent prayer at the altar. Today he saw something glowing in the sunlight that spilled onto the altar. He walked slowly up the center aisle, climbed the two steps into the chancel and saw that there, in the offering plate, was his cat, Boots. He could see, however that Boots was not sleeping. His eyes were glazed and open. His mouth twisted into a

Centerville

snarl and his head hung at an awkward angle because of his broken neck.

The preacher let out a brief shriek and sank to his knees before the altar. Who, he wondered, could have done something like this? Who could be so evil? The sun slowly set and the sanctuary grew darker. He didn't know that the darkness was only beginning.

Centerville

Chapter 8
Carnival – Part 1

The annual firemen's carnival was the major fundraiser for the fire company. People attending the carnival were donating to the cause willingly, even those who lived outside the coverage area of the local company; spending their money eating, drinking and playing games. Every town and village that had a volunteer fire department hosted a carnival. There were traveling carnival companies that spent the mid to late summer simply going from town to town, setting up their rides and game concessions. Charging the local firemen enough to squeeze a good of a profit and leave the same firemen with funds to maintain their companies and equipment.

But money was also made by the locals with their own concessions and games. Bingo was by far the most popular. Every prize was donated and every game made a profit. Cake wheels, the penny pitch and all the rest were pure money makers. The ladies auxiliary made soups, cakes, pies and more. Along with hamburgers, hot dogs, chicken corn soup and bar-b-que chicken they made a killing. The carnival was always good. Lasting a week and ending with fireworks it was by far the high point of the year for the village and for the children.

Jimmy and Ben walked the short distance from Jimmy's house, down the street and across it, then over the field cum parking lot and onto the grounds themselves. This year there was a Ferris wheel, a carousel, a Whirl-A-Gig and a Tilt-A-Whirl. Kiddy rides included a train, pony rides and more. The rides were arrayed at the west end of the grounds. To the north, along the woods, were the Bingo stand, the cake wheel and various games such as Jimmy's and Ben's favorite, the penny pitch. The boys headed there first.

"Let's pitch a few pennies before we get anything to eat. I feel lucky."

Jimmy, jangling the trove of pennies in his pocket readily agreed. They approached the game. The rules were simple; the player could lean over the rail but not step across it or reach under it to pick up stray coins. Pennies tossed had to be completely inside a numbered box without touching any part of the border. The board consisted of a grid of squares twenty-five on a side. Each square was numbered from three through five. Landing in one of those squares would pay back the amount printed in the square. In the center was a large circle containing four much smaller circles each worth twenty five cents. In the very center was one worth one dollar. Tonight covering the dollar spot was a shot glass with a ten dollar bill in it. A target like that was irresistible. Lost pennies add up and many would be lost in the coming week going after that ten dollar bill. The bill was arranged in such a way that it was impossible to put a penny into the shot glass but that would stop nobody.

Jimmy and Ben arranged themselves next to the rail and carefully tossed their precious pennies. The trick was to toss with a flat trajectory so that the penny would land flat and not roll. A little bounce was all right. Almost immediately Ben hit a nickel square. He shouted to the attendant who verified the win and counted out five cents into Ben's waiting hand.

"I'm ahead already!" He shouted as he pounded Jimmy's arm, thus ruining a perfect ten dollar shot. Ben quickly lost the five cents and another eight as well before he won back three pennies. And so it went for the boys. Win a few and lose more. Those were the rules and they obeyed.

Centerville

As their coins diminished Jimmy finally said, "I'm getting hungry. Let's get something to eat and see what else there is to do."

Ben thought that sounded good and so they set off towards the Ladies Aid food stand. The line was long but it moved quickly and soon they were able to place their orders. Hamburgers, fries and a coke were the order of the day. Ben put vinegar on his fries. Jimmy hated the thought. He didn't even like ketchup on his fries but he did like it, along with onions, on his hamburger. They quickly found seats in the pavilion and ate.

At the same time, down on the bandstand, The Shade Mountain Boys were warming up. The bandstand was quite an affair for such a small town. Most places had a simple stage and some even had roofs. But this one boasted a roof, wings and a painted backdrop of a western desert sunset. Bullhorn speakers were permanently mounted near the roof and spotlights were strung behind the fascia. Behind the backdrop were long rooms where waiting acts could relax. In former years amateur theatrics had been held here in the spring and summer and the actors remained behind the backdrop until ready to enter the stage. Tonight they were empty.

The guitar twanged and the fiddle screeched as the band prepared for their first set. People were putting blankets on the ground and settling in for tonight's concert. It promised to be a good one. Near the cake wheel the bell of the High Striker would occasionally ring as a young man impressed his girlfriend with his strength.

Jimmy and Ben finished their meal and began the first of many circuits around the carnival grounds. As they passed, the first Bingo game was starting as Mr. Billman turned the basket crank, tumbling the balls and then releasing one.

Centerville

"Welcome folks, we're ready to start. Clear you cards and let's begin. Good luck. Our first number; under the N, number thirty eight," Billman called. And the weeklong Bingo tournament had begun. Every night until eleven Jimmy, and half the town, could hear Billman, or his replacement, calling Bingo, even over the sound of the bands in the bandstand.

While Jimmy watched Ben tried the ring toss and then each put down a nickel to pick a duck floating in a zinc trough. Everyone won picking ducks. Ben got a whistle and Jimmy Chinese handcuffs. A squeal of feedback announced the beginning of the first set of music. The boys continued their circuit, not talking but, instead, taking in the atmosphere. They were slowly making their way back to the magnetic penny pitch.

The afternoon turned into evening as the sky turned purple and then black. Moths and a myriad of other bugs circled and attacked the spot lights, hung high on poles, in an unending attempt to fulfill their natural urges. Bats happily circled the same lights as did a few swallows, swooping out of the dark like bright black meteors before disappearing back into the darkness; a moth clenched in their beaks. In the nearby woods katydids and crickets tuned up as though competing with the country western band on the stage.

The boys gravitated towards the stage themselves and sat on the grass to listen to the music. Jimmy wasn't that fond of country western music but it was something to do; a respite from the constant circling of the carnival grounds.

"And naow we're gonny play a new song by the great Homer and Jethro. It's called *The Billboard Song*." The Shade Mountain Boys leader announced with a twang. When he wasn't on stage his accent was the same slightly German accent that everyone else in the area had. He was a car salesman by day. The banjo and guitar struck up the tune and they began to sing.

The song was about a man who was reading the remnants of tattered billboards after a storm. Most of the song was nonsense created by garbled messages overlaid on the billboard advertisements. The audience laughed and clapped at the song.

Jimmy and Ben rolled on the ground laughing when they heard the band sing, "*Simonize your baby with a Hershey's candy bar.*" They roared and howled through the length of the song.

When the song was over, the boys rose and staggered away, laughing harder than they had in a long time. Somehow they found themselves back at the penny pitch. Pennies in hand they began to play, inveterate gamblers at the age of twelve.

It was close to nine o'clock when the boys, learning the hard truth that the house always wins, decided to call it a night. But the scream brought them to instant and rapt attention. Near the High Striker a girl came stumbling from the woods and stopped near the cake wheel. Hands to her face, she would not stop screaming. The boys, along with many others, ran to see what was happening. Jimmy could see that the girl's eyes were wide and that she was very frightened. He could also see that her white blouse was torn down the back exposing the strap of her bra. Her skirt was crooked and dead leaves clung to it as thought she had lain on the ground. He felt embarrassed for her.

Jimmy thought he saw a shadow move swiftly through the woods in the light of the nearly full moon as he approached the girl. He knew who she was, Judith Mecklenburg, who lived only a few houses away. She was sixteen and sometimes, when he was younger, "watched"

Jimmy and Pete when their parents went out. Tonight she was panting, crying and clearly near panic.

A woman, Richard's mother, came to her and put her arms around Judith. She steered her to a place to sit by the cake wheel and tried to calm the distraught girl. "What is it?" she asked.

"Uh, uh, uh," Judith tried to speak, each utterance rising in pitch. "Uh a man. Big man. Tried to hurt me. Truh, truh, tried to pull me into th, th, woods," the girl cried, wiping her eyes with her fists. "He tore my blouse and truh, truh, he threw me to the ground. I screamed and ran. He's still out there! In the woods!" She then collapsed into Richard's mother's arms, sobbing and gasping. Jimmy could see bruises begin to darken her arms where someone had tried to hold her tight. By then Judith's mother was there, taking her daughter into *her* own arms and leading her to a place of safety.

"He was going to rape her," one of the women stage whispered, loud enough for all to hear while the band played on only a few yards away. Someone called Oppie Fenster who soon had a posse of fire police stumbling through the woods.

"B twelve," Mr Billman called into the night.

Centerville

Chapter 9
Carnival – (Part 2)

It wasn't long before Oppie's men were thrashing randomly through the woods, bumping into each other, shouting and scaring any predator into the next county. Jimmy, though concerned for Judith, couldn't help but think that these were the very same men who fought the fire only a couple of weeks ago and were just as effective now as then.

While fire police stumbled through the woods Fred, looking carefully in all directions slunk out of the woods near the Bingo stand. He sat on the end of the bench, watching the commotion near the cake wheel after Judith ran from the woods; his black, flat eyes unblinking in the darkness. His heart was still pounding from the excitement. He could feel the hardness in his groin and knew that he almost had had her. He could feel her arm in his grasp and still hear the sound of her ripping blouse. It was so close! If only she hadn't fallen as she pulled away from him, scratching his burnt arm as she fell. Thank god it was dark; he knew she had no idea he was the one. Well it wouldn't happen the next time. And he knew there would be a next time. Soon.

It seemed strange to Jimmy that while Judith was sobbing and clutching at her mother, the rest of the carnival went on as usual. Mr. Billman continued calling Bingo numbers, the band played into the night and people still laughed, ate and walked the circuit. It was almost as though what had happened in this little corner meant nothing to the rest of the carnival goers.

Though he was partially right what he didn't know was that Judith Mecklenburg's mother was a sister to the county sheriff and *he* would take quite an interest in finding his niece's attacker.

Centerville

But now things were beginning to calm down and it was getting late. Jimmy and Ben decided to call it a night, an exciting night at that. They had almost a whole week to spend at the carnival. Little did they know that it would be a week never to be forgotten. But lying in bed that night, listening to the continuous Bingo games and the Shade Mountain Boys that was a future he couldn't imagine.

* * *

The following morning at breakfast Jimmy's father said, "You were there when Judith was attacked, weren't you?"

"Ben and I were at the penny pitch but when we heard her scream we ran over to see what happened. Why?"

"The sheriff wants to talk to you, that's why."

Jimmy got cold, physically cold. He hadn't done anything but the thought of having to talk to the sheriff chilled him to the bone. "Why? I didn't do anything."

His father smiled, "No, you didn't do anything but someone said that you and Ben were there when Judith came out of the woods. Sheriff Shambach wants to ask everybody who was there what they saw or heard. He's holding a hearing at the carnival ground at eleven. I'll go with you."

"But why? I don't know anything!" Jimmy was actually afraid but for no good reason.

"You don't have to worry. It won't be about you or what you did. He just wants to find out who attacked Judith and who knows what someone, even you, might have seen or heard. He just wants your help."

For the rest of the morning Jimmy was frightened and anxious. There was no good reason for it but the thought of having to talk to the sheriff made him nervous. It would make any twelve year old nervous. But Ben would be there too, so that was good. The time passed and then his dad came from the post office and took him to the carnival ground.

When they got there he saw that there were about fifteen people there including Judith and her mother. Bruises were clearly visible on her arms. Ben, his father and others, mostly adults, were watching as well. They met at the Bingo stand where there were places to sit. Sheriff John Shambach stood at the Bingo caller's table and the rest stood or sat on the benches.

"Thank you all for coming. This isn't any kind of legal inquest; I'm not going to swear anybody in or anything like that." He smiled. "I just want to find out who attacked Judy. I want to put together the set of events and see if anyone, or more than one of you, might have seen or heard anything suspicious last night. So just think back and let's talk and see if we can arrest the offender.

"I want to start with you, Judy. I know it may be hard so take your time and tell us what you remember."

Judith, standing close to her mother but appearing very calm, paused for a moment, "I was talking with Sally Stample over at the cake wheel and thought that I saw a friend of ours over by the bell ring game. Sally and I started walking over but then someone called to her so she went off towards the bandstand. I went behind the bell game because there was a line of people there in the front and I didn't want to have to go through them.

"I thought I heard my friend say, 'over here' and so I went towards the woods. It was kind of dark but there was enough light that I could see what I thought was my friend, so I went into the woods. But it wasn't my friend but this big man and he grabbed my arm and pushed me to the ground. I hurt my knee and he scared me so I screamed. He grabbed at me and I think I scratched his arm because he made sounds like I hurt him. He grabbed my blouse and tore it but I got away and ran back out of the woods. And that was it. I was scared for a minute but..."

"Did you get a look at who it was?" the sheriff asked.

"Not really. It looked like a big man with a white shirt. That's all I can remember."

"Did he say anything?"

"No, I don't think so. I thought I heard 'over here' but now I'm not sure."

"Was the friend you thought you were going to see a boy?"

Judith hesitated until her mother nudged her arm and then she said, "I thought it was Tony Marsh."

The sheriff said, "But it wasn't." Everyone knew that Judith was sweet on Tony Marsh.

Judith shook her head. Sheriff Shambach then questioned a number of other people but got very little from them. John Rogers thought he saw a big man running from the woods up towards the school but he couldn't be sure. Another said they saw Judith walk into the woods. Then the sheriff called for Jimmy.

Jimmy stepped forward, his father right behind him.

"Hi Jimmy, how you doin?" the sheriff said. "I don't expect that you know a whole lot but someone said that you were there when Judy came out of the woods and I'd like to know what you saw or heard. You heard other people here tell their stories so don't be afraid. Just take your time and think. If you didn't see or hear anything then that's what I need you to tell me."

Jimmy thought and then spoke, "Well Ben and I were losing at the penny pitch when I heard Judith scream."

"What did you do?"

"I ran, of course, I wanted to see what was happening and we were losing anyway."

"Don't we all," the sheriff smiled as some of the people chuckled, "and what did you see."

"Well Ben and I got up there by the bell ringer game when Judith came out of the woods. I saw that there were dried leaves on her skirt and that her blouse was torn down the back. She was all excited and everyone came running at the same time to see what was happening."

"Did you see anyone in the woods?"

Jimmy paused, "I don't know. I thought that I saw something in there but I'm not sure. It was so fast and I was watching Judith anyway. It all happened so fast."

"You thought you saw something?"

"It was just a blur. It might have been a man in a white shirt but I wouldn't swear on it."

"That's good to know," said Sheriff Shambach. He thanked Jimmy and then turned to Ben, "So Ben, what did you see?" It seemed like the sheriff knew everyone by their first name, even Jimmy and Ben. Of course it was their parents that the Sheriff knew, in this small county he knew just about everybody.

Ben stepped forward and said, "Pretty much what Jimmy said but I didn't see anything in the woods. I just heard her scream and came over to see what was happening."

In the end it was the general consensus that a large man in a white tee shirt had lured Judith into the woods and had attempted to attack her. Luckily she got away. But now the sheriff had to find a suspect. Everyone

Centerville

believed that it must have been one of the carnival workers but which one? They all seemed to fit the description.

As the meeting broke up, Jimmy and his dad walked back home. "See, it wasn't so bad, was it?"

"No, I guess not. I was nervous though. I didn't know what he wanted to do."

"I wonder what he *will* do. Just about everybody that works for the carnival is big and wears white tee shirts. I can't see how the sheriff can possibly arrest anyone." But he was surprised when later in the day he heard that Sheriff Shambach had actually arrested a man on an assault charge.

Immediately after the meeting the sheriff met with the carnival boss. He questioned and examined every man that worked there. One had his particular interest; it was the man who ran the Tilt-A-Whirl. At the time of Judith's attack the ride had been shut down while the mechanics worked on it, giving the man the opportunity he needed. He also had scratches on his arm. When the sheriff asked about them the man replied that he had scraped his arm on the steel supports of the ride while he was trying to figure out what was wrong with it.

Sheriff Shambach arrested him on the spot and hauled him off to jail. There he sat for the rest of the week. The circuit judge wouldn't be around until next week, so no bail could be set for the man.

Never the less he protested his innocence loud and long; just what the sheriff liked to hear. The more they protested the guiltier they were. Sheriff Shambach liked to quote, "I think thou dost protest too much!" and assumed that meant guilt.

The village rallied around the sheriff and would have hanged the man if given the chance. It was obvious to everyone that he was guilty as sin. Judith was the village prize, lovely and destined for great things. The guilty carny was simply a brute from somewhere else. He was guilty and would pay the price.

But not this time.

Centerville

Chapter 10
Carnival (Part – 3)

The arrest of the carny ride operator was enough to soothe the worries of many and so the carnival was as popular as ever that night. The imprisoned man protested his innocence and the carnival boss had to run the Tilt-A-Whirl himself. He was pretty sure that the man had done nothing to the girl but he also knew the ride operator was not present while the mechanic was working on the machine. He decided to fire the man when he got out of jail. Pay him off and let him go. There were plenty of men looking for work and all a man needed for the job as some muscle and half a brain. Now if he could find someone to take *his* place at the Tilt-A-whirl.

The previous night, in fact, the now imprisoned ride operator had been hiding with a friend behind one of the carnival trucks sipping cherry vodka when Judith was attacked. A firing offense for sure.

Tuesday at the carnival passed uneventfully.

The Wednesday crowd was not as large as the previous days and it would remain smaller until Friday. Saturday, with the fireworks climax, would be the big night for everyone. The carnival grounds would be packed.

But tonight, Wednesday, was Jimmy's lucky night. Now, for once, the penny pitch would pay off, big time! He started with about fifteen cents but quickly racked up a couple of wins, including two five cent wins, almost back to back. There were a fair number of pennies on the board and Jimmy knew that soon the attendant would use his long handled squeegee to push the coins into the troughs at the side of the pitch. Jimmy waited for the board to clear and a few seconds later it *was* cleared.

Centerville

Now he had a clean board. The players were already tossing pennies but now they would often roll in large circles, sometimes even rolling off the playing surface. Jimmy took aim at the center and carefully tossed his coin in a flat trajectory but it bounced on the oil cloth game board and began to roll. Jimmy watched the penny roll across the numbered squares and then enter the center high price area. It circled the twenty five cent target in an ever tightening spiral. His heart leapt as it finally spun briefly and flopped over into the circle but not completely; instead it barely touched the bounding edge of the target. Moments later, as if by magic, a thrown penny skidded across the surface and just nicked Jimmy's. It hit hard enough to push it completely into the circle, making it a winner.

"I win! I win!" shouted Jimmy as he pointed to his penny. "That's mine. I won twenty five cents." It was rare for anyone to actually put their coin inside the small target. The game attendant scrutinized the penny and finally, almost grudgingly, counted out the winnings into Jimmy's eager hand. As soon as he had the pennies he thrust them into his pants pocket satisfied at the weight they made and continued playing. Amazingly his luck held. It was not long before he snagged a ten cent win and then another. The attendant began watching Jimmy to see if somehow he was cheating.

Finally after another miraculous ten cent win and a number of three and four cent wins the attendant said to Jimmy, "Maybe you ought to take your winnings somewhere else and give someone else a chance." He had paid out close to seventy five cents to Jimmy and wasn't happy about it.

Jimmy tapped Ben on the shoulder and said, "Let's get out of here."

Centerville

Ben shrugged and the two began another of the endless circuits of the carnival ground.

"I know what! Let's ride the Ferris wheel. I'll even pay. After all I'm rich." And so they ran off to stand in line at the ride. They hadn't been on this ride yet this season. As they neared the head of the line Jimmy counted out twenty cents for the ride operator and when their turn came they climbed into the car.

Almost immediately they were swept to the very top of the ride. Bathed in the moonlight the whole carnival ground spread out before them in all its glory. It was a magical sight that wasn't lost on the boys. Spread before them was the panorama of light and sound. At the High Striker the boomping sound of a mallet hitting the rubber pad and then the bell ringing out a winner played a counterpart to the country western band on the stage stomping their feet and strumming their guitars. Bingo to the left, rides to the right and the tiny penny pitch, way over there. Everything laid out like a living, moving carpet far below. Next to the bandstand they could see a couple dancing in the grass.

To them it always seemed as though they stayed at the top on every Ferris wheel ride but they didn't understand that the wheel had to be balanced. A good operator emptied and loaded cars opposite each other so that the opposing set of cars always had riders. And so they spent their minute at the top rocking the car with the whole world spread out before them. In the distance they could see heat lightening silhouette the mountains.

"There's your dad." Ben pointed. Jimmy could see his dad walking from the High Striker towards the Bingo stand. Not far behind him he also saw Fred, almost as though he was following his dad, or someone. Then the wheel lurched and they rolled forward to stop near the bottom as the next car was loaded. It seemed to take as long to load the wheel as the actual ride itself. They lost sight of Jimmy's dad, and of Fred.

After the ride ended the boys again cruised the circuit. On the bandstand the group was wailing, "Your Cheatin' Heart" for all they were worth. In Jimmy's estimation they weren't worth very much. He knew he would have to listen to them when he was back at home in bed. That and the Bingo caller. As they passed the penny pitch Jimmy was tempted but then decided that he had had enough luck for one night.

And so the evening passed. As they were finally walking to their homes they agreed to meet at the lime kiln the next morning. They'd do a little fishing and exploring the area. They already knew it like the backs of their hands but they never knew what they might find.

Thursday dawned hot and promised to get even hotter through the day. As Ben's dad liked to say, it would be a real scorcher. And indeed it was.

They met at Ben's place and walked across the fields until they encountered the Dry Run. Then they turned left and followed its bank to the lime kiln. When they reached the kiln the stream split. To one side it came to a rather deep pool, perhaps as much as five feet deep. That's where the best fishing was.

The other fork was dammed so only a small amount of water flowed over the dam and disappeared into the earth, gurgling deep into what everyone knew was a cave. But no one had ever managed to open it up.

Years back, it was said, when most of the stream drained here, a local farmer had poured a colored dye into the hole. Half a day later there was a red stain in Cave Creek about two miles away, where a spring flowed out from among the roots of a tree and into the river. The story went that the farmer had even dynamited the place where the water drained but he had no luck.

Centerville

Occasionally the boys would dig around the hole but there was too much rock to accomplish anything. A close examination would reveal that the hole was an eroded opening in the limestone streambed that did lead to a cave. If one listened carefully the water could be heard falling a number of feet into the darkness with a slight echo. But there was no loose rock to dig, just solid limestone. No way to get inside.

Ben led the way to the lime kiln pool and they settled in for a morning of fishing. They lazed back on the bank, propping up their fishing poles on forked sticks they had thrust into the earth. In their laziness they did more tree top and cloud watching and talking than fishing but that was just fine with them. Nobody was depending on them for a meal. They passed the morning hours and caught nothing.

Finally Ben suggested that they climb the opposite bank and explore the remains of the kiln. They put their rods on the bank knowing they were safe until they picked them up later. Hiking upstream they came to a shallow and narrow part of the run and crossed. Turning back downstream they walked to the brick ruins of the kiln oven.

There was very little left. When it was in operation there were three ovens but now they were mostly mounds of earth covered rotting brick. One stump of a chimney still remained but it was only about six feet high and vine covered.

As they clambered over the ruins Ben came upon an area where the bricks looked clean and well aligned. "Look at this," he said.

Jimmy joined him and curiosity got the better of them. They started to dig at the bricks and soon dislodged one. Lifting it out they found a hole in the mound of the kiln. They soon pulled out the rest of the bricks to reveal a small brick lined vault.

"Wow, would you look at that?" Jimmy said.

"Yeah," replied Ben as he reached into the hole. He brought out a large hunting knife in a sheath. As he slid it from its scabbard they could see that the steel was shiny and the knife was sharp.

"I wonder whose it is."

"I don't know but I could make a guess. What else is in there?" Jimmy asked as he looked around. The last thing he wanted was to get caught but he wanted to see what other treasures might be in there.

Ben reached in again and pulled out a cigar box. Lifting the lid he revealed a few coins, three .22 caliber bullets, what looked like the skull of a squirrel and two pair of women's panties.

Suddenly anxious Jimmy said, "Put it back. It must be Fred's and if he catches us here he'll kill us!"

Nodding, Ben returned the items to the box and placed it and the knife into the vault. Carefully they put the brick cover back in place and brushed earth over and around them in hopes of concealing their activity.

"I think we had better get home before he comes around. I haven't seen Fred in a while and for now I don't want to." Said Ben.

Jimmy agreed and so they headed back to their fishing gear and then walked back upstream to where they could cross the field. As they crossed the pasture and entered the alley behind Ben's house Jimmy turned and saw Fred crossing the field a few hundred yards downstream and headed for the lime kiln.

"Boy that was close" he breathed.

That night both boys stayed home from the carnival. They needed a break from too much of a good

Centerville

thing. They also knew that Friday and Saturday would be much better, more exciting.

Centerville

Chapter 11
Carnival (Part – 4)

Betsy Smith was restless. She had waited all day for her mother to take her to the carnival and now that she was here she had to sit at the Bingo stand while her mother played. She wanted to go on the merry-go-round, the Ferris wheel and oh how she wanted a pony ride. She wanted cotton candy and to run around the grounds, having fun. But now she had to wait. She fiddled with the dried corn kernels that were used to mark the Bingo cards and wished her aunt would hurry up.

"Mommy, when is Aunt Mary going to get here. It's been forever." She moaned.

"Hush and be patient. We haven't been here more than half an hour. She'll be here in plenty of time. It's still early. Now don't you go putting corn on the numbers. If you accidently win I still have to pay for the card."

Betsy pushed the corn off the card with a huff and shook her long blonde ringlets. She was dressed in a light violet dress with frilly sleeves, white socks and shoes. On her left wrist was a small bracelet with a charm bearing her name; Betsy. It was her favorite dress and she had insisted that she wear it tonight. Nothing else would do. Her mother, knowing how stubborn Betsy could be gave in and let the girl have her way.

Betsy continued to squirm on the bench, the rough wood scratching her bare legs, while her mother played. She sighed as loud as she dared.

"Your aunt and Sally will be here soon enough! Why it's not even six o'clock yet. There'll be plenty of time, now let your momma play a little Bingo."

It was Friday and the grounds were filling. Many farm families had done the milking early so they could come to the carnival for their supper and a good evening of fun and entertainment. They would visit with each other and talk, play Bingo and more. The men would chew on stalks of long grass or tobacco or smoke, and talk about crops, cows and whatever; spitting in the weeds if they had a chaw. Weekend evenings at carnivals were great social events.

Boys and girls, sometimes hand in hand, walked the circuit endlessly, stopping to talk with friends or play one of the many games or just to stare into each other's eyes. Later, when the band would begin to play they would sit on blankets and listen to the music. Some of the braver ones might sneak off into the woods to steal a kiss or cop a feel. Few were brave enough to go much beyond that, that close to the public. Though some might dare as the hours turned late but while it was still light all were on their best behavior.

Jimmy and Peter were lazing along, watching people play games but not playing anything themselves. Jimmy knew that later he would be inexorably drawn to the penny pitch but like a thirsty man drawn to that first shot of whiskey he did his best to delay his gratification. He was really far ahead and he didn't want to lose all his money on the next to last night. That would be no fun. He wondered where Ben was. He hadn't seen him all day.

Ben, the subject of Jimmy's thoughts, was just leaving his house with his father to walk to the carnival grounds. He hadn't completed all of his chores around the house that day and so he had been kept on a short leash. He was hoping his father would let up later, or get busy and forget about him. Then he could meet Jimmy and have a good time. The last thing he wanted to do was stay with his dad on Friday evening at the carnival.

Fred, as usual, was lurking. For a while he had been sitting by the bandstand but then went across the grounds to the woods and watched from the brush and trees. Constantly looking around he worked his way through the woods from the High Striker to the Bingo stand. He knew these woods, like every other grove in the area, like the back of his hand. Having a mother in a wheelchair had its advantages. He was always on his own and took care of himself. And he knew how to keep out of sight.

The food stands were doing a brisk business, especially the Ladies Aid. Farmers were lined up out and around the back of the building waiting for their turn for soup, a sandwich and a slice of pie. The chicken bar-b-que was doing a tremendous business as were the hot dog, hamburger and French fry stands. No matter where a person stood, they could smell the goodness coming from these cornucopias.

It seemed as though food was everywhere this night. Even the caramel corn stand had a line and it seemed like every other child had pink or blue cotton candy. People were playing the cake wheel, hoping that the number on which their dime lay would be the winner. While they ate or waited to eat, people talked and laughed enjoying the warm evening and the good company of their friends.

Behind the Bingo stand a few men had a few tubs in the back of their pickup trucks and had plenty of beer, Genesee, Ballantine's, Schlitz and Black Label, cooling on ice. They weren't selling the beer; that would be illegal. Instead they were taking *donations* for the fire department. Next to the trucks there was an old battered Chevy. For twenty-five cents a man, or boy, could take a swing at the car with a ten pound sledge hammer. The headlights and all the glass were long gone. The doors, hood and trunk were nothing but dents.

Children scrambled over the fire trucks, pretending to put out fires. A few boys pretended to drive,

Centerville

either roaring like sirens, or grinding through the gears as they shifted into high and roared off to imaginary emergencies. None of them even thought to fight the already infamous tabernacle fire.

The sun finally began to set behind Keel Mountain and the evening sky sprang into a flaming red and orange. At the same time the full moon slid up into the darkened eastern sky, huge and as orange as the western sky. On her front porch on the upper street, Geraldine Koester eased her ageing legs while she watched the moonrise. "Blood moon," she muttered under her breath. "No good in that."

The band began to tune their instruments, preparing for their first set. People gathered in front of the bandstand, spread blankets on the ground and began to settle in for the evening. It was going to be a good night.

Betsy's aunt and Sally finally arrived and the four walked the circuit. The girls rode the merry-go-round, the Ferris wheel and the ponies. In fact Betsy talked her mother into two pony rides. Later they sat at the tables near the Ladies Aid stand and ate soup and slices of fresh cherry pie. Betsy wanted French fries but her mother said no. She also wanted cotton candy and was promised maybe she could have some, later.

The moon rose and darkness covered the carnival. The field lights sprang into brightness. The band began their first set and people gathered on the lawn in front to listen and maybe dance. Occasionally the sound of the bell clanged in the evening air, a sure winner at the High Striker. As a counterpoint the thud of a sledge hitting the wrecked Chevy at the other end of the carnival traveled low to the ground.

Centerville

Ben and his father encountered Jimmy and Ben's father finally said, "Oh go ahead. Take off but mind your mother in the future."

Whooping Ben and Jimmy headed straight for the penny pitch like sailors on their first night of shore leave. Neither would win this night.

As the darkness settled the car bashing came to an end. It was simply too dark for the hammerers to do any more damage to the Chevy. Besides, there was no more beer. As he packed up the back of his truck, Jim Keister spat on the ground, bared his tobacco darkened teeth in a grimace meant for a smile and wished his friends a good night. He pulled his truck out onto the dirt path leading away from the carnival grounds and went home for the night. He left behind a dark shadow next to the woods, not far from the Bingo stand. The rest of the crew also began to disburse. Harvey Miller, a bit drunker than the rest, staggered off into the woods to take a piss. Afterwards he sat at the base of a tree and passed out.

Fred saw Jim Keister drive off as he watched the Bingo stand and anything close to it. Somehow he missed Harvey going off to relieve himself. That's when he saw Betsy. He unconsciously licked his lips and smiled, the corners of his mouth turning down instead of up. The knot in his chest, which had not loosened for days, began to tighten even more. The heat in his body became intense as he began to sweat like he had never before. He found a dark place to sit and hide while he watched the girl and her mother.

Betsy, Sally and their mothers approached the Bingo stand. Betsy's mother's sister, Mary, had come from beyond Middlebury, leaving her drunken husband to fend for himself for once in his lifetime. She'd be happy if he drowned in his own beer but sadly knew that he would not. But at least tonight she would have a good

Centerville

time with her sister June. June had no husband so maybe after the carnival they would go to her house to have a glass of wine and Mary could forget, for the moment, what was waiting for her at home. If she got home late enough there wouldn't be a problem. No beatings, just snores.

June and Mary found seats on the bench near the back of the Bingo stand, close to the prizes and the woods. It wasn't as crowded back here and they could actually hear themselves talk while they played.

Betsy and Sally sat on the bench. Having little to do they watched and talked. Not having mutual friends their conversation soon became a discussion of nothing. Betsy, easily bored, began to fidget while Sally, who was two years older and understood the rules, began to play Bingo. She slid two dimes from the pile of coins next to her mother's elbow to pay for her games, a nickel a piece.

Now totally ignored Betsy cast her eye to find anything exciting. She couldn't sit still and wanted more rides, more cotton candy and more of everything. Playing with her curls she moved to the end of the bench and gazed first at the bandstand and then turned to the woods. There in the shadows she thought that she saw something move. Maybe it was a ghost.

Heart pounding, she licked her lips in anticipation of seeing the apparition glide through the darkness but instead was disappointed when a sheep dog loped along the edge of the woods, looking for its master or an evening rabbit. Betsy thumped herself onto the bench and sighed. But her mother didn't notice the bored girl. Neither did her cousin or aunt.

Fred noticed, however, from his seat in the shadows of the cake wheel and pick-a-duck stand. He rose and carefully made his way to the cotton candy stand, only a few feet away. After purchasing a cone of the sugary fluff he slowly, carefully edged his way into the woods. Once there he moved deliberately towards the Bingo stand, keeping to the shadows with plenty of brush and low trees between him and his prey His dark blue shirt blending into the darkness..

Once he found the perfect place he smiled. Sliding out onto the path leading into the woods he looked directly at Betsy and waved. The girl saw him almost immediately and waved back. Fred pointed at the cotton candy and raised his eyebrows. "Want some" he mouthed widely.

Betsy nodded, looked around, and seeing the coast was clear, walked into the woods.

"Want some cotton candy?" asked Fred in the sweetest voice he could manage. Nodding Betsy reached for the treat. As she did so Fred backed into the darkness and Betsy followed, not thinking of anything except the sugary sweet candy. As she approached Fred, already tasting it, she stretched her arm, anticipating the cotton candy.

Quick as lightening Fred reached out and grabbed her hand and pulled her into the brush lining the path. He put his hand over her mouth and the other on the back of her head, preventing her from shouting, or even breathing.

The girl kicked as he dragged her deeper into the woods and the shadows. His heart was pounding and there was a hardness and tension between his legs that threatened to burst his blue jeans as he pulled Betsy deeper into the darkness of the trees.

Struggling Betsy came close to breaking lose. Fred, in a fury even he did not recognize, threw her to the ground, knocking the breath out of the girl and stunning her at the same time. Betsy lay on the earth struggling to breathe.

Centerville

Chapter 12
Fred

Fred, shaking like a leaf from the adrenalin rush, raced through the woods the long way, heading for the elementary school on the other side of the woods and at the top of the hill. From there, in the light of the full moon, he kept to the alleys until he made it to his home on the Lower Street. As he approached from the street he could see the flicker of the black and white television as his mother watched the Friday Night Fights. Turning aside he crept in through the back door but still she heard him.

"Fred?" she screeched. "What are you doing comin' in the back door? I thought you was at the carnival."

Fred entered the darkened living room and said, "I was but it was boring, so I came home and saw Franky down the street. We went out back to the barn and shot a little pool."

"I'll bet you was smoking down there. Don't you burn that place down!" She shouted. Fred's mother could never talk at a normal pitch or volume. Because she was crippled and in a wheelchair she thought that everyone was deaf.

"Mom, you know I don't smoke." He complained. "I'm going to bed." Before she could respond he hustled up the steps to his bedroom and locked the door, though his mother could never get up the stairs and there was nobody else in the house.

This one wasn't like Patsy. When that had happened he was excited and a bit scared but he knew that there was nobody to see him. And it happened without thought or planning. Tonight, though, was different. He had a rage building inside all week since he failed to take control of Judith and he just had to let

102

Centerville

something loose. He was careful but almost anyone could have seen the girl go into the woods – and not come out. Almost anyone could have seen *him* there, enticing her with cotton candy. At least she didn't make much noise like Judith had. He was thankful for that.

He lay on the bed and, trancelike, he replayed the scene in his mind. His heart pounded and loins tingled. He felt himself getting hard once again as he recreated the event. He couldn't think of it as rape or murder, he wasn't that mature. Instead, for the rest of his life, he thought of it as the girl thing.

He undressed and lay naked in his bed, the warm breeze wafting through his open bedroom window. The moon cast a sharp but short shadow on the linoleum floor. He masturbated as he thought about the girl thing and fell asleep in the hot summer night. And dreamed.

Though he could barely remember him Fred dreamed frequently of his father, Robert. Now, as in most dreams, his father was carrying Fred on his shoulders, playing in the back yard. They were laughing as Fred bounced on his horsey ride. But the dream subtly changed and the boy was thrown to the ground and his father towered over Fred's cowering body. He could smell the grass and he watched as his father raised his booted foot to press it on Fred's tiny chest. The pressure became greater and greater until Fred could not breathe. Then at the last possible moment before his father crushed him Fred woke, holding his pillow tightly to his chest and sweating in the humid night air. Gasping he sat in the bed trembling. He watched the moon from his window until he was calm enough to lie back down in the sweat soaked bed to try to sleep once again. As he drifted back to sleep he could hear Jimmy Powers calling the Gillette Cavalcade of Champions main event on the television down below.

Centerville

His memories of his father were only as a misty figure that towered over everything and had a deep voice. Fred's father died on D Day in the Normandy invasion. His was an ironic and incongruous death. When his Higgins boat ground to a halt on the beach Robert stepped off the lowered ramp and into a hole fifteen feet deep. The weight of his gear, ammunition and rifle immediately pulled him to the bottom where he drowned trying to escape. His rifle strap was entangled with his back pack and he could not dislodge anything in the short panicky time he had. His last thought was that he probably would have been shot anyway. All Fred knew was that his father died a hero on the beaches of Normandy, fighting the Germans. Fred was three at the time. He barely remembered horsey rides his father gave him before he left forever to invade France.

As he slept his mother, Sarah, watched the fights. She hadn't always been in a wheelchair. In fact she had been able to walk like a normal person until Fred was seven.

That long ago summers' day he had been playing trucks in the kitchen as she worked, baking some rhubarb pies for the upcoming county fair. She always baked for the fair and won her share of ribbons. Her rhubarb pies were consistently judged the best. That day her friend and neighbor El Kaiser had been visiting to talk while she baked. They spoke in German, which always made Fred laugh, though he never knew quite why. Descended from the Pennsylvania Dutch both women were quite fluent in what they called Dutch as well as English. They were not of Amish or Mennonite extraction, at least they didn't think so, it was just that as descendants of German immigrants they grew up in a bilingual society.

Centerville

Fred had been playing in the short hallway that led past the cellar door to the back room. There was the front room where Sunday visitors talked and then the back room where Sarah did her mending at the Singer treadle sewing machine as well as her ironing. She was constantly telling Fred to pick up his trucks from the hallway and put them upstairs in his room or in the back sunporch. Just somewhere out of the way.

This day Fred was still angry because his mother had scolded him about his trucks in front of El. He ran them back and forth, motoring with his mouth but after a while he got bored. Then he got an idea. He looked around the corner to see the two women talking a mile a minute in German, not caring a bit about him. He opened the cellar door and parked one truck on the next to the top step in the darkness. Then he closed the door and carried the other two trucks to the sunporch, like a good boy. Then he told his mom that he was going out back to play. She nodded, barely paying attention.

Later in the afternoon Sarah went to the cellar to get some canning jars. Opening the door she reached for the light switch as she stepped down and onto the truck. Its wheels spun and shot out into the darkness. Overcoming her lost balance Sarah pitched forward and fell down the stairs, landing on her back on the cement step at the bottom. She lay in the darkness for what seemed like an eternity; calling for Freddy constantly. Finally the boy came and saw her lying on the dirt floor in the darkness at the bottom of the steps.

"Freddy, run, get help. I can't get up. Your momma's hurt. Get Jenny next door. Run!" she gasped.

Fred stood there and looked at her, not saying a thing.

"Go, get help. I can't get up and I'm hurt. Go get Jenny!"

Centerville

Finally, Fred ran to the neighbor's house, shouting all the way and soon Jenny Miller came running back. She flipped the light switch and saw Sarah crumpled on the ground.

"Freddy, you stay here with your mother while I go to the post office."

Neither family had a telephone so she rushed to the post office where there was a telephone and to spread the news.

What seemed like an eternity later the ambulance came and Sarah was carted off to the hospital. There she stayed for six weeks, never to walk again. In the excitement nobody noticed the truck, kicked into a corner of the cellar.

While his mother recovered in the hospital and for months after that Fred lived with his Uncle Jack and Aunt Mildred. He helped out on their dairy farm as little as he could, hating every minute of it. Milking the cows twice a day; early in the morning and right before supper was more than he thought he could bear. To the small boy the cows were big, smelly and rather frightening. The one thing that he *did* like was that there were dozens of cats and kittens on the milk farm. There were more of them than cows but they paid their due in rodent control. It seemed like no one ever missed a kitten that disappeared now and again. Not even the one that Fred threw down the well.

When Fred finally returned home his mother had changed. Before, she had been harsh but loving. Now she was shrill, almost always shouting, constantly in pain and angry that she was captive to a wheelchair. Fred had to take up more than what he thought was his fair share of chores and work around the house. His only refuge was the barn and the upstairs of the house. Neither place his mother could go.

Centerville

So Fred became self-sufficient and spent as much time away from home as he could. As the years passed he grew from the spindly boy of seven to the husky almost man that he was at fourteen. He explored the woods, fields and streams for as far around as he dared; sometimes not coming home for days, which only infuriated his mother more than ever. But Fred didn't care, not any more.

Fred, almost from birth, was a difficult child. It was obvious that he had a mind of his own and a rebellious streak a mile wide. Even while in diapers he found ways to infuriate his mother. Once he crawled under the sink and refused to make a sound as his mother became frantic searching for him. The spanking was something he remembered all his life.

Almost as soon as he could walk he began to get into everything he could, trying dangerous stunts like opening kitchen cabinet drawers like a staircase so he could climb up them to the kitchen counter where, of course, his mother found him and spanked him; it seemed it was something she enjoyed. When he was five he managed to find a way to climb to the top of the refrigerator. There he knocked to the floor his mother's favorite cake stand which shattered.

"This is going to hurt me more than it will you," his mother had said as she laid a blistering beating on his small bare back and buttocks. The welts hurt for days but it didn't slow him down at all. The beatings just made him madder at her and ultimately the world.

As soon as he was able to leave the house on his own to play in the back yard and alley his explorations began. Of course he didn't keep to the bounds of the yard and he took the beatings when his mother discovered his disobeyance.

Centerville

When he entered the elementary school at five years of age, he soon became the class bully. He got into fights in the schoolyard at almost every recess; that is those which he was permitted to be outside.

He was a mediocre student. Fred could have done much better but he didn't try. Of course that meant that a bad report card meant another beating. By this time in his young life he was used to them and he began to resent his mother to the point of near hate. His frustration was that he was in her thrall and could do but little but refuse to obey; and take the beatings.

As time passed and he grew larger and stronger he began to take out his frustrations on the occasional stray cat that he could catch. He would hang them by their tails and then wring their necks. He managed the same with the occasional smaller dog. Once he entered a chicken coop and wrung the necks of a number of chickens. The owners thought there was a fox in the area.

When he did these things he usually got an erection. He was too young to understand what the hardness was all about but it did feel good. It was when he was nearly ten and beginning to get pubic hair that his rubbings suddenly generated a pain, almost like having to urgently urinate, and then a flood of something white and sticky. It felt so very good. Killing anything generated an erection and he became to associate sexual feelings with death. And he looked forward to shooting all kinds of animals with his BB gun and he was quite an accurate shot. As he grew older, into his teens, he began to trap and hunt – a dual vocation earning money for trapped furs and meat for the table as well as his sexual satisfaction.

Centerville

Chapter 13
The Search

Back at the carnival grounds the band was finishing up its second set and silence flowed from the bandstand as folks gathered their blankets and headed for their cars. At about the same time, while the Bingo attendant called the numbers from the winning card, there was a brief silence. June Smith looked up from her card and realized that Betsy was not where she was supposed to be. She also realized that she had not heard her whining or complaining for some time. She looked around and saw Sally with her Bingo card but not her daughter.

"Betsy," she called as she rose from the whitewashed bench and turned completely around as she looked for her daughter. "Mary," she said as she turned to her sister, "Sally. Have either of you seen Betsy? Do you know where she went?"

Both mother and daughter looked up from their cards and at the same time shook their heads.

"Sally, weren't you watching her?" Mary asked.

"No. I was playing Bingo. The last I saw of her she was sitting at the end of the bench, over there." She pointed to the spot not more than ten feet away. "She was just sitting there, looking around, and watching people."

"Betsy!" June shouted, "You come here right now! You hear? Betsy, where are you?"

There was no answer.

By now a small group of people had gathered, looking at June as well as at each other. Most were questioning what was happening.

"Have any of you seen my daughter? She was wearing a light purple dress and white shoes. She was sitting right there." June pointed to the vacant bench.

Centerville

The people, as one, shook their heads in the negative and looked around and at each other. Shrugging their shoulders they looked away.

Jim Brocious, one of the sheriff's deputies, the one assigned to the carnival, stepped forward.

"What's the problem, mam?"

"My daughter, Betsy, I don't know where she is. She was sitting here a little while ago but now I can't find her."

"Do you think she may be playing with other children?"

"No, she wouldn't do that without asking me."

"What were you doing?" he asked.

"I was playing Bingo and she was sitting next to me."

"Is it possible that she did ask you to let her go play and you didn't hear her?

"No," replied June. "No I would have heard her and no, she didn't ask."

"OK, you stay right here and I'll get some people to help look around. She's probably playing somewhere close by."

"Find my baby!" June cried. "Something has happened to her!"

"What does she look like?"

"She has blond hair with long ringlets, is wearing a light purple dress and white shoes. She's about this tall." June held her hand, palm down, about three feet off the ground. "Her name is Betsy. She's only six years old" She swept her hair behind her ear and then put her hand to her mouth. She started to shake.

"We'll find her, mam."

Mary took June by the shoulders and pushed her back down to sit on the bench. "It'll be OK. She's probably close by. You just be calm, they'll find her real soon."

Centerville

Deputy Brocious gathered the first three fire policemen he could find and instructed them to comb the carnival grounds looking for the girl. The men branched out and covered every inch of the place. They talked to people, describing Betsy as best they could having never seen her.

Brocious divided the grounds into four parts and assigned the men to their individual areas to search. Edgar Johns had the food and small game stands to cover. He looked behind every food stand and inside most of them. He looked under every table.

Jimmy saw him pass the penny pitch and noted how intense the man was. Jimmy wondered what was so important that he was looking like that. Then he turned and tossed another penny. It landed on a line, another loser.

Another policeman, Bruce Walter, examined the rides and the lines leading to them. He looked at every person on the rides as well as those leaving or entering. He also looked at all the people playing the bigger games, though there the people were mostly adults or older teenagers, no little girls.

The third, Willard Musser, combed the parking lot. He walked down each row and looked between the cars. He didn't think to look under the cars, perhaps instinctively knowing that no little girl in a dress would crawl under a greasy car.

Deputy Brocious searched the bandstand and even went up on to the stage to look out over the thinning crowd as the band was packing its instruments and equipment. The brightness of the full moon flooded the field with enough light that the electric ones might not be needed. All in all the light was more than enough to reveal a little girl wandering alone in the carnival grounds. But there was none

Centerville

A long half hour passed. By then June Smith was near panic. She knew that something horrible had happened to her little girl and it was all her fault. She should have been paying attention to Betsy. She should have taken her on more rides and gotten her cotton candy. She should have let Betsy have fun instead of playing Bingo and ignoring the little girl.

Mary held her close, her arm wrapped around June's shoulders. Sally tried to look scared or sad but she really didn't care. Betsy was just a pest.

Jim Brocious gathered his men and heard their negative reports. He removed his hat and brushed his hand over his crewcut head. He looked around, "You men have flashlights. Let's look in the woods. Maybe she went in there and fell asleep or got lost."

They walked single file along the path that led into the woods by the Bingo stand. Their flashlights cast bright cones of light as they looked both left and right. A few feet into the woods Brocious pointed to a small path and told Bruce Walter to search down that way.

Bruce turned right and stepped onto the path. He hadn't gone more than twenty feet when he saw something shimmering in the dimly dappled moonlit woods. He stepped close and pointed his light at the light smudge lying on the leaf cluttered ground.

"Oh God no." he sighed, "Not again. Not me!" He knelt next to the fragile body and touched it. It was still warm but he could tell that she was dead. Tears began to involuntarily flow as he rose and turned.

"Here! Over here. Come quickly." He waved his flashlight down the path until he saw the others coming his way. Then he knelt again and held his head in his hands as he wept. "Why here, why now, why me?"

Centerville

His thoughts leapt back to that hot day, only a few weeks ago, when he had pulled the cover from his well. "Not again," he sighed.

Then Jim Brocious and the others stumbled onto the scene, their eyes widening as they saw Bruce and the crumpled body of Betsy Smith.

"Don't touch a thing. You didn't touch or move anything, did you Bruce."

"No, I just touched the girl to see if she was alive. I don't think she is. I didn't touch anything else."

"This is a crime scene, right now. Christ, I gotta call the sheriff. He's not going to like this. Bruce, you come with me. You other two, stay here and don't let anyone come close, you hear?"

The men nodded and stepped onto the path shielding Betsy's body from anyone who might come by.

Instinctively realizing that June Smith would immediately run to her daughter, Deputy Brocious and Bruce turned from the woods and the path and walked around the far side of the Bingo stand and to his police car parked near the firetrucks.

Once there he keyed the microphone on his radio. In seconds the dispatcher responded. "Sheriff's dispatch. Who is this?"

"Jim Brocious. Get the sheriff and a couple more deputies over here to Centerville. We got a bad one."

"What is it?" The dispatcher asked.

"I'd rather not say. Too many people could hear and I want to keep this as quiet as possible. I'll wait here until I hear back from Sheriff Shambach."

"10-4. I'll call the sheriff. Stand by."

After what seemed like an eternity the sheriff called on the radio.

"What you got, Jim?"

Forgetting his own admonishment to secrecy, Brocious said, "We have a little girl and she's dead. It looks like someone killed her."

"Damn! Then we need to have the staties come too."

"I think so. How soon can you get over here?"

"I'm already on my way. I called out a couple of fellas as well, so they should be along soon. I'll be there in ten minutes."

"Roger that. I'm going back to the scene. Bruce Walter will be waiting for you near the firetrucks."

"Roger, out."

"Stay here until the sheriff arrives and then bring him back. I'm going to go up there to keep order. Don't you tell a soul what has happened."

Bruce dumbly nodded his head and leaned loosely against the police car.

When Deputy Brocious returned to the woods there was already a small crowd gathering near the path leading into the darkness.

"Move along, move along. There's nothing to see here, nothing for you to do, so please move on." The group slowly dispersed as Jim Brocious entered the woods, only to gather again once he was out of sight. Guided by his flashlight he made his way to where Ed Johns and Will Musser waited with Betsy at their feet.

Brocious knelt next to the body. He could see by bruises that had formed on her neck and arms that she had been brutalized. He touched her cheek and could feel the cooling beginning to move in. Her torso was partially covered by her torn dress and her legs were splayed apart. Her mouth was stuffed with her panties and her hands were clenched.

Centerville

He examined the area around the body but in the dim light could determine nothing. And then he heard the scream.

* * *

Meanwhile the sheriff arrived and parked next to the deputy's car, his deputies were following close behind. Bruce guided him to the woods, passing the Bingo stand. When she saw the sheriff, June Smith screamed at the top of her lungs and threw herself at him. Immediately Bruce and Mary pulled at June; Mary trying to calm her, so the sheriff could get through. The crowd began to thicken.

"Over there," someone pointed towards the woods, "You should go over there where the deputy is."

The sheriff pulled June's hands from his uniform. "When the deputies get here, tell them to control these people," he said to Bruce as he turned to the woods. Ed Johns was waiting for him on the path entering the woods.

"This way," Johns said, as he led Sheriff Shambach into the dark woods and down the side path. In moments he could see Deputy Brocious. He stepped up to the spot where Betsy lay and slowly shook his head.

"How long ago did this happen?"

Brocious shook his head, "I really don't know. Not more than an hour, I would think."

"Well the coroner will know. He should be here soon, along with the State Police." He turned to Will and Ed. "You two go back and make sure nobody but police officials come back here. Nobody else, understand?" Both men nodded and rushed off down the path, glad to be away.

Centerville

Sheriff Shambach knelt next to Betsy's body and instinctively touched her cheek, also feeling the coolness spreading through her flesh. He shook his head and whispered, "What a waste."

He quickly stood as he heard shouting and thrashing in the woods back down the path. "Stay here, Jim." Shambach rose and walked back down the path to discover a knot of men struggling in the woods not far from the path.

"What's going on here?" he shouted at the men. Then he saw that Ed and Will were holding Harvey Miller to the ground, despite his struggles.

"We caught this man coming out of the woods over there." Ed pointed in the direction of where the body had been found.

"What were you doing back there?" the sheriff asked.

"Nothing, I just went back to take a leak and must have feel asleep."

"Stand up and let me get a look at you."

Will pulled Harvey to his feet. Harvey's plaid shirt was littered with leaves and the pocket on the front of his shirt was torn and hanging loose. Harvey's hair was mussed and he had scratches on his face.

"How'd you get those scratches on your face?"

"I don't know. Your men here were beating me up. They probably did it.'

Ed and Will shook their heads, "No, we didn't beat him. We saw him sneaking though the woods from back there," he pointed, "And we grabbed him. He must be the one that done it. Just look at him."

"I *am* looking at him and I don't like what I see. What's your name?"

"Ha, Har, Harvey Miller. What did I do? I didn't do nothin'."

Centerville

"Hold out your arms." Miller did so and the sheriff put handcuffs on him. "Harvey Miller I'm arresting you on suspicion of murder. You two," he pointed to Ed and Will, "Take him down to my cruiser. If you see the State police or my deputies tell them what you witnessed and hand him over to them."

Now, he thought, I have to go talk to the mother.

Centerville

Chapter 14
The Village

June Smith looked around in near panic. She saw people everywhere, especially a small knot of men near the woods. Then she saw Sheriff Shambach go into the woods and only a minute or two later come back out to disperse the crowd. Then he walked towards the parking lot. Again, a few minutes later he came back and again chased the men away and went into the woods. The next time he came out of the woods June was struck by the horror of the realization that there was only one reason all this was happening. She knew it was her baby, her Betsy.

Jumping to her feet she headed towards the woods but Mary, her sister, held fast and prevented June from moving. In pure desperation June filled her lungs and released a scream that came from the very core of her being. The scream pierced the night and rushed over the carnival ground, seeming to stop the entire place for a long static second. The anguish of it stopped people in mid-step.

For a moment nothing seemed to move. The full moon bathed the carnival grounds with its almost luminescent radiance. And then movement began once again, people looking around, others gathering their belongings from the grass at the bandstand and began the walk to their cars.

Jimmy and Ben heard the scream as well. Remembering seeing Edgar Johns searching around the stands Jimmy put the two together and poked Ben in the ribs.

"Come on, there's something better than the penny pitch going on. We're losing anyway. Let's go!" He turned and began running towards the source of the scream. Ben was right on his heels. In less than a minute the boys were at the Bingo stand on the outer edge of a knot of people, all looking to see what was going on.

"Let's go around back," Ben pointed, "maybe we can see more from there." The two boys quickly walked around the crowd and made their way between the benches until they were only a few feet from June Smith and her sister.

Wide eyed Ben whispered, "Wouldja look at her? Something bad happened, that's for sure." Jimmy nodded in agreement. While they watched and waited they saw two men hustling Harvey Miller from the woods and towards the parking lot. The moonlight glinted off the handcuffs binding his wrists in front of him.

Jimmy poked Ben, "I told you something was going on. I wonder what it is? It must be bad if the cops are here and they got that guy cuffed like that.

When June saw Harvey she screamed even louder and longer at the realization that she was looking at the man who had done some unspeakable thing to her daughter. She struggled with all her might and broke from her sister's grip. June ran to Harvey and began beating at him with her fists, pummeling his head and shoulders, screaming all the while.

Ed Johns and Will Musser were taken aback by this sudden attack and found their hands full with a struggling Harvey and June relentlessly pounding him. Harvey's nose was now bleeding and one eye was beginning to puff. Pulling away from June the two men began to drag Harvey away while Mary and another woman pulled and clutched at June, trying to calm her and take her from the scene at the same time. Finally in sheer exhaustion June collapsed to the ground. Sobbing she weakly hammered the earth with her fists.

Centerville

The two women gathered June to her feet and helped her back to her seat at the Bingo stand while Jimmy and Ben, wide eyed, drank it all in.

A few moments later the sheriff walked back out of the woods and came towards June. As he sat beside her, he took June's hands in his own large, strong, hands and gently squeezed them.

"Mrs. Smith, June, I'm so sorry to have to tell you this. It *is* your daughter in there. It pains me to tell you that she is dead. But we got the man that did it and he'll be punished for it, I can promise you that."

Sobbing uncontrollably June sank into his chest as the sheriff put his arms around her and held her tightly. Rocking back and forth he caressed her hair, suddenly feeling both non-professional and totally inadequate to deal with this devastated mother.

"I want to see my baby. I want to see Betsy. Please let me see my baby." She cried.

There was no way that the sheriff would take her to the crime scene and he was troubled because he was not sure what to do. She had a right to see her child but not like she was now. Not with the little girl's panties still stuffed in her mouth and laying naked on the dirt floor of the woods. Not revealed in the harsh light of a flashlight with policemen standing all around. No; not like that.

Soothing her as best he could he said, "As soon as the ambulance comes and we bring her out I promise you that you can see her. If you want you can ride to the hospital with her. I'm sorry but I have to do my job and that means that only police can go back into the woods right now. But I promise you'll be able to see her."

He looked almost pleadingly at Mary and the other woman for them to take care of June until they brought Betsy out of the dark woods. They nodded and moved close as though to protect June from the harsh universe surrounding them.

A few moments earlier Coroner Hackett had arrived along with two policemen who took a stretcher into the woods. The coroner was led to the place where Betsy still lay on the hard ground among the leaves and scuff marks. It took him only a few moments to determine that she had died by strangulation and that rape had been the intended motive.

He pulled her panties from her mouth and stood up. "Put her on the stretcher boys, and cover her up. Smooth her hair down a bit first in case her mother wants to see." He turned and walked from the woods. Meeting the sheriff by the Bingo stand he shook his head.

"We'll take her to the hospital where they can examine her properly. I'd like to get my hands on the bastard that did this." He said as he thought of his own granddaughter who was about the same age.

"Her mother wants to see her. Is she presentable?"

"She's as presentable as we can make her in these circumstances." He waved the two policemen carrying the stretcher to a halt. Meanwhile the sheriff signaled Mary to bring June to his side. Once there he led her to the stretcher. With one arm around her shoulders Sheriff Shambach lifted the corner of the blanket covering the body exposing Betsy's head and curls.

He felt June collapse with a long drawn sigh as she saw her daughter; cold and still, on the stretcher. Picking her up and carrying her in his arms he turned to the stretcher bearers and said, "Let's go."

They silently walked to the ambulance. There they gently placed the stretcher inside and helped June into it as well. Nodding to the nurse he said, "take care of this woman. She's had a shock." The ambulance doors were closed and it silently drove off into the night.

Centerville

Then the sheriff went back to the woods to collect whatever evidence remained and to take Harvey to jail.

* * *

"Did you see the body? It was a little girl. I was this close to her." Ben held his hands about two feet apart.

"Of course I saw it. I was beside you." Jimmy replied.

The boys were walking home after all the excitement had died down. Once they had taken Betsy's body away in the ambulance there wasn't much to see; just a bunch of lights in the woods and not much else.

"I wonder if they'll have the carnival tomorrow night, after all this?" Ben asked.

"Of course they will," replied Jimmy.

But he was wrong.

The next morning it seemed as though the entire village gathered at the post office. Whenever there was big news the post office became the clearing house for every rumor, bit of gossip or buzz floating through the town like pollen in allergy season.

Jimmy's dad had nothing to do with it and contributed nothing as well. Never the less people gathered in the vestibule where the mailboxes were as well as outside the building itself.

The vestibule was nothing more than a converted sun porch, fifteen feet long and about five feet deep. Four people made it crowded and this morning it was more like a mob.

"They tried to rape that Mecklenburg girl just last Monday. She was lucky she wasn't killed, and now the little Smith girl. Poor thing, I hear she was raped and tore up something pitiful." One woman said with a faint smile on her face.

"Yeah and I hear that old Harvey Miller was the one that did it. I never did like the look in his squinty eyes." Said Stanley Roberts. "I know he likes his beer an awful lot," he said as if in condemnation as he spat tobacco juice onto the sidewalk.

"I saw Sheriff Shambach haul him away to the jail. He looked like he could strangle old Harvey, he did."

"Well I wouldn't get too cock sure about 'Old Harvey' if I was you. Yep, he likes his beer but so do you Bill! I saw you over by the beer trucks myself last night. How do we know 'Old Harvey' didn't just have too much to drink and passed out in the woods?"

"You stickin up for the bastid, John? I wouldn't if I was you."

"Well you ain't me and I never said I was sticking up for him. I just said he was pretty much like every one of us. It could'a been anybody that did it, or no one, so don't get so high and mighty, Bill."

Sounding like fighting words Bill took off after John and in an instant they were in a tussle on the sidewalk. Clutching each other close so neither could get in a punch they wobbled around in a circle until cooler heads prevailed and they were pulled apart, nothing hurt including their defended pride.

Just then Jimmy's father, Eldred, came out of his office and tried to chase the crowd away.

"There's people who actually have business here and this is U.S. Government property. There is no loitering allowed. Please take your discussion somewhere else."

The people in the crowd looked at him as though he had just grown eyestalks on his head. But grumbling they moved a few feet down the sidewalk to stand in front of Martin's restaurant, some even climbing on the porch, to continue their argument.

Preceded by the squealing of tires, Rufus Ott's beat up Chevy truck barreled around the corner and screeched to a stop in front of the restaurant as though showing his nonexistent racing prowess to the crowd. He leapt from the cab as though his pants were on fire and shouted, "Have you heard?"

In rapt attention the people turned as one to pay full attention to the new town crier.

"They let Harvey Miller out of jail! Can you imagine that? Said there isn't enough evidence to hold him, even with his shirt torn to threads and scratches all over his face and his zipper down. What do they need? He's guilty as hell for killing that little girl and they let him loose! Can you imagine?"

The crowd had grown larger by this time and the grumbling grew in volume.

"Hain't right," shouted Herb Marks, "they should'of strung him up."

The crowd agreed with various shouts and grunts of agreement.

"I can't imagine that the Sheriff would let him out unless he found out that he was innocent. You know he isn't guilty until proven so in a court of law." Shouted Dick Strasser.

"Piss on that, I say. The man's guilty as hell and we all know it. What more is there?" said Herb as he spat on the sidewalk. "They should of hung him up last night when they had the chance."

"Herb, you know better than that! This is still a democracy and we have to abide with the rule of law."

"Fuck the rule of law," Herb shouted back at Dick. "The law ain't workin' here and we all know it. We ought'a do something."

Centerville

"Yes, you should," shouted Eldred Harris, the postmaster, "you should all go home and wait for the police to do their job. Mobs, even tiny ones like this one, don't rule around here. Go home and cool down. If you don't I'll call the sheriff myself!"

"You tell 'em Ned." Someone shouted from the safety of the back of the crowd.

Grudgingly the small crowd began to disburse. On his way Herb Peters spat tobacco juice at the feet of the postmaster.

Returning to his office Eldred wondered whether he should call Sheriff Shambach anyway. He had never seen people in the village so riled up about anything before. Of course the murder and rape of a little six year old girl was enough to get anybody upset.

'They'll probably go home and simmer down,' he thought. 'But again, Harvey lives just down the street and he lives alone since his wife walked out. He could be an easy target. Maybe I better call, just in case.'

But he never did.

* * *

Earlier that morning, after examining Harvey, looking at the evidence and talking with a few of the known witnesses at the beer trucks it became apparent that Harvey had nothing to do with Betsey's murder. His shirt pocket had been torn when he got to the carnival and the scratches on his face came from struggling in the brush in the woods when he was captured. He truly was at the wrong place at the wrong time.

That would teach him to drink too much in public. At least he slept it off in safety and not in the woods.

So Sheriff Shambach released Harvey Miller that morning. At the same time he issued an order to close down the carnival. He didn't want any excitement in Centerville on Saturday night.

Centerville

Chapter 15
A Gathering Storm

It was by chance that Jimmy had decided to visit his father at the post office that morning but he hadn't expected to find a crowd there. As a result he hung in the background, watching, listening and learning until his father had chased them all away.

Seeing that the coast was clear he went into the post office and opened the door to his father's office. Though nobody ever tried the door, it was always unlocked when the postmaster was in. But few, if any, knew that fact and Jimmy kept the secret.

"Dad, did you see that crowd out there? What did they want?" he asked but he already knew.

"Whenever there is any kind of trouble in town all the people gather here to talk about it. I wish they wouldn't but they do. Today it was about what happened last night. I hope you kept away from all that."

"I saw them bring the little girl out of the woods, dad. Everybody did. And I saw the sheriff take her mother to the ambulance and that man to jail. What's going on around here, dad? I mean, Patsy when school let out, then Judy last Monday and now this? What's going on?"

"Jim, I'm not sure I know. Yes, something is happening in town but it isn't as bad as you think. Sure bad things happen but that doesn't mean that they are all connected. We don't know. And *you* know very well that Patsy fell down the well and drowned. Sometimes a number of unconnected things happen that just don't look that way. I think this is just one of those times."

"I'm not sure, dad. And what about the fire? Everyone thinks that it was set by someone. Maybe that same person is doing all of this? What could be next?"

Centerville

"Jim, now you are going to extremes." His father said with a stern look. "I know that it must be frightening for you to see all of these things and that you naturally try to relate them to each other. But they aren't related. Sure, the fire might have been set, but then again it might have been natural. We had a thunderstorm the day before the fire. Lightening could have struck and started a slow smoldering fire that didn't really catch on until the next day. And Patsy, Judy and Betsy Smith, because that was the little girl's name, don't have to be related. Sometimes things just happen. For no rhyme or reason, they just do. And things aren't always as black and white as people think or want. For example though he arrested Harvey Miller last night the sheriff released him this morning because there is no evidence that he actually did anything but some people still think so. Harvey was just at the wrong place at the wrong time. The sheriff understood that but some people don't."

Jimmy tried to follow his father's reasoning but came up short no matter how hard he tried. How does a kid reason with an adult? He could bring up Patsy's pants zipper again but it probably would have no effect. He could share his suspicions about Fred but even Jimmy knew there wasn't nearly enough evidence to prove anything. He knew that right now his arguments would be lost in his father's logic. Better to let it go – for now.

"I guess you're right, dad. It's just too much. I wish it would all go away."

"Son, don't we all." His father replied. "What are you going to do today?"

"I'm on my way to Ben's and then we'll figure out something to do. Maybe go down to the kiln."

"Sounds good but be careful."

Centerville

Jimmy nodded as he left the post office and set off down the street. Dads were like that. Of course he and Ben would be careful.

As he walked along the Lower Street, scuffing his shoes on the uneven slate sidewalk he thought about Betsy and Judy and Patsy. He couldn't help it. There was a connection there and he knew it. But try as he might he couldn't put it together. And he believed that he and Ben were the only people who believed that something more had happened to Patsy than just falling down into a well. His troubled mind deepened as he neared Ben's house.

On the Lower street, for some reason, all of the houses stood directly on the street with only the narrow slate sidewalk separating the street from the houses. Here and there a large chestnut or maple tree grew directly from the sidewalk, the roots lifting the slate in crazy angles and pushing the curb, lopsided, into the narrow street. Ben lived on the next block but still only a few doors down from Harvey Miller's and as Jimmy came close he saw a small group of men gathered on the sidewalk at Harvey's front door.

Feeling cautious Jimmy crossed the street as he continued his walk. He had seen Harvey many times but never, until now, knew his name. Next he passed Fred's house which was directly across from the Miller household and catty corner to Ben's place on the next block. Having passed the knot of men who were discussing something in low voices that seemed ominous, Jimmy crossed back over to Ben's house.

He went around to the side porch and knocked on the kitchen door. Friends never came in the front door but at least they knocked. Ben opened the door and came out onto the porch. He held up his hand to signal quiet.

"Mom has another of her migraines, so we better be quiet."

Jimmy nodded as they walked into the side yard.

"Have you seen the crowd in front of Mr. Miller's house?" Jimmy asked.

"Well it isn't quite a crowd, but I did see it 'cause I was across to Mrs. Kleckner a few minutes ago. She had some ground cherries for mom. God I hate those things but mom likes them and wants to bake a pie." He made a sour face as though in anticipation of having to taste the future pie.

"I don't know how big the crowd was back then but there are about eight or ten men out there now," Jimmy said.

"That sounds about what I saw. I wonder what they're doing?"

"Whatever it is they aren't talking about the fireworks at the carnival tonight."

"Haven't you heard?" Ben asked. "They cancelled the carnival for tonight. There won't be any fireworks. I guess what happened last night was too much. Dad said that the sheriff shut it down. That little girl's death must have been too much."

"Her name was Betsy," Jimmy said absently.

The boys continued to talk as they walked from the side yard and onto the sidewalk. Looking down the street they could see that there were now more than a dozen men gathered a few doors down.

"That doesn't look good," Ben said.

"No it doesn't. Do you think we ought to tell my dad?"

Ben shrugged as they crossed the street and turned towards the post office as though the decision had already been made. A few minutes later they arrived and entered the post office. Jimmy led the way behind the counter.

"What's up fellows?" Jimmy's father asked.

Centerville

"There's a bunch of men down at Mr. Miller's house. I know he was arrested last night and that the sheriff let him off because he doesn't think he did anything. But I think these men think he did," Jimmy stuttered. "Most of them are the same men who were here arguing here a little while ago."

"How do you know about Mr. Miller?"

"Like I said I was outside when all those people were arguing in front of the post office a little while ago. I heard what they were talking about and I heard how mad some of them were. And I know what you told me about Mr. Miller.

"But they still sound pretty mad. Do you think they'll do something?"

"I don't know that they will but I'll keep my eye on them and if the crowd gets bigger I'll call the sheriff. How's that sound?"

"Thanks dad, I guess I'm just worried."

"I understand. I'll keep an eye on them. You boys go along now; things will be OK. I promise." Jimmy's father spoke as he turned back to his work. Jimmy and Ben left the office and walked down to the wooden bridge to find something to do. Jimmy's dad, involved in his own studies, put the event to the back of his mind.

When they arrived at the bridge Ben began to climb on the girders. Once again he said that one of these days he was actually going to be able to climb to the top and walk across the bridge high above the stream. And once again Jimmy told him that he would fall to his death on the rocks below. It was an ongoing litany the boys carried out every time they crossed the bridge.

As they reached the other side Ben looked down at the muddy banks and said, "Would you look at that?" He pointed at the sleeping Bart Tuttle. It seemed that his favorite place to sleep off warm summer afternoons was there, at the base of the bank by the bridge his feet almost in the shallow water.

Jimmy laughed as he pointed downstream, "Let's go that way and see what we can find." The boys knew the stream like the back of their hands and so they didn't really expect to find anything new or different. But this day they were a bit surprised.

One hundred feet away on the downstream side of the bridge and at the edge of the water they discovered a large pile of rocks. Some were sunken into the earthen bank, the water lapping at them. They all looked like they had come from somewhere else. They were, for the most part, large and round, some close to a foot or more across. They had to be heavy and the way they were sunken in the mud it looked like they had been dropped from some height, perhaps from the top of the steep bank; their presence looked recent.

"I wonder what that's all about?" Ben asked.

"I don't know. Maybe someone is collecting those stones to build a dam across the run. I know they do it down at Cave Creek. In fact my dad works on the dam down there every summer. He collects rocks from all over below the dam and puts them in a pile near it. Then when he has enough he builds them into the dam. Maybe someone is doing that here." Jimmy believed that he was an expert in dams because he helped his dad and his dad's friends every summer as they rebuilt the dam at the creek. That raised the water so the swimming was better but it also improved the fishing in the rapids below the dam. He had caught a nice whitefish a few weeks back when he and his dad went there to collect hellgrammites for fishing bait and then tried them out in the rapids. At first he had thought that his bait was just dragging until his rod bent and pulled. Then he knew he had something big, and it was. Though the fish was naturally bony his dad knew how to grind it up to make fish cakes. With fried potatoes it made an excellent meal.

As the boys followed the bed of the stream the afternoon sky darkened and they thought they heard a rumble of thunder over Keel Mountain. It was typical of August days to have thunderstorms in the afternoon and it looked like they might get a soaking.

Never the less they continued downstream heading in the direction of the lime kiln. Pants rolled up and carrying their shoes they waded in the water, pausing now and again to try to catch crayfish in the shallows. They would carefully turn over rocks and watch for the tiny lobster like creatures to back away from them at lightning speed. Once in a while they did catch one but more often than not they chickened out fearing they would get pinched by their claws.

As they neared the lime kiln they heard the first strong peal of thunder. "Maybe we should head over to my place in case it rains." Ben suggested.

Jimmy agreed and so they turned their backs on the lime kiln and crossed the field to the alley paralleling the Lower Street.

It was probably a good thing because Fred was prowling around the lime kiln. He was restless and full of energy and had no outlet or target on which to vent.

Chapter 16
Fireworks, of a Different Sort

When they arrived at Ben's back door Ben turned to Jimmy and said, "Let's go over to the store and get a soda. I have enough to buy two if you're short."

"I still have money from the penny pitch, if they don't mind taking a lot of pennies." Jimmy replied as they turned to Musser's store just down the street on the corner across from the fire house.

A few minutes later they crossed the street and entered the store. The interior was dark, and quiet, as always. Floyd stood behind the counter smiling broadly and nodded to them as they entered. Floyd Musser was tall and gangly and reminded Jimmy of Ichabod Crane from the story of the Headless Horseman.

Indeed Floyd was well over six feet tall and thin as a rail. It was said that his crazy wife wouldn't feed him anything healthy and that he was starving to death right before the town's eyes. In fact he was just a tall thin man with a grin so wide the corners of his mouth seemed to touch his ear lobes and his large white teeth shined, especially in the darkness of the store as they did today as he greeted the boys when they entered. In the gloom his white shirt was almost ghostly as he faded into the shelves.

"What can I do for you boys today?" he asked.

"We're just here for a couple of sodas." Ben replied as they crossed the room to the cooler in the alcove near the shoe counter.

Musser's store was a treasure trove. Almost anything one could want could be bought there from barbed wire, to clothing (in limited supply) and even coal in the winter. Jimmy often went to the store for bread and milk. When he entered Floyd always provided the goods and said, "Here you are son, a quart of bread and a loaf of milk." Jimmy would giggle but after a while it got old.

Once in a while he would get cereal as well. When he asked for cereal he always asked for something on the top shelf, high near the ceiling. The Cheerios were up there. Then Floyd would get this marvelous device that had rubber coated yellow pinchers at one end and squeeze handles at the other. He would raise the yellow claws to the cereal and squeeze the handles at the other end and pluck the cereal from its perch high atop the shelves. Then when the cereal box was straight overhead he would release it and catch the box with one hand. With a flourish he would put it in the counter and Jimmy was always amazed at the thin man's dexterity.

Today the boys rummaged around the soda cooler looking for something cold to drink. Jimmy was hoping they would have ginger ale. That was his favorite. As they sorted through the loose bottles and discussed the relative value of the various brands they dimly heard the bell ring as the door to the street opened. They didn't look up from their work.

Had they been paying attention they would have heard footsteps cross to the counter but the boys never turned from their quest.

"I need some kerosene." A deep voice said. "I need a gallon. Can you give it to me in a jug; I don't have anything to put it in."

Floyd figured that he could provide the kerosene in a glass gallon jug. But it would cost a nickel extra. The voice agreed and Floyd left the room and the building, grabbing an empty gallon jug on the way. He went outside as the voice followed to watch him fill the jug from the pump behind the store.

Centerville

Inside Ben finally selected a Royal Crown Cola and Jimmy got his Canada Dry, *"the Champaign of ginger ale."* They turned and saw that Floyd had gone so they sat on the bench in the shadowed corner near the wood stove. In the winter men gathered here daily to discuss the news and solve the problems of the world. But in the summertime the corner was deserted while all the men worked on the farms and in the fields.

While they waited, Floyd and the voice, actually a man both boys were familiar with but didn't know his name came back into the store.

"That damn Harvey Miller; he's going to get his." the man said as he paid his fifteen cents for the kerosene. "The sheriff may have left him off but we won't!" He took his jug and left the store.

Jimmy and Ben presented their sodas to Floyd and paid him.

"I don't know what you boys might have heard but don't pay a mind to Bob there. He doesn't mean anything by what he said. Don't forget to bring our bottles back. There's a five cent deposit for each one."

The boys knew very well that there was a reward for bringing the bottles back. At least once a week they scavenged for soda bottles around the village and would sometimes find a few, occasionally enough to trade for a soda each.

Floyd uncapped their bottles for them and they left the store. As they stood under the second story overhang, sipping the sweet effervescent goodness, they looked to their right and saw Bob and his jug walking towards a group of men across the street from Harvey Miller's place.

"I don't like the look of that," said Jimmy as thunder rumbled in the distance over Keel Mountain.

Centerville

"Maybe it'll rain and chase them away," Ben nodded.

"I wonder if we ought to tell my dad," was Jimmy's reply. But instead they turned the other way and returned to Ben's place.

On the far side of the mountain the thunder storm gathered itself and began to roar down the Cave Creek valley, pounding rain and wind as it gathered force. Over the village, still far from the storm, the skies began to darken and the air became still.

Fred looked up from his work, building a fish trap and decided that it was time to go home before it rained. The trap could wait for another day.

Ben and Jimmy sat on Ben's back porch drinking their sodas and talked baseball.

Bob Zartman rejoined the group standing in the street in front of Harvey Miller's house, presenting his jug to his fellow compatriots.

"That's just the thing we need," someone said. "Just the thing."

"Harvey!" someone shouted and threw the apple he had been gnawing at the front window of Harvey's house. The apple ineffectually bounced off the glass and rolled across the porch. Someone laughed.

"Damn," someone else muttered and picked a small rock from the street and hurled it at the same window. To the men gathered there it gave a resounding and satisfying crash of broken glass. Someone cheered.

Fred crossed the street at the corner by the store and saw the gathering of men across from his own house. He could tell that there was going to be some fun. He hurried to his home, hoping his mother would leave him alone. He snuck through the back door and up to his room. He raised his bedroom window. There he had a front row seat to whatever was about to happen.

Centerville

"Get your ass out here Harvey! We want to talk to you. We know what you did." Someone shouted.

Though none of the men saw it, a corner of the curtain in the second floor bedroom of the house lifted and a single frightened eye looked out over the crowd of men filling the street. As it watched more men arrived to swell the ranks.

"I know he's in there. I saw him this morning and his car is out in the shed behind the house."

By now the sky had darkened considerably and the storm began to roll over the crest of the mountain and onto the village. Lightening flashed and thunder rolled. The charged atmosphere seemed to bring the men in the street to action.

As the darkness lowered the men flowed onto Harvey Miller's porch and some began to pound on the door demanding entry. Others crunched through the shattered glass to peer through the broken window into the interior darkness. A sudden flash of lightening bathed the empty room in stark brightness. Thunder quickly followed as the wind quickened.

Fred, wide eyed and excited, watched from his room. The excitement in his chest made his heart pound and rise in his throat as though it would jump from his mouth. He felt excitement in his groin and his breath got short. This was almost as good as being there himself. He grasped at the window sill as he watched the frenzy on the street below, his pupils so wide that his eyes became as black as the approaching storm.

Then the storm broke on the town. Rain poured and wind swept down the street, howling as it tore at the trees lining the street. The fury of the storm drove the men on the porch to pound savagely on the door and break it open. They flooded into the house like a stream breaching a dam.

Centerville

"He's in here somewhere", someone shouted. "Let's get the bastard!"

Spreading through the first floor of the house while others went up the stairs the men searched for Harvey Miller who had taken refuge in a bedroom closet hidden behind some clothing left by his wife in her hasty departure a few months back. But he wasn't hidden well enough.

Breaking through the bedroom door Bob Zartman and his fellows ransacked the room and tore at the closet door. Pulling it open Harvey tumbled to the floor.

"There's the son of a bitch that killed the little girl. He started; it now let's finish it!" someone shouted as they dragged him across the floor and threw him down the stairs. Flailing and kicking Harvey tumbled down the steps and landed in a heap at the base.

Jim Bateman, stood there and looked up to watch Harvey tumble. When Harvey came to a stop he kicked fiercely at Harvey's head with his heavy steel toed work boot. Harvey's head snapped sharply to the side and he lay still. More men stumbled on the stairs and across the room to join in the kicking and stomping of Harvey's now still body. Blood flowed from his temples and nose. His mouth was crushed and the stumps of his teeth were all that were left in his bloody mouth. His tongue was nearly bitten through.

Outside thunder roared and hail pelted the street, houses and trees. Fred could only see blurs of movement through the windows of Harvey's house until there was a sudden flash of red and orange through the front room windows.

"We better get out of here," Bob hollered as he poured kerosene from his jug onto Harvey's body and the floor around him. "Move it!" he shouted as he threw the

Centerville

jug against the wall where it burst, spraying the balance of the fuel onto the walls and floor.

As the men flooded through the front door Bob put a match to Harvey and watched the flames quickly flow over the body and across the floor. Within seconds the room was filled with fire and the crowd had no choice but to flee into the wind and the rain. Thunder set the tempo of the rain, wind and hail as the men ran, arms covering their heads to protect themselves from the elements.

Someone called the fire department but the siren could be barely heard in the fury of the storm. And nobody came to fight the fire.

Fred watched, eyes like saucers, as the house burned to the ground, consuming Harvey's body in the flames of hate and malice. He rubbed his erection and grinned like an idiot in his glee as he felt the heat of the flames cover his already sweating body.

Finally the house collapsed in upon itself, sending sparks and embers upwards to be blown by the wind; fireworks of a different sort than had been anticipated on this Saturday night.

Centerville

Chapter 17
Ashes to Ashes

A few hours later the sheriff, state police, fire marshal, Oppie Fenster and the coroner, all accompanied by deputies and hangers on were combing over the ruins of Harvey Miller's house.

"I guess I shouldn't be surprised that there were no witnesses to this tragedy. Nobody saw anything. Nobody heard anything. Hell, the fire department, for the little it's worth, didn't even come to fight the fire. Afraid they might get wet or they hoped that the storm would put the fire out." Sheriff Shambach was talking with a State Police corporal. "This is becoming some sorry assed town this summer, especially the last week or so. I just don't know where it's going to end but I hope this is it."

Just then the coroner, Ray Hackett, and his assistant stumbled from the wreckage and across what was left of the front porch. He approached the sheriff, "There's a body in there. At the base of what used to be the stairs. Can't tell who it is but I suppose it's the man who lived there. He's burnt pretty bad. Won't be able to tell much more than that until after the autopsy."

"Well, for now, I'm going to assume that it's Harvey Miller. This was his house. If you need help to get him into the ambulance get a couple of my deputies." Sheriff Shambach turned to the state policeman. "Wonder what the marshal will find?"

"I'd guess he'll find evidence of an accelerant, probably kerosene or gas. We'll know soon enough." The two men continued to talk as they watched the coroner move back into the ruins with a stretcher and two deputies.

Centerville

About five minutes later they emerged into the street carrying the litter, the body covered with a blanket. Not long after that the fire marshal approached.

"What do you think Glenn?" asked the sheriff.

"It looks like arson all right. I could see that something was poured on the floor and on the body; by the scaling it's pretty obvious. I also found the pieces of a glass jug in the living room. The base of the jug is pretty well intact. Probably what they carried the fuel in. I think it was probably kerosene because it burned slower than gasoline burns and there isn't any sign of explosion, just slower moving flames. That's about all I can tell right now. Maybe in the daylight I'll be able to see more."

The state cop shuffled his feet and said, "Sheriff, do you really need me here? It looks like you have this pretty well under control."

Sheriff Shambach nodded, "Yeah, I got it under control; as much as I can and is possible. For now I don't think I need anything. But if this turns into some kind of mob outrage, which I think it might, I may very well need you, maybe a lot of you. Keep your ears open."

The statey nodded and walked back to his grey and blue cruiser. He started it and turned in the street, his headlights leading him out of the village and away from the blackened ruins.

"Brocious," he called to his chief deputy as he signaled him to come over. The deputy walked over from the remains of the front porch and nodded.

"I don't think much is going to happen tonight but I want you to post a rotation of men here for the rest of the night anyway. I don't want any towns folk coming here to pick through this stuff. It's a crime scene now, so we have to keep people out."

"I'm on it," replied Jim Brocious. "I'll rotate two man teams until morning. Then I'll come over myself."

Centerville

"Sounds good. I'll meet you here around 7:00. Tell the men that if anyone comes around tonight to question them about what they know – if anything. And then send them packing. To be honest I'm not hopeful that we'll learn much of anything from these people. They're going to be pretty closed mouth, I think." He spat as he turned towards his car. "I'll see you in the morning."

Thunder rumbled in the distance as he slowly drove away.

* * *

The next morning the Reverend Hummel opened the Reformed Church worship service, not with his usual greeting, but with a somber yet fervent prayer for the safety of the village and for sanity to prevail. The service did not follow the usual format but instead, after a somber hymn, he launched into a sermon the likes of which few had ever heard,

"My fellow Centervillians." He quietly began. "A double tragedy has befallen this peaceful village and it is at the hand of man that it has happened. A girl," he sighed, "a little girl, was brutally murdered on Friday night at the hands of we know not who. And last night a villager was killed in his own home when a crowd of unknown men burned his house to the ground. I know some think that he must have done the evil deed.

"Where is the mercy, where is the humanity?" he shouted at the surprised congregation. "What brings us to this state, this place of hate and horror? And who is the Judas who betrayed Harvey Miller and led the mob to his house?"

He paused and looked across the upturned faces. "Evil things have happened in this village this summer. We all remember poor Patrick Marks who drowned in the

143

well. And the fire that took God's tabernacle in the woods. These events were accidents. But the brutal attack on the young lady last week at the carnival, the death of little Betsy Smith and the horrible death of Harvey Miller were not accidents!" His voice rose in pitch and volume.

"It is the evil of men that have brought these ashes to bear. It is the wickedness of men that tore the girl from her mother and our fellow man from our midst. We must not succumb to evil. Not here in this place. Not now. Not ever!

"Pray, pray, my friends, that God has mercy on our very souls. And pray for justice, justice for Miss Smith and her mother. And pray for justice for Harvey Miller. And pray for *mercy* from God the almighty for those who have perpetrated these horrendous crimes. Pray for mercy from God for I fear there is no other mercy in this town."

With that he turned and left the church to walk to his parsonage where he locked the doors and wept in grief, fear and rage.

Centerville

Chapter 18
Inquest (Part 1)

That afternoon found many of the villagers looking over the wreckage of Harvey Miller's home. There were whispered comments among them that Harvey did get what he deserved. It seemed that the whole village believed the dead man guilty of murder. None of them seemed to feel that there might be murderers among themselves. Many didn't believe that he was murdered but, instead, that justice had been done.

In the daylight Fred could openly watch and examine the ruins. He stood close to the rope the sheriff's deputies strung around the property to keep people out. He was close enough to be satisfied. Then he noticed that Jimmy Harris, Ben Snyder, Darryl Wheems and a couple of other boys were gathered right there with him.

"Didja see it happen, Fred? Didja?" one of the boys asked.

Fred nodded, "I saw it all right. How could I miss it? I saw the whole thing from my bedroom window." He puffed out his chest a bit as he spoke.

"Wow," another boy said. "It must have been something."

"It was something all right, and it was hotter than hell. I'll tell you that."

"Do you know who did it?" another asked.

Fred shook his head and the conversation died off as the sheriff came from around the back of the burned house.

"You boys run off now. There's nothing here for you to see. Run along, I said."

Reluctantly the boys turned from the scene of the crime and went their different directions. Fred lingered

145

the longest but at last he, too, turned and ambled down the street towards the restaurant.

Two days later, at the supper table, Jimmy's father said, "I want you to come down to the post office tomorrow morning at 10:00."

"Sure, what for? Do you have some work for me?" Sometimes Jimmy would be hired to pack mail bags. They seemed to gather into a large pile. Then Jimmy would get the paying job of stuffing bags into one or two others for the delivery truck to haul away the next day. It was easy money.

"I might have some bags to stuff but it's something else I need you to be there for." His father said nothing more than that.

The next morning Jimmy arrived on time. True to his word his father gave him work stuffing mail bags. While he was working his dad called him from the back storage room to the front office. When he arrived he saw the sheriff standing there. Immediately he was afraid but didn't know exactly why.

"Don't be nervous, Jim," Sheriff Shambach smiled and actually shook Jimmy's hand. Then he took a piece of paper from his shirt pocket and handed it to Jimmy, not his father.

"This here is a summons. I called your dad yesterday to tell him I was coming to serve it to you. What it says is that you have to come to the coroner's office next week, on Tuesday at 9:00am, to testify. Floyd Musser said that you and Ben Snyder were in the store the day of the fire and the coroner wants to know what you might have seen or heard." He paused, "now don't get excited. It won't be much different than the meeting I held at the carnival ground last week. It'll just be a couple of simple questions. Your friend Ben will be there too."

"What about Fred? Will he be there? He said he saw the whole thing from his bedroom window. And he lives just across the street."

"Fred who?" asked the sheriff.

"Fred Swope. Like I said he lives right across from Mr. Miller's house." Jimmy replied.

"His mother is in a wheel chair, right?"

"Yes," Ned said, "She fell down the cellar steps a number of years ago and was paralyzed."

"Yes, I remember something about that. A real shame," said the sheriff.

Shambach rubbed his jaw. "The coroner didn't say anything about Fred Swope but who knows. He might be called too." In fact Jimmy's question made it a certainty that Fred would be called.

"Now don't worry about this. I know it must make you feel anxious but you haven't done anything wrong. You are simply a possible witness to an event or events that may be important to figuring out what happened on Saturday night. What you might say may not even be important. So don't get into a sweat over this. OK Jim?"

Jimmy nodded nervously.

"Your dad will be there with you, won't you Ned? And, oh yes, don't talk about Saturday to anyone, not even Ben or your father, until after the inquest. OK?"

Finding it hard to swallow and not being able to speak, Jimmy simply mutely nodded.

"He'll be just fine sheriff. We'll be there on Tuesday."

Sheriff Shambach nodded, turned and left the post office.

"Jim," his father began, "I want you to know that this is serious business. Mr. Miller is dead and the circumstances make it look like someone in town had something to do with it. So please do not talk about what you may, or may not, have seen. And don't be afraid. I think you *are* right now and I don't blame you, but you're safe and nobody will bother you. The coroner just needs to understand what happened and maybe you can help."

"OK dad. But I don't know what they'll ask. But I'll do my best. Let me finish the bags and then I think I'll go home." With that he turned towards the back room to finish stuffing his mail bags.

The week slowly passed and when the two boys were together there were often long and awkward silences. They played a lot of whiffle ball. Neither saw any sign of Fred and neither went to Musser's store.

Much of the time that week the village seemed to be almost deserted. Few people gathered at the post office, restaurant or anywhere else. When they did meet no one talked about the fire. The ring leaders themselves were not seen anywhere.

The following Tuesday Jimmy and his father arrived promptly on time at the coroner's office. They went inside and were advised by a secretary to have a seat until called.

Inside the hearing room Coroner Raymond Hackett called the inquest to order with the hammering of a gavel onto his desk. The room was large enough to seat the jury and had space in the gallery for perhaps fifty people. The ceiling was high and dusty windows filtered what sunlight was available. At one time it had been a part of the courthouse and had been a courtroom in its own right. Now the coroner used it for his inquests.

"Order, order please!" He called. "This inquest into the death of one Mr. Harvey Miller is now in session. Anyone who has been summoned as a witness must now leave the room. I'll not have any witness present before they have testified.

Centerville

"This is not a court of law. We are not here to charge anyone for a crime. We are not here to arrest or accuse. That is not our function; that is the job of the police. We are here today simply to determine, as best we can, what happened in Centerville on Saturday, August 13, 1955.

"On that evening a fire occurred, which destroyed the home of Mr. Harvey Miller. Mr. Miller was in the home at the time and his burned body was discovered that same evening.

"A jury has been selected from the voting rolls of the county and will now be impaneled. Jurors, please rise and raise your right hands."

The six men of the jury rose.

"Do you solemnly swear that you will diligently inquire and a true presentment make, how, in what manner and by whom or what Mr. Harvey Miller of Centerville, Pennsylvania came to his death; and that you will deliver to me, the coroner of this county, a true inquest thereof, according to such evidence as shall be given to you, and according to the best of your knowledge and belief. So help you God."

The jurors responded in unison, "I do."

"You may be seated," intoned Coroner Hackett.

"Gentlemen," he continued speaking to the jury. "During these proceedings you will hear testimony from a number of people. I will question each witness. When I complete my questions you may provide written questions which I will ask. You may take notes if you so desire. When testimony has completed you will retire to the jury room to reach your verdict. You will receive instructions at that time.

"Before we call the first witness I will make a brief account of my findings as the coroner of this county. The complete report is available as public record. Now I will summarize that report.

"On August 13th I investigated a suspicious death in Centerville at the home of Mr. Harvey Miller. Mr. Miller's home had been burned and I discovered his body in the living room of the home at the base of the steps leading to the second floor.

"Mr. Miller suffered injuries consistent with being beaten or kicked about the head and torso. He was missing a number of teeth that had been broken out in the beating. His skull was fractured on the right temple. There was evidence that an accelerant, probably kerosene, had been poured on his body and then ignited. The autopsy reported that there was no smoke residue in his lungs. That means that Mr. Miller was dead before he was burned. His injuries were not, I repeat not, consistent with having fallen down the stairs. They are also not consistent with being pushed or thrown down the stairs.

"Because of the facts gathered at the scene Mr. Miller's death is considered a suspicious death and is thus being considered a homicide. Homicide is simply defined as a death caused by another human being.

"Call the first witness, Sheriff John Shambach."

The sheriff entered the room and was sworn in. He sat in the witness box.

"Sheriff, we know that you were present at the scene of the fire. Would you please describe what you saw?"

The sheriff began, "I arrived after the fire had pretty well burned itself out. To the best of my knowledge the Centerville fire department did not respond. At that time the ruins were too hot to examine but about an hour later, what with all the rain, the remains of the house were cool enough to enter. You, Mr. Coroner, came from the house and informed me that there was a body inside. I assumed that it was Mr. Harvey Miller. Not long after that the fire marshal, Mr. Glenn Bowersox informed me that it was a probable case of arson. At that time I declared the scene of the fire a crime scene and I appointed my deputies to rope off the area. I also had them stand watch for the balance of the night to keep onlookers away."

"Did you interview any witnesses?"

"Only one, Mr. Floyd Musser. He was not so much a witness of the fire but, instead, he spoke to me about what may have been a related incident at his store."

"And what was that?" asked the coroner.

"Mr. Musser told me that shortly before the fire a Mr. Bob Zartman bought a glass gallon jug and had it filled with kerosene. He also told me that Mr. Zartman spoke about Mr. Miller, quote, 'getting his'. I spoke to no other witnesses.

"I returned Sunday morning to examine the ruins but could not locate anyone who had been witness to the fire."

The jury had no questions so with that the sheriff was released. He took seat in the gallery. Coroner Hackett next called Fire Marshal Bowersox.

After the Fire Marshal had been sworn and seated the coroner asked, "Marshal Bowersox, we are aware, through testimony, that you were present at the scene of the fire and examined the remains of the house. Will you please state your qualifications and then describe for the jury what, if anything, you discovered."

"My name is Glenn Bowersox and I am the Pennsylvania state fire marshal for this district. I am certified by the state and have been marshal for the past fifteen years. Prior to that, I was assistant fire marshal for another ten years. I have investigated hundreds of fires during my carrier.

"I examined the front porch of the structure as well as what apparently was the living room. I saw signs of broken glass on the porch. The glass showed no signs of heat or flame. Inside the house at the same general location I found more glass which showed a small amount of heat damage. Based on that I determined that a window had been broken inward prior to the fire

"Inside what was left of the dwelling I observed the body of Mr. Miller. It was lying at the base of the stairs leading to the second floor. His body was charred pretty badly.

"Near the inside wall of the living room I found broken glass that had definitely been in the fire. Among the fragments I found, in almost complete condition, the glass base of what remained of a gallon jug. It also showed signs of being in a fire.

"Near and around the body I found strong evidence of the use of an accelerant. Because of the way it spread, as well as the type of char, I have concluded that kerosene was most likely the accelerant used. There was also significant alligatoring or scaling, of the charred wood and it was in such a pattern that arson can be concluded. It also appears that the jug may have been smashed against the wall because there was a definitely different burn pattern on that portion of the wall that was not present elsewhere.

"I also noted that the front door had been broken. It looked like it was kicked in. But that is not indicative of arson. It could have been kicked in so that someone could have entered the house to attempt to rescue Mr. Miller. The door, being open, however did add a source of air, a draft which helped enhance the fire."

Centerville

"Have you definitely concluded that this was an arson fire?"

"Yes I have. There is no doubt in my mind."

"Does the jury have any questions for this witness?"

In this case the jury did and a piece of paper containing the written question was passed to the coroner. He unfolded the page and read, "Will you please describe in more detail what you mean by alligatoring?"

"I'd be happy to. Wood itself doesn't actually burn in a fire. The wood gives off flammable gas. It is this gas that does the actual burning. The intense heat of the fire chars the wood, turns it into charcoal, if you will. This is called pyrolysis. Alligatoring is the process of the wood charring because of the intense heat so that the char itself takes on the look or form of large scales, such as those you might see on an alligator in Florida. As a result we call this alligatoring. Along with the burn patterns and the flow of the kerosene across the floor I can conclude this fire was set."

"How do you know it was kerosene," Coroner Hackett asked.

"Simple. There was no sign of explosion. If it was gasoline there would be signs of an explosion and the fire would have spread more rapidly. Also the heat would not have been as intense at the point of origin."

His testimony completed the fire marshal left the stand.

"It's getting on to lunch time, so I'll call one more witness then we'll take a break for lunch. Call Mr. Floyd Musser."

Tall, pale and gaunt Floyd Musser entered the room and was sworn in. He took the witness seat.

"Mr. Musser, earlier sheriff Shambach testified that you told him that a Mr. Bob Zartman had been in your store shortly before the fire. Would you tell the inquest what happened?"

"Well, Jimmy Harris and Ben Snyder had just come in and were rummaging through the soda cooler, and I wish they'd be faster about it and not let in the warm air."

Many, including the coroner, chuckled at this but the coroner said, "Please just stick to the facts Mr. Musser. So what actually happened?"

"Like I said the boys were getting sodas when Bob Zartman came in and wanted to buy some kerosene. But he didn't even have a jug. I had to sell him one before I could pump the kerosene."

"Did he say anything about why he was buying the kerosene?"

"No, he didn't talk about that but he did say that Harvey Miller was going to get something."

"Can you tell us exactly what he said?"

"Yes, I remember it, I guess because of the fire later. He said, 'That damn Harvey Miller; he's going to get his.' Then he said that the sheriff let him off but 'we', whoever 'we' was, wouldn't let him off. That's pretty much all he said."

The coroner asked, "Did the boys hear what Mr. Zartman said?"

"Yes, I'm pretty sure they did. In fact, I told them not to pay any attention to Bob. He's more bark than bite."

"Did you see where he went when Mr. Zartman left?

Floyd shook his head, "No, I didn't see a thing. By then I was collecting the boy's money and reminding them that there was a deposit on the bottles."

At that moment they could hear the courthouse clock ring out the noon hour.

Centerville

"I'll call a recess until one O'clock. Jury, don't discuss this among yourselves until testimony has been completed. Until then talk about baseball. We're adjourned until one." And he banged his gavel.

Centerville

Chapter 19
Inquest (Part 2)

All morning Jimmy waited nervously. Not knowing what was happening inside the hearing room made the wait that much longer and harder. He only nibbled on the sandwich that his father bought him at the lunch counter across the street. He did drink his cherry coke. That was a treat. By the time the hearing resumed the waiting room was hot and stifling. Then the bailiff opened the hearing room door and in a loud voice said, "Calling James Harris, calling witness Harris."

Startled Jimmy rose and, followed by his father, stiffly walked through the hearing room door. The bailiff led Jimmy to the witness chair.

"Please raise your right hand." The coroner said and Jimmy, shaking slightly, did so.

"Do you solemnly swear that the testimony you are about to give to this inquest, concerning the death of Mr. Harvey Miller, shall be the truth, the whole truth and nothing but the truth, so help you God?"

A lump about the size of an apple suddenly filled Jimmy's throat and his legs shook. Somehow he managed to croak, "I do."

"You can sit down on that chair there. How's your grandpa? I haven't been to his store in a while."

Surprised Jimmy turned to the coroner and said, "He's doing pretty good." Up until that moment he hadn't considered that the coroner was a human, just like everyone else or that he knew his grandfather who ran a bakery just a few blocks away.

"Well, next time you see him tell him Hacky said 'Hi' he'll know who you mean."

Much more relaxed Jimmy nodded.

Centerville

"Now, Mr. Harris, you have been called to testify today because we understand that you were at Musser's store on the day of the fire. We know that because Mr. Musser told us so.

"In your own words will you tell us what you saw and heard while you were in the store? And take your time, son."

Jimmy thought for a moment. He remembered that afternoon clearly and in detail.

"Well, sir, my friend Ben and I had been out playing. We were hot and so we went to the store to get a soda."

"What is Ben's last name?"

"Uh, his last name is Snyder. Anyway we went into the store to get a soda and were back in the corner where the soda cooler is and we were picking through the bottles trying to find something good.

"Then this man, I didn't know his name then, in fact I still don't know his last name, came into the store. He said he needed to buy a gallon of kerosene but he didn't have a jug and could Mr. Musser sell him a jug too."

Jimmy paused. "Then what happened?" the coroner asked.

"Well they went outside to pump the kerosene. So Ben and I picked out our sodas and then sat on the bench and waited for them to come back."

"What kind of soda did you get?"

"Got ginger ale, it's my favorite."

Coroner Hackett smiled, "mine too," and then asked, "What happened next?"

"The man came in first and then Mr. Musser. The man was carrying a jug of kerosene. While they went to the counter the man said something like, Mr. Miller was going to get his and he used the D word, you know. He had a really deep voice."

The coroner nodded.

"Then," Jimmy continued, "He said that the sheriff had left Mr. Miller off but that he wouldn't. Then he left the store. When we paid for our drinks Mr. Musser told us not to pay any attention to 'Old Bob' as he called him because he didn't mean anything he was saying. And then we left."

"Did he see you and is there anything else you want to add?"

"No, I don't think he knew we were there. While they were outside pumping the kerosene, like I said, Ben and I sat on the bench in the corner and when they came back in his back was to us. When we left the store we saw him carrying his jug towards Mr. Miller's house and there were a bunch of men standing around in front of the house."

"Thank you. That's it and you can go and sit with your dad now. You did good."

Relieved Jimmy walked to his father and sat next to him. His dad leaned over and whispered, "You *did* do well. And see? It wasn't that bad."

"Call Benjamin Snyder," the coroner said.

A few moments later Ben entered the room and was led to the witness stand. He was sworn in and looked as nervous as Jimmy had been not long before. 'I wonder if that's how I looked?' Jimmy thought.

"Mr. Snyder, do you like baseball? Somehow I think you do," asked Coroner Hackett.

Surprised Ben nodded his head and said "Yes."

"What's your favorite team, young man? I like the Phillies."

"So do I," said Ben and Jimmy could see him relax. Jimmy realized that the coroner knew how to get people to be at ease. That's why he asked about his grandfather.

Centerville

"Mr. Floyd Musser and your friend Jim Harris over there," he pointed at Jimmy, "both told us that you were in Musser's store the day of the fire. Can you tell us what you heard and saw that day?"

Jimmy could see Ben swallow and then he glanced at Jimmy.

"Jimmy and I went into the store to get a couple of sodas and while we were there this man came in and wanted to buy a jug of kerosene. So he and Mr. Musser went out to get it. While we waited Jimmy and I sat on a bench in the corner and waited."

"What happened when they got back?"

"Well the man was talking and he had a very deep voice, I remember that, and he said, 'That damn Harvey Miller; he's going to get his.' Sorry about the swearing."

"That's all right but how do you remember so exactly?"

"I don't know but I know that's exactly what he said. I'm sure of it. Then he said that the sheriff left him off but he said, 'we won't' and then he left.

"After that Mr. Musser told us not to pay attention to "Old Bob", as he called him, because he didn't mean anything by what he said. When we left the store we saw Old Bob carrying the jug to Mr. Miller's house. There were about ten men waiting for him. And then we went to my place and sat on the back porch."

"Do you think he saw you in the store?"

"I doubt it. His back was to us and where we were sitting it was kind of dark. So no, I don't think so."

"Anything else you can think of?"

Ben shook his head. Moments later he was dismissed and sat behind Jimmy in the gallery.

"Call Mr. Fred Swope to the stand."

After a very long wait the bailiff led Fred into the hearing room and guided him to the witness stand.

Centerville

The coroner swore him in and he was seated.

"Mr. Swope, we understand that you live directly across the street and that you witnessed the fire at Mr. Harvey Miller's home. Is that true?"

"Yeah, I saw it." Fred nodded.

"In your own words would you tell the jury what you saw?"

"I was down at the run but it started thundering so I decided to go home. When I got there I went to my bedroom and heard shouting out in the street. What I saw was a bunch of men there. They were shouting for Mr. Miller to come out but he didn't."

"Then what happened?"

"Someone threw a rock through the window and then they all went up on the porch and pounded on the front door until it opened and they all went inside. I couldn't hear much but they were shouting and then I saw fire. After that they all ran away and the house burned down."

The coroner asked, "Did you recognize anyone."

Fred took a long time answering. "It was pretty dark and was starting to rain but yeah, I think I recognized one man. It looked like, I don't know his whole name, but they call him "Old Bob". He's kind of tall and has a deep voice. And that's all I can tell you."

Shortly after that Fred was dismissed. He left the room, not bothering to hear any more testimony.

The shadows were lengthening as the coroner wrote something on his notepad, looked up and called out, "Call Mr. Robert Zartman to the stand."

It seemed to Jimmy like it was a very long time before Mr. Zartman came into the room. As he walked to the witness stand he looked around the room as though looking for enemies. Jimmy thought that maybe he was doing just that.

Centerville

Zartman was sworn in and he sat on the witness chair.

"Mr. Zartman, there has been testimony here today that places you at or near the home of Mr. Harvey Miller on Saturday, August 13. There has also been testimony that at the time you had in your possession a gallon of kerosene. Would you tell us about that?"

"I didn't have no kerosene," he replied in his surly deep voice, "Not at all."

"I remind you that you are under oath. It has also been testified that you purchased that kerosene from Mr. Floyd Musser at his store not far from Mr. Miller's home."

"I didn't buy anything from Musser that day. If he said so *he* was lying!"

"Mr. Zartman, we're trying to determine what happened to Mr. Miller. I remind you again that you are under oath. I'll also tell you that we have heard testimony from three reputable individuals that you bought kerosene and that you didn't have a jug and had to buy that too."

Zartman shook his head and began to speak but coroner Hackett cut him off.

"In fact there were two other individuals in the store at the time. They clearly saw and heard you purchase the kerosene and jug. They also clearly heard you and in fact quoted you making threats against Mr. Miller. Would you like to change your testimony?"

"I ain't changing nothin'. I said what I said and I ain't saying nothin' else!" With that he rose from the witness chair and marched out of the hearing room.

Sheriff John Shambach followed him through the door. The people in the room began to chatter among themselves.

"Order! Order!" shouted the coroner. "We're not through here. Call the next witness, James Klingman."

Centerville

The inquest continued with only three more witnesses. After that the coroner charged the jury.

"Gentlemen," he began. "You have heard testimony from the coroner's report, the sheriff, the state fire marshal and from numerous witnesses. Your task, as you have previously been instructed is to determine what happened in Centerville on August 13th of this year. You may return a verdict of accident or misadventure, negligent homicide or willful homicide. If your verdict is homicide you may state the name or names of anyone you may suspect is involved in the act. That does not mean that a true writ will be entered against that person or persons. In other words it doesn't mean they'll be arrested. Your verdict need not be unanimous and I, as the county coroner, do have to right to overrule your decision but that rarely happens. I now release you to the jury room and your deliberations."

The jury rose and left the room. Then the coroner rose as did everyone else in the room. Now it was time to wait.

"Now what happens?" Jimmy asked his father.

"We wait until the jury returns with their verdict. If the verdict is homicide then the coroner will report it to the sheriff and the district attorney. After that there will be an investigation and if they have enough evidence they'll go to the grand jury. They will hear the sheriff's evidence and if they believe a crime has been committed they'll issue what is called an indictment against someone who will be arrested and charged with a crime. After that, who knows? But first we need to hear from this jury. And that's about everything I know about the legal system.

The wait for the jury was barely half an hour before they trooped back into the room. The coroner gaveled order and said, "Gentlemen, have you reached a verdict?"

"Yes sir, we have," the foreman replied.

"Please read your verdict."

"We the jury find that Mr. Harvey Miller, on August 13, 1955 died at the hand or hands of one or more persons in his home. We further find that Mr. Robert Zartman had a part in the killing."

"Your verdict is so recorded. I thank you for your diligent attention during this hearing. You are dismissed with my thanks and the thanks of the people of this county."

Coroner Hackett rose and left the room. The inquest was over.

Centerville

Chapter 20
A Troubled Village

Sheriff Shambach followed Bob Zartman from the hearing room. As they crossed through the waiting room he nodded to a deputy to follow. Zartman left the room and the building. As he stood on the sidewalk, lighting a cigarette, the sheriff approached him and said, "Robert Zartman, you are under arrest on suspicion of murder and suspicion of arson."

Zartman, startled, turned and spat at Sheriff Shambach's feet. "You ain't got no cause to arrest me sheriff. I done nothin' wrong."

Shambach nodded and said, "By what I heard at the inquest there is enough evidence to arrest you and hold you. The DA will be looking into this by tomorrow. So let's go. If you come peacefully I won't put the handcuffs on you."

Zartman spun around as though to flee but ran directly into the arms of deputy Johns who was waiting for him. The deputy threw him to the ground and in seconds had his handcuffs out and bound the fallen man's wrists behind his back.

"Very slick, Ed. Nice work! Book him. I'll be there in a few." He watched as Ed Johns pulled Zartman to his feet and began to march him off to the jail which was a short distance away.

"Let's go," Deputy Johns said as he marched his prisoner off.

"I said I ain't done nothin' wrong."

"We'll see," muttered the sheriff, "we'll see about that." He turned and walked next door to the courthouse where the district attorney had his office. He was hot by the time he climbed the three long flights of stairs in the stuffy air. He entered the prosecutor's office.

Centerville

"Ralph in?" he asked the secretary.

She nodded towards Clark's office door and said, "Go on in."

The sheriff knocked and hearing a faint response entered the office of District Attorney Clark.

"How doin' there John? Ready for a rematch?" Clark smiled in greeting.

"Not today, Ralph. No," he sighed, "I just arrested Robert Zartman of Centerville."

"Charges?"

"The murder of Harvey Miller and arson. I heard enough testimony at the inquest to have a reasonable suspicion that he instigated and participated the whole thing. Of course he claims innocence. I suppose he'll have a bail hearing tomorrow unless you can do something."

"Well sit down and let's have a good talk about this."

The sheriff sat across from the district attorney and sighed. "Ralph. That is one troubled village. Somehow I don't think we've seen the end of this. I hope, but..." he trailed off shaking his head.

"Maybe you need a little of this," the DA replied as he reached into a bottom desk drawer and pulled out a bottle. "Perks of office," he said as he poured a finger of whiskey for the sheriff and one for himself. "It's been a long dry day already. Did the jury reach a verdict?"

"Not as of yet but I suppose another hour will see it through. I think everyone is already pretty sure that Zartman had a lot to do with it?"

* * *

"Were you scared?" asked Ben the next day as he and Jimmy walked down the alley scuffing their shoes.

"Nah. Nothing to it."

"Yeah," replied Ben, "me too! Do you think Mr. Zartman done it?"

Jimmy thought for a moment, "I think he must have. I definitely think he started it. He was in the crowd at the post office that dad chased away. They must have gone right down to Mr. Miller's house after that."

"Yes, but I wish we knew for sure. All we know is that he bought kerosene and said Mr. Miller was going to get his. For all we know he was going to get his kerosene from Mr. Zartman."

"Do you really believe that?" Jimmy scornfully asked.

"Not for a minute but..."

"Yeah, I see what you mean. I bet Fred knows more than he said yesterday."

Ben stopped and turned to Jimmy, "Yeah. He probably does. He said he saw it all and from his bedroom he could see directly into the house across the street. Maybe they should have asked him more questions."

The boys pondered the results of the inquest as they continued their way to nowhere in particular that hot August Wednesday morning.

* * *

The Reverend Hummel rested his head against his arms as he sat in his study. Nothing would come. He usually began the outline for his Sunday sermon on Wednesday but today the page, just like his mind, was blank. He was tired and thought maybe it was time to think about retiring. Head down, he dozed.

In a dream he was reaching for his cat, Boots, but every time he came close, the cat ran away. It ran from the parsonage which was attached to the church and into the sanctuary and finally jumped onto the altar. The pastor admonished the cat, 'you know you aren't allowed in here, especially not on God's altar.' But the cat didn't listen and settled itself into the empty offering plate and closed its eyes. The minister rapped his knuckles on the altar and said, 'you get out of there right now.' And he continued rapping.

Slowly the knocking on his office door drew him from sleep. Still a bit groggy he called, "Just a minute." He rose, smoothed his hair out of habit and crossed to the office door and opened it.

"William, what can I do for you?" Hummel asked William Stancel

"Can I come in Pastor? I need to talk to someone."

Reverend Hummel turned sideways and motioned the man to come in. Stancel was a member but did not regularly attend. He was knows as a C and E, he attended church on Christmas and Easter. Still he was one of the flock. The minister motioned his visitor to a seat and took his own at his desk.

"What can I do for you William?"

The man paused for such a long time that the pastor believed he wouldn't speak. Then Stancel let out a long almost painful groan and cried out, "Oh god! I can't stand it."

"Can't stand what?"

"I was there that day. I was there when we burned down Harvey's house. I'm covered in his blood and can hardly live with myself." He hunched his shoulders as though trying to curl himself into a ball there in the chair.

"Oh William, how can I help?"

The man began to sob. "I didn't mean to do anything bad I just went along with the crowd. All I really did was throw a rock through his window and go inside. But I'm as guilty as the rest of them who kicked Harvey and burned his house. I didn't even go upstairs. I should have gone home after the post office."

Pastor Hummel rose from his desk, walked around it and put his hand on the crying man's head.

"Confession is good for the soul. Why don't you tell me what happened."

"You won't tell anybody will you?"

"As a man of God I promise you that what you say will stay between the two of us and nobody else."

And William Stancel began to talk.

"I never thought it would actually come to anything like that. It started at the post office. Bob Zartman and Jim Bateman were the ring leaders. They just knew that Harvey killed that little girl. They said that it didn't matter that the sheriff let him off but that he was guilty and they knew it.

"It started getting loud at the post office until Ned Harris chased us all off. I thought we were just going to go to the restaurant but instead Bob led us to Harvey's house. There must have been six or eight of us by then. Some were calling for Harvey to come out, some wanted his blood. They said that justice had to be done.

"I don't even know why I was there. I should have been tending my pigs, not taking part in a riot. I don't drink but some of them had been drinking. Jim Bateman smelled like whiskey. I know he likes it.

"So we were outside his house and more came up until there were about a dozen of us. All were yelling for Harvey to come out. But he didn't. Someone threw something at his window but it didn't break, so I grabbed a rock and threw it through the window. And that's all I did! Then everyone ran up on the porch and began to break down the front door.

"We all got inside and it was crowded. Bob and some others went upstairs and found Harvey hiding in his closet. They dragged him out and pushed him down the stairs."

Stancel's words were rushing and almost tumbling over themselves as he tried to get it all out.

"Go on," whispered the minister.

"He landed on his back in the front room and Jim Bateman kicked him in the head so hard that I could actually see Harvey's head bulge out around Jim's boot. He kicked him something awful I don't know how many times. Around the head and body, all over. That's where he kicked him. But after the first kick Harvey didn't move anymore and I knew he was dead.

"Bob said, 'Oh shit. Look what you did Jim.' He said that. Then he said, 'we gotta fix it up.' And he poured kerosene on Harvey's body. Then he set him on fire."

William Stancel shuddered and sobbed deep in his chest. Pastor Hummel simply waited silently. After a few minutes Stancel resumed.

"The fire spread and we all began to run outside. Bob threw the jug against the wall and hollered, 'let's all get the hell out of here! Nobody says nothing. Ya hear me? Nobody!' and I thought he looked at me when he said it.

"I don't know about the rest of them but I can hardly take it. What should I do reverend? What should I do?"

"Pray," whispered the minister. "Pray for your eternal soul. I won't condemn you but I can't offer forgiveness either, only God himself can do that. But I am bound to secrecy, so I will not say anything about this to anyone. But to save your soul I tell you that you must go to the authorities and confess your part and what you know. I know it will be hard for you to do but that is what you must do. Now will you pray with me for God's forgiveness?"

Centerville

A long and agonizing silence followed while Reverend Hummel gathered his strength to pray for this man.

Centerville

Chapter 21
Dusty Exploration

A hot dry wind skirled down the Lower Street, slowing here and there to gather a handful of leaves or dust from the gutters. It worked a whirlwind over the ashes of the Miller house and carried them on down the street to Musser's store. There it exchanged the ashes for leaves and dust. Jimmy and Ben, standing on the sidewalk beneath the overhanging roof watched the display.

"Pretty cool," said Ben.

"Yes, it is," agreed Jimmy. He sipped his ginger ale as they stepped out onto the deserted street.

"Sure is quiet today. You can't even hear a bird or even a dog barking. It feels kind of strange, you know what I mean?"

"Everything has felt strange this summer, especially the last two weeks. I almost wish that school would start so that something different will happen."

Ben nodded his head, "Yeah, I know what you mean." The two boys continued across the street and then down Kuhns street towards the field next to the Dry Run. They ambled, not sure where to go or what to do.

Clouds scudded rapidly across the sky as though in a hurry to get somewhere as the boys turned and walked along the alley back towards the post office. A hundred feet down the dirt lane they came upon Harvey Miller's barn.

"Let's go in," Ben said.

"I'm not sure. We could be trespassing, it isn't our property."

"Come on, Jimmy, who's going to know? Or care, for that matter. Mr. Miller sure won't."

171

Centerville

Not totally convinced but having nothing better to do Jimmy joined Ben as they turned and began to scout the building, looking for an open door or window.

"Here, look at this," Ben pulled at the sliding garage door and pulled it a foot away from the wall. Turning he squeezed through. Jimmy followed close behind.

They found themselves in a large twilit room. The ceiling dripped and flowed with cobwebs and dust motes hung in the air. The room smelled of oil soaked earth and dead straw. The dirt floor was clean and hard packed. Harvey's beat up Ford stood parked next to the wall but the remainder of the large room was clear and open. Tools hung on one wall over a work bench and a wheelbarrow leaned against the far wall. A stairway climbed along the same wall to the loft above their heads. Beneath the stairs were a number of boxes and a barrel.

"Have you ever been in here before?" Jimmy whispered.

"No, but I looked in once when the back door was open. I even talked to Mr. Miller, or at least I said 'Hi.'. But I didn't see anything much inside. Let's look upstairs, maybe there is something interesting up there."

The boys crossed to the stairs and began to climb. The treads creaked and groaned as though they hadn't taken any weight in years. Jimmy secretly hoped that they wouldn't collapse and break their bones. Ben, on the other hand, forged ahead as though he were on solid ground. He reached the top while Jimmy was still only halfway.

"Come on," he waved his arm. "There's all kinds of stuff up here."

Jimmy finally stepped onto the loft floor. In the shadows he could see dust shrouded boxes, barrels and even what looked like an old sleigh. Chains hung from the rafters and ropes hung coiled from pegs in the beams. Sunlight filtered through the slots between the board siding and a small window at the western end of the building, above the stairway. It was enough to light their way through the maze of things that Harvey had gathered over the years. There was surprising order and neatness in the collection.

The boys looked through boxes and into barrels. One box was filled with nails while another had a number of horse shoes. Ben picked up a horse shoe and pretended to throw it at an imaginary hob. Jimmy was afraid he would throw it and make a loud noise.

Looking into the sleigh they found a buggy whip standing in its holder and a blanket in the seat as though it was only waiting for a good snowfall to go gliding across the winter fields. Jimmy sneezed as they raised dust while sitting in the sleigh. Ben pretended to be driving a horse, snapping an imaginary whip. Looking around Jimmy pointed to something pale and ethereal in a corner.

"What's that?" he whispered. "It looks like a ghost but I know there aren't such things." Ben immediately jumped from the sleigh and crossed the room. Jimmy was not far behind. What they discovered both thrilled them and frightened them at the same time.

Hanging from a peg was a very dusty white robe with a faded red cross on the breast. Next to it hung a tall but floppy, hood. Behind the hood hung a noose.

"A hangman's noose!" Ben exclaimed. "Wouldja look at that? It's a KKK uniform. I would've never guessed. Mr. Miller was like that? He seemed like a nice man..." he trailed off.

"Let's get out of here. I've seen enough." Jimmy replied, "Let's go. Now!"

They turned towards the stairs when they heard the sound of the sliding door opening below and then the sound of voices.

"I heard that he hid stuff somewhere in here," someone said. It was a familiar voice to the boys but they couldn't place it.

"Do you think it's in the car?" another voice asked.

"Might be, or maybe upstairs. Bob said it was somewhere in this barn"

Jimmy immediately held his finger to his lips as though he thought Ben would make a noise. The boys looked around the room, trying to find a place to hide. Ben pointed to the sleigh and whispered, "On the other side, next to the wall."

The boys began to creep slowly towards the hiding place, praying that the floor would not give them away.

The men below opened the car doors and talked among themselves, covering any sound that the boys might have made as they crawled into the hiding place. Crouching next to the wall they heard the trunk of the car open.

"There, I told you we'd find something."

"Would you look at that," the other voice said. "It looks like a little girl's dress and underwear. Looks like Bob was right. Miller *was* a monster."

"We'll just leave that here for now but I have you as a witness. He went after little girls and this will prove to the sheriff that we were right! Now let's get out of here."

The boys heard the trunk lid slam shut and a moment later the garage door close. Still they sat there for at least five minutes before moving or even talking.

"Did you hear that?" Ben asked. "That was Jim Bateman, he helps my dad sometimes, but I don't know who the other man was. Let's go down and look for ourselves."

Now almost boldly the boys came from behind the sleigh and crossed the room. This time the stairs held no fear for Jimmy. They crossed the dirt floor to the automobile and Ben twisted the trunk handle and raised the lid. There, almost as though it was carefully laid out, lay a small pink dress and a pair of panties.

"Oh," Ben gasped, "It's true?"

Jimmy looked carefully at the dress as doubt filled his mind. He wasn't ready to comment but to him things didn't look quite right.

"Let's get out of here, I've seen enough." Jimmy said. And so this time the boys rolled open the garage door and passed out into the alley. In the daylight they could see that they were covered with dust.

"We need to sweep each other off. Let's go to my place." Said Ben as they closed the door and turned back down the alley. His house was only a few hundred feet away and in minutes they were standing on his back porch taking turns with the broom, sweeping the dust off each other's pants and shirts.

"Do you think Mr. Miller was like that? That he did go after little girls?" asked Ben.

"No, I don't," Jimmy's thoughts were still roiling as he answered. "It looked all wrong to me. The dress was folded to neatly and the underwear was folded too. And they were right in the middle of the trunk. It just looked too convenient to me. It seems to me that if Mr. Miller actually did things like that that he would hide the evidence, if he kept anything at all.

"And I haven't heard of any other missing girls or attacks or anything like that. If someone was attacking little girls we would have heard about it, don't you think?"

Ben nodded.

In a flash it came to Jimmy, "No! But somebody wants to convince the sheriff that Mr. Miller killed Betsy Smith and maybe attacked Judy so he planted the dress and stuff himself. Then he brought a witness and," he air quoted, "'found' the dress in Mr. Miller's trunk. He's trying to frame a dead man!

"But here's the thing, the sheriff left him off and he had to have a good reason for it. Bob Zartman is in jail for murder. I'll bet that he had someone plant the dress and then had someone else find it just to make him look a little better. At least in his mind's eye."

"Woah," Ben's eyes became as large as saucers. "But what about the KKK outfit?"

"I don't know about that but I know that my uncle has one too. He said that he got it from some guy so he could add it to his collection. Besides I never heard of the KKK doing anything around here. That's only in the south. Maybe he had it for Halloween. I don't know."

With enough fodder to keep them talking for a week the boys sat on Ben's back porch and talked the afternoon away.

Centerville

Chapter 22
Conspiracy

Within hours the village was flooded with rumors of Harvey Miller and his supposed crimes. Jim Bateman had wasted no time telling everyone he could about what he and Rufus Ott had discovered. No one seemed to wonder how it was that they had trespassed into Harvey Miller's barn and searched his car, or why.

Whispers passed from mouth to ear, each tidbit becoming more embellished until it seemed that Miller must have been a most depraved monster, preying on children throughout the area. But, unlike Jimmy, nobody bothered to follow things through to discover who these children might be. Nobody bothered to count these nonexistent children, missing or dead.

Ned Harris told more than one villager that the rumors were untrue and that they should know better but he was treated with pure disregard for his logic. Finally he gave up and retreated back behind his cage at the post office to sort the arriving mail and sweep the floor.

Word even got to Middlebury and to Sheriff Shambach. 'What now?' he thought. To his deputy he said, "Miller's barely in the ground and already they're concocting stories about him. Damn, I just know I'm gonna have to go over there and knock some sense into them. Picking on a dead man isn't making my job any easier."

Not long after that the sheriff received word that Bob Zartman wanted to speak with him. 'Just what I need' he thought as he crossed to the jail.

Entering the jail he passed the deputy on duty and entered the cell block; in reality nothing but a dimly lit hall with cells on either side. As he approached Zartman's cell he could see the man standing there, hands grasping the bars.

"I told you so, sheriff. I told you that Miller was no good. Now you see."

"I see nothing and even if he was the devil himself you had no right to do what you did."

"I ain't done nuthin' and you know it!" Spat Bob. "For all you know Harvey fell down the steps and died."

"Did he set himself on fire too? I don't think so."

"Well, I sure didn't set no fire."

"We'll let the jury decide that," returned the sheriff.

"But you know they found little girl's clothes in the trunk of his car. That's gotta mean something." Zartman said.

"All it means to me is that the clothes were there. They could have been a gift for a niece or someone. It's purely circumstantial. And who told you about that already?"

"I just knowed," shot back Zartman. "Well, sheriff, you ought to at least take a look."

"I'll take a look, all right, don't you worry about that." The sheriff turned and left the jail. As he passed back through his office he waved Deputy Brocious.

"You doing anything? Let's take a ride to Centerville and check out this damning evidence."

As they drove the deputy asked, "What the hell is going on over there? Every time I turn around something else is happening. What do they think they're trying to prove now?"

"They're trying to create mitigating circumstances for Bob Zartman. But in the process they're stirring up a hornet's nest. That town has been simmering for a couple of weeks and I'm afraid that it isn't going to get any better any time soon. We may have to have an almost constant presence if things don't settle down over there."

As they pulled into the village the sheriff said, "We'll stop at the post office. Ned will probably know as much as anybody and he's more trustworthy." Brocious nodded. As they entered the building they encountered Jim Bateman.

"Why, Sheriff Shambach, you're just the man I wanted to see," said Jim.

"That so, Mr. Bateman. What about?"

"I want you to come and see what I saw this morning over in Harvey Miller's barn."

"Funny thing," said the sheriff, "that's exactly what I came over here to look at. Get in the car and we'll drive you over there." The three men got into the sheriff's car and drove the short distance to the alley where the Miller barn was located. The three approached the rear of the building.

"It's right in there," Bateman pointed as he led the way and pushed open the garage door. "Right there in the car's trunk."

The sheriff crossed the room and opened the trunk. The three men looked at the contents.

"Damned if it is," said the sheriff as he turned to Jim Bateman. "So what were you doing trespassing on this property? Who gave you permission to be in here and who told you to look in the trunk of the car? Hmmm?"

"Wh, wh, wh" Bateman stuttered

"Oh hell, I'm not gonna arrest you – yet. Just tell me what brought you here?"

"Well, I kinda heard Bob say something about finding something in here that would show what kind of person Harvey was."

"Really now? So did Bob tell you to come here and specifically look in the trunk of the car?"

Bateman began to nod his head and at the same time said, "no," in a rather unconvincing voice.

"Stand right there while I take a look at this *evidence*. I mean it, don't you move a muscle. Keep an eye on him Jim."

Sheriff Shambach turned and looked closely at the dress and panties in the trunk. He could see that they were both folded and laid out neatly instead of being thrust under the burlap bags and tools scattered on the floor of the trunk.

"One would think," He wondered out loud, "that someone would want to hide evidence like this, maybe under the bags or even somewhere else in this barn." He turned to Bateman, "Are you sure this is how you found them?"

"Yessir, just like that."

Turning back to the trunk he carefully felt around the dress, turning the edges over as though looking for evidence of a crime.

"No blood," he said. "But oh, look at this. Jim, come look at this, I want you to witness this."

Deputy Brocious approached the trunk and looked inside as the sheriff pointed to a price tag attached to the collar of the dress.

"That," Brocioius said, "is pretty damning evidence, sheriff. What do you think?"

The sheriff turned to Jim Bateman and said, "I think it's a lot of bullshit! You missed the price tag on the dress, Mr. Bateman. Looks like it was bought at Miss Judy's Dress Shop, for three dollars and ninety-eight cents. What do you think of that? You had better get out of here before I change my mind and take you in for interfering with an investigation." Bateman turned and sped from the barn like an Olympic sprinter.

Centerville

Shaking his head the sheriff gathered the dress and panties. "Let's pay Miss Judy a visit. Maybe we can find out who bought this, and when." The men closed the trunk and barn door.

Miss Judy's Dress Shop was located near the center of Middlebury, just off the town square. Fifteen minutes later the sheriff and deputy entered the dress shop where Miss Judy herself greeted them.

"Hello sheriff," she said. "What can I do for you?"

Sheriff Shambach placed the clothing on the counter and asked, "Do you have any idea who bought these cloths and when?"

The woman looked at the dress for a few moments and nodded. "Yes, I do. A man came in here a last week and bought both of these pieces. I asked him if he wanted matching socks but he said 'no'. He didn't want them wrapped either even though he said he was getting them for his niece for her birthday."

"Can you describe the man?"

"He was tallish with dark hair and had a very deep voice."

At that the sheriff drew a photograph from his pocket and showed it to Miss Judy. "Might this have been the man?"

"Yes, that is the man. He's the one who bought the dress and panties. I'm sure of it."

"Thank you mam. Have a nice day." The sheriff tucked the mug shot of Bob Zartman back into his shirt pocket and gathered the clothing, now as evidence, and turned to the door.

'I guess it's time to give Bob another visit,' he thought. 'Then take this to the D.A. He'll want to see it for sure.'

A few minutes later, standing in front of Bob Zartman Sheriff Shambach held up the dress for the other to see and said, "Is this what you were talking about? This dress and panties?"

"Thems the ones."

"Are you sure?"

"Yes sir, I'm sure. I knowed that Harvey Miller had stuff like that, that rapist."

"Well that's an interesting story. But Miss Judy, from the dress shop down the street, identified you and told me not only when you purchased it but that you were buying it as a gift for a relative and didn't want it wrapped. Oh yes, and you forgot to pull off the price tag, that's how I know. What did you do it for, Bob?"

Zartman just turned his back on the sheriff and sat on his cot.

"Thought so." Said Sheriff Shambach as he walked out of the cell block and headed towards the office of the district attorney.

Centerville

Chapter 23
Dog Days

To a country boy in the dog days of August there is no better time than that waiting, rod in hand, for the electric shock of an unseen fish taking the bait and silently tugging the line. Jimmy was seated on the bank not far downstream from the bridge waiting for this electric moment. So far it hadn't come.

Ben had crossed the stream and was seated on a small island, fishing in the same pool as Jimmy. This was one of the few places, other than the deeper water at the lime kiln, where the stream pooled deep enough to harbor larger fish.

The boys lazed in the dappled shade, feeling the slight breeze as it ruffled through the leaves of the trees and bushes. Somewhere not too far off they could hear the cry of a hawk. The high pitched, almost catlike, cry of the hawk perplexed them. A bird of that size and power should have a call to match. In the field across the stream red wing black birds balanced on the tops of the tall weeds; thistles and milk weeds and made their raucous calls as though scolding the boys for their lazy ways. A ground hog snuffled the edge of the field not far from the entrance of its burrow. It was the kind of day that could induce a sleepy stupor over the strongest man. Boys didn't stand a chance.

Just as he was dozing off, his rod beginning to dip towards the water, a tug pulled Jimmy immediately awake. He pulled back on the rod hoping to set the hook and began to reel in his line. He knew right away that he had caught something and visions of a prize winning bass filled his imagination as he battled his invisible foe.

"Don't rush it!" Ben called across the water.

Centerville

Jimmy knew better than that but this was still a small pool of water, so the landing of the fish would not take long no matter what. Jimmy stood and worked the fish to the shore. He could see it flashing in the shallow water beneath the surface and then he had it on the bank.

"It's a cat fish. Don't see many of them this far up. You see them mostly in Cave Creek."

"Watch out for the stingers, they're poison, you know." said Ben.

Fully aware of the poisonous danger the cat fish whiskers, or barbels, Jimmy was not about to take any chances getting stung by this one. The fish itself was close to a foot long and flopping madly in the mud. Jimmy could see his hook protruding from the corner of the fish's mouth. He squatted, trying to get a closer look.

"If I was you I'd cut the line and let it go," advised Ben.

Jimmy was inclined to agree except that it was the only hook he had with him today and didn't want to lose it.

"No, you put your foot on it and I'll try to dig it out with my pocket knife. Don't squash it but hold it tight so it doesn't wiggle."

Ben obligingly pressed his sneakered foot over the fish just behind its flat head. Jimmy squatted and pulled on the fishing line while trying to get the blade of his small knife between the fish's jaw and the hook. Still thrashing as best it could the fish would not hold still so Jimmy braved the danger and pressed his left hand on the very top of the fish's flat head. Now, the fish totally immobilized, Jimmy pushed and twisted the knife blade until the hook came free.

"That was fun," said Ben as he kicked the fish into the water.

Centerville

"Let's move down a bit, maybe we can catch something in the riffles," Jimmy nodded as he rinsed his hands in the stream and then rubbed his palms on his pants. The riffles were an area of faster flowing water not far from where they now were. The pool opened to a wider area before the stream narrowed, thus creating riffles.

"All we'll catch in the riffles will be chubs and they're not worth keeping."

"I don't want to keep them," said Jimmy, "I just want to catch them and throw them back. That's the fun of it." And so the boys continued downstream to the riffles where they did, indeed, catch a number of chubs. Most of them were less than half a foot long but it was still a lot of fun. The little ones grabbed the bait, on this day worms, and pulled it off the hook. They were too small to get the hook into their mouths and so made excellent thieves. After half an hour of this the boys decided to move on to other adventures.

"Want to explore the cave?" asked Ben. "We can leave our rods here and pick them up when we come back."

Getting tired of fishing Jimmy thought this was an excellent idea and so they crossed the stream and climbed the bank to the field beyond. It really wasn't a cave so much as it was a limestone outcropping that had been weathered to the point where there were a few openings in the rock wall as well as eroded arches. It was all a part of the root system of a huge maple tree. One part that was overhung by the bank of the hill actually exposed what looked like flowstone, a sure indication that at one time there had indeed been a cave here. The boys hoped that they could find a spot where digging would actually open a cave passage. But their mining forays had so far yielded nothing.

Centerville

Clambering over the rock wall they found a spot that had not been excavated and so, finding a couple of strong sticks they began to poke and dig, hoping for the motherlode. After a few minutes of digging, the hole narrowed and pinched off.

They turned and sitting with their backs against the sun warmed rocks they contemplated little and discussed nothing. It was being too good a day to ruin it by talking about the weighty matters of the times, such as baseball, fire or murder. So they leaned back and soon were overcome by the sleepiness that Jimmy experienced before hooking the cat fish. Far overhead the dozing boys a few buzzards circled, catching thermals as they coasted across the land.

After a time a bothersome fly began to torment Ben, buzzing and dive-bombing his head and crawling over his nose. Waving proved to be ineffectual at ridding himself of the fly and so fully awake he sat up, nudging Jimmy in the process. Making one last swat at the fly Ben said, "Maybe we had better get back to our rods and head downstream and home."

Jimmy yawned, "Yeah, I could use something to drink."

Soon they retraced their steps to the stream and their fishing rods and shared tin can of worms. Gathering their equipment they continued their lazy way downstream heading for the lime kiln. They hadn't gone far when Ben saw something.

"Would you look at that." He said as he pointed across the stream.

Jimmy's eyes widened when he saw where Ben was pointing. "What is it?" he asked.

"I don't know but it looks like a bunch of rocks that were dropped on some watermelons. But why? And who did it?"

Centerville

Across the stream at the base of the stream bank were a number of rocks in a small pile. It was obvious that the rocks had been dropped or thrown from the top of the bank onto one or two medium sized watermelons. The rocks had sunk into the melons, cracking them open and scattering some of the pulp onto the stream bank. It was clear to the boys that the rocks had been dropped onto the melons and not the other way around. Even from across the stream the boys could see ants and flies enjoying the sweet bounty of the watermelons dashed shells and pulp.

A sudden flash of memory brought Jimmy up short.

"Wow! Do you remember a couple of weeks ago? We saw a pile of rocks at the bottom of the bank, down that way?" he pointed. "This looks like that, except for the watermelons. I wonder if someone was practicing for something?"

"Could be, but what?"

Jimmy shook his head but at the same time something began to nag at his thoughts. He felt the same way as he did when he had a word on the tip of his tongue but couldn't quite remember or say it. Something was on the edge of his consciousness, something so tangible that he could almost touch it. Something real but at the same time he felt it was something he didn't want to know. His heart pounded in his chest as he looked at the rocks and watermelons and wished that he hadn't seen them at all.

"Let's get out of here. This is too weird." Jimmy said as he turned away and continued towards the lime kiln.

Unsure of what Jimmy meant Ben shrugged, kicked a stone, turned and followed him downstream.

A hundred yards later Jimmy stopped. "Notice that?"

"Notice what?" asked Ben.

"Did you notice how quiet it suddenly got? Notice how the wind stopped blowing. You can't even hear a bird. We're gonna get a thunder storm. I can smell it."

Ben knew that Jimmy had an almost uncanny way of predicting thunder storms. If he said that he could smell a storm it would probably rain as predicted. He looked to the sky. Clouds were forming, tall in the afternoon sky.

"Maybe you're right. It does feel kind of strange."

"Yeah. Let's call it a day and go to your house for a little. I'm getting pretty thirsty and the run doesn't look that appetizing." At that the boys turned and crossed the field to the alley and then to Ben's house. Later, as they sat on the back porch, they began to hear distant peals of thunder and the clouds gathered.

"That means something. I know it but I can't figure it out." Jimmy spoke.

"What are you talking about? The thunder?"

"Those rocks and watermelons. There's more there than meets the eye. I know that it means something, it's like it's on the tip of my tongue but I can't spit it out! It's going to drive me crazy."

"Don't get yourself all worked up about it. Someone was just having some fun. I wouldn't mind smashing some melons."

"I guess you're right," Jimmy sighed, "but seeing this and remembering that other stack of rocks just kind of put themselves together and my mind wants to make something of it." He paused.

"Well it's getting kind of late. I had better get home before it rains and get cleaned up for supper. I'll see you later." And with that Jimmy rose to leave. Ben walked with him to the front of the house and watched his friend walk up the street. He shook his head and thought that sometimes Jimmy was wound way too tight and thought too much about unimportant stuff. Then he turned back to his own home to get washed up as well. He smelled of creek and fish.

* * *

The storm struck while Jimmy and his family were eating supper. The wind howled and screamed around the eves of the house. The rain lashed the windows and drummed on the roof. Hail pelted the trees, shredding the leaves from the branches and covered the earth in a false winter wonderland.

Trying to talk above the storm Ned asked, "What did you boys do today?" as he scooped mashed potatoes onto his plate.

"Ben and I went fishing. I caught a cat fish in the pool near the bridge. It must have been this long." He held up his hands portraying a fairly accurate length of the fish.

"Then Ben and I saw where someone threw some rocks and smashed some watermelons. Ben says I'm crazy but I think it means something?"

"Oh really?" his father asked. "Sounds to me like someone was just having a little fun."

"That's what Ben said, but it's nagging at my mind and I don't know why."

"Well I'm sure, if it is anything, it'll come to you. What about you, Pete? What did you do today?"

The conversation continued through the storm and around the table until the meal had ended. They all cleaned the dishes and prepared to watch television. But it was then that with a loud crack of lightening the lights went out.

Centerville

Power was lost to the entire village and then spread out through the surrounding area as the electric system was overwhelmed by the demand and the storm.

From the basement Jimmy's dad got a Coleman lantern that they used for camping and pumped it up. He lit the mantel and bright light flooded the living room as the lantern hissed in the night. They played a few games while the unabating storms pummeled the town. Finally the family gave up and all went to bed; hoping to find sleep between the thunderclaps and rain.

Jimmy fell asleep quickly even though his mind seemed to be racing. Somehow the rolling thunder lulled him into a restless sleep and into dark dreams.

He was back at the stream, alone, looking across at the rocks and the watermelons. But even in the dream state he could make nothing of what he saw. He turned and glided, his feet did not appear to move, to the pool where he had caught the cat fish. Now it was filled with fish, squirming and splashing, roiling over each other and trying to find deeper water.

Across the stream someone was walking, heading towards the bridge. But he couldn't tell who it was. The far bank was shrouded in fog, making it difficult to see. He shouted and waved but the person did not respond but kept on walking into the mist.

As dreams do, he suddenly found himself on the road walking towards the bridge. There was no fog, the sun was shining but it felt dark. He walked to the edge of the road and arrived at the bridge. Then he reached out and grabbed the beam and began to climb the superstructure; to walk across the bridge on the high beams. He reached the top and stepped out on the level beam.

Centerville

He looked down. The stream looked like it was hundreds of feet below him and the wide steel beam suddenly narrowed until it was not much wider than a railroad track. His heart leapt into his throat as his gaze traveled to the far side of the stream.

There lying on the bank was a man whom he knew without thinking. There lay Bart Tuttle, on his back, sleeping in his favorite place. But then his head changed and became smashed watermelons, smashed by rocks thrown from the bank. At this sight Jimmy lost his balance and fell to the streambed far below. At the same time a car drove across the bridge rattling the boards like thunder.

With a jerk he awoke to the rumble of thunder. Sweating and entangled in his bedsheet he gasped in horror. The nagging was no longer on the tip of his tongue. Now it was stuck in his throat, preventing him from crying out loud. Now it was clear as a bell.

Bart was next.

Centerville

Chapter 24
Confession

Sheriff Shambach was doing his hated paperwork. Once each month he had to report on the activity of the sheriff's office, the number of arrests, prisoners housed, calls made and all the rest. He worked on it every week instead of having to do it all at one time. This report seemed to have the name Centerville in it far too often.

He sighed as he began a paragraph on Bob Zartman and the Harvey Miller murder. 'When will it ever end?' he wondered. He was deep in thought when Deputy Brocious knocked. As the sheriff looked up the door opened and Jim stuck his head through the opening.

"Got someone here to see you."

"Who is it?"

"Fellow named Stancel, says he's from Centerville. Won't talk to anybody else. Just you."

The sheriff sighed again, rubbed his hands over his face as though trying to wash away the weary feeling Centerville gave him. He closed his report book and said, "Send him in." He rose as William Stancel entered the room. The man looked around, not sure what to do or say.

The sheriff gestured to the chair facing his desk. "Good afternoon Mr. Stancel. Have a seat and tell me what I can do for you."

Stancel shuffled across the room looking old and weary. His face was haggard and he did not look like the thirty nine year old pig farmer that he was. He took off his hat and sat, gazing at the floor.

Sheriff Shambach took his own chair again and said, "What can I do for you?"

After a long moment Stancel gathered a deep and shuddering breath and replied, "I need to tell you about how we killed Harvey Miller. And who did it. I can't live with myself any more if I don't talk about it. It's just so wrong."

The weariness lifted from the sheriff. "Take your time, I have all day."

After another long pause William Stancel spoke. And once he started he couldn't stop. His story started the night Betsy Smith had been killed at the carnival.

"I was there when you arrested Harvey that terrible night. And like everyone else I believed that he did it, that he killed that little girl. I wasn't sure of it but I believed it and I was satisfied when you hauled him off to jail.

"Bob Zartman was downright happy about it. I don't know if you know but there was bad blood between the two of them, Bob and Harvey. It goes back a while when Bob thought that Harvey was stealing from his traps. Harvey said he didn't take anything but Bob never believed him. Then last year he accused Harvey of going into his coop and stealing a chicken and eggs. But I don't think Harvey did either thing but Bob swore he did and would get him for it. Personally I think a fox got the chicken. I seen one down by the run near Bob's place off and on." He paused.

"Tell me more."

Stancel began to talk and wound a long story that finally led to the day they accosted Harvey.

"It began at the post office. Bob and Jim Bateman were raising hell outside and a bunch of men gathered and some joined in. Bob was all for stringing up Harvey from the nearest tree. But none of us believed him.

"'Bout then the postmaster, Ned Harris, he came out and told us to break it up and get off federal property. I thought we were going to the restaurant but we kept on going down the street to Harvey's house. Bob was leading the way. Jim pulled out a bottle of something every once in a while and was getting pretty liquored up, if you know what I mean."

"Who all was with you?"

"Well there was Bob and Jim. I was following along in the back and I guess there were four or five others, Stan Knapp, Bill Ott and some others... I can't think right now."

The sheriff nodded, "Just take your time."

William nodded, "We got down to Harvey's place and were standing in the street shouting for Harvey to come out but he didn't. Then Bob went down to Musser's store and came back a little while later with a jug of kerosene. I didn't know what he was going to do with it

"Then all hell broke loose. Someone threw something at the house and then I threw a rock through the living room window and before I knew it they were smashing down the front door.

"I went inside with all the rest but didn't do anything else. I just stood by the front door and watched. Bob went upstairs with a couple other fellows. There was a lot of shouting and then they threw Harvey down the steps.

"He landed on his back and Jim kicked him in the head something awful. Harvey didn't move after that. I figured that Jim must have killed him. And then Bob set the place on fire."

Stancel shuddered, "All I did was throw a rock but I'm as guilty as all the rest of them. I should have never gone down to the post office that day.

"Oh god, sheriff, we killed that man, for no good reason. I think Bob was just trying to pay him back and we all helped. I'm ready to go to jail and pay the penalty. I'm guilty as sin just as much as Bob and Jim. We all are."

"Are you willing to testify in court and tell everything that you saw on that day?"

Centerville

William Stancel nodded his head and looked at the floor.

"Stay here, I'll be right back." The sheriff left the room and told Jim Brocious to watch that Stancel stayed there. Then, rather than walk to the courthouse and climb three flights of stairs, walked to the county tax assessor's office next door to use their telephone. He didn't want to use the only other telephone in the office, the one at the reception desk, for this kind of conversation.

In a few moments he was talking to the district attorney.

"I've got a man here who is confessing to everything that happened at Harvey Millers place. He's naming names and giving good details. Name of William Stancel. He directly implicated a man named Jim Bateman. The name doesn't ring a bell with me.

"Here's my problem. I have more than enough to arrest Stancel but right now the last place I want him is in the same jail as Bob Zartman. That man would eat him alive, right through the bars. I think Zartman could scare him enough that he wouldn't testify to anything. I think I'm going to tell him to consider himself under arrest and send him home. I don't think he'll go anywhere but I wanted to run it past you first. What do you think?"

"Tell him to come back in tomorrow so that I can talk with him." Clark replied. "And tell him not to talk with anyone else. Keep me posted."

The call ended and Sheriff Shambach returned to his office to find Stancel still sitting, looking at the floor and rubbing his hands together.

"Mr. Stancel, here's what we're going to do. I'm not going to arrest you today. In fact I'm going to send you home because you are cooperating. Can you come back in tomorrow to talk with D.A. Clark?"

Centerville

Stancel nodded at the floor, "Yes, I think so."

"Ok, I'm going to let you go. Deputy Brocious will take you to your vehicle and I want you to go straight home and don't talk to anybody about this. You hear? Nobody."

"Yes sir."

"Now go home. But come back tomorrow at the same time as today."

A very surprised William Stancel left the office. Accompanied by the deputy he went to his truck to return to his farm not far from Centerville. In a numbed state, wondering what had just happened, he slowly drove home. The enormity of what he had just done filled him with fear. He was far more afraid of Bob Zartman and Jim Bateman than of going to jail. In fact he'd be safer in jail.

But what should he, or would he, tell his wife. Sarah had to know. She'd probably file for divorce and he wouldn't blame her. She wouldn't want to be married to a convicted murderer.

Finally arriving at his farm he parked the truck and slowly walked to his house. Once there he almost painfully climbed the three steps to the front porch and sat on the bench. He looked out over the sunlit yard but didn't move. He knew that he had to slop the pigs but that could wait for a few minutes while he gathered his thoughts.

The last thing he expected was to be released by the sheriff. He had expected to be arrested for murder and thrown into jail. Never to see his farm again. Never to see Sarah again. He didn't see himself as a star witness, only as a bloody killer, even if all he did was to throw a stone.

Centerville

Then Sarah came out onto the porch. "What are you doing sitting there?" She paused, "Are you feeling ok? You look a little peaked."

William looked miserably up at her and shook his head. "I don't know, I just feel so worn out I can hardly move."

"Why don't you take care of the pigs now and then get some rest? A hot meal and then a good night's sleep will do you a world of good."

The man nodded and slowly rose to his feet. Almost painfully he shuffled off the porch into the sunlight and across the front yard. The walk to the hog house seemed to take forever.

Once there the routine kicked in. He mixed the feed and poured buckets of it into the troughs. The pigs snuffled and grunted as they pushed each other aside. William shook his head, they acted like they hadn't eaten in days but in fact they were well fed, and often.

He looked around the work area and decided to clean up a bit. He had slacked off the past week or so and the place looked like the pig pen it was. He gathered a number of burlap bags and threw them into the growing stack. It would really have to be hauled off one of these days.

Then he turned to the tools. Scattered across the work bench he put them back on their hooks and pegs. He swept the floor until he was satisfied that the place looked the way it should; clean and businesslike.

After that he sat on a keg and removed his boots and socks. Then he crossed the room and got the tool he needed and returned to the keg. He took off his hat and carefully put it on the floor. With care he cocked the tool, his twelve gauge, and put the butt on the floor. Opening wide he put the barrels into his mouth. Placing his big toe on the trigger, he pulled it.

Centerville

Centerville

Chapter 25
The Stone Collector

The day was quiet and hot and Fred was bored. He almost wished school would start just so he would have something to do. He would be entering the seventh grade this year and a new school, not to mention the bus ride, opened great new possibilities for him. He knew that he was large enough to pass as an upper classman. But right now he was restless and wanted something to do.

With no specific plan he left his house. Standing on his front porch he scanned what was left of Harvey Miller's burnt house. Most of it had been cleaned up and removed. A couple of days after the fire, dump trucks and a front end loader came and the remains were scooped into the trucks to be hauled to the town dump for disposal. Now there was nothing but a hole and the foundation walls.

Fred crossed the street and walked between the burned foundation and the neighboring house. Then he entered what was left of the cellar. The sun beat down on Fred as he dug through the ruins. Looking for nothing in particular he sifted ashes and rubble, hoping to find something worth his while, maybe some tools or anything interesting. But finding nothing he moved out of the clutter and crossed the back yard to Miller's barn. Fred was aware that something had been found in the barn that was supposed to prove Miller's guilt. Fred grinned as he thought of the frame job someone wanted to pull on the dead man.

And now that Harvey *was* dead, Fred figured that nobody would mind if he rummaged around and helped himself to anything that was interesting or useful. So he went into the alley and squeezed through the slightly opened garage door and entered the dusty and hot barn.

There before him was Miller's car with the trunk still opened wide. He looked into it but saw nothing worth taking.

He scanned the work bench but still found nothing of interest. He didn't need hammers, wrenches or screwdrivers. Then, as he peered into the dimness beneath the stairway he saw exactly the kind of thing he wanted. There hanging from the wall were almost new, clean and shiny traps. When the trapping season came along in a few months these would surely help Fred expand his trap line along the run.

There were more good places than Fred had traps for but now there were an extra dozen new traps that would surely increase his chances of getting more muskrats or maybe even a mink. Trapping in the winter put good money into his pockets. He already had almost enough to buy a new hunting rifle, something more powerful than his .22, when he turned sixteen. Now with more traps he could earn even more money.

Looking around he found a burlap sack and stuffed the traps into it. Not bothering to look upstairs he left the building as he had come and openly carried the sack down the alley, up the side street and into his own barn to place the traps with his collection. When he looked at his own traps he felt a tinge of guilt that he hadn't taken as good care of his traps as Harvey had. Fred decided that one day soon he would clean and polish his traps to look just as good.

Getting the traps was fun but he still had a long day ahead and nothing to do. Cave Creek was too far a walk on a hot day and he didn't feel like fishing at the lime kiln. That was getting too much like kid stuff. He wanted something more interesting, more exciting. He could feel his blood heat and the urge coming so maybe it was time to collect more rocks.

Centerville

Leaving his barn he angled through the neighbor's yard to the sidewalk as he headed for the bridge. He decided that he needed at least four good sized boulders. He wanted something round and heavy. Rocks like that weren't easy to find though there might be a few along the streambed. The trick was finding and moving them without being seen. He already knew the exact spot he wanted to put them.

* * *

Jimmy was at loose ends. Ben was away for the week visiting his cousins who lived near Woodmere Lake. Pete wasn't interested in playing whiffle ball and it seemed like there was no one else around. He didn't feel like fishing and though he had a couple of good books he wasn't interested in reading either. Finally he decided to get his BB gun and go exploring along the run. There were always chipmunks down there as well as other targets of opportunity.

He walked down through his back yard to the alley and then headed east, away from the wooden bridge. He wanted to hunt down by the old tractor bridge instead. This bridge wasn't used anymore and the deck was falling to pieces but often he would see snakes on the bank and occasionally in the run itself. It was a good place to practice shooting. At times he was tempted to take his dad's .38 revolver but he knew that he would get a good hiding if he did so without permission and he didn't think his dad would give that.

At the McMaster's farm he turned to the field behind the barn and followed what remained of the old tractor road down to the bridge and stream. The field wasn't fenced in and was no longer cultivated. Trees were creeping in from the small woods on the far side of the

Centerville

Dry Run. Beyond the woods was open farmland that was accessed from a different direction and was part of a large farm a good mile from the dilapidated bridge.

As he crossed the field he spied a ground hog trundling through the weeds. He took aim but had no intention of pulling the trigger. A BB wouldn't kill the creature but it could injure it and would make it run like mad. It might be fun to see but wasn't worth hurting it, even a little, for no good reason.

Arriving at the bridge he walked out to the center of the span on one of the long steel beams. It was safer than walking on the wooden boards crossing the beams. He could see how rotted the wooden planks were. He knew the steel was safe. He picked a spot near the center and carefully sat. This bridge was only a couple of feet above the water and so the thought of falling did not bother him. He looked at the crumbling stone foundations and knew that in a few years this bridge would fall into the stream, perhaps to create a dam in the process.

It didn't take long for a black snake to slither along the bank not more than ten feet from Jimmy's perch. Carefully cocking the gun he took aim, lining the cross hairs of his scope on the snakes head and pulled the trigger. The shot was true and the snake began to writhe and roll, tying itself in knots on the bank and rolling down into the water. There the stream turned slightly red as the snake's blood stained the water. He fired a few more shots at the snake, hitting it most of the time, until it lay still half in and half out of the water. It twitched occasionally. He was grimly satisfied and at the same time slightly saddened that he had done such a thing.

He sat and watched the snake as flies quickly found the body and began to feed. He sat for a while longer but saw nothing else move except birds and minnows in the run. Growing tired of inactivity he rose and crossed the bridge to the far side of the stream.

It wasn't often that he walked this side of the Dry Run. The only times were when he and Ben dug in the lime kiln or explored the fields on the other side of the wooden bridge. Today he turned upstream and patrolled the area.

As he walked he searched for targets but nothing worth shooting at appeared in his sights. A hawk was winging overhead but he would never think of shooting at a bird like that. He didn't even shoot at blackbirds, just snakes and the occasional chipmunk.

He continued slowly, zig zagging back and forth for about fifteen minutes, in and out of the tree line at the base of the hill. In that time he rounded the bend in the stream at the lime kiln. He stood there looking down the steep bank at what remained of one of the ovens. A few bricks protruded from the clay earth as he wondered what the place had looked like in its heyday.

Then he turned upstream and it was a straight shot to the wooden bridge. He decided that when he got there he would head for home and maybe climb into the treehouse to read for an hour.

Walking in a crouch, as though stalking a deer, he saw movement ahead of where he was and down by the bank of the stream. He stopped to watch, to see what was happening. He crept slowly forward hoping to gain a better vantage point. Assuming it was another kid fishing he pretended that he was a scout on a mission behind enemy lines assigned to monitor the enemy's actions.

Stopping behind a fallen tree he crouched to watch, his air rifle leveled over the trunk. It was then that Fred stood up and was carrying a large and apparently heavy stone upstream. Jimmy watched as he carried it up and across the road to the top of the stream bank on the far side of the wooden bridge. There he dropped it and turned back to search for another.

With growing alarm Jimmy watched as Fred scoured the stream bank and base of the hill until he found another boulder that seemed to satisfy him. He carried the second one to the same place and deposited it next to the first. Then he returned, again, to his search.

His heart pounded and a lump formed in his throat as Jimmy quietly retreated backwards until he felt it was safe to stand and run. Then he ran downstream until he found a place to cross and pounded his way through the fields, alleys and yards until he was safely home. He climbed into his treehouse, taking his BB gun along as though for protection.

Panting and in near panic he looked out over the lower village. '*It's Fred,*' he realized in a flash of horror and understanding. '*It's been Fred all along! And he's going to kill Bart. He's going to wait until Bart's sleeping and he'll drop rocks on his head and kill him. Just like he smashed the watermelons.*

'*He must have killed Betsy too. And he set the fire, I saw his burned arm, my god he did all of that and nobody ever knew. Who would suspect a kid? I guess he must have attacked Judith and when that didn't work he picked Betsy. What else has he done that nobody knows about?*

'*Oh god, what do I do? Will anyone believe me? I'm just a kid and nobody believes a kid. They just don't! What do I do? Who do I tell? Oh I wish Ben was here. Did Fred see me? Did he? No, I don't think he did but I'm scared anyway. What do I do?*'

Jimmy sat for the rest of the day; there in the treehouse, agonizing over this sudden revelation, his

Centerville

thoughts tumbling over each other until his brain was filled with utter chaos.

At the same time Fred calmly and methodically continued his search for the perfect stones, large and heavy. He didn't want anything puny, he wanted killer rocks and he couldn't wait to use them.

Centerville

Chapter 26
Law and Anger

Sheriff Shambach turned from the body of William Stancel and shook his head. He had already examined the pig barn and found it almost too tidy. The remains of Stancel's blood and brains on the wall next to the work bench, threw a stark and horrific contrast to that neatness. Gazing around the room he saw the tools in their place and no signs of a struggle, not that he expected any. Outwardly calm he turned back to the body and the coroner.

"There is no sign of foul play or even of a struggle. It was suicide all right. Look at his bare foot. It's amazing what people will do. I'll bet that he swept the floor and put all of his tools away before he did it. Get him into the ambulance and out of here."

Coroner Hackett directed the attendants to lift the body onto the gurney and watched, along with the sheriff, as they moved it into the ambulance and closed the doors.

"I'll see you at your office," the coroner said as he climbed into the ambulance for the ride to the morgue.

As the ambulance drove away the sheriff examined the scene once again. He finally picked up the shotgun, which had been lying near the body, and carried it to his car. He carefully placed it in the trunk, not worrying about fingerprints.

Returning the barn he turned to one of the deputies, "The man's wife doesn't have to see any more of this or have to clean it up. Get someone to take care of this mess.

"God, I hate this place. I'm going back to my office. You clean up here and then get back." He turned and stiffly walked to his car.

Centerville

As he drove to Middlebury he beat on the steering wheel as his anger mounted. 'Right now,' he thought, 'if I had Bob Zartman in my hands I'd wring his scrawny fucking neck!'

The deputies, back in Stancel's barn, took the burlap sacks that had just been tossed onto the pile and used them to clean the mess on the wall. They scrubbed with water from the trough until there was no stain left. Then they turned off the lights and closed the door. Later they would burn the bags to remove all trace of William Stancel.

Arriving at the courthouse the sheriff climbed the stairs to the District Attorney's office. He entered Clark's office and slumped into the chair across the desk from the DA. He shook his head and sighed.

Looking up he asked, "Is there any statute on wrongful death, or anything close to that, that I can charge Zartman with? It's his fault that William Stancel killed himself. He wouldn't have done it if he wasn't terrified of the man."

"I suppose his wife could file a wrongful death suit but there's nothing on the books I can think of that he can be charged with, at least nothing worthwhile."

"I'm so angry right now that I could wring his neck! He makes me sick; that whole damn town makes me sick. What's wrong with those people?"

"John, it isn't the whole town and you know it. Yes, there is a handful of people who may not be worth much, but not all of them. I know you're stressed and angry. Justice will be done and even if we can't charge him with anything more, we will put Zartman away for a very long time, I promise you that.

"It's been a long day, a long week, hell, a long month. Look at it this way, there can't be many more like this. If there are I'll have to get another bottle. Right now

Centerville

I think you could use a sip." With that he reached into this desk and retrieved the whiskey bottle once again and poured a stiff finger for each of them.

Shambach took the glass, turned it in his hand and said, "I surely hope you're right. I don't know how much more the town, or I, can take." He slumped back into his seat and took a sip.

Next door Deputy Brocious walked back into the cell block closing the door behind him. He slowly strode the length of the hallway until he faced Bob Zartman. Zartman rose from his bunk and came to the cell door. Grasping the bars he said, "What do you want?"

"I want to tell you that you had better be extra nice to the sheriff for a while. He's awful angry right now, mostly at you. He's over at the DA's office and Lord knows what the two of them are talking about but somehow I think you're in that picture."

"What do you mean?"

"Your buddy, Bill Stancel, spilled his guts to the sheriff this afternoon. Told him all about how you, Jim Bateman and all the rest killed Harvey Miller. Told him everything. Left nothing out, right down to *you* throwing Miller down the stairs and Jim kicking him to death. Yeah, your buddy Stancel left nothing out. And boy is the sheriff pissed."

Zartman snuffled, "I didn't do nothin'."

"That's what I hear. But you might want to change your tune 'cause the sheriff isn't the only one who's mad at you. I am too!"

"Why are you mad at me?"

"Because I just don't like you or your kind, that's why." He then stepped close and swung his fist through the bars and hit Zartman hard in the stomach. The man doubled and fell away from the bars.

Centerville

"Sorry about that, I was just trying to check the lock. My hand must have slipped." With that Brocious turned and left.

Bob Zartman groaned as he lay on the floor muttering curses at the deputy, the sheriff and anyone else he could think of, especially William Stancel. That man could cause a lot of trouble, he already had. Suddenly Bob devoutly wished William Stancel was dead.

He should have been careful what he wished for.

Half an hour later the door opened again and footsteps drew near to Zartman's cell. This time he stayed in his bunk as he heard the sheriff speak.

"Get over here Bob. I want to talk to you."

"What do you want?" the man groaned.

"Come over and find out, otherwise I'll come in there after you. I mean it! Move!"

Zartman rolled off his bunk and shuffled to the gate but he stayed beyond arm's reach.

"What do you want sheriff? I don't think I have anything to say to you."

"You may not but I have something to say to you. So you listen to me and you listen good.

"Your buddy Bill Stancel came in today and spilled his guts. He told me everything. I know that you and Jim Bateman were the ring leaders. I know that Jim was the one who kicked Harvey Miller to death but it was *you* who threw him down the steps and *you* who set the house on fire. You're the one who instigated the whole thing.

"Bill filled in all the holes that were left after the inquest - in great detail. I know everyone who was there by name and every one of them will be charged as being an accessory to murder. And I'm just sure that one or two of them will spill their guts, just like Stancel.

209

Centerville

"You're gonna be charged with first degree murder and arson, for a start. The DA's still working up all the charges. We'll arraign you tomorrow and you can be sure that you'll spend the rest of your scrawny life in jail. Right up until the day they hang you.

"If I had my way I'd wring your damn neck right now but that would deprive the state of giving you a fair trial."

"I don't know what you're talking about. I keep tellin ya I aint done nothing. Why don't you believe me?"

"Because I know you're a goddamn liar and Stancel told me everything I needed to know, like I said, and in great detail. You'd best give it up while you still have a chance. You're gonna have company tonight. Your buddy Jim will be just down the hall, but over in the women's side. We don't want you talking now, do we?"

"Sheriff, what do I gotta do?"

"Fess up, be a man." Sheriff Shambach abruptly turned and rapidly walked from the jail before he could lose his composure and beat Zartman to a pulp. As he left he turned off the lights and slammed the door.

On the other side he slumped, his back against the door and wiped his forehead.

"How did it go in there?" asked Jim Brocious.

"I don't know. I sure hope I put the fear of either God or the noose into him. Back there I wanted to save the state the time and money. But as for now, I'm going home. Tomorrow come hell or high water, I'm going to turn him. I'm going to have him begging for mercy. And you can help.

"But first I want you to grab one of the fellows and go out at about 5:30 tomorrow morning and arrest Jim Bateman on suspicion of murder. Then here's what I want you to do."

Centerville

"Got it," Jim Brocious said with a smile. "This could be fun."

* * *

For Deputy Brocious the arrest the next day went without a hitch. He and Ed Johns pulled up to Jim Bateman's house at precisely 5:30 that morning. The lights were burning in the house and they could see someone moving. Brocious motioned Johns to follow a little to the side as he approached the house.

He knocked on the kitchen door, only strangers knocked on the front doors of houses in the country. He stepped to the side and waited.

A few moments later Jim Bateman opened the door. "Why didn't you just come in Bill? I'll be ready in a minute." He looked around apparently expecting to see a friend and not the law.

"I'd hate to come in without an invite," said Deputy Brocious. "But now that you're out I have something for you."

"What's that?"

"This," said the deputy as he grabbed Bateman by the arm. Ed Johns stepped into view. "I have a warrant for your arrest, so it's time to go."

"For what," Bateman asked. "I ain't done nothin."

"That's not what I hear. Let's make this easy on everybody and let's go. I'm arresting you on suspicion of the murder of Harvey Miller. Like I said, let's go." With that he hustled Bateman off to his cruiser. The man was so shocked that he didn't put up even a token protest. Forty minutes later Deputy Brocious had Jim Bateman locked up in the women's jail.

Centerville

Later that morning the sheriff nodded to Jim Brocious and then headed for Bob Zartman's cell. With a nod Jim turned towards the hall to the women's jail.

He walked to Jim Bateman's cell and brought him out into the hallway leading to the rest of the jail and sheriff's office.

"I'm taking you out to be booked. Don't you dare say a word unless spoken to. Understand?" Bateman mutely nodded as the deputy led him from the women's jail. As they passed through the door the deputy pulled Bateman to a halt and said, "We'll wait here for a minute."

As if on cue the sheriff escorted Bob Zartman from the men's jail, across the large room and into the interrogation room. Along the way he ensured that Zartman saw his buddy Jim Bateman handcuffed and in the presence of Deputy Brocious. Bateman looked shocked and Zartman turned pale.

Grimly the sheriff led Zartman through the interrogation room door and pushed him into a chair.

"Let's get started." He said. "I want you to tell me everything that happened at Harvey Miller's house. And you had better tell me before your buddy tells my deputy. He could be ratting on you already.

"Your friend Stancel told me just about everything there is to know from the fact that you threw Miller down the stairs to how you bought the kerosene and started the fire by setting poor Harvey on fire. So what have you got to say."

"Sheriff," Zartman whined, "It ain't like you think or like Bill Stancel told you. I didn't do anything. Bill just told you that because he's afraid of me."

"Why would he be afraid of you?"

"He stole from my traps last winter and I got the proof."

Centerville

"So what does he think you'll do? Thrown him down the stairs and set him on fire?"

"That's not fair, sheriff. You know I wouldn't do that."

"Maybe not but what I want to know, from your mouth, is what happened in Miller's house. This is probably the only time that you're going to have the chance to bare your chest before Bateman talks. And you know he's going to talk, and hang you if he can.

"Listen, I'll make it easy for you. I got a pretty clear picture from Stancel. I know who was with you and that you came down from the post office after Ned Harris chased you off. I know you all broke into the house and found Harvey hiding in his closet. That you dragged him across the upstairs of his house and threw him down the stairs.

"I also know that it was Jim Bateman who actually killed Harvey when he kicked him in the head. You're still an accessory but it may help that you didn't do the actual killing. But you had better speak up and do it fast."

Bob Zartman looked at the table top as though hoping for a miracle to emerge but nothing happened. After a long time he sighed.

"All right sheriff. You got me. I was there all right and I did the all stuff that Bill Stancel told you about."

"That's a good start but tell me more, in a lot of detail. It's the only thing that's going to save your ass."

"Well, when I heard that Miller killed that little girl it just tore me up inside. And when you let that murdering coward go I just got mad as hell."

"Why do you think I let him go?" asked the sheriff.

"I don't rightly know but you must have had a reason."

"Did you ever think that the reason I let him go was because I knew he was innocent? Ever cross your mind?"

Zartman stared at the table top.

"Let me tell you something. I knew that Harvey Miller was innocent because later that night the coroner brought me a piece of evidence. Little Betsy Smith, in her struggles, tore a small piece of her killer's shirt and was clutching it in her hand when she died. It was still there when she was taken to the morgue."

"Yeah, I know. It was Harvey Miller's pocket. Everybody know that."

"Ah, but Harvey was wearing a plaid shirt. The scrap of cloth in the girl's hand was dark blue. And it was thin cotton, like a tee shirt, not the heavier flannel that Harvey was wearing. That's why I let him go."

"But what about the scratches?"

"There was no evidence under the girl's fingernails that she scratched anybody. Harvey got scratched in the scuffle with the deputies. He was an innocent man.

"And you killed him!"

"Jim did it! Jim did it! I didn't kill him, I just got him downstairs. Jim did it and I couldn't stop him. It was all Jim's fault.

"You know what Bill Stancel told you. He saw it. He'll testify to what Jim did. He already told you all that. He must have. He wouldn't lie."

"Bill Stancel did tell me enough. So are you admitting to what happened at Harvey Miller's house? Will you write a confession?"

"Yes sheriff, I'll write a confession. Looks like I got no choice, what with what Stancel must have told you and all. And I saw Jim Bateman out there when you brought me in. He didn't look too friendly either."

Centerville

Sheriff Shambach got a tablet and pencil from a cabinet in the corner of the room and slammed them down in front of Zartman.

"Now write! Write to save your life because it's on the line."

Bob Zartman bent over the tablet, stuck his tongue into the corner of his mouth and began to slowly print. Occasionally he would lick the tip of the pencil and then continue. He worked for the better part of an hour. Finally he finished and pushed the tablet away.

"There it is, sheriff. And that's all I got to say."

The sheriff read the confession, nodding here and there. Finally he passed it back to his prisoner and said, "Now sign it. Sign your confession."

Laboriously Bob Zartman signed his name to the last page and passed the tablet back.

"Now let's get you back to your cell. I think you probably need a rest, your brain must be awfully hot and tired."

With that he led Zartman back through the waiting room and to the cell block. Zartman looked around the room as they passed through it.

As they walked the long hall, passing mostly empty cells, the sheriff said, "The DA will probably want an arraignment later this afternoon or tomorrow. That's when you will be officially charged. If I were you I'd probably start thinking about getting a lawyer cause you're gonna need one. I can promise you that.

"Oh yes, one other thing," he said as he locked Bob Zartman into his cell. "Your buddy Bill Stancel blew his head off with a shotgun yesterday afternoon. Right after he confessed."

Centerville

Chapter 27
Agony

The wait for Ben to come back home from his visit to his cousins was excruciatingly long for Jimmy. Though it was only three more days this wait was probably the longest of his life. Time passed as though encased in January molasses. Nothing helped pass the time.

The anxiety that Jimmy felt would have caused a heart attack in an adult. As it was his heart was constantly pounding. He couldn't concentrate on anything, he could barely eat. Sleep was nearly impossible. It was a wonder that his parents didn't notice his distress.

His mind was constantly flailing over what little fact he knew along with all that he suspected. He extracted and assumed facts constantly; mulling them over and over until they were like a thick paste in his head.

And he could talk with nobody. Who would believe him based on a pile of rocks beside a stream? Certainly not his father or any other adult that he knew. Ben would listen and understand but he was the only one. Jimmy's mantra became, '*no one listens to a kid.*' And he drilled it into his mind with the constancy and urgency of a well drilling rig going after oil.

Never the less there were things that he knew. He knew that there was indeed a pile of rocks beside the Dry Run and he knew that the rocks were there intended to crush Bart Tuttle's head. He knew that it was Fred Swope who would drop those rocks. And he knew that Bart would be sleeping when it happened.

What if he told his dad all of that? Would he think Jimmy was crazy? Would he think Jimmy was making things up? Would he even listen or if he did would he just brush it aside as a childish fantasy? No, he couldn't tell his dad.

What if he told Fred that he knew? What would happen then? Fred would probably kill him, what else could he do? Jimmy knew too much. Besides the last person Jimmy wanted to get within eyesight was Fred.

But Jimmy knew, or suspected even more. Over the past few days he had done nothing but think. Pouring over facts and conjecture; things he definitely knew and those he suspected. Hour after hour he sat in the treehouse pondering.

The first thing he pondered was the fire. Was that only last month, barely six weeks ago? There was so much in such a brief period of time. But the fire was what started it all. And he was sure that Fred had set the fire. He and Ben had seen Fred running from the rear of the Tabernacle that day and he remembered seeing Fred with his injured arm. And Fred said that he had burned it trying to put out the fire. If that was the case then Fred had to have been there when the fire started. And if he was there when the fire started then he must have been the one who started it. They saw no one else running from the fire that day and Jimmy, Ben and the rest had been there from the start and had front row seats. The fire had to be Fred's doing; that was the fact.

And, he remembered, that he had seen Fred favor his right arm the day after the attack on Judith. And Judith had said that she thought that she had scratched her attacker's arm. If she scratched the injured part of his arm he would probably favor his arm for a day or two. She had said it was a big man and Fred was pretty large for his age. In the dark Fred could be mistaken for a larger man. No doubt about it.

Then there was Patsy. If Fred was responsible for Patsy's death then the fire *wasn't* the first thing Fred had done. And nothing added up when it came to Patsy. First his pants *had* been on backwards. There was no doubt about that, why even Oppie Fenster had seen that, so the state cop and the deputy had to have seen it as well. And the coroner too! Jimmy and Ben had seen it and talked about it often enough but nobody ever mentioned it.

Then there was the well cover. Sure, someone could have pushed it back into place after Patsy went in but if he fell into the well there was no way that Patsy could have pushed it back himself. And the final verdict was that Patsy had drowned.

What if Patsy and Fred had been playing and things got out of hand and Fred hurt him? What if Fred thought Patsy was dead? He probably would have panicked and tried to get rid of the body. Fred was big enough to move the well cover and he was big enough to carry Patsy to the well and drop him in. And if Patsy was alive when he was thrown in he would have drowned in the darkness.

The pants still didn't make any sense unless the two boys had been playing doctor or something like that but that didn't make any sense.

But then it hit Jimmy like a blow to the stomach. He remembered Ben's story of being at the lime kiln with Fred when Fred asked Ben if he knew what a cog was and then started to take off his pants. Is that what happened with Patsy? Did Fred ask Patsy the same question and did that result in a fight? A fight that Patsy lost; lost everything?

Was Fred a killer of more than one person? Did he kill Patsy *and* Betsy too? Maybe he wanted to kill Judith and when he failed he waited a couple of days and tried again with someone smaller and easier to handle.

Jimmy's brain almost hurt with all the emotions and suspicions barreling through it. And then there *was*

Centerville

Betsy. Jimmy had no knowledge or facts to implicate Fred in her death; nevertheless he suspected that Fred was responsible. After all nobody had been arrested except Mr. Miller and he had been released, not that it did any good.

But Fred had been at the carnival that night and Jimmy had seen him. But, now that he thought if it, he hadn't seen Fred after Betsy had been attacked. That wasn't much but it was enough for Jimmy to hang his hat on, just enough. If Fred had done all of those things, and Jimmy was sure that he had, then Fred was a very dangerous person. And Bart was in a lot of trouble.

God he wished Ben were home. He needed to talk to him about all of this and see what Ben thought, though he knew deep inside that Ben would not be able to change Jimmy's mind. Not at all.

The next two days were the longest in history. But finally Ben came home and Jimmy couldn't wait to talk with him. He rushed to Ben's house right after breakfast. He knew that Ben had arrived home the evening before but knew better than to go to his place then.

As soon as they met Jimmy blurted, "We have to go somewhere to talk. Somewhere very private."

"How about your treehouse?"

Jimmy nodded and the boys headed back to Jimmy's house. They clambered up into the treehouse and made themselves comfortable.

"So what's so important that we have to have this private talk?" asked Ben.

"I know it all. I know everything and I know who did it."

"What are you talking about? It's too early in the morning to have mysteries. I haven't even digested my Cheerios yet." Ben laughed.

Centerville

"It's not funny! I know who killed Betsy Smith. I know who set the tabernacle on fire and I know what will happen next. I know it all."

"So," replied Ben. "Tell me already."

"It's Fred."

"Fred what?"

"Fred did it all. He killed Patsy and the girl. He set fire to the tabernacle, and attacked Judith and he's going to kill Bart Tuttle. It was Fred all along. But I have to tell you first because I need you to help me decide what I'm going to do.

"I was down by the run a couple of days ago and I saw Fred. He was hunting for big rocks and when he found one he would pile it on the bank right above where Bart likes to sleep. There next to the bridge. I watched him do it and later I went to look at the pile of rocks. And that's when it all made sense to me."

"How could it make sense? All you saw was Fred collecting rocks."

"I know," Jimmy sighed. "But I promise you it all came clear at that moment. And I've been thinking about nothing else for the past three days.

"Think about the fire, that's the obvious place to start. We all saw Fred running *away* from the fire and he even admitted to me that he got his arm burnt when he said he was trying to put out the fire. If he was a normal kid he would have stayed to watch. He might even have told someone that he got hurt. That would be heroic. But he didn't instead he ran away and like I said, we all saw it, you and me. Darryl and Richard saw him too?"

"Did you ask them?"

"No," Jimmy moaned. "But they were right there with us watching the same thing. They had to have seen Fred running away, they had to."

"Ok, so Fred set the fire. What about the rest?"

Centerville

"You remember when you told me about Fred and you down at the lime kiln? What he said and did."

"Of course. He asked me if I knew what a cog was and he started to take off his pants. And I told him I'd hit him with a rock if he went any farther and then I left."

"That's it! I'll bet everything I have that that's what happened with Patsy, except Fred went a lot farther than that. You know Patsy couldn't have uncovered the well by himself. But Fred could. And Patsy would never put his pants on backwards just for the fun of it. But if Fred made him take off his pants and then hurt him and had to dress Patsy himself, Fred might have made that kind of mistake. Especially if he was nervous or scared. I don't really know what happened but I'll bet Fred was involved."

"Might be but you can't tell anybody that. Everyone has decided what really happened and you're a kid. Nobody listens to us!"

"That's right. Nobody does."

"Well what about the girl? What about Betsy?"

"I don't have any proof or anything, really. But I know he was involved. He was at the carnival grounds all night until *that* happened. I didn't see him after that. He should have been curious if he was there and innocent. He would have hung around to see what was going on.

"Oh I know none of this sounds like much but I know I'm right. And what if he does kill Bart? Then what?" Jimmy groaned.

Ben thought for a moment. "Show me the rocks. I want to see them and then we'll decide."

The boys climbed down from the treehouse and walked down to the bridge. As they approached Jimmy pointed and said, "It's on the far side, up there."

"Let's go and see."

Centerville

Jimmy led the way as they approached the bridge. But he didn't cross the bridge. Instead he led the way to the bank across from where Bart always slept, the vantage point where they usually saw him. As they approached both boys could see that Bart was already there, sleeping in his accustomed place. Feet stretched out, almost touching the water in his peaceful repose.

But Bart wasn't sleeping. His arms were splayed out and his legs weren't crossed, as usual. And his head wasn't readily apparent. In its place were rocks. And the pulp where his head had been looked nothing at all like crushed watermelons.

Centerville

Chapter 28
Premeditated

In sheer terror the boys turned as one and ran full tilt the two hundred yards to the post office; their feet stamping on the already hot macadam of the August day. Their lungs bursting as they charged like horses from a burning barn. Jimmy's dad would know what to do, that was sure.

Fred, watching from a hiding spot, crawled away. He had seen what he wanted to see; the discovery. And it was close up. Interesting that it would be Jimmy and Ben but then they seemed to be snooping around almost all the time. Fred carefully crossed the road and climbed up to the cave diggings. There he would have a good view and hiding among the rocks he wouldn't be seen. Shortly now the fun would really begin.

Bursting into the post office lobby and then into his father's office Jimmy shouted out, "It's Bart, it's Bart!"

"Woah boys, what are you shouting about? Bart what?"

Breathlessly Jimmy began again. All in one breath he rushed his words. "It's Bart, dad. He's dead down by the run where he likes to sleep. He was murdered and I know who did it! Ben and I just saw him, you gotta go look and do something. You gotta!" He gasped for breath.

"Ok, calm down. You aren't making this up are you?"

"No," both boys nearly shouted.

"It's just like Jimmy said, Bart was killed down by the run. If you go look, you'll see for yourself and then you can call the sheriff, or something." Ben said.

Centerville

"How do you know he's dead and not sleeping. He sleeps down there all the time."

"Oh we know," Jimmy groaned. "And you will too. It's his head."

"His head?"

"Oh dad, it's crushed. With big rocks. Just go *look*." Jimmy pleaded.

"Ok, I'll go but you boys stay here. Better yet, go home. Stay at home. Ben, you go with Jim." With that Ned Harris turned and left the post office. He quickly walked down the road towards the bridge but like his son and Ben, he went to the right of the bridge and looked from across the stream.

His heart leapt to his throat as he saw Bart lying there. He could see that his head was indeed crushed by a number of rocks. His stomach turned as he knelt on the bank and looked across the stream at the body.

'What in god's name is happening in this town. One death was more than enough but now this. And Bart was a harmless man. I have to call the sheriff.' And he rose and turned back to the post office.

In the meantime the boys reluctantly left the post office. Looking over their shoulders at Jimmy's dad, now standing on the stream bank, they both wanted to be there *and* as far away as possible. With one last long look they turned and walked to Jimmy's house.

When they arrived Ben suggested they go to the treehouse. Maybe they could see some of the activity there. They climbed to the platform and sat.

"You were right all along. Now your dad will believe you? You can tell him later and then he can call the sheriff, or whatever."

"Yeah, I guess I could but…"

"But what?" asked Ben.

Centerville

"I wonder how long it will take before the whole town knows what I told him. How long will it take before Fred knows? He'll be after me next. I just know it."

"But not if the sheriff arrests Fred first."

"But Fred's smart enough to know that someone had to tell the sheriff and he's smart enough to know that it could have been me. He might even figure it out first. I'm scared, Ben."

"But you'll be safe. Your dad and the sheriff will take care of that. Tell your dad today and maybe the sheriff will arrest Fred right away."

"And maybe he won't."

Just then they could hear sirens approaching the village from Middlebury. That had to be the sheriff.

"Let's go down to the corner and watch. We can see better what's going on from there instead of from up here." Ben suggested. So the two boys climbed down from the treehouse and walked the short distance to the street corner and looked down towards the bridge. The bridge was only a few hundred yards from where they stood and they could see all of the activity clearly.

A sheriff's car turned from the lower street onto the road leading to the bridge and pulled off to the right. Immediately behind it was an ambulance. The boys could see the sheriff get out of his car and talk to Jimmy's father. Then the sheriff and a deputy crossed the bridge and climbed down to the stream.

"Oh no!" moaned Jimmy.

"What?" asked Ben.

"The sheriff will ask dad how he found Bart and dad will have to tell the sheriff that *we* found him. And then the sheriff will want to talk with us and I can't tell the sheriff yet. I just can't."

"But he might go and get Fred right way. He wouldn't wait, would he?"

Centerville

"I don't know if he would wait or not," Jimmy groaned. "Oh I wish I didn't know anything."

"Oh but you do, Jim. You know it all and you'll have to tell sometime. And Fred won't be able to hurt you. He'll be in jail."

"I don't know. I just don't know." Jimmy moaned.

* * *

Ned Harris watched as the sheriff pulled up and parked on the berm next to the bridge. John Shambach got out of his car and walked to where Ned was standing. He looked across the stream at Bart's battered body.

"Shit." He shook his head, "That's all we need; another killing in Centerville. Is it ever going to end? Jim," he signaled to Deputy Brocious, "Let's go and take a look." He turned to Ned, "You stay right here."

"I'm not going anywhere, sheriff."

The sheriff and his deputy crossed the bridge and gingerly climbed down the bank and approached Bart's body.

"Would you look at that. It wasn't no accident, I assure you that. Someone deliberately dropped those rocks on the poor man. In fact it had to be premeditated. Those rocks didn't end up on the top of the bank, or on his head, by themselves." He looked around.

"In fact," the sheriff continued, "there aren't any rocks like those anywhere close. Someone had to go hunting them and then haul them to this spot so they could drop them on Bart. But why in Hell would anyone want to kill old Bart. He never hurt a soul." He sadly shook his head. "Who would do such a thing?"

Looking up he saw that Coroner Hackett was looking from across the Dry Run. He waved to him to

Centerville

come across. The coroner turned and made his way across the bridge and down the bank to the sheriff's side.

"Ray, who would do such a thing?" the sheriff asked.

"That's your job, John. I just haul 'em away." He stooped and examined the remains of Bart's head and the rocks that had crushed. He rose, shaking his head.

"Did a pretty good job of it. Must have waited until he was asleep, or passed out from what I hear. It looks like the first one would have been enough. At least he didn't feel anything. We'll have an autopsy in a day or so but I can tell you with some confidence that it was blunt force trauma to the head that caused his death."

He turned and looked across the stream bed to the ambulance attendants. He waved and shouted, "Get a litter over here and get this body out of here."

"What the hell is wrong with this town. Haven't they had enough killing for one summer?" he asked the sheriff.

"Appears not, Ray. Appears not." Turning to Jim Brocious he said, "Let's get out of here."

Though they could near nothing the boys watched as the body was loaded into the ambulance and driven away. Then they saw the sheriff scramble up the bank, cross the bridge and turn to Jimmy's dad. By now there was a good sized crowd that the deputies had to disburse.

The sheriff and Jimmy's dad seemed to talk for a long time before the sheriff finally climbed into his car and left.

Jimmy's dad turned and headed up the hill towards the boys.

Centerville

Chapter 29
Jimmy Tells All

The boys waited at the street corner as Jimmy's father walked up the hill and approached them.

"Let's go home and talk." He said as he turned and led the way.

They walked single file to Jimmy's house and into the kitchen. They all sat, the boys eyes downcast and looking at the oil cloth covered table. The sink dripped in the quiet background.

"Ok, spill it. You obviously know something and I want to know what it is. I didn't tell the sheriff anything except that you two found the body. I also promised him that I'd bring you over to his office the day after tomorrow. Tomorrow I have a big meeting in Harrisburg and I can't miss it. I guess the sheriff thinks that Bart can wait another day.

"But you, Jim, you know something about this and it sounds like you think you know who did it, so you had better talk."

Jimmy, looking terrified asked, "Am I in trouble? But I didn't do anything."

"No," his father sighed, "No, you aren't in trouble. This is just such a shock and the way you came into the post office shouting; I know that you know a lot more than you have ever told me. So I want to know what you know before we see the sheriff."

"He didn't do anything. He's just as smart as Sherlock Holmes, or Joe Friday. That's all." Ben said.

Ned Harris smiled. "Oh, I know that for sure. Nobody is in trouble here but please tell me what you know."

And so Jimmy started.

Centerville

"Dad, most people don't believe kids, even when they do know stuff. So please believe me, I'm not making anything up.

"I'm positive that Fred Swope killed Patsy Marks, Betsy Smith *and* Bart. I'm just as sure that he set the fire at the tabernacle. I'm pretty sure he also attacked Judith as well. But I can't prove any of it."

He turned to Ben, "Should we start with Patsy? I'll have to tell him about you and Fred down at the run."

"Go ahead," said Ben.

"But first, dad, please, please, *please* don't tell anybody but the sheriff. If people find out Fred will find out too and he'll kill me. I mean what has he got to lose?"

"Fred won't kill you, I promise you that. And I'm not going to tell the sheriff, or anybody else anything. You're going to do that when you meet with him on Thursday. And as long as you sound reasonable he will listen to you. And, if need be, he will protect you but he won't arrest you for anything or put you in jail. You aren't a bad guy, neither of you are. He'll just need your help. That is if what you know is worth his hearing."

"Oh it is," Ben said, "Oh it is."

"Ok, now continue," Jimmy's father said.

"Do you remember when I told you that Patsy's pants were on backwards?"

"Yes, I remember that but it didn't make any sense and so I thought you were mistaken."

"But Oppie saw it first and so did the statey. And Ben and I both saw it at the same time that they did. Now what if Fred was with Patsy and something happened?"

"What would happen that would make Patsy put his pants on backwards?"

"But what if Patsy didn't? What if Fred put them on Patsy backwards?"

"Now why would Fred do that? You're not making any sense, Jim."

"Ben," Jimmy turned to his friend, "You tell my dad what happened down at the run?"

For a long minute Ben sat there silent and still as a statue. Finally he spoke. "It was a couple of days before we went camping down at the river. I went down to the lime kill to fish and while I was there Fred came up to me and sat down. He didn't say much for a while but then he asked me the strangest thing.

"He asked me if I knew what a cog was. Now the only cogs I know about are like gears but I knew that he wasn't talking about that. Then he did the scariest thing. He stood up and started to take off his pants. That's when I figured out he must have been talking about a guy's peter. I got up and told him that if he did anything else I'd bash him on the head with a rock. Then I grabbed my fishing rod and ran like heck."

"Dad, what if the same thing happened with Patsy? What if Fred went to Patsy's place and asked him if he knew what a cog was? We all know that Patsy wasn't nearly as big as Fred. Maybe Fred took off his pants and made Patsy do the same. Maybe things got out of hand and Fred panicked and knocked Patsy out.

"Then Fred could have got scared and thought Patsy was dead. He dressed him but got his pants on backwards and carried him to the well and threw him in. Patsy couldn't have opened the well himself but Fred could. Not only that but if Patsy fell in he couldn't have put the cover back."

"But the coroner said that Patsy drowned." Jimmy's father said.

"That's right, I heard it too. He said that Patsy must have hit his head when he fell in and it knocked him out and he drowned. But what if Fred hit him on the head with a rock and knocked him out. Patsy was alive but Fred didn't know that. All he knew was that he had to hide Patsy and the well was a good place to hide him, so he threw Patsy down the well."

"I'll grant you that does make sense; if that's what happened. It's awfully circumstantial. Your story does help though, Ben. But what else, there has to be more."

"There is, dad. How about the fire? Ben and Darryl and Richard and me were playing basketball up at the school when the fire started. When we saw the smoke we ran to see what was burning. When we got there we all, at least Ben and me, saw Fred running away from the back of the tabernacle where the fire started. He never stayed around to watch. And it *was* worth watching.

"A day or so later I saw Fred and he was kind of holding his arm. I asked him about it and he said that he got burned when he tried to put the fire out. But I think he got burned when he started it. I know it doesn't mean much but that's what I think."

"Go on. Are you telling me this in some kind of order?"

"Yes. I'm saving the best for last.

"You remember what happened to Judith and how the sheriff talked to us at the carnival ground. Well I remember that she said that she scratched the man who attacked her and thought that she hurt his arm because he sounded like he was in pain. Well I saw Fred the next day and he was favoring his arm, as though it hurt. He was even using his left arm to do some stuff.

"I think he attacked Judith and she did scratch his arm and it did hurt. Maybe that's why he didn't do more. I saw him all over the carnival that night but not after the attack. Suddenly he was nowhere to be seen. I think he got scared and ran off."

"Yes, but Judith said that it was a big man."

"I know but if I was a girl and I was scared because I was attacked in the dark I might think that the attacker was a lot bigger too."

Jimmy's dad nodded, "You have a point there. What else?"

"Well, just about the same for Betsy, except that this time Fred succeeded. It was just like Judith. I saw him all over that night. He was spending a lot of time around the Bingo stand. But afterwards he was gone. I didn't see him anywhere. I know he could have been hiding in the dark but I don't think so."

"Were you looking for him?"

"Well, no."

"Then how do you know he wasn't there? That's all pretty weak, Jim. Now tell me about Bart."

"A week or so ago Ben and I were down by the run and we saw a pile of rocks that looked like they were thrown down the bank. They were half buried in the mud. We didn't think anything about it then. But a few days later we saw another pile of rocks but this time they had smashed a watermelon or two. They were at the bottom of the bank by the run. Ben said that it looked like someone was just having fun but I didn't think so."

"Yeah, it was just like that, both times." Ben said.

"But get this. Last Saturday I was playing down by the run and I saw Fred. He was below the bridge hunting for something. I watched him and he found and carried a pretty large rock up the bank. Then he took it across the road and put it down on the bank right above where Bart likes to sleep. I watched him carry three or four rocks and put them all in the same place. That's when I knew. That's when everything all kind of came together and I knew that Fred was going to kill Bart.

Centerville

"This morning I told Ben all about it and then we went down to the bridge so I could show him the pile of rocks and decide what to do, whether to tell you. But you know what we saw when we got there. Bart was already dead. If I hadn't waited for Ben I could have stopped it." At that point Jimmy stopped talking. He gulped a couple of times and burst out in tears.

"I could have stopped it but I waited."

"Jim, you didn't know for sure. You suspected it, maybe, but you didn't absolutely know. Why wait for Ben. Were you afraid to tell me?"

Sniffing Jimmy nodded his head to his father and wiped his nose on his sleeve.

"All I know is that Fred did it all. I believe it with all my heart and he has to be stopped. Will the sheriff arrest him?"

Ned Harris shook his head, "I don't know son. Some of what you say makes sense, especially about Bart but I don't know if there is enough there for the Sheriff to go on.

"It's getting late and I have to go to Harrisburg tomorrow. But the day after tomorrow we'll go visit the sheriff. You can tell him what you told me and then he can make a decision. You will have done your best.

"Right now you need to calm down. It's been a long and tragic day for you and you need to take it easy. I think you should go up to your room and lay down for a while. As hard as it is, try to think of something else."

They rose from the table and Ben left. Jimmy slowly climbed the stairs to his bedroom and exhausted he lay on his bed. Within minutes he was fast asleep.

Chapter 30
By the Lime Kiln

Jimmy's dreams were troubled in the night as thunderstorms rumbled through the area but they were nothing but misty memories by morning. He woke feeling rested but still anxious. After breakfast he could find nothing to occupy himself. Ben was at the dentist and wouldn't be back for hours. Jimmy became restless.

Climbing into the treehouse he sat for a long time looking over the lower part of the village thinking about all that had happened the day before, not only discovering Bart but telling his father everything about Fred. And just as he expected his father didn't believe most of it. But Fred was guilty of it all and Jimmy knew it.

But if Fred got even a hint of what Jimmy knew he would be after Jimmy for sure. Jimmy had no doubt that Fred would kill him if he got the chance. If Jimmy talked to the sheriff then people would find out and then Fred would find out. The sheriff had to arrest Fred or it was all over.

What if Fred saw him yesterday when he and Ben found Bart? What if Fred saw him when he was watching Fred collect rocks?

Jimmy truly feared Fred, feared that Fred would hurt him when he found out what Jimmy knew. Jimmy was beyond reason and logic. He was in a near state of panic. He felt cold, inside and out, even though the day was already hot.

From the treehouse the village looked so peaceful and quiet. A light breeze brushed through the leaves of the tree surrounding him. Birds hopped from branch to branch and in the distance a dog barked. Someone drove over the wooden bridge and the planks sounded like

Centerville

distant thunder. But inside there was nothing but turmoil and fear.

Then he thought of what was in his father's bureau and that his father was away. In the drawer was a .38 revolver. His dad called it his post office gun but Jimmy never saw it at the post office.

When they went camping his dad usually took the gun along and in the past couple of years Jimmy had shot it often. At first he was afraid of the kick but now he was used to it. He wasn't a very good shot but he enjoyed shooting it with his father. And his father taught him how to handle the gun, how to load it, to keep one cylinder empty and keep the hammer over that cylinder. How to half cock the gun, fully cock it and how to return it safely to half cock. Maybe if he took it down to the lime kiln and fired a couple of shots it might help relieve the tension he was feeling. For some reason he always felt good, calm, after shooting the gun. Maybe today would be no different. He needed to do something, sitting here in the treehouse all day wouldn't help at all.

His dad was away all day and Jimmy knew not only where he kept the gun but where to find the ammunition as well. Usually there were bullets scattered on the bottom of the dresser drawer as well as in a small box the ammunition came in. Yes, firing a few rounds would really help settle his nerves. It would give him a feeling of power, not helplessness.

And nobody would know.

Climbing down from the treehouse Jimmy entered the house by the back door and went to his room. As he passed through the kitchen his mother asked what he was up to.

"Nothing," he replied. "I'm thinking of going down to the lime kiln to fish for a while."

"That sounds nice, just be careful."

"I will," he said over his shoulder as he crossed the living room to the stairs. He climbed the stairs and entered his bedroom. He went through it to the back attic, to his secret stash. There was his Army knapsack. He removed the aluminum canteen from it to make room. Then carefully he crossed back through his bedroom and into his parent's.

He went directly to this father's dresser and opened the top drawer. There, wrapped in a cotton cloth and underneath some socks was the gun. Jimmy carefully lifted it from the drawer and flipped open the cylinder. There were no bullets in it. He looked through the drawer and found a handful of bullets rolling loose among his father's socks. He put the gun into his knapsack along with the bullets. Then he carefully closed the drawer and went downstairs and through the kitchen.

"I'll see you later, mom."

"Have fun and good luck fishing," she said as he entered the back porch to retrieve his rod. He went down the back steps and across the yard. He had no intention of fishing but the rod would be good cover. He continued down through his back yard to the alley where he turned left and walked to the corner. Then right and down the street to the field and across it to the lime kiln.

It was really a short walk.

When he arrived on the banks of the Dry Run he sat on a log and pulled the gun from his knapsack. He fished out the bullets and fully loaded the gun. He put the remaining bullets back into the pack and then put the now halfcocked gun into the pack as well. Placing the knapsack at his side he reached into it and touched the cold steel of the gun. For some reason it made him feel calm.

Centerville

And there he sat, mulling everything over and over in his mind. It was going to drive him crazy but he had to *think*. Was there anything that he missed? What exactly should he tell the sheriff and in what order? He knew that what he said and how he said it was vital. He only had one chance to do it right. If he screwed up and the sheriff didn't arrest Fred then Fred would figure out that Jimmy talked and that would be that.

The subject of Jimmy's thoughts was only a few hundred feet away. He had just that moment seen Jimmy sitting there as Fred, himself, came around the end of McMaster's barn and headed for the lime kiln for his own amusement.

Without being especially stealthy he, nevertheless, came upon Jimmy and caught him almost unawares.

"Watcha doin?" Fred asked.

Startled Jimmy turned to Fred and with what felt like a hand clenching his heart managed to say, "Not much. I thought I would fish for a while."

"After last night's rain you might catch some suckers."

Jimmy nodded as Fred sat, five feet away, on the end of the same log Jimmy was occupying.

"Yep, might be good fishing at that." Fred paused, "Did you hear about poor Bart?"

Again Jimmy nodded, "Yes, I did hear about it, I watched from the corner near my house when the sheriff came."

"Is that all the closer you got? You didn't see anything else?" Fred asked in a slightly mocking voice, "Nothing else?"

With a growing weight in his chest Jimmy asked, "Why do you ask?"

Centerville

"I thought maybe you and your buddy Ben might have actually gone down to the bridge and seen Bart for yourself. In fact I seen both of you heading out that way."

Mutely Jimmy shook his head as cold terror began to flood his veins.

"As a matter of fact I thought I saw you guys down there looking right at Bart. Standing there; next to the bridge. I even thought that I saw you run off towards the post office. You didn't get your daddy, did you?"

"Yeah, maybe that is what happened," Jimmy whispered through a dry mouth. His heart pounding so hard he was sure that Fred could hear it.

"What's that? Can't hear you. Cat got your tongue?"

Swallowing, hoping to get some moisture into his mouth Jimmy croaked, "Yes, maybe that's what happened."

"Thought so, cause I saw you. I saw you standing there looking at Bart like two scared ninnies. And then you ran to your daddy."

"What if we did? Were we supposed to leave him there to rot?" Jimmy's voice suddenly came back with force. He felt anger begin to flood into his veins.

"Sure, why not. He was only a drunk anyway. Wasn't worth anything."

"But you didn't have to *kill* him Fred!"

Suddenly Jimmy's heart stopped and time stood still. His blood froze as terror welled from within. '*I'm dead meat.*' He thought.

"What did you say, Jimmy boy? What did you say? Did I hear you right?" Fred taunted.

Without knowing where it came from Jimmy blurted, "And I know you killed Patsy too! And you probably killed that little girl! You set the fire at the

Centerville

tabernacle and attacked Judith. You did it all. You're evil Fred. You're evil!"

Turning pale with a look of pure fury on his face Fred stood and faced Jimmy. He put his fists on his hips and stared at him. If looks could kill, they would have.

Jimmy, his hand still in the knapsack, slowly and carefully cocked the gun. Then he grasped it in a deathlike grip, finger on the trigger guard.

In full fury and with a voice filled with death Fred said, "I can't believe that you said that. You must be crazy and nobody would believe you." The fury turned cold within Fred and then a heat rose in his loins and his heart began to race. Suddenly he knew that everything was all right. Everything would be fine. He knew what he had to do. He put his hands on his belt buckle and he cruelly smiled.

"Jimmy," he asked. "Do you know what a cog is?"

Book III
Crime and Punishment

Centerville

Prologue
By the Lime Kiln

The buzzard lazily circled above the field by the lime kiln. The tips of its wings flicked as it thermaled in a large circle in the still air. Something below had its attention. Two things, really, but then one of the things was still and the other went away. The bird was in no hurry, it was still early.

After a while another different thing moved into the field. It moved in the direction of the thing that was still. As it approached it began to move faster. Then it grew close and stopped by the thing that was still. Had the vulture been capable of thought the word 'competition' might have flitted through its brain. But there was competition in the air as well as another bird of prey entered the thermal that warm summer's morning.

Centerville

Chapter 1
By the Lime Kiln

Ben Snyder clattered around his house looking for something to do. He had just returned from the dentist and was bored. He figured that his best friend Jimmy Harris would not be interested in doing much of anything after what had happened yesterday but Ben was restless. He thought of going fishing at the lime kiln but decided that he probably couldn't keep still long enough to catch anything. But maybe he could find a couple of arrowheads down by the run. That would be something to do.

In the past Ben had found Indian artifacts around the lime kiln area and in the fields bordering the Dry Run after they had been plowed. Maybe he would get lucky. It sure beat doing nothing. He would be almost glad when school started in another two weeks. Almost.

He pounded down the rear steps and crossed his back yard as he headed towards the alley. Idly kicking a stone ahead of himself, he followed the stone and the alley to the east until he came to the spot where he could enter the field. There he shimmied under the barbed wire fence and into McMaster's field. Formerly a pasture now the field was overgrown with weeds.

Almost stumbling through the knee high weeds he headed towards the lime kiln. He'd dig around there first and then decide where to go. As he neared the far side of the field he thought he could see a splash of color, bright blue, near the stream bank but it was too far away to tell who or what it was. Never the less it gave Ben a good destination, so he altered his course ever so slightly.

Thinking of very little, Ben approached the blue object. Perhaps it *was* Jimmy. He had a bright blue shirt. It was too bright a color for Ben but Jim liked it. If it was Jimmy he must have been sleeping, leaning back against the log where they often sat and sometimes cooked freshly caught fish over an open campfire.

"Jim!" Ben shouted but there was no response. As Ben drew closer an involuntary shiver ran down his spine. Suddenly he noticed how quiet the day was. He looked up and saw a vulture floating high overhead.

He quickly approached the log and could clearly see that someone was sitting there, slumped against the log, as though asleep.

"Jim, Jim, wake up." Ben crossed in front of the log and saw that it was indeed Jimmy Harris sitting by the log. His head was thrown back and a large bloody gash streaked across his temple. Blood soaked the blue shirt and had puddled on the log before dripping down the far side and soaking Jimmy's blue jeans.

"Holyjezumcrowmotherfuck!" Ben clasped his mouth with both hands, not so much to hold in the curse than to stem to gorge rising in his throat. A heat rose in his chest, his heart pounded and he thought it would burst. 'What happened to you Jimmy? Who did this to you?'

He knew, however, who had done this terrible thing to his best friend and he knew, just as well, that he was probably next in Fred Swope's sights. Turning, Ben blindly stumbled through the field to his home. His dad wasn't home but his mother would know what to do.

High above a second vulture, and then a third, joined the air dance in the sky.

Centerville

Chapter 2
Will it Never End?

"Mom! Mom!" Ben screamed as he stumbled up the steps of the back porch and into the kitchen.

His mother turned from the sink to see the panic stricken Ben sobbing breathlessly, his chest heaving as he stuttered trying to talk.

"Mom! It's Jimmy! Mom! He's down at the lime kill. Help! He's bleeding something awful. Fred killed him. Get the sheriff!" He gasped the words out almost in a continuous stream, barely pausing between his words. Then he reached for the table and collapsed.

Janet Snyder helped her son to sit at the table, his head resting on his arm as he sobbed.

"What's this all about, Ben? Take your time and tell me."

"Mom, Jimmy is down at the lime kill and he's blood all over! He was hit in the head and I know Fred Swope did it. Now he'll be after me! Oh God, mom, get the sheriff, get the police."

"Are you sure Jimmy's..."

In fury Ben jumped from the chair and shouted, "He's dead, mom. And it was Fred who did it."

"Ok, ok. I'll call the sheriff and I'll call Jimmy's dad down at the post office."

"Just call the sheriff. Jimmy's dad is in Harrisburg at some meeting. Just get the sheriff!"

Janet finally turned to the telephone on the wall and dialed the emergency number for Sheriff Shambach, from the list on the calendar hanging there.

* * *

Centerville

"Sheriff, you need to take this," said Jim Brocious the chief deputy. "It's from Centerville and doesn't sound very good."

Sheriff John Shambach rolled his eyes as he took the receiver from the deputy. "This is Sheriff Shambach." He sat and listened for a few moments.

"Jimmy Harris? Are you sure?" he asked at one point. Then he nodded and said, "ambulance." A few seconds later he hung up the telephone.

"Grab your hat, Jim. Call out the ambulance to follow us and get the coroner as well. We'll probably need him. Have them meet us in Centerville at the end of the alley on the Lower Street, at McMaster's barn." He shook his head, "Will it never end?"

As they drove to Centerville the sheriff shared what little information he had.

"Looks like Jimmy Harris; Ned Harris' son, has been killed. Had his skull smashed in. His friend Ben Snyder found the body and says he knows who did it. And he just might. He and Jim were best friends. Ned called me yesterday afternoon and wanted to meet with me tomorrow. Said that Jimmy had some important information to tell me."

They drove in silence the rest of the way to Centerville and parked at the McMasters' barn. The sheriff and his deputy walked across the field to where Ben's mother had said to look for the body. Soon they could see the bright blue of Jimmy's shirt standing out among the greens and browns of the field and stream bank. Far above a number of vultures circled, watching everything that was transpiring.

"Christ almighty," muttered the sheriff as he looked down at Jimmy Harris' savagely beaten head. "Who would do something like this? We'll have to talk to the Snyder boy." He paused, "look around here for evidence of a struggle while I examine..." he pointed towards the body. "This."

245

Centerville

He knelt to examine the body. The skin was cool but not yet cold. He couldn't have been dead for very long. Flies had gathered on the pooled blood and on the head. He brushed them away as he continued his examination. The boy's right hand was inside a backpack that lay at his side. The sheriff reached into the backpack and felt the familiar cold metal of a revolver and the hand that was still grasping it.

Carefully he pulled the backpack away from the body revealing the boy's hand which was clutching the fully cocked .38 revolver. The finger was on the trigger guard and not on the trigger itself. 'At least he was taught how to use a gun properly. Looks like maybe he should have used it, though.'

Gingerly he removed Jimmy's hand from the gun and moved the hammer to the half-cocked position and then lowered the hammer to the safe position.

"See anything?" he asked Deputy Brocious as he waved to the ambulance to cross the field to where they were standing. "Let's get this taken care of and then see the Snyder boy. Take some photos before the ambulance gets here and everything gets trampled."

He walked to his car and radioed his office. "Get a couple of deputies over here to Centerville to rope off the scene and comb for evidence." He turned to Jim Brocious, "You stay here until the other deputies arrive, then come find me. Keep the rubberneckers away. You know the drill." He turned back to his car and silently drove to the Snyder home.

A few minutes later he knocked on the front door. Ben's mother opened it and ushered the sheriff into the kitchen. An ashen Ben sat at the table, an untouched glass of water in front of him. The sheriff took a seat across from Ben and said, "Want to tell me what happened, Ben?"

For a few moments Ben looked down at the table. Slowly he raised his head to look at the sheriff.

Centerville

"Fred Swope killed Jimmy. I know it and he'll kill me if he gets the chance. I know that too."

"Before we get into that, just tell me what you know. What you did this morning, what you found down by the run. Let's start with that, and then we'll talk about what you think you know."

"It's not what I think I know, it's what I *know* I know!" Ben said in a firm and convincing voice.

"Ok, ok, but let's start at the beginning."

"All right," Ben sighed. "I went down to the lime kill thinking I might be able to find some arrowheads. It rained last night and sometimes you can find arrowheads on bare ground and in the fields after the rain washes them out.

"While I was walking through the field I thought I saw Jimmy sitting on a log where we sometimes go to fish and talk. I thought it was him because of his bright blue shirt. When I got close I hollered to him but he didn't answer." He paused and a shudder passed over his body.

"When I got there I could see that he was covered in blood and he wasn't moving." Ben froze for a moment and he gasped, "Oh my god! His eyes were open! His eyes were open! And there were *flies* on his face." He bent to the table and sobbed into his arms. His mother rubbed his back and made soothing noises.

The sheriff watched, an outsider caught up in a painting of sadness and misery. After a while he asked, "Anything else you can think of?"

Ben shook his head as he sniffed and raised his head to look at the sheriff. "No sir, that's it."

"Ok, now how do you know it was this Fred fellow?"

"Jimmy should be the one to tell you that because he figured it all out."

"I think he was," said the sheriff. "He and his dad were coming to see me tomorrow. So you'll have to tell me what Jimmy knew."

Centerville

"It was Fred," said Ben. "Everything was Fred. He killed that little girl, he killed Patsy and Bart. He even burned down the tabernacle and everything."

"How do you know this?"

"Like I said Jimmy figured it all out, he was smart like that. I guess what started it all was that Patsy's pants were on backwards." Ben began to talk and for the next hour and a half he told Sheriff Shambach everything that he could remember or think of. And it was a lot.

Centerville

Chapter 3
Fred

Killing Jimmy had been pure impulse. His internal rage had been at a slow smolder ever since he had killed Bart. He thought it would go away but it lingered reminding him of the deed.

He hadn't intended to do more than bully Jimmy a little, there in the field but when Jimmy blurted, "And I know you killed Patsy too! And you probably killed that little girl! You set the fire at the tabernacle and attacked Judith. You did it all. You're evil Fred. You're evil!"

Fred's internal fire suddenly turned cold and with a look of pure fury on his face Fred stood and faced Jimmy. He put his fists on his hips and stared at him. If looks could kill, they would have.

In full fury and with a voice filled with death Fred had said, "I can't believe that you said that. You must be crazy and nobody would believe you." The fury turned cold within Fred and then the heat rose back in his loins and his heart began to race. Suddenly he knew that everything was all right. Everything would be fine. He knew what he had to do. He put his hands on his belt buckle and he cruelly smiled.

"Jimmy," he asked. "Do you know what a cog is?"

Confused Jimmy mutely shook his head and made the mistake of looking away. In that instant Fred grabbed one of the larger rocks in the fire pit and struck Jimmy with all his might. He heard and felt a satisfying crunch as Jimmy's skull caved beneath the rock. Fred struck again and again. In a matter of seconds Jimmy was dead and slumped against the log.

Fred rose and tossed the rock into the nearby stream. Then he turned and quickly headed for the McMaster's barn. 'Time to hustle,' he thought.

Centerville

Fred saw the sheriff's car as it drove down the Lower Street. He didn't have to guess why it was there or where it was going. He knew that Jimmy's body had been found. In fact he watched as Ben, Jimmy's best friend, discovered the body. Right now he was crouched in the upper haymow of McMasters' barn and watched the activity out in the field. The sheriff was talking to his deputy but then turned and walked back towards the barn.

As soon as Fred had seen the sheriff's car he headed for the barn and the cover of the straw in the second floor. As he watched the sheriff walk back to the patrol car, Fred knew that he had to get to a better hiding place. It wouldn't be long before they would be looking for him. Strangely he didn't feel frightened or nervous but, instead, confident that he would be ok.

But he knew that he would have to do some fast talking. He didn't know what Ben would tell the sheriff but he knew that Ben knew everything that Jimmy knew. And now Fred knew that Jimmy knew just about everything. He didn't know how Jimmy had put everything together and that really didn't matter. Jimmy, and thereby Ben, knew enough to hang Fred. That was for sure. Maybe it was time for him to disappear for a while.

He knew of a cave down by Cave Creek. Nobody knew it was there because Fred, himself, had discovered it. He had been rummaging around in the weeds near the eddy in the creek when he discovered a small spring seeping from the side of the hill. He began removing stones and soon had discovered a small cave. Going back

250

with a flashlight he found that past the small crawlway of an entrance there was a larger room, perhaps twenty by thirty feet and a good fifteen feet high. A few small passages led away from the single room but they went nowhere.

Now he knew that this would be the perfect place to hide. He could take some food, candles and his sleeping bag to the cave and stay there for a few days until they stopped looking for him. Maybe they'd think that he ran away.

With a plan in mind he watched and waited until the police had left the field. Then he carefully made his way to his home. He snuck through the field, staying in the tall grass as much as possible, not worrying about the burrs. He thought that he should take his fishing rod as well as the rest of the things he needed.

When he got home, Fred was glad that his mother was sleeping, she took a lot of naps, so, he began to gather together the necessities for his trip. Before he knew it he realized that he had much more than he could carry in one trip. Thinking carefully he bundled some canned food, a frying pan, his fishing rod and tackle, sleeping bag, flashlight and all the rest into three burlap bags. Carefully but quickly he moved the bundles to the cellar of the burned house across the street, the one that Harvey Miller had lived in before they killed him.

Then from there taking the food he worked his way down the alley and then along the fence row and headed out of the village. He knew that at some point he would have to cross the highway and then he could stay in the fields until he reached the woods. After that it was a walk through the woods and down the foot of the mountain to where the cave was located. All in all it wasn't much more than a mile.

When he reached the end of the fence row he stumbled on a small abandoned tool shed. He had known that it was there but had completely forgotten it. He realized that this would be a very good place to store everything and would be much safer that the ruins across from his house. He stowed the bundle of food in the shed and returned for the rest of his goods. It took him two more trips but by then he was a lot closer to his destination and a lot safer.

Fred rested for a few minutes and then took the first bundle and headed for the cave. As he crossed the highway and entered the woods he decided that again it might be a good idea to stash the rest of his stuff there before moving everything to the cave. And so, once again, he moved back and forth, shuttling his supplies to the new stash point.

Finally he began the last part of the trek, going down the mountain and to the cave. In little more than an hour he had everything safely packed into the cave. It was then that he discovered that the candles provided pitiful light and would not last very long. He needed a better light, a kerosene lamp would be best, he thought, but where to get one. It was getting late in the day and he was tired but he wouldn't rest until he had better light. He thought of building a fire but decided against using that for light. The cave was chilly and he knew he might need a small fire later for cooking and to keep warm.

Fred crawled from the cave and gathered some brush and branches that could be used to cover the entrance. The creek bank was rocky, so he didn't worry about footprints. As he worked he continued to think and worry about light. Then he remembered a cabin about a mile upstream from the cave. It would be empty because it wasn't used much until hunting season came around. It just might have a lamp and maybe more things that he could use. It would be worth the walk to see what might be there.

He covered the cave entrance and headed upstream. It was now late Monday afternoon and he knew that people might be looking for him, so he had to be careful and keep as hidden as possible. He didn't think that they would be looking for him down here yet but he didn't aim on getting caught. There was a rough path going upstream, the remnants of an old logging road that made the trip to the cabin a short fifteen minute walk.

When he arrived Fred peered through the windows. From outside he couldn't see much in the dim interior. On the back porch, however, he immediately found a half full can of kerosene. This was more like it. With two sturdy pushes against the back door its flimsy lock gave way and Fred stumbled into the kitchen. As he rummaged through the drawers he discovered a can opener and some flatware. He realized then that he had cans of food but no way to open them! This was a tremendous find. In a storage room off the kitchen he found the lamp, already filled with kerosene and a box of barn burner matches. Those were the kind that you could light by scratching them against just about anything. Matches; something else he had forgotten. The few book matches he had would not last very long.

Rifling through the cabin he found a few more odds and ends that he had either forgotten or now realized that he could use. And finally he discovered a burlap sack in which he could put everything but the lamp and the can of fuel. He could carry those by their bails in one hand and the sack in another. He was all set.

It wasn't long before he was back at the cave. His last act was to gather wood for a small fire to help stay warm in the chilly and damp air inside. Then he pulled the brush and branches over the small entrance and settled in for the night.

Inside the kerosene lamp gave a cheery but dim light, enough to get around. Fred laid out a small circle of rocks and in it built a fire so that he could cook his supper. He was pleased with the fire. It gave even more light and luckily the smoke seemed to be pulled back into the cave. It might be downright comfy for the night.

Centerville

Tomorrow he would try catching a bass in the creek. After heating and eating a can of soup he settled into his sleeping bag and watched the fire dwindle in the darkness.

'They'll never find me here,' he thought. And then he slept.

Centerville

Chapter 4
The Investigation

Sheriff Shambach leaned back in his chair and looked at Ben and his mother. "That's an amazing tale and I can see a lot of sense in it. Believe it or not I was aware that the Marks boy's pants were on backwards. But because the coroner said that the boy drowned I never put much thought into it. I still don't know what it means. The thing is that a lot of what you tell me is purely circumstantial. There isn't much of anything in the line of physical evidence that points to the Swope boy. That could prove to be a problem. However we will keep a sharp eye on him to make sure that nothing more happens."

A quick flash of fear crossed Ben's face.

"Don't worry, Ben, you'll be safe. I promise you that. For now I want you to stay home and out of sight. Can you do that?"

Ben nodded as his mother said, "Don't worry, Sheriff. He's going nowhere until you get Fred Swope."

He rose to leave. "Good. Now I have more work to do." The Sheriff found his deputy, Jim Brocious, waiting outside the house.

"We have to see the Harris family. I want you to come with me." The two drove the short distance to Ned Harris' home. Sheriff Shambach knocked on the front door of the house. Carol Harris, Jimmy's mother, opened the door. Shambach could immediately see that she had already heard of her son's death. She wordlessly stepped aside and ushered the sheriff and deputy into the living room.

"I know why you're here, Sheriff. Won't you have a seat?"

Centerville

All three sat, the sheriff and deputy leaning forward, elbows in their knees, appearing almost like matching statues at the entrance to a building.

"I'm so sorry to have to tell you this, Mrs. Harris. I know you are in great pain and I can't make it any less. But, yes, we did find Jimmy down by the run. And yes, it does look like he was killed by someone."

"Do you know who? Was it Fred Swope?"

"We just had a long talk with Ben Snyder and he indicated that Fred is responsible. I was going to meet with Ned and Jimmy tomorrow and I'm pretty sure that Jimmy was going to tell me what Ben told me today; that Fred Swope is responsible for a number of events that happened over the summer."

She nodded, "I tried calling Ned down in Harrisburg but couldn't get him. I don't know for sure what time his meetings will end. He may not be home until after seven or even eight, tonight."

The sheriff thought about asking whether she knew that her son had a gun in his possession but thought better of it. He would discuss that with Ned, if not tonight then tomorrow. "I'll want to talk with your husband. I would prefer this evening, if he is up to it but if not then tomorrow."

Carol Harris nodded. "Will you arrest Fred today?"

"I don't think so, ma'am, I have to talk with the DA and determine whether we have enough evidence, or probable cause, to make an arrest. But I do promise that he'll be taken off the street as quickly as we can. We've seen enough evil this summer, we don't need any more. I have to go, now, please know that you have my sympathies."

"And mine too," said Deputy Brocious.

"Will you ask your husband to call me tonight?" He and the deputy rose as Jimmy's mother slightly nodded. "We'll let ourselves out." But just as they turned

Centerville

to the door there was a knock. The sheriff opened the door and found the Rev. Hummel standing outside. The sheriff stepped aside and let the minister enter.

"Sheriff," the pastor said and nodded as he came into the house. "I'll take over now." He turned to Carol Harris and took her into his arms as she finally lost her composure.

The sheriff signaled the deputy and they both silently left the house, closing the door on the muffled sobs behind.

"I don't know about you but I'd just as soon arrest Fred Swope now under suspicion, than wait for the DA to make up his mind. You know how slow he can be at times."

"I agree Jim. There's enough sadness and tragedy here today. We don't need fear added to the mix. No matter how much we keep this investigation under wraps, the word will get out. We all know what happed to Harvey Miller. We don't need another vigilance committee hunting down this kid. I know where he lives, just down from the fire hall, across from the burned out Miller house. You drive down, I think I'll walk. Let's go find him."

Sheriff John Shambach walked down the sidewalk as the deputy climbed into his cruiser and drove the short block to the Lower Street and parked near the fire hall. There he sat, thinking, while he waited for the sheriff. 'Is this kid really as bad as all this? If he is, we won't find him at home. We may not find him for quite a while. He sounds like a smart cookie. He'll probably run off.'

Just then the sheriff rounded the corner. Jim Brocious climbed out of his car and joined his boss as they made their way down the street to the Swope house. When they arrived the sheriff knocked on the front door. A few long moments passed until the door opened, just as the sheriff prepared to knock again. There, inside, they found Sarah Swope, confined to a wheelchair.

"May I help you sheriff?" she asked.

"Mrs. Swope, may we come in? And is your son Fred at home?"

She opened the door wide and the two men entered the house. "I'm sorry but I haven't seen Fred since this morning. He doesn't tell me where he goes or what he does. He's at that *difficult* age, I guess, where he thinks he knows everything. What do you want to see him about?"

"We have some questions we would like to ask him about what he may have heard or seen this morning."

"Is this about that poor Harris boy? Marybell Spence, my neighbor, told me what they found down at the lime kiln this morning. It must be awful for his poor mother."

"It is. When your son comes home tell him to stay inside until we find out who did this. It may not be safe for him. Too many children have been hurt lately. Tell him we just want to talk to him. We'd like to find out what he might have seen or heard"

They let themselves out of the house and stood talking on the sidewalk. "Who is keeping an eye on the Snyder boy? Tell him to watch for Fred Swope to come home and let us know the moment he sees him."

"John, do you think that maybe Fred already knows we're looking for him? This kid is no idiot and if he's as guilty as Ben Snyder says he is, then he may be way ahead of us. He may be on the run this very minute."

"I'm very aware of that, Jim, but I have to start somewhere. If he doesn't show up today or tonight then we'll start searching for him in the morning. In the meantime I have to speak with DA Clark. I'd rather have an arrest warrant in my hands when we do find the Swope kid. You know where I'm going. You're in charge here, call if anything happens, anything at all."

Centerville

The sheriff turned and walked back the way he had come to where his car was parked at the Harris house. Twenty minutes later he was at the court house, climbing the steps to the District Attorney's office.

"What have you got, John?" district Attorney Ralph Clark asked as the sheriff entered the room.

"I guess you heard by now that a kid was killed over in Centerville. He was bludgeoned with a rock, I would guess. I don't know for sure because we found no weapon at the scene."

"Yes, I heard. Who was it and any idea who did it?"

"It was Jim Harris, Ned's son. You know Ned, the postmaster, don't you?"

"Yes, I do, we went to school together. How about who did it?"

"I spoke with Harris boy's best friend, Ben Snyder. He tells me that a boy by the name of Fred Swope is the killer. I also spoke with the victim's mother who mentioned the same name. To cap it off I had an appointment tomorrow morning to meet with Ned and his son. They wanted to talk about all the happenings in Centerville this summer. I now understand that Jim was going to tell me that Fred Swope was responsible for all of it; including the murder of the little Smith girl, Bart Tuttle and that the Marks boy didn't drown but was murdered as well.

"Jim Harris must have been expecting trouble because I found a cocked .38 in his hand – inside a knapsack, at the scene. It looks to me like he was prepared to defend himself against whoever killed him but missed the chance."

"Do you have anything that isn't circumstantial?" Clark asked.

"Not at this time. We don't even know if the Marks boy was murdered. The coroner said that he drowned in the well. Do you remember that?"

259

Centerville

The DA nodded.

"Well today the Snyder boy told me that the Marks boy had his pants on backwards. I was aware of that but put no significance to it but now get *this*. Ben Snyder believes that Fred Swope and Patrick Marks may have been involved on some kind of sexual play. He didn't know what but he told me this story:

"One day he was fishing down at the lime kiln behind town when this Fred Swope came up. After talking for a while Swope asked Ben whether, and I quote, he knew 'what a cog was.' Swope then proceeded to take off his pants and demanded that the Snyder boy do the same. Snyder believes that this is what happened to the Marks boy but that it went farther and that in a panic Fred Swope knocked the boy out and then dumped his body into the well and *covered it back up*.

"Thing is, is that the boy was not dead when he went into the well and so he drowned. The coroner determined that he hit his head on the stone wall as he fell into the well and then drowned. But nobody could figure out how the well got covered back up. Bruce Walter, who owns the farm the well is on, claimed that the well was always under cover.

"Well what if Ben Snyder is right and this Swope kid did kill the Marks boy by hitting him on the head and then dropping him into the well and covering it. What if they were naked and Swope pulled the Marks boy's pants on backwards in his panic to get rid of the evidence. This is all beginning to make a lot of sense to me."

"That's an interesting theory but it's pretty thin. Even if we could take the Snyder boy's story about cocks, or cogs, and Fred Swope taking off his pants it will be hard to link to what is officially an accidental drowning to murder. What else have you learned?"

Finally the sheriff sat and they began to talk.

Centerville

Chapter 5
The Search Begins

After an hour Ralph Clark said, "That's a lot of information John. But I'd really hate to go to trial with just that but it *is* compelling. Come back in the morning. I'll talk to Judge Spicer and see if I can't get a warrant on suspicion. That should be enough to get him off the streets. Maybe you'll be able to get a confession. In the meantime, keep digging."

John Shambach returned to his office to write his daily reports. He sat at his desk and as he began to write he was overcome by a sense of futility and deep sadness. How could it be that something like the events at Centerville could happen, on his or anyone else's watch? As he struggled with the report his telephone rang. He dreaded picking up the receiver because he knew it was going to be Ned Harris.

It was.

"Shambach."

"Sheriff, this is Ned Harris. My wife asked me to call you."

Shambach sighed and then inhaled deeply, fearing the coming moments. "Mr. Harris, Ned. I am so very sorry for you and your family. I am so sorry for what has happened and that I have to ask you a few questions. We can do this over the telephone, if you wish, or I can come to your house this evening. Because of the nature of the investigation I don't believe that tomorrow can wait."

"No, sheriff, let's talk now. I'm exhausted and," his voice broke, "this is a hell of a welcome to come home to."

"Ned, I know this is painful and I want to keep our conversation to a minimum, so please bear with me. I have some questions to ask you and rather than make this difficult just tell me the minimum for now. Later we can go into details, if we must."

Centerville

"Go ahead sheriff."

"You and your son Jim were scheduled to meet with me tomorrow. Will you please tell me why?"

There was a long pause. It was so long that Shambach began to think that line had been cut. Finally Ned Harris spoke.

"Sheriff, as you know the past couple of months have been like a terror to us here in Centerville. We lost so very much. First Judy Mecklenburg was attacked. Then only a couple of days later Betsy Smith was killed. After that Harvey Miller was murdered and finally, Bart Tuttle. Then there was the fire at the tabernacle. Each of these was horrible in itself but nobody really connected them to a single source.

"But Jim, my son..." Here Ned Harris caught his breath and stumbled over his words. "Jim somehow put all of these events together and came to the realization that they were all connected and were committed by the same person.

"To be honest, sheriff, I didn't believe him at first but his friend Ben Snyder helped Jim to convince me. The kicker was that they both saw a pile of rocks along the stream bank that were used to smash a number of watermelons. It was exactly the same, they said, as what they saw when Bart Tuttle was killed.

"When they saw the smashed watermelons on the stream bank. The boys didn't think much of it at the time but then Jimmy told me that he saw Fred Swope collecting stones and piling them near where Bart usually slept. That's when Jimmy put it all together. And when Bart was killed, he knew it for sure. And I'm pretty sure that Ben did as well."

The line went silent as Ned stopped talking. After what seemed like an hour the sheriff spoke, "Ned, I heard much of what you have just told me from Ben Snyder earlier today. I've talked with the DA and am hoping that I will have an arrest warrant for Fred Swope by morning.

Centerville

But, to be honest, I will need a lot more detail. I know you may not be able to provide it all but I'm hoping that between you and Ben we can get enough to secure an indictment. In the meantime the DA is working on obtaining that arrest warrant."

"So will you arrest Fred when you get it?"

"I would like to but we don't know where he is. It looks like he fled right after he killed your son."

There was a gasp followed by a long silence.

"I'm sorry, Mr. Harris. I didn't mean to sound that coarse."

"John, you didn't and weren't. It's just... so hard to even comprehend that this has happened."

"I understand. And I'm sorry that I have to say that there is no evidence yet but that's what I believe. After all that I have heard today I can't image who else could have done it. It isn't and will not be easy for you and your family. That's why we are here, to give you as much support as we can. The next few days will be rough, I won't deny, but we'll get through it and we will bring Fred Swope to justice. On my honor I promise you that."

The next morning DA Clark called the sheriff. "I have your warrant. Judge Spicer seemed to think that there is enough evidence to arrest Fred Swope on suspicion of murder. So he's all yours."

The Sheriff thanked the DA and called his deputies into his office. As they gathered together in his small office he spoke, "I have an arrest warrant for Fred Swope, of Centerville, on suspicion of the murder of James Harris. To the best of my knowledge nobody has seen Swope since yesterday morning. For those who don't know Fred Swope is fourteen years old. He looks a good bit older. He's large for his age.

"Jim and you, Ed, I want you to come with me to Centerville. Take Jim's Car. The rest of you stay around here unless you're called out. I want to be able to get to you quickly. I have no idea where this kid is but we'll find him. And never forget that he is dangerous. According to what I have been told, not that it has been proved, is that he has killed at least three other people in the past couple of months. I don't know if he is armed but assume that he is if you encounter him. I'll probably get together a search party if we don't find him quickly. Now let's go."

The men moved from the room. Jim Brocious and Ed Johns headed for Jim's cruiser while the sheriff climbed the stairs to the DA's office in order to get a copy of the warrant. Then he too drove to the nearby village of Centerville.

* * *

Fred woke in the chill blackness of the cave. In the deep silence he could hear the occasional drip as water fell from stalactites. A rock ground into his back as he rolled over to sit up. He fumbled in the darkness for the flashlight. Finding it he switched it on. In its dim light he managed to lay out a fire and get it burning. The damp wood slowly caught and became a low smoky blaze. Next he lighted the kerosene lantern and looked into making himself something for breakfast. He was again pleased that the smoke from the fire seemed to be drawn deeper into the cave.

In his pack he found a can of beef stew. While it warmed in the pan he walked to the other end of the large room to relieve himself. Soon he was eating the beef stew and contemplating the day ahead. He couldn't stay in here all day. Even with the fire it was too chilly. He could see his breath, but it was warm, if not hot, outside. He still liked the idea of catching a nice bass and frying it up for his supper.

After he ate he collected his fishing rod and prepared to leave the confines and darkness of the cave. He put out the lantern and left the fire smoldering as he crawled through the cramped entrance. Pushing the branches that covered the entrance aside he exited the cave. The sunlight was strong and the heat of the day was building. Fred actually shivered as the heat enveloped him. 'Now to find some bait.' He thought.

That same morning Elwood Loss was fishing about a mile downstream. The action was slow to non-existent and so his mind wandered. Already the heat of the day was making him sweat. He wiped his brow with his red paisley handkerchief and looked up along the mountain where it dove beneath the creek. He saw a haze of smoke about halfway up the side of the mountain and wondered whether lightening had struck and caused a tree to smolder.

He decided that maybe he had better report it to the fire department in Centerville. It didn't look like much but it could get worse. Besides the fish weren't biting at all. So he packed his rod and tackle box into his battered Ford truck and headed for town.

There was no one at the fire station, it was all volunteer after all, but he had seen a sheriff's car as he drove down Center Street; he could tell them. So he circled back to the Reformed church where he had seen the sheriff's car. As he approached he saw two deputies standing by the car talking.

"Deputy," he said as he pulled up, "I think there's a fire up on the mountain. Ain't nobody at the fire hall so I thought maybe you might could do something about it."

"We're kind of busy right now," replied Jim Brocious. "The best we can do is call the fire department in Middlebury. Maybe they can send someone to investigate. Where is it located."

Loss pointed towards the mountain, "Right there."

Brocious turned and could clearly see smoke rising in a thin column from the far side of the mountain. "Doesn't look like much to me."

Centerville

"It may not be now but it could spread," Elwood Loss insisted. "Somebody ought to do something about it, just in case, you know."

"Ok, we'll radio Middlebury and have them take a look."

Elwood Loss climbed back into his car and decided to find a nice cold beer somewhere. At least that beat fishing. As he pulled his car out onto the road the sheriff turned into the parking lot to meet his deputies and to plot out their search.

As they strategized the deputies forgot about the fire.

"Let's start with the Swope home. I suppose there's a small chance that he did actually return home last night. After that we'll just spread out. Maybe we can figure out where he likes to go and check those places out."

A few minutes later Fred's mother answered the knock on her door. "Yes sheriff, come in." she wheeled her chair backwards as she made room for Shambach to enter the living room.

"I haven't seen Fred since yesterday," she said in answer to sheriff Shambach's question. "In fact I think he must have gone camping. I saw that a frying pan is missing from the kitchen. When he goes camping he often takes a pan with him to cook in."

"Where does he like to camp?"

"Often down by the lime kiln and sometimes down at Cave Creek. He likes to camp and fish there by the eddy. Once in a while he'll bring home a nice bass that he caught and I'll fry it up for him.

"Any other places you can think of?"

"Not really," she replied. "He just likes to go off. He rarely tells me where." She paused, "He's not in trouble, is he?"

The sheriff paused to think. He decided to be less than truthful. "I think that he may know, or may have

266

Centerville

seen something, about what happened to Jimmy Harris yesterday and I want to talk to him about it. It would help us a lot."

"Well I'll certainly tell him when he gets back home. He's never gone more than a day or so."

"Thank you," said Sheriff Shambach. "Don't bother. I'll let myself out." The sheriff left the house and joined the deputies in the street.

"She said that he might be camping down by Cave Creek." He spat in the gutter, "You might want to take a drive down there to take a look. She said he likes to camp by the eddy. Do either of you know where that is?"

"I do," said Ed Johns, who lived in Centerville. "It's just a few yards down and across from the dam and that's a popular swimming hole. The eddy is on this side of the creek."

"Well check it out. Maybe you'll get lucky."

"That reminds me, some guy came by the church and pointed out a fire on the mountain. While we're over there maybe we'll take a look."

"Don't take too long at it."

The deputies climbed into the cruiser. Brocious, who was driving, made a U turn in the street and headed for the creek. Ten minutes later they were parked at the dam and swimming hole. Looking along the mountain they saw no evidence of smoke.

"Looks like the fire went out," Ed pointed out.

"Didn't look like much anyway. If we see more smoke later we'll call it in. For now let's walk along the creek to look for a camp site."

"I doubt we'll find anything on this side. Mostly summer cabins here. My wife's cousin has one right down there," he pointed. "If anyone is going to camp out around here it will be on the other side." Again he pointed but this time at the area of the eddy on the far side of the creek.

Centerville

Jim Brocious looked towards the eddy, "Think it might have been a camp fire up on the mountain?"

"Naw. It's too steep and rocky for that. The only good camping is right along the bank. There's an old road that goes partway to the eddy. We could drive down it and walk the rest of the way. It's not that far."

Brocious nodded his consent as they returned to the car. They leisurely drove back down the creek road to the intersection. There they turned right and crossed the bridge. Immediately on the other side of the bridge they took another right and drove past the old mill and down a rutted road. "We had better be able to get back out of here," Jim said as they bounced along.

About one hundred yards down the road he stopped the car and they continued on foot. "The eddy's up here only a few hundred feet. I camped here myself when I was a kid. It's good fishing too. Wouldn't be surprised to find signs of him camping here."

At that Brocious loosened his holster and became much more alert. The two deputies moved slowly down the road, looking for signs of recent activity. At one point they found the remains of a long dead fire, the ashes cold and damp. Ed shook his head and they continued on.

As they walked a squirrel chattered at them from the branches of a walnut tree. Here, already, the mountain side was steep and foreboding. 'I'd hate to have to climb up that bank,' thought Jim Brocious.

Within a few minutes they arrived at the eddy and examined the shallow creek bank for any signs of camping, footprints or anything. Nothing disturbed the soft earth. They walked a little farther in the quiet morning and then turned back.

Three hundred feet upstream from where they turned Fred Swope crouched beneath a mountain laurel bush, holding his breath. Not daring to move he watched them slowly return to their car. He did not move until they were long gone.

Centerville

Fred had seen them earlier when they were on the far side of the stream. As soon as he had seen the cruiser slow to a stop he hid in the cluster of pine and laurel that covered the rocky banks of the creek. He saw Ed Johns point to the eddy and when they left Fred assumed that they would come to the eddy to check out the area.

For a few moments he wondered whether he had covered the cave entrance and finally remembered that he had. After covering the entrance he had walked on the rocky ground that rose steeply up into the mountain so to leave no footprints. He moved to a place with a better vantage point and hid deep within the thick laurel. He knew that someone could walk past him only a few feet away and never know he was there.

When the police were gone he knew that he was safe; there was no reason for them to come back to the eddy again. He breathed a sigh of relief.

Chapter 6
Caught

The sheriff looked for likely places and settled first on McMaster's barn. He knew that Fred would not be there but he guessed that it might be a place that Fred frequented. Gaining permission he entered the large bank barn.

The stable and milking parlor on the ground floor were clean and deserted. Cows hadn't been here for a number of years. He was not surprised when he found nothing but dusty and cobwebbed milking equipment. On the next floor up, the threshing floor, he found the solid wooden floor worn smooth by years of threshing corn and wheat. Pigeons cooed in the rafters far above his head. The air was hot, dry and dusty.

Parked on this floor were an old hay bailer and a wagon. On both sides, to the front of the barn were empty granaries. On either side of the large rolling doors were stacks of hay bales. The McMasters still made hay, and straw; perhaps to be sold as they had no cattle themselves. Suspended above him above the doors was another floor. He climbed a ladder to this floor and made his first discovery.

The floor was covered with straw. There were a few wooden milk crates scattered about, two of them set up and covered with some worn planks to form a table. On the table were a few fish hooks, a screwdriver, rusty knife and a couple of muskrat traps.

A nest, of sorts, was formed along an inner wall and a bale had been placed beneath one of the windows. Looking out of the window Shambach could clearly see across the field to the place where Jimmy Harris' body had been found. Suddenly he was very certain that Fred had been watching his every move the day before. It made him shiver.

Centerville

After leaving the barn he drove down the alley and came upon the burned out remains of Harvey Miller's house. On impulse he stopped. He got out of his car and entered the ruined cellar. There on the floor he saw a clean wooden spoon. 'What is that doing here?' he wondered. The cellar looked like it was regularly used. Across the street from Fred Swope's house it might be the perfect place for Fred to cache things. Bemused, the sheriff left the cellar. As he turned he saw marks on the floor, recent marks of something being dragged across the floor. Something like a burlap bag.

Returning to his car he heard Jim Brocious calling on the radio. "Go ahead Jim."

"We checked out the swimming hole and then crossed the creek to look around the eddy. We didn't find anything."

"10-4 on that. I didn't find much myself but I *did* find something. Let's meet back at the church and regroup. Out here."

Within ten minutes they were again in the parking lot of the Reformed church in the center of the village. Comparing notes the deputies were empty handed. The sheriff described his discoveries in the barn and the cellar. "I believe that's a clear indication that Swope was there. And the drag marks on the floor tell me that he was transferring something to somewhere. The wooden spoon was odd but I guess he was planning on cooking with it but it was dropped and overlooked. Now my question is where did he go with at least one bag of goods and did anybody see him?

"You two canvass the lower street heading east. I suspect that he might have headed that way. I'm going to examine the alley going that way as well. Maybe we'll get lucky. Let's meet back here," he looked at his watch, "at two thirty and we'll see what we've got."

They got into their respective cars and headed off. The sheriff returned to the burned house and parked

271

behind it. Then he walked slowly down the alley, looking for any signs of passage. After about a quarter of a mile he came to the end of the alley, not far past McMaster's barn. There only a path led along a fence row. Shambach carefully walked, head down looking for evidence of passage. Again his luck held. He found a spot of crushed grass and weeds where perhaps a bag had rested. Not far beyond that he came upon the abandoned tool shed. He found nothing there but he had a suspicion that Fred had passed this way.

From that point, however, the sheriff found nothing. The trail, such as it was, went cold. Looking in all directions he had no idea of which way to go. After gazing around for a long while he sighed and retraced his steps. Maybe his men would get some information from their canvass of the neighborhood.

Maybe not.

When they again met at the church the two deputies confessed that they had found few people at home and those who were reported seeing nothing out of the ordinary or in seeing Fred Swope at all. Shambach shared the little information he had discovered.

Meanwhile Fred was having great luck. Sitting on the bank of the eddy he hooked a large mouth bass that had been hiding in the waters beneath a fallen tree. It gave him an exciting fight. When he finally landed it he was proud of his success. He cleaned the fish there by the creek and threw the remains into the water. Then he carefully carried the fillets into the cave and put them on a plate. With the fillets and some fried potatoes he would have an excellent supper. He returned to the creek with the frying pan and scrubbed it clean before returning to the cave. Next he looked for some good dry wood for his evening fire. He didn't want the green or damp wood that didn't burn well. He wanted some heat, for cooking and to hopefully raise the temperature in the cave. He had almost frozen the previous night.

Centerville

Forgetting that he was a fugitive he was thoroughly enjoying himself.

Having brought a good deal of firewood into the cave Fred decided to light a new fire and hopefully drive some of the cold from the cave. Soon the flames were leaping higher than he had anticipated. Painting moving shadows on the cave walls the flames danced as the wood spit and snapped. Again Fred was pleased that the smoke flowed into the depths of the cave.

"Is that the fire you were talking about earlier?" Sheriff Shambach pointed to the mountain as he and the deputies discussed their unsuccessful afternoon.

"Sure looks like it," Jim Brocious said. "The smokes a lot heavier than last time though. Maybe we *should* call the fire department."

"Maybe," said the sheriff, "we should go check it out ourselves. Maybe it isn't a lightning struck tree. Maybe it's Fred Swope at his camp site. Follow me down to the dam and let's take another look."

The two cars pulled out and drove the short three miles to the dam and swimming hole. From the vantage point of the parking area – a wide spot in the gravel road – they could easily see the side of the mountain.

"As high as it is up the side of the mountain I don't see how it could be a camp site. I've tramped all over that side. It's nothing but rocks and is too steep to camp. You could hardly get comfortable up there." Ed Johns shrugged his shoulders. "It must be lightening."

"Well it doesn't look like it's that far up. Let's go over and see if we can get up there. Maybe we can knock it down ourselves. You guys game?"

The deputies reluctantly nodded their heads as they got back into their cars and drove back to the rutted road by the old mill. When they arrived the sheriff took an axe from the trunk of his car. "I keep forgetting to put this back in my garage. Good thing I still have it. Let's go."

273

Centerville

The men walked down the old road to a point where they felt they were below the smoke. Turning to the slope they began to climb. It was indeed as steep and rocky as Ed had said and soon they found themselves pausing to catch their breath. As they sat on the rocks they could faintly smell the smoke and even imagined that they could see a slight haze in the forest above them.

"Let's go and finish this before I change my mind and let the firemen deal with it," the sheriff grimaced. They rose and began once again to scramble up the side of the mountain. A few hundred feet farther they knew that they were approaching the source of the fire. The air was definitely hazy and smelled of burning wood.

The men stumbled over the rocks and steep terrain until Jim Brocious said, "There it is!" He pointed to a spot about fifty feet away. They made their way to the source of the smoke but found no fire, no sign of a tree struck by lightning. Instead the smoke was coming from the ground.

"What the hell?" said Ed Johns.

"Son of a bitch!" said John Shambach. "Ed, is there a cave around here?"

"Not that I know of, sheriff. I've never seen one."

"I'll bet you a dollar that there is and that Fred Swope, himself, is camping inside the cave. This is the smoke from his camp fire and he doesn't know it. Let's get back down to the cars but don't you dare fall and break a leg. And keep it quiet too. We don't want him to know we're here." The three followed a shallower and more diagonal path back to the cars than they had taken to get up the mountain.

Fifteen minutes later they were back at the cars. "Let's go back to the church," said the sheriff. When they arrived and gathered the sheriff said, "I've thought about it while were driving and here's what we're going to do."

* * *

274

Centerville

At four thirty the next morning the sheriff and five deputies met at the church parking lot.

"Ok men. Here's the deal. As you know we think that there must be a cave down along the creek." He pointed to a spot on a topographical map. "This is about where the eddy is and I'm guessing that there's a cave entrance somewhere close to that. Ed," he nodded to Ed Johns, "says that there is a spring that comes out of the mountain side just about there."

"I've done a lot of fishing down at the eddy and never thought anything about it; the spring, that is. But I suppose that it could be coming out of a cave." Spoke Ed.

Jim Brocious said, "There's gotta be something. We definitely saw that smoke coming out of the ground and I don't think a volcano smells like burning wood." He laughed at his own joke.

"You're right there, Jim. Now here's what we're going to do.

"Frank, you and Jake take the canoe up above the dam a little ways and paddle across the creek. Keep it quiet. Make your way down towards the eddy but stop a good hundred feet away from this point." He put his finger on the map just where the eddy would be.

"Bill, I want you there at the dam in case Swope decides to cross the creek. If he does it's your job to stop him, chase him down. You might get a little wet.

"Jim, Ed and I will go up the road to as close as we can get to the spring and will take cover in the brush there. It's pretty thick. If Fred Swope is in a cave there he'll have to come out sometime and when he does we'll be ready. He may very well try to run so be ready to chase him down. I don't believe he is armed but you should definitely consider him dangerous. He's very big for his age and will put up a hell of a fight, so be prepared.

"Oh yes, another thing, you know enough to be quiet but I don't want any of you smoking out there. If he

275

comes out and smells cigarette smoke he might go back in and we don't know if there is another way out."

"Hell, sheriff, we don't even know if there is a cave there at all? Maybe there *is* a volcano in the mountain." Frank Pierce laughed and spat a stream of tobacco juice between his feet.

"Well we'll know soon enough. I don't have to tell you to keep it quiet and don't show any lights. You guys on the other side of the creek, park behind trees or bushes so your cars don't show." He looked at the sky. "It's getting light enough to see what we're doing and where we're going, so let's do it. Good luck and be careful. Let's move out."

The sheriff and his deputies got into their cars while Frank and Jake climbed into Jake's pickup truck which was carrying the canoe. In moments they were on their way. Within ten minutes all were in place. The canoe was in the water and the two deputies were beginning to paddle across the slowly flowing creek in the early morning twilight.

Deputy Bill Underhill sat on a rock by the creek behind an elderberry bush. He was just able to see across the creek and the eddy to where the supposed cave entrance was. The sheriff, Jim and Ed Johns moved silently down the rutted road to vantage points only a few yards from where they believed the cave entrance might be; based on Ed's knowledge of the area.

"You two take the mountain side over there," the sheriff pointed. "I'll take cover behind those bushes and fallen tree by the water. Let's go." The men carefully went their different directions and found themselves good places to hide.

And then the wait; nobody knew if Fred was even near there or if there actually was a cave. Nobody knew, if he was there, how long they would have to wait for Fred to show his face. And no one knew what would happen if or when he did.

Centerville

The day awakened around them while in the cave Fred had little awareness of the passage of time. He didn't have a watch and the only way he knew if it were day or night was by what little light seeped in through the low entrance. He did sleep deeply, however, and did not awaken until well after dawn. When he did finally open his eyes it was nearly eight am. While he moved around the cave room building a fire and taking a leak, the sheriff and his deputies were stiffening from not moving for nearly three hours. They all wished something would happen.

Deputy Underhill noticed the smoke first. He could see it rising from the side of the mountain not long after Fred had lit the fire in the cave. An errant breeze wafted the smoke in the direction of the sheriff, Jim and Ed. They smelled it and knew that Fred was awake and moving. They all tensed, watching for any movement along the base of the mountain.

In the cave Fred wishing that he had a couple of eggs instead opened a can of Spam and fried large chunks in the pan. He ate his breakfast in the light of the kerosene lantern and planned his day. The fish supper had been good last night. He still had a couple of potatoes so maybe he could catch another bass today. But he would be happy with some sunfish or rock bass. He knew that he would have to raid the hunting cabin again. He needed more canned goods if he was going to be staying here for a while. It would be nice if he could find some coffee in the cabin. He would kill for an RC Cola. He could also use a saw or axe to cut more firewood. It burned a lot faster than he had imagined. The easy windfall branches were nearly gone. He had to have a better and longer lasting supply. Finishing his Spam breakfast he extinguished the lantern and made his way to the entrance and crawled out into the daylight.

The sheriff saw branches begin to move, exactly where he had been staring for the past ten minutes. At one of the spots that he thought might be the hidden entrance to a cave the brush just looked wrong. It was too dry and the leaves were wilted. Taking a chance he crept across the road, signaled the deputies and stood up his back to the rocks near the moving brush. He drew his gun and unconsciously held his breath. The branches moved away from the side of the mountain and Fred Swope stuck his head out into the morning air. The sheriff waited until Fred was almost completely out and ready to stand.

"Hold it right there Fred. I don't want to shoot you but by god I will! So just stand up slowly and put your hands above your head."

Stunned Fred slowly rose. Thoughts of running flitted through his mind until he saw deputies step onto the road to his right and then more deputies quickly move down the path to his left. There was only one place to go and that was into the creek to try to swim for it.

"I wouldn't do it if I were you. I have another deputy on the other side and he has a gun too."

Fred raised his hands, "I don't have no gun, Sheriff, don't shoot me. It would kill my mom."

"Wouldn't do you much good either," said Ed Johns.

"Cuff him up, Jim. Is there anybody else in the cave, Fred?" The sheriff already knew the answer but he had to cover all of his bases. Fred shook his head and Jim Brocious pulled Fred's hands behind him and put Fred in handcuffs.

"I'm arresting on the suspicion of the murder of James Harris. Jim, you and Ed take him to the jail. I'll be right behind you." He turned to deputies Pierce and Thomas. "Good work men. You can paddle back across the creek and then get back to the office. Tell Bill that I said good job. I'll see you back at the office." Then the sheriff turned and followed Jim Brocious and Ed Johns

to the cars and then followed them to the county jail in
Middlebury.

Centerville

Chapter 7
In the Jail

Fred was stunned as he was led into the county jail in Middlebury. He posed for his mug shot and then was led into a cell. As they pushed him into the tiny cell they slammed the barred door shut behind him. It was at that moment that he believed that his doom had come. He sat on the only bed and looking at the floor fought back tears. But they were tears of anger and frustration, not remorse. And they didn't last long. He wondered how long they would keep him. Surely they didn't suspect him of anything other than Jimmy Harris' death and hopefully they couldn't even prove that. And, after all, he was just a kid. They had to go easy on a kid.

How could they have caught him? He had been so very careful to hide his tracks. He had kept out of sight and had made sure that he left nothing behind that would show that he had been in the area. And how was it that they were exactly at the cave entrance? Nobody knew about it except himself. How had they found him? As he pondered, across the hall a now sobered and repentant man in the drunk tank clamored to be released.

Fred sat in the cell, barely moving, for what seemed like an eternity before the sheriff came.

"Fredrick Swope. Is that your full name?" the sheriff asked.

"It's Fred, not Fredrick, and my middle name is Henry."

"Well, Fred Henry Swope, in a couple of hours you'll be seeing the judge. In the meantime do you want anything to eat? It's getting onto lunch. It ain't much, some fried ham and potatoes. But it'll do you good. We'll bring you a tray if you want."

Fred shook his head.

Centerville

"Suit yourself. Supper won't be 'till six." Sheriff Shambach turned and went to the drunk tank. "Let's get you out of here, Ralph, you look like you've sobered up." The cell door rang as the sheriff released the man and led him from the cell block. Fred heard the door close as the sheriff and Ralph exited and things were quiet once again.

"Hey, what's you in for?" The voice came from across the hall and another cell.

Fred looked up and then rose. He walked the three short steps to his cell door and looked out. He saw a man's arms resting on the cross bars of a cell opposite Fred's.

"I'm in for stealing a pig, not that I did it. But what's a kid like you doing here in jail?"

Fred shook his head. For a while he said nothing then finally said, "They think I killed some kid. But I didn't do it!"

"Really?" the man said. "Well they certainly can't do much to a kid. You're too young to know anything. They'll probably let you out in a day or two. You might as well enjoy the food while you're in here. It ain't half bad. No it ain't."

Fred shook his head. "Hope you're right. I'm only fourteen. I hope they just let me go home."

"I'm sure they will," the man said. "Ah, here comes lunch."

The door to the cell block opened and a deputy brought a lunch tray to the man. Then the deputy turned and asked Fred, "You sure you don't want anything?" Fred shook his head and went back to the bed and sat, staring at the wall.

What seemed like hours passed before a deputy, Jim Brocious, came and unlocked Fred's cell door. "Time to go see the judge. Let's go." He motioned to Fred who rose and came to the door. "I'm not going to cuff you if you promise not to give any trouble."

Centerville

Speechless, Fred shook his head as the deputy took his arm in a viselike grip and led him from the cell block. He guided Fred down halls, through doors and up the stairs to finally end up in the courtroom. Though different, it reminded him of the courtroom in which he had testified only a few weeks earlier. And Fred could see that it was the same judge. Brocious led Fred to stand at a railing a few feet from the judge.

"Mr. Fred Swope," the judge said. "Do you know why you are here?"

Fred looked at the floor and shook his head.

"Let the record show that Mr. Swope indicated that he does not know why he is here by a shake of his head. Young man, I think you *do* know why you are here. You are charged with suspicion of the murder of one James Leroy Harris, from Centerville."

Fred heard a gasp from somewhere behind him in the courtroom. He turned and saw his mother sitting in her wheelchair in the front row. He didn't know how he had not seen her when he had entered the room, even if he *was* looking at the floor.

"I'm not asking you for a plea at this time. That will come in a day or two. Right now I want to know if you have a lawyer. You're gonna need one."

"No sir, I don't," Fred shook his head.

"Your honor, he'll have one," the voice came from the gallery.

"Who are you?" asked the judge.

"I'm Sarah Swope, his mother, and I will hire a lawyer for my son."

"Very good. For now, Mr. Swope, I'm going to hold you in jail until you have a lawyer and have had a bond hearing. Then we'll decide what to do. Mr. Brocious, take him back to his cell. And make sure he eats something."

"May I speak with my son first?" Mrs. Swope asked.

Centerville

"Jim, let them visit for a few minutes before you take him back." The judge rose and left the courtroom.

Jim Brocious led Fred to the front row of pews and pushed him to sit facing his mother.

"Can we have some privacy here?" Fred's mother asked. "He won't go anywhere."

"I'll be right over there. You," he pointed to Fred, "behave yourself."

Fred swallowed and nodded to the deputy.

"You didn't do it, did you? *Did you?*"

"No, mom," Fred lied. "I didn't do nothin'"

"Good. Are they treating you ok? Do you need anything?"

Fred shook his head, "I'm ok mom."

"I'll get a lawyer before I go home and try to get him to see you today. Whatever you do, don't say anything to anybody except the lawyer. Say nothing, because if they hear you they'll remember it." Viscously she whispered, "Keep your damn mouth *shut!*" She waved the deputy over and said, "Take care of my boy."

"Yes mam," replied Jim Brocious, as he took Fred's arm and led him back to his cell.

On their way back to the cell block Fred asked, "Can I get a little to eat, now."

"Normally I'd say no but because the Judge said so I'll see what I can dig up, but it won't be very much." A few minutes after locking him back into his cell the deputy brought Fred a ham sandwich and some water.

"This'll carry you to supper." He said as he passed the tray under the cell door.

Suddenly ravenous Fred swallowed the sandwich in a few large bites and he drank all of the water. Then, with nothing to do, he sat on the bed and looked at the wall. He wished there were a window in his cell but the wall was hard blank stone.

Time passed slowly and as the day progressed, Fred began to think. What would he say and what would

283

he do. What would he tell the lawyer? Obviously he couldn't tell anything even close to the truth. If he did that they would surely hang him. And they'd ask him why and he wasn't sure himself exactly why he killed Jimmy. Maybe it was in self-defense. After all Jimmy would have ultimately told someone and eventually they would have come for him.

'But why,' he thought, 'was he hiding in the cave? I wasn't hiding, I was camping out, having a good time fishing and swimming and then the sheriff came along and ruined it all.' Yes, that's what he'd say.

'But what about Jimmy? What will you say about that? I don't know nothing about that. I wasn't there and didn't do anything.' He thought that sounded just about right.

The opening of the cell block door broke his thoughts and he heard footsteps in the hallway. They stopped at his cell. He turned as the cell door was unlocked and a stranger was let into his cell. After he entered the cell door was locked again and the deputy walked away. Fred watched the man, tall and thin, wearing a rumpled grey suit and tie. He had a fedora on his head.

"Fred? Fred Swope?" the man said.

Speechless, Fred nodded.

"Mind if I sit on the bed? Shame you don't have a chair." The man sat at the end of the bed facing Fred. "I'm your attorney, Bill Ranken, your mother hired me to represent you. Are they treating you ok?

Fred nodded and mumbled, "Yes."

"Do you understand why you are here?"

"Yes. They said that I killed Jimmy Harris. But honest to God, I didn't do it. I was just camping down at the creek when the sheriff up and arrested me. They even put hand cuffs on me. And I was really scared. I still am." He tried to sob but nothing came out.

Centerville

"Yes, I'm sure you are scared. Well I'll do everything I can to help you out. I'm sure you are wondering what will happen to you so let me fill you in. Tomorrow or the day after you will be called to be arraigned. This is a hearing where they will formally charge you for the crime you were arrested on. They may charge you with anything from involuntary manslaughter to murder. They will give enough evidence to convince the judge that you should be tried on the charge the District Attorney will suggest. Then you will be asked to enter a plea and we'll say 'not guilty' no matter what the charge. After that the judge will set bail. Bail is an amount of money you have to pay in order to be released from jail. It also ensures that you will appear for your trial. In a case like this he may not set bail. That means that you will stay in jail until your trial.

"I'll do everything that I can to get you released and even, if possible, to have the charges dropped. What happens then is all up to Judge Spicer. He is a good and fair man, so we'll try hard to have him go light on you. Now I know you just told me that you didn't do it but I have to ask you; did you kill, or did you have anything to do with the death of Jimmy Harris?"

Fred shook his head and vehemently said, "I didn't do nothin! I don't know what happened to him but I know it wasn't me."

"Ok, I hear you. There are already rumors starting, they always do, about Bart Tuttle and you having something to do with his death. I'll tell you, it doesn't look good. So listen to me carefully."

Fred did not respond. "*Look* at me!" the lawyer nearly shouted.

Fred who had been staring at the floor jumped at the ferocity of the lawyer's voice and looked at Bill Rankin as if seeing him for the first time.

"That's better. Now listen to me and listen good. You're in a deep pile of shit here boy. So you listen to everything I tell you and do everything I tell you to do, exactly. And the first thing is that you keep your mouth shut. Do not say anything to anyone unless I tell you otherwise. And if I do tell you to talk you will say exactly what I tell you to say, nothing more and nothing less. Do you understand?"

Fred nodded dumbly and finally croaked, "yes sir."

Having put the fear of god into Fred the lawyer smiled and stood up. "The hard part is done. I hate to use strong language like that but I need to get you to understand how serious this is. I'll do everything within my power to help you. For now I want you just to think. I have to start working on your case, talking to people, talking to the DA and the sheriff. I'll be back tomorrow afternoon at the latest and maybe sooner. Until then keep your mouth shut."

He walked to the cell door and rattled it against its lock as he looked back at Fred. "Do you want some books or comics to help pass the time?" Fred nodded to him. "Deputy! I'm finished here."

Centerville

Chapter 8
The Village Abuzz

The Reverend Hummel was preparing for the Harris funeral which would take place tomorrow, Thursday. He began looking for the slate shingle that he used on special occasions, in this case to hold the brass vase that would contain flowers for the coffin. The slate, with its felt pads, prevented the vase from scratching the wooden stand it rested upon. But he couldn't find the slate, anywhere.

"You idiot!" he muttered as he slapped his head. "You broke it, remember?" And indeed he did remember. He had dropped the slate shingle on the concrete walk a week or so ago and forgot to replace it. The piece of slate was a remainder of the slate shingles used to cover the church roof. Well there was a stack of the shingles in the attic. He would just climb up and get another. He would also need a piece of felt as well. But he had plenty of that in the Sunday School room.

He left his office and walked the length of the sanctuary, down the inside aisle. He pushed through the tall swinging doors and turned right into the cloak room. Attached firmly to the wall was a ladder that led to the attic and ultimately the belfry. The pastor began to climb. When he reached the ceiling he pushed aside the trapdoor and continued upward. He passed through the false ceiling and continued another ten feet. There he passed through a second trapdoor and into the church attic. The attic was really just a large room directly beneath the roof and over the sanctuary. A cobwebbed window filtered sunlight into the room from the far end. The attic had no other purpose than to be used for storage. To one side were stacks of moldering hymnals from a long past era. A pair of wooden candlesticks lay dry and crumbling on the floor. To his left was the stack of slate shingles. As he turned in the dusty light, the smell of dryness and summer heat invaded his nostrils. And there, before him, about ten feet away was a nest. Or at least that's what it looked like.

He slowly approached, his eyes widening in shock. There before him he saw a collection of rotting pew cushions, arranged in a semi-circle; the open end faced a makeshift altar. On the altar, made of stacks of hymnals supporting a plank, were two candle stubs. Between them was an upside down cross and in front of that was what looked like the skeleton of a small animal. Rising between its ribs was a knife, stabbed deeply into the plank. To the right was the dried skin of a snake and to the left what looked like the skull of a rat – or a squirrel. In front of all of this, leaning up against the altar, was a tattered and torn bible; its pages stained a dark red.

Stumbling backwards, the minister clattered down the ladder into the safety of the sanctuary; chilled to the bone in the warm air of the sunbathed church. He knew beyond a shadow of a doubt he had discovered Fred Swope's place of worship. But what kind of worship was it? He staggered to the parsonage forgetting the slate and the upcoming funeral.

A block downhill a small crowd had gathered at Musser's store. The usual congregating spot was the post office but in view of what had happened the store was a more neutral place and there was more room outside under the roof sheltering the sidewalk. Vultures circled overhead on this day as their equivalents discussed the events of the day far below.

"I'll tell ye, I ain't surprised that Fred Swope did it. I never did think much of him creeping around and snooping in people's sheds and stuff. Why one time I caught him in my barn and it looked like he was after my chickens." One man said as he spat at the gutter and missed.

Centerville

"And he was always sneaking around with that twenty-two of his. Wouldn't put it past him to shoot at dogs and cats. Lord knows he was never friendly to any dog that I knowed." Said another.

"Yeah. Well I heered that he was piling up rocks down by the bridge for no good purpose. And then they found Bart... Ya think he killed old Bart with those rocks? Somebody sure did," said Jake Swengle as he plugged his thumbs into his bibs.

There was general agreement that Fred was not one to be trusted and there were even a few nods when the conversation turned to Bart and his smashed head.

"And I heard that Jimmy Harris and Ben Snyder, Jr. had something on him. Don't know what but I heard that they were talking to the sheriff. Well they got him now, locked up good and tight. Hope they throw away the key." Sherm McMaster took one last pull at his Lucky ,threw the butt onto the sidewalk and ground it out with his booted toe.

"Don't you think they ought to find him guilty first?" asked Stan Yeager.

Cattycorner to the Reformed church Melba Keister and Nancy Loss rocked on the Keister's side porch. Enjoying the shade as Melba snapped beans while they talked.

"Have you seen Carol Harris? How is she holding up?" asked Nancy.

"No, I didn't get the chance to talk with her. I'm fixing up some ham and string beans to take over for their supper tonight. Poor thing doesn't need to worry about cooking. The Lady's Aid is taking turns cooking for them and it's my turn tonight. Just picked these beans fresh this morning. I do hear that she's pretty well out of it, according to Arla Snook."

"Do you know if anyone has looked in on Sara Swope? Seems that she could probably use some help and support herself; what with her son in jail and all."

"I do suppose she could," said Melba. "It's got to be a burden on her soul as if Fred hasn't already caused her enough heartache."

"What do you mean?"

Melba rocked forward and lowered her voice, "Well all of this, of course. And I shouldn't say but Jenny Miller told me before she left Harvey – Jenny, she was the one that found Sarah lying at the bottom of the steps, you know; all those years ago when Fred was a little boy." Nancy nodded. "Well Jenny went down to help Sarah after she called the ambulance. And she said that Sarah was lying on a toy truck and it looked like it had been stepped on. Sarah said she always wondered whether Fred left it on the cellar steps and that's what made her fall. Now I don't know if it was on purpose or not but you hear things, you know."

Nancy gasped and covered her mouth. "You know," she whispered, "I always thought he was some kind of evil, or at least bad. Sometimes I think I wouldn't be at all surprised if he did do that to poor Jimmy."

Melba continued to snap her beans, rocking and nodding all along.

On the Upper Street Sam Greenleaf was splitting firewood. The back of his lot bordered on the Holiness Grove. From where he stood he could still see the remains of the tabernacle. Most of it had been cleaned up but there still was some remaining framework of the building scattered on the ground and, of course, the stone altar and font.

He had worried about the tabernacle fire spreading to his property and burning his outbuildings. He had an equipment shed and a small barn where he raised a couple of pigs and some chickens. Sam used to have a dog but it disappeared around the time the tabernacle burned. He still watched for it but he figured the fire must have scared it away. But today he too was thinking about the murder of Jimmy Harris, not that he

Centerville

was friends with the family. Oh he knew Ned all right, everybody did. After all Ned *was* the postmaster. It was just that too many things had happened in Centerville this summer. Why they hadn't had four murders in a century! And the tabernacle fire? Some strange things were happening. He just hoped that they had seen the end of it.

'God I hope.' He thought as he split another piece of maple.

And on the Lower Street, confined to her wheelchair, Sarah Swope sat thinking; thinking about her son Fred. 'The grief I've had over that boy and now this. It's enough to drive me to my grave. I'll do everything I can for him but after this he's on his own.' She frowned and shook her head. She had known for some time that her son was a wild one and had suspected that he might have had something to do with some of the goings on in the village this summer. But this was too much. She believed that her heart ached for the Harris family but mostly it ached for herself. Wallowing in her own self-pity, her pain fed her already hardening heart towards her only child. He could take care of himself after this; after all he had been doing so all his life. But now who would take care of her? The village would surely turn against her, punishing her for the sins of her son.

She wheeled from the window and sighed.

Ben shuffled through his back yard. Doing nothing but feeling the heavy weight of having lost his best friend in an act of murder. Murder! The word overwhelmed him as though it were a weight chained to him, dragging him slowly – to nowhere. The day was hot, quiet and still, as though waiting for a thunder storm to come roaring through. Not even a bird sang in the stillness of the afternoon. The sky was more of a dusty gold color than the normal blue. Sweat dripped from Ben's forehead as he continued to shuffle back and forth in his yard.

Centerville

'I should have been with him,' he thought. 'I know I had to go to the dentist – but still...' his thought trailed off into nothingness as the numbness once again overwhelmed him. Finally he crumbled to the ground and face in the grass he cried for his friend.

The Reverend Hummel called the sheriff to tell him about the makeshift altar that he had found in the church attic. As he hung up the telephone sheriff Shambach sighed. One more thing in this summer of pain, sadness and horror.

Centerville

Chapter 9
A Funeral for a Friend

Thursday came all too quickly for Ben. He didn't know if it was a blessing or a curse. He wanted this day to be gone; over and done with. It wasn't going to be an easy day, not for Ben or anyone else in the village. His anxiety for the day had begun the moment he woke and, he was sure, it would stay for at least the rest of the day if not longer. As Jimmy's best friend he had been asked to be an honorary pall bearer. Thank god he wouldn't have to actually help carry the coffin. He didn't know if he could do *that*. He had been told he was to just walk directly behind the coffin as it was carried from the church to the hearse and again as it was carried to and placed over the grave in the cemetery. He supposed he could manage that but he knew he would be nervous.

This wasn't going to be like Patsy Marks' funeral. Yes, he and Patsy were friends but they weren't *best* friends like he was with Jimmy. That made a big difference. Though he wouldn't think of it *that* way he did love Jimmy almost as much as he hated Fred, and after Jimmy's death, Ben hated Fred with a passion that had no end. He would rather see Fred in the coffin and Jimmy standing next to him, looking at dead Fred. As he thought of it he cracked a faint smile at the rhyme that he made but it wasn't that funny. But yes, he would much prefer a dead Fred right now. Very much.

As the lunch hour passed he took his required bath and put on his Sunday suit; the neck tie far too tight and the jacket far too hot. He sweated the rest of the brief afternoon until two o'clock rolled around. About fifteen minutes before the appointed hour Ben and his parents climbed into the family car and drove the short two blocks to the Reformed church.

They walked in.

Centerville

"If it's too hard for you to do then you don't have to go up and look in the coffin. But it will be good if you did. Be good if you said goodbye to Jimmy." His father said as they entered the sanctuary. As much as he did not want to look, Ben felt a need to see his lifelong friend one more time and to say his goodbyes to him in person. He understood fully well that his words of parting would not mean a thing to Jimmy but he also knew it was something he needed to do, if only for himself.

The organ was playing softly as Ben and his parents walked slowly up the suddenly long center aisle to the casket resting on a dais surrounded by dark maroon velvet. As Ben looked up he could see sprays of flowers everywhere. He could also see that the head end, or what he assumed was the head end, of the casket was open while the lower portion was closed and covered with flowers. He saw that the candles on the altar were lit and that the large room was brightly lit by the sun through the windows on what should have been a dark and gloomy day.

He approached the casket and, steeling himself, looked in. Ben was surprised to see that Jimmy looked just like he was sleeping. Totally at rest, his eyes closed, Ben looked; expecting to see the chest move at any moment as Jimmy breathed. But of course, there in the coffin he did not breathe.

Ben reached into his pocket and pulled out a battered and much thumbed baseball card featuring Yogi Berra, Jimmy's favorite Yankee. He looked at it and then looked at his father. Questioningly he asked, "Can I?"

"Of course you can. Put it in his hands if you want."

But Ben took the card and tucked into the pocket of the suit jacket that Jimmy was wearing; just a little bit of the card peeking out. There it would be close to his heart.

Centerville

Suddenly his heart seemed to swell to more than fill his chest. His throat constricted, his head became stuffed and he could hardly breathe. He struggled to finally chokingly whisper, "Goodbye Jimmy. You were the best friend anybody could ever have. You're with God now so behave and don't drop your shoulder when you are at bat." Then his eyes filled with tears and he began to sob. His father guided him by the arm to their seats in the second pew, right behind Jimmy's parents.

The organ finally stopped.

The pastor, Reverend Hummel, slowly walked into the sanctuary from a side entrance. He paused in front of Jimmy Harris' casket and then turned to face the congregation.

"In the name of the Father and of the Son and of the Holy Spirit. Amen" he intoned and made the sign of the cross. "We are gathered here today to celebrate the life of James Leroy Harris. Cut short in the prime of life and rendered up to God the Lord and Father of mankind. May his soul rest in peace." His sing song voice tapered downward as though he were chanting.

Jimmy's mother, Carol, began to sob as Ned, his father put his arm around his wife's shoulders. The sound of weeping could be heard from other parts of the church as well.

A hymn was sung and then, once more, the pastor spoke. "Again, and let's beg God in Heaven, for the last time, we bury our young who have been cut down in the prime of life." Carol Harris' sobs became stronger and she shook as though she were cold. "Here before us lies Jimmy Harris. His name was James but we all, even I, knew him as Jimmy; a boy who had a smile that could light a room even on the brightest day, a boy who never knew an enemy."

Ben thought differently about that statement.

"Jimmy was a gentle boy, full of love and kindness. He was a friend to all and an enemy of none.

295

He was an acolyte in this church and served admirably. And he, this treasure of his family and of the community, was cut down even before the prime of his life. Cut down in a senseless act of cruelty for no reason that we can comprehend."

The pastor's droning voice soon lulled Ben into a sleepy daze. His eyes closed and in the heat of the day he began to drift. As he drifted the scene before him changed to the field next to the lime kiln. To his dreaming eye he could see Jimmy sitting in the place where Ben had found his lifeless body. And as his dream became clearer he saw Fred Swope come up to where Jimmy was sitting. Ben could see them talking, as though he were a third party present at the event. He saw Jimmy shout something at Fred and then turn away. Ben could see Fred pick up a large rock and approach Jimmy.

"No...no...no," he thought in his dream. "Get up. Run!" the last word he shouted, not only in his dream but in the midst in the service as well. "Run, Jimmy! Run!"

The room became silent as the pastor stopped mid-sentence and the large congregation gave a communal gasp, as though waiting for more. Ben, as though pulled by marionette strings, jerked straight in the pew and opened his eyes. His father bent over to look at him.

"Are you OK?" his father whispered.

"Yes. I I'm sorry." Ben whispered back. "I must have been dreaming."

"Well try to keep quiet for the rest of the service."

Ben nodded as pastor Hummel continued his eulogy.

Ben thought it would never end but finally the last amen was said and the congregation was led from the church. Ben and his family remained, along with the Harris family and the four uncles who would carry the coffin. One of the undertaker's helpers directed Ben to the front of the church and whispered to him to follow the

Centerville

casket to the hearse. The four bearers lifted Jimmy's last resting place and solemnly carried it down the center aisle and out of the church to the waiting black hearse. Ben dutifully followed until the casket was pushed on the rollers into the hearse.

They closed the doors.

Ben was directed to his car which was the third in the funeral procession. Headlights on the ever growing column of automobiles made its way down Center Street to the Reformed cemetery only half a mile away. There the funeral procession wound through the dusty streets of the cemetery to the place where Jimmy would be buried.

Once again Ben was directed to the hearse and he stood there while the casket was pulled from the black vehicle. Again Ben followed it, this time to the grave site. There he saw a platform over the open pit of the grave and he was struck to the core of his being with a cold that would not leave him for days. This, not the coffin, was Jimmy's final resting place. He would be lowered down into the dark and would be covered with dirt. Forever. His chest heaved as Ben tried to control himself.

The pall bearers lowered the casket onto the platform and stepped away. Ben was the last to turn away. He went and stood beside his father facing the casket as the pastor moved to the grave side.

The graveside service was brief. The pastor said a few words and prayed. He ended his prayer with the words, "Ashes to ashes and dust to dust." He scattered some earth onto the coffin and then turned away. Jimmy's mother placed a rose on the top of the closed casket and was led away. Ben, his family and all the rest turned from the grave as the coffin was lowered into the earth. As Ben looked back he saw Jimmy's father, dressed in black, standing, all alone, hat in hand, looking at the lowered casket. He was shaking his head as though he were in total disbelief.

Centerville

Ben and his family, along with many others, returned to the fellowship hall at the church to share in a memorial lunch. The thought of eating turned Ben's stomach. All he wanted to do was to go to his room and cry.

Centerville

Chapter 10
The Investigation Begins

Howard Moyer left the cemetery with all the rest. He too looked back to see Ned Harris, by himself, standing over his son's grave. He sighed as he climbed into his car. Some days he hated his job and this day was one of them.

Moyer was the chief, and only, detective of the Stone County District Attorney. He was built like a linebacker and wore ill-fitting suits. He almost always had a pipe clenched between his teeth. He was now directly involved with the prosecution of Fred Swope. It was Moyer's job to investigate the murder of Jimmy Harris and the activities of defendant Swope. To gather evidence that DA Clark would need at trial. He already knew that the sheriff had heard from Ben Snyder and that was a good place to start. But the sheriff's job ended with the arrest. Moyer had suspicions that there was much more to know and that the sheriff would have a lot to tell him. With everything else on his plate he had put this interview off far too long but now it was time to get moving.

That Friday morning Moyer was fortunate that the sheriff was in his office and available to talk, so he walked downstairs to begin the process.

"Welcome Hard, have a seat." The sheriff said. When he was a teenager Howard had earned a reputation for being a hard fighter and the local Pennsylvania Dutch dialect added to the reputation by pronouncing the *"ow"* of his name as a short *"a"* and so he became Hard for the rest of his life.

"I suppose you want to talk about the Harris murder. Well, sit down and let's talk."

Centerville

Detective Moyer sat across from the sheriff, pulled his pipe from his mouth and said, "Tell me what you've got."

"I've got a lot more than you need to know and more that may surprise you. But at the same time I may not have enough of what you are really looking for. To start I don't have any concrete evidence to pin this on Fred Swope. It's all circumstantial. It's strong but I don't have a smoking gun if that's what you're looking for. I don't even have a smoking rock and that's what we think he used."

"Just give me what you've got John and I'll make heads and tails of it. Give me names of people I can interview."

For the next hour the two men talked. Sheriff Shambach gave Moyer everything he had heard from Ben.

"So you're telling me," said the detective, "that Fred Swope may be responsible for the fire, the attempted rape, the murders of Patsy Marks and Betsy Smith and the death of Bart Tuttle. John I have to tell you that is a big and dirty list."

"Don't I know it! But I believe Ben Snyder and Ned Harris told me as much as well. Jimmy was going to put it all together for me but Swope got there first. I'm not sure that Jimmy Harris had much direct evidence either but it is all very compelling.

"I'll be honest with you Hard, I don't envy you in this case. But I surely hope you come up with some solid evidence because personally I believe Fred Swope is guilty as hell and should be put away for a very long time."

Moyer nodded, "I tend to agree but I have to find the proof first. Did anybody go into the cave Swope was using? Maybe he had some souvenirs there. And a search warrant will be the first thing that I request. I definitely want to see his belongings."

Centerville

He rose and shook hands with the sheriff. "Thanks, John, you have been helpful. If you think of anything else you know where to find me." Moyer left the office and climbed the stairs to his own office and the office of the DA. There he began the process of requesting a search warrant.

The probable cause portion of the warrant was not too difficult to write. He had to include enough to get the warrant without being too specific about multiple crimes. The same was true of the description of the items he wanted to search for. He didn't know what, specifically, he was looking for and that created a problem. He would search for notebooks and diaries and personal items that might have belonged to the victim. That should give him enough leeway for now.

He placed his pipe in an ashtray while he laboriously one-finger typed the information into the printed form, listing in as much detail as he could the things he wanted to look for in Fred's home. Any other place, such as the cave, or the spot in the McMaster's barn would not have to be listed. As he was working a secretary entered to tell him to talk with DA Clark regarding the current matter. He finished the warrant and took it through the office to DA Clark's office.

"Boss, Here is a preliminary search warrant on Fred Swope's house." He placed the form on the desk.

"I'll get the judge to sign it at his next recess, which shouldn't be long now. I just got a call from the sheriff who passed this on to me; you need to see the pastor of the Reformed church in Centerville. According to Shambach he has something you ought to see."

Moyer nodded, "I'll be back for the warrant in about an hour and then I'll head over to Centerville. I'll be there most of the afternoon as I have a number of places to visit. I'm going back down to the sheriff. I have a couple of new questions for him."

Centerville

Wishing the building had an elevator, once again he negotiated the stairs to the sheriff's office. There he spoke to him. "John, I asked but you never said; did anyone search the cave where Swope was hiding?"

"Yes, I sent one of the smaller deputies in to take a look. He found nothing but a frying pan and cooking utensils, a kerosene lamp and the like, sleeping bag; just normal camping stuff. There's a list around her somewhere, I'll find it and have it sent up to your office."

"Did he bring any of this stuff out?"

"No but if you need anything on the list let me know and I'll send him back to get it."

"I may want it all, just in case. Have him go and get it all but tell him to photograph the scene before he moves anything. In this case anything even that slim may be a good piece of evidence. Clark told me to see the preacher at the Reformed church in Centerville. Want to tell me why?"

"No, Hard, from what I saw I think you ought to see it for yourself."

"Ok then, well now I'm off to see the coroner" Moyer replied as he turned and left the sheriff's office followed by a trail of smoke from his pipe. The coroner's office was a few blocks away but it didn't take Howard Moyer long to walk the distance. There he found Ray Hackett in his office.

"What can I do for you Hard?" Hackett asked.

"I need to know a couple of things. First what is the official cause of Jimmy Harris death?"

"Blunt force trauma, probably from a rock."

"Right, just what I expected. How big a rock?"

"Oh like this," Hackett held up his hands. "Probably ten to fifteen pounds. It was multiple blows but it was also a single blow that killed him so it had to have some mass behind it."

"Got it. I also need everything you put in your report on the death of Patrick Marks. For instance do you have any photographs of him with his pants on backwards? I know I'm officially investigating the death of the Harris boy but it seems that a lot of things are intertwined here."

"Yes, I did take photographs and they're in the report. I can have it sent over to your office. You know I ruled the death an accidental drowning. There was definitely water in his lungs. I assumed that he fell into the well, hit his head on the way down and was knocked unconscious. He drowned as he lay in the water"

"That is the most likely scenario," replied Detective Moyer "but these backwards pants are causing a problem for me. That and the fact that the well cover was in place. Bruce Walter the property owner said that he never uncovered the well or put the cover back in place." He paused, "Now that's a problem and I don't like problems." He shook his head. "Well, have that report sent over to my office so I can take a look. Thanks."

Hackett nodded as the detective left. Returning to his office Moyer found the signed search warrant on his desk. He called Isaac Martin, one of the DA's office flunkeys to join him in his afternoon's search warrant execution.

"Ike, get the car ready. We're going to Centerville."

Chapter 11
Searching for Evidence

Ike Martin served more as a witness than anything else. He drove the car but Howard Moyer could have done that.

"We've got a couple of places to go this afternoon. First I want to go to the Reformed church to see what the preacher found. Then I want to see what is in the McMaster barn and then we'll focus on Fred Swope's house." He didn't have to tell Ike anything but he felt that it never hurt.

They pulled into the church parking lot. As the detective got out of the car he banged the bowl of his pipe against his shoe heel and then deposited the pipe in his pocket. As they climbed the steps of the church he said, "I have no idea of what we're going to be looking at. I hope it's worth it."

They entered the sanctuary from the rear. The room was spacious and brightly lit by sunlight streaming through the stained glass windows. As they looked around Moyer noticed that a dove in the one window had a spall of glass broken out. 'Looks like some kid shot a BB into that window.' He mused, 'If he was aiming at the bird – good shot.'

Not knowing where to go they wandered down the center aisle and turned to the Sunday School room door. Just as they entered Pastor Hummel came into the room from the opposite side. "May I help you gentlemen?" the minister asked.

Displaying his badge Moyer said, "I'm detective Howard Moyer from the District Attorney's office. I was told that you had something that you want to show me."

"I'm Reverend Hummel, the pastor of this church. Yes, I do have something to show you. Come with me. I hope you don't mind ladders because we're going upstairs." He pointed upwards as he spoke. "I really don't know what it means, if anything, but I thought the authorities should see it. Actually the Sheriff was over and I thought that would be enough." As they entered the cloak room the pastor said, "I have to warn you gentlemen. It will be hot up there. You might want to leave your jackets down here."

Ike did remove his jacket but Howard Moyer did not. He was armed and did not want to expose the .38 in his shoulder holster. The minister started up the ladder attached to the wall followed by Moyer and Ike Martin. They pushed through the trapdoors and climbed even higher until they reached the level of the attic floor. There the minister led them to what he thought of as the nest.

He pointed, "This is what I found the other day when I was looking for a piece of slate."

Detective Moyer examined the nest from all angles. He directed Ike Martin to photograph the area from numerous angles as well. "Does all of this stuff come from the church itself?" He asked.

"Yes, I believe it does, except for bones and knife, of course. I don't know where they came from or what the bones are."

"Ike, get close ups of the altar and then bag the knife and all the bones. Get the Bible too." He turned to Pastor Hummel, "Do you mind if I look around up here."

"Help yourself Mr. Moyer. As you can see the place is pretty empty so I don't think you will find much of anything. Do watch your step over there," he pointed. "I don't want you taking a fast trip down stairs."

Moyer looked and could see that there was one spot in the floor that was open to the ceiling of the sanctuary below. He carefully reconnoitered the large dusty dry room. He circled back to the ladder and looked up.

"What's up there?" he asked.

"That leads up to the belfry."

Moyer began to climb the makeshift ladder that wound its way around the sides of the steeple into the darkness above. He pulled the flashlight he always carried from his jacket pocket and shined the light around the belfry. He climbed higher until finally encountering a long iron hook attached through a ring in a trapdoor directly above his head. He pushed up on the trapdoor and saw sunlight break through. Pushing the trapdoor aside he was able to stick his head out into the steeple with the bell hanging directly overhead. He surveyed the village from this vantage point and was secretly delighted at what he saw.

Then he looked down and saw the letters FHS carved into the floor of the cupola. 'Our friend Fred was definitely here.' He thought. He called down into the depths below, "Ike bring me the camera, I need to take a photo of something." Ike gingerly climbed the ladder, grimly grasping each rung and wrapping his arms around each and every one. He obviously did not like this particular climb. He finally handed the camera to the detective who took it and photographed the initials. He also took a few photos of the panorama around him before passing the camera back to Ike who just as gingerly climbed back down to the safety of the attic floor. Howard Moyer followed.

Once back in the attic he asked the pastor, "Do you see any significance in the positioning of the altar or the objects on and around it?"

"No, I really don't. I'm pretty sure that Fred Swope used it for some kind of worship but I surely don't know what. Maybe he was just playing but somehow I don't think so."

"Well I think we're done here. Let's go back down and get out of this heat." With that the three men climbed back down the ladders to the cloak room below. Once again on the ground floor they thanked the pastor for showing them Fred's nest.

"Is there anything else we need to know?" The detective asked.

The minister paused, shook his head and then said, "I don't know but a few weeks back I came into the sanctuary and was horrified to discover my cat lying dead in the offering plate on the altar. Its neck was broken. I don't know if it is related or not. Until now I haven't told anyone about it. I'd prefer to keep it that way."

Moyer nodded, "I'll keep it confidential to my office. Thanks again for your time." They turned to leave. Their next stop was Sherm McMaster's barn.

After the four block drive they found Sherm working in his front yard. Identifying themselves they asked to see the area in the barn that the sheriff had marked off. Sherm led the way to the haymow of the barn. There Moyer was surprised to find another nest. Bales of straw had been placed in a rough semicircle facing an open window in the wall of the barn. A straw bale rested on the floor beneath the window.

The detective discovered what the sheriff missed. In the center of the nest buried in a pile of straw was a small cardboard box and in it a collection of bones and another animal skull. They photographed and bagged them both and continued their search. Nothing more worth noting was found in the barn, so they left, thanking Sherm McMaster as they returned to their car.

As they climbed into the car and Howard Moyer lit his pipe, Ike said, "Sure looks weird to me, Hard, those things actually look like big bird's nests, almost."

"Yes, they do. I wonder what, if anything, it means. Let's go to Fred Swope's house. It's up that way," he pointed. "Two blocks. White house with blue trim." They found it in no time.

The wait after knocking on the front door was so long that they almost turned away. Finally the door opened to reveal Sarah Swope and her wheelchair. "May I help you?" she asked.

Moyer identified himself and Ike Martin. "I have a search warrant for your home, specifically your son's bedroom." He handed a copy of the warrant to the chair bound woman.

She read the document and said, "And what if I don't let you into my house?"

"I'll be back with the sheriff, mam. This is a legal warrant and I'm sorry but you don't have much choice."

She sternly said, "I don't want you tearing up my house looking for stuff. I can't get around that well, as you can see and cleaning up any mess you make will cost me money I can ill afford."

"I assure you that Isaac and I will not disrupt your household. We'll respect your property and will return anything we move to its proper place. We aren't cops like you might see on the television."

Reluctantly she rolled her chair away from the door and allowed the men to enter. "Don't you dare break anything either," she admonished.

"We'll be careful Mrs. Swope. We want to start with your son's room or rooms. Where can we find them?"

"They'll be upstairs. I don't get up there, as you can see. I haven't been upstairs in weeks."

Moyer led the way to the second floor. There they found a room across from the stairs looking out onto the Lower Street. By the clutter they could tell that this was a boy's bedroom."

"Let's start there." Moyer pointed.

They entered the room and almost immediately noticed the semi-circle of pillows and cushions facing one of the windows. Beneath the window was a plank shelf supported by bricks. On the shelf was, not surprisingly, a small skull.

"He definitely has a thing about skulls and nests. Take a photo and the skull." Ike nodded in agreement as

Centerville

he did as requested. Moyer turned to the desk facing the wall. Its surface was cluttered with coins, a pocket knife and other things that a fourteen year old boy would normally carry. As he searched through the detritus he came upon an odd item to find on a boy's desk.

It was a bracelet. While examining it Moyer read the name engraved on the bracelet. "Betsy." He shook his head. He knew it was important but couldn't remember why. He directed Ike to photograph the desktop while he thought. Then, in a flash, it came to him. Betsy Smith! The young girl murdered the previous month at the firemen's carnival here in Centerville.

"Ike, get a good close up of this bracelet." After the photo was taken Moyer carefully tagged the bracelet himself. This was evidence of a crime other than the one he was investigating. He would need to file a piggy back warrant to cover the bracelet. What else might he find here?

He took a small yearbook like photo stuck into the frame of the mirror above the desk. It was of a pretty teenage girl. He flipped it over and on the back in script was the written the name "Judy." His eyes widened. "Very interesting, Ike. I may need another piggy back." He tagged the photo and moved on.

The search revealed no diaries or notebooks. One drawer in the bureau revealed a number of pairs of panties and a couple of bras. Somehow the detective didn't think that Fred wore them but probably did other things with them. Were they souvenirs of other crimes or where they the results of raids on women's wash lines? Moyer assumed the latter.

Under the mattress he found, in fact he almost expected to find, girlie magazines. What teenage boy didn't have a couple hidden somewhere? Ultimately the search of Fred's room revealed nothing pertaining to Jimmy Harris. Maybe they would have better luck elsewhere in the house.

Centerville

The remaining rooms upstairs revealed little. The bathroom was surprisingly clean compared to Fred's bedroom. But then again a maid could be taking care of that. The two other rooms were empty save for beds and bureaus, neither of which had anything in the drawers. In the bedroom nearest the stairs they did find a wheelchair. Thinking little of it they moved on to the attic. Again they found a tidy space and nothing worth noting.

"We won't have better luck downstairs, I guess." Said Moyer, "but maybe the garage will have something." Ike nodded in agreement as they returned to the first floor.

"Did you find anything?" Fred's mother asked as they entered the kitchen.

"No, nothing relating to Jimmy Harris but even if we did I couldn't tell you about it. We want to take a quick look down here and then we want to look at your garage."

"Suit yourself but you won't find anything here."

He turned away and then back, "by the way. Does your son have a girlfriend or maybe a relative named Betsy?" He didn't know exactly why he asked it, maybe to put a scare into the woman.

"Not that I know of, why do you ask?"

"No particular reason, just something that came to mind."

Sarah Swope frowned and nodded. 'He didn't ask that question for nothing,' she thought.

Moyer suspected that she was right about the rest of the house and the garage. They carefully inspected the three rooms on the lower floor as well as the musty basement. They found nothing to incriminate Fred. Everything appeared to be neatly in its place but what would you expect with a cripple in the house. They obtained the key to the garage and left the house.

The garage was another matter. There was no car. Things were piled in an almost haphazard manner but somehow related. On one wall hung a surprisingly large number of animal traps; those used for trapping muskrats and the like. On examining them Moyer could see that the name tags on many did not say Fred Swope. The traps were clean and well cared for.

On the work bench he found a number of hand tools, a couple of hammers, screw drivers, pliers and the like. On the dirt floor was a foot locker. Inside they found a well-cared for .22 rifle and a few boxes of ammunition. They also found a 20 gauge single shot shotgun and shells as well as a gun cleaning kit. There was also a cylinder for a revolver but no hand gun.

Not surprising at all there was a row of four small animal skulls adorning the wide window sill. And traced in the dust, between two of the skulls Moyer could clearly read, "Jimmy knows"

"Ike," he almost shouted, "Get a number of photos of this," he pointed. "Get a few different angles to be sure that the letters in the dust are clearly visible. We may have our smoking gun. I wish there was a way to preserve this."

Ike came close to the window sill and examined it carefully. Then he proceeded to take photographs of it from all angles. "I think I got it good." He finally said.

They locked the garage, returned the key and drove back to Middlebury. They were satisfied that they had at least one piece of evidence pertaining to Jimmy Harris.

"I don't get it," said Ike.

"What's that?"

"What it is with all these nests. Everywhere we go or everywhere Swope goes we find a nest. Is he a fuckin bird or what?"

"I'd like to figure that out too, Ike. Maybe we can find a psychologist who can tell us. I'm sure the DA will have one interview Swope. I'll make sure that DA Clark knows to include that in any questions the shrink might ask.

After the detectives left Sara Swope laboriously climbed the stairs. One step at a time she used her strong arms to lift herself up until she got to the second floor. She did this occasionally so she could get a real bath, as there was no bathtub down stairs. She worked her way into the closest bedroom and managed to hoist herself into the wheelchair she kept there. She hadn't been in Fred's room in months but, she thought, it was time that she took a look.

She found the usual boy's room clutter and the room looked much the same as the last time she had seen it. But this time she noted the nest by the window. This was new and she wondered what it meant. 'He's been up to no good for a long time. This time he may have hung himself. And who was this Betsy?' She sighed, then a chill ran down her spine. 'It couldn't be! What was that little girl's name? *Was* it Betsy? Oh God, now what? I'll do what I can but if he did it, he'll have to pay.' She frowned as she contemplated the long climb back down the stairs. Maybe she would take a bath, now that she was up here.

Centerville

Chapter 12
The Investigation Continues

Later that afternoon Howard Moyer reported to the DA all that he had seen and done in the search. "Thing is, I didn't find anything directly in reference to the Harris murder but I did find two interesting and troubling pieces of evidence.

"For example," he produced the bracelet that he assumed belonged to Betsy Smith. "This was in plain sight on his desk. I have to follow up but I'll bet my badge that this bracelet belonged to the little girl who was murdered in Centerville at the Fireman's Carnival." He passed it to the DA.

"And then there's this," he produced the photo of 'Judy'. "I need to follow up with this one too but I'll also bet it is a picture of Judy Mecklenburg, I just checked and it is the girl who was attacked at the same carnival. Interesting coincidence; finding both these pieces in Fred Swope's bedroom."

"Do some digging on those two. If anything comes of them we'll issue a piggy back warrant to cover them. See the little girl's mother about the bracelet."

He nodded. "Oh yes, and I did ask Mrs. Swope whether Fred has a girlfriend or relative named Betsy. She said no."

"Really? Why did you ask that?"

"I'm not sure. I think I wanted to see if I could get a reaction."

"Did you?"

"She didn't bat an eye. Anyway the only other thing we found was in the garage. In the dust on the window sill was written '*Jimmy knows*'. Ike got photos of it but I wish there was a way to preserve it. This may be the closest we can come to a smoking gun."

"It may be an important piece of evidence. We can have the State Police lab take a look. Maybe they can do something." Ralph Clark replied. "Do you have anything else?"

"Nothing concrete, really. We did note a few odd things." He air quoted the word 'odd'.

"Like what?"

"Well first, in the Reformed church, we found what can only be described as a nest that we assume Fred Swope made there in the attic. Pillows and the like formed into a semi-circle around a homemade altar. On the altar were some bones, a skull and a knife. We took photos and collected them as evidence. The preacher also told us that his cat had been killed a few weeks back, neck broken, and was put in the offering plate on the church altar. Nobody knows that except us. And I'm pretty sure it was done by Swope, I found his initials freshly carved in the belfry.

"Then in the McMaster's barn we found another nest made of straw bales. I also found a skull there, among other things. And finally in Swope's bedroom there was a nest of pillows and blankets in front of the window that looks out onto the street, across from a burned out house. And again we found a skull. Oh yes, and there were four skulls lining the window sill in the garage. I don't know about all these skulls. We bagged them so somebody can identify them. There were a bunch of small animal traps in the garage, so they might be muskrat skulls or something like that. Could be cats, too."

The DA nodded. "It looks like Mr. Swope has a thing about dead animals and maybe death in general. I'm having a psychologist, Dr. Kenner, interview him on Monday, I'll mention the skulls and nests to him so he can use that information as part of the interview. See what he gets."

Centerville

"I have photos if that will help. Other than that, that's about it," Moyer said. "I'm going to take the skulls to a vet to see if they can be identified and I'll get in touch with the Smith woman, see what she tells me." He turned and putting his pipe between his teeth left the room.

After her bath Sarah Swope wasted no time in getting to the telephone to call the attorney she had hired, Bill Rankin. "The police were over here today, just a little while ago, with a search warrant. They went over the house and garage pretty well. I don't know what they found, if anything, but I thought you ought to know."

"Anything that they found as evidence will have to be released to us through discovery. I'll be sure to contact the District Attorney about this. I'm going to see your son later today. Did they say anything worth mentioning? Is there anything you want to send to Fred or any message you might have?"

"I don't have anything here that Fred needs." Then she cryptically said, "But you can ask him about his girlfriend Betsy. And you can tell him that I'm praying for his soul and that he should appreciate what I'm doing for him."

The lawyer shook his head at her comment and said, "Yes mam, I'll be sure to tell him."

Next he called the office of the District Attorney and requested information on the search warrant. DA Clark, himself, took the call. "Mr. Rankin, what can I do for you?"

"I just talked with my client, Fred Swope's, mother. She said that the police were there with a search warrant."

"Yes, my detective was there serving a warrant."

"Did he find anything?"

"Mr. Rankin, you know that I won't answer that question this soon after the search. I really don't know what he found and I won't until I receive his official report. As you know, Mr. Swope hasn't been officially

315

charged with a crime. He was arrested and is being held on suspicion. But as I said, you know that."

"I know that alright but I also know that you are going to charge him in the next day or two for the murder of James Harris. You have to admit that."

"Well actually," DA Clark replied, "I don't. I can't charge anyone on suspicion alone. We're gathering evidence and when we have satisfied ourselves then we'll make a decision."

"Well what about bail?" The defense attorney asked.

"That's for the judge to set at the arraignment."

"Mr. Clark, I feel that I'm getting nothing but a runaround here. I don't think you have anything on my client and I'm going to press for his release."

"Go right ahead, either way, I'll see you in court."

Flustered and angry Bill Rankin hung up the telephone. 'They don't have anything on my client. They're looking hard but have nothing. They can't hold him on suspicion forever. I'll file a writ for his release next week. It won't hurt the boy to stay in jail over the weekend, Monday would be soon enough. Might as well walk over to the jail now and see him. Get it over with.'

Fred was bored. He had nothing to do but sit and think and he wasn't a deep thinker. All he could do was imagine the worst. They would keep him in jail forever, he would never get out. He didn't want that. But surely they wouldn't find anything.

While he worried his lawyer arrived.

"Fred, the District Attorney's detective was over to your house today. They searched the entire house from attic to the cellar. I'm sure they tossed your bedroom pretty well. Is there anything they might have found that I should know about?"

Fred shrugged, "no I can't think of anything."

Centerville

"Ok, so here's what we're going to do. They don't have a thing to charge you with. On Monday I'm going to file a writ of habeas corpus, do you know what that is?"

Fred shook his head.

"It means that I'm going to ask the judge to let you go home because they have no evidence that you are involved in anything, especially murder. They'll have to let you out."

"That would be good. I hate it in here, there's nothing to do."

"Well you'll probably only have to wait until sometime Monday and you'll be free."

"But it's Friday, can't you do something today?"

"Sorry but it will take some time to file the paperwork and for the judge to review it. You'll have to wait. I'll have some comic books and magazines sent over to tide you through the weekend." He paused, "by the way, your mother said to tell you that she is praying for you and asked about your girlfriend Betsy."

Fred stiffened. Rankin saw immediately that the name had meaning for Fred, a strong meaning.

'Shit,' he thought. 'Just what I need now. I hate surprises.'

"Spill it. I can see that the name means something to you, better tell me now rather than have the police tell me later."

Numbly Fred shook his head. He thought furiously, then, "It was just a girl I liked. But she didn't like me. I didn't think mom knew. That's all."

"I certainly hope that's all. If you think of anything else have the sheriff call me." Bill Rankin left with a sudden sour taste in his mouth.

Alone in his cell Fred Swope alternately shivered and sweated. He knew that the police had found the bracelet, the one with Betsy's name on it. That meant that they had found Judy's picture. Had they found Patsy Marks school picture hidden in the girlie magazine under his mattress? The one he found tucked in the pocket of Patsy's pants when he pulled them back onto his body?

Fred knew that he was as good as dead. If they knew that they knew that he was responsible for a lot more than Jimmy's death. 'Fuck' he sighed as he lay face down on his cot.

Centerville

Chapter 13
Truth in Small Bites

Howard Moyer looked at his watch. It was still early enough that he might be able to see June Smith, the mother of the murdered girl, Betsy. As he drove he decided that he would ask for more than the identification of the bracelet. He would ask about the night that the little girl was killed.

He found June Smith at home. Invited into her kitchen he sat. "Mrs. Smith, I know that this might be difficult for you and I apologize. But let me start with this." He pulled the bracelet from his pocket.

"Do you recognize this?"

She gasped as she took the bracelet from his hands. "It's my baby's! I gave her this for her birthday. It was her favorite. She was wearing it that night..." Tears began to fill her eyes and she quietly wept. After a few moments she wiped her eyes. "I'm sorry. Can I keep it?"

"I wish I could say yes but I'm afraid it is evidence. When we have completed our investigation then I'll bring this back to you personally. Would you please tell me about that night at the carnival?"

For a long time the woman sat there at the table, wringing her hands and occasionally wiping her eyes with a Kleenex tissue. "I had promised Betsy that we would go to the carnival in Centerville. She was so excited. I even let her wear her favorite dress and the bracelet. When we got there we walked around just looking at things for a little while and then sat at the BINGO stand waiting for my sister, Mary. She and her daughter, Sally. I was playing BINGO while we waited. I guess it must have been around six o'clock. It must have been around seven or seven-thirty before Mary showed. Betsy was fit to be tied by then, having to wait so long.

319

"When Mary and Sally got there we did the carnival. The girls rode all the rides and some twice. Betsy would have ridden the ponies all night if I had let her. Finally, around nine we went back to the BINGO stand to play and rest our feet. Sally was old enough to play but Betsy wasn't. I should have thought about that but the carnival only comes once a year..." She paused to wipe her eyes and to steel herself for the rest of her brief tale.

"I got involved in the game and the next thing I knew time had passed and," she paused to swallow and take a deep breath, "Betsy was gone." Her chin quivered, "I didn't know what happened to her and nobody had seen her. I went crazy trying to find her and when they did, it was too late."

"I know you've been asked but sometimes memories come back. Did you see or hear anything or anyone that might have stood out, or looked suspicious? Anything at all out of the ordinary, *anything*."

"No, once she went missing I don't remember much at all and before that... I was paying too much attention to the BINGO game. I'm sorry."

"No need to be." The detective patted her hand. "You've provided enough information. Thank you." He rose to go.

"Where did you find it? The bracelet, that is."

"I'm sorry but I can't tell you that, at least not yet. Thank you for your time and I *am* sorry for your loss." Moyer left himself out. Sometimes he hated his job but this time, 'I can't wait to nail that little bastard!'

The next day, Saturday, came clear and hot. It seemed like this hot weather would never break. That morning Moyer sat at his kitchen table smoking and drinking coffee as he pondered his investigation. There was little he could do this day, all the offices he needed were closed, but there were still witnesses and principals who could be interviewed. He would like to see Judith

Centerville

Mecklenburg and her mother. It was a long shot but she might remember something. And he wanted to talk with Ben Snyder again. He had to read the sheriff's report on both incidents as well. He would start at the sheriff's office first anyway. Maybe he could talk to any deputies who were at the carnival those nights.

In small towns like Middlebury everything was close to everything else. Everyone knew everyone. Even a short trip to the A&P could get a person totally caught up with the local news and rumors. So Moyer wasn't surprised when he walked into the sheriff's office to be greeted with expectation.

"I was wondering how soon you would get here." Jim Brocious said. "What can I do for you Hard?"

"Hi to you too, Jim. I need a couple of things. First I'd like to see your reports on the Mecklenburg attack and the murder of Betsy Smith."

"They're still open cases so there is no final report but I guess you can see what we have. Mind if I ask why?"

Moyer sat across the desk from the deputy. "Keep this quiet but I'm beginning to believe that Fred Swope is involved in both of those cases. I have some physical evidence on both girls that links directly to Swope. Now don't you tell a soul! Not even the sheriff – I'll talk with him myself. It could be nothing but I am inclined to think that what I have is important. But I don't want word of this to prejudice my investigation."

"Got my word on it, Hard. You know me better than that anyway."

Howard Moyer nodded, "Yes, I do, but I have to keep a tight lid on this."

"I'll get the reports myself and you can read them here at my desk. Nobody will bother you and I have some things to do anyway."

"Thanks, after I read them then I want to talk."

"Sure thing."

321

Centerville

A few moments later he had manila folders on the blotter before him, one for each girl. He opened the file on Judith Mecklenburg first. There was little in it. Stapled to the top left corner of the first page was a copy of the same photo he had found in Fred's room. He quickly scanned the pages. There was general agreement that a large man wearing a white shirt, Moyer assumed a tee shirt, had lured Judith into the woods and attacked her there. Apparently Judith had thought it was her boyfriend who called to her and so willingly went into the woods. In a small town like this it would be very possible for a girl and boy to sneak off into the woods for a little one on one time.

Judith herself had little to tell. Only that it had been a large man in a white shirt, which by then everyone knew. She had a few scratches and bruises, he blouse was torn but she wasn't harmed in any other way.

A carnival worker had been arrested and released; no one else had been arrested.

Fred was large for his age. In the dark, in moments of stress, he could easily be taken for a large man. Judith's attacker had apparently said nothing, so though his voice was lowering, Fred's couldn't be compared to a man's voice at the time.

The folder on Betsy Smith was much thicker. But his perusal of the documents proved to be disappointing. There was, of course, no eye witness evidence. Witnesses to the event after the discovery of the body were inconclusive at best. Nobody reported seeing anybody in the actual woods area. One man, Harvey Miller, had been arrested but he, too, had been released. Miller's subsequent murder was appended only as a footnote.

What forensics that had been performed by the coroner and the state police provided much detail but little actual evidentiary information.

The crime scene itself had been carefully described and photographed. It had been determined that the little girl had been grabbed near a path running through the woods and dragged down another path at right angles to the first. The scuffle ended a short distance from the intersection of the paths. The assumption was that the assailant had carried the girl deeper into the woods. The ground where her body had been found showed obvious signs of a struggle. Dead leaves had been kicked aside and the small amount of undergrowth had been flattened.

Howard Moyer examined the photographs carefully using a magnifying glass. There was little that he could discern that was not in the descriptive text. He did realize that a good bit of the trampling was due to deputies and other people moving over the area. One thing did stand out in one of the photographs. Against the dark greens and browns of the wooded shrubbery there lay, next to the path near the intersection, a long white cone with clumps of cotton candy still clinging to it. Moyer checked and determined that it had not been taken as evidence. 'I wonder if it's still there?' he thought.

The interviews provided almost nothing. Everything was after the fact. Moyer was disappointed that the report did not have any real concrete information. The cotton candy cone was interesting though. It probably meant nothing but it was still something to consider. Maybe, when he had the time, he would go and look for it.

As he sat making notes Jim Brocious returned to the room. "Here, Jim, you can take these. I got all that I could from them." The deputy took for folders and returned them to the filing room. When he had returned he found Moyer seated in the visitor's chair facing the desk. He sat.

"I don't have a lot to ask you. Mostly I'd like to know whether you noticed anything at either scene that isn't in the reports."

Centerville

Brocious thought for a few moments, "Nothing extra stands out. There was so much going on and the fire police were everywhere. I wouldn't be surprised if evidence was destroyed by those amateurs."

"In one of the photographs at the Smith scene I saw a white paper cotton candy cone lying by the path. It still had some cotton candy on it. Do you remember seeing that?"

The deputy thought, "No, I don't. Of course if I had seen it I might not have thought much of it. Why?"

"I'm wondering whether the killer might have used it to lure the girl away from the BINGO stand and into the woods."

"That's an interesting thought."

"The more I think about it the more I want to go and see if there is any chance that it's still there. I think it might be important."

Brocious nodded his head. "It might be, if you can find it. Think you might find prints on it?"

"That would be great but I doubt it after all this time. But it would add to the circumstantial evidence. Yes, it may be worth a look." He stood. "Well I think I have all that I need for now. Thanks Jim." As he turned away he pulled his pipe from his pocket and clamped it between his teeth.

As he left the sheriff's office he decided that the Centerville carnival ground was next on his agenda. He just had to know.

Centerville

Chapter 14
Fred Sweats

Fred sat thumbing through a magazine his lawyer had sent over. He now had a few magazines and comic books. But he wasn't really interested in reading. Thoughts of the bracelet whirled through his mind. He knew that the police had found it. Why else would his mother ask that question? He had taken it on impulse. It had broken from the girl's wrist and had fallen to the ground. It glimmered in the mottled moonlight that had filtered through the trees. He saw it and took it. He should have left it where it was.

He wondered what else they had found in his bedroom, or in the garage; surely they had searched there too. Did they see what he had written on the window sill? Doing that was stupid but he was pissed that day. Was that really only a few days ago? It seemed like years. The whole summer seemed to be telescoped into such a short time frame and yet the events seemed to have happened ages ago.

If they found the bracelet then they also had found the picture of Judith Mecklenburg. They probably found the photo of Patsy. He guessed that they had taken the cat skulls in his bedroom and the garage. Had they figured out that most of his traps were stolen? What else did he have that they might have found and taken?

With the evidence they had they would throw the book at him. He would spend the rest of his life in jail. His lawyer wouldn't be able to do anything for him. They'd just take him to Rockville and throw away the key. If he ever got out he'd be an old man.

At least they didn't have any proof that he had anything to do with Bart Tuttle's death. Fred hadn't taken any souvenirs from Bart. Nobody saw him do anything not even Jimmy had any proof. But of course

Jimmy was dead. But what about Ben? He only knew what Jimmy told him, so that wouldn't be much, if anything.

Then he remembered the watermelons, the ones he had smashed as he practiced his aim dropping boulders over the stream bank. He had smashed a number of melons that way and left them there, beneath the rocks. If Jimmy saw them he would have remembered them when he and Ben saw Bart. That's what he meant when he shouted that Fred had killed Bart.

Maybe they did have proof about Bart.

Fred now truly realized that he was in a heap of shit. Deeper than even his lawyer suspected. He had the feeling that he was going to be looking at bars for a very long time. He lay back sweating, even though the cell was cool.

While Fred sweated Howard Moyer fretted more about the cotton candy cone. Even if it had no prints he might be able to use it as evidence enough to frighten a confession out of Fred Swope. Finally he grabbed a camera and evidence bags and headed for Centerville.

When he arrived he drove right through the carnival grounds, there was nothing to stop him, until he got to the BINGO stand. There he parked the car and walked towards the woods. On impulse he stopped at the stand and sat where he supposed Betsy Smith and her mother had sat the night of the little girl's murder. Sitting at the end of the bench Howard looked around. Directly to his left there was a path going into the woods and he assumed that was where the girl had been looking when she might have seen Fred entice her with cotton candy.

He rose. She would have walked down the path only a few feet to where the side path intersected and where Fred was waiting. Moyer could almost see it. He felt the hairs on the back of his neck rise as though he, himself, were in danger. He turned right and entered the second path. He could see Fred, in his mind's eye, as he enticed the girl further into the darkness of the woods. He could almost hear the BINGO caller in the hot night.

Not fifty feet down the path he came upon the trampled clearing where the body had been found. Surely in all the commotion evidence had been destroyed and now nothing was left. But he scanned the ground thoroughly anyway. He quickly found the paper cotton candy cone. Much worse for wear it lay where it had been photographed. He took new photos from different angles and then carefully bagged the evidence. There was no longer any sign of the cotton candy on the cone. Hopefully there would be a trace of a fingerprint but he doubted it.

Finding nothing more he continued down the path and soon emerged from the woods behind the now empty cake wheel stand. There was no wheel but the 2x4 whitewashed frame was still in place. This, he realized, was where Judith Mecklenburg had been attacked, right on the edge of the woods.

Howard Moyer walked back to the BINGO stand. He took out his pipe and stuffed tobacco in the bowl and lit it. He sat while he scanned the carnival ground. Now there was nothing remarkable in this place.

As he smoked he began to put his case together. He believed that he had enough to charge Fred Swope with murder of Betsy Smith and the attempted rape of Judith Mecklenburg. He wasn't sure about Jimmy Harris as there was no direct evidence but he had a feeling that it wouldn't matter. The writing on the window sill, even if only photographic and circumstantial evidence should be enough and if the state police could lift it off the window sill it would be even better.

What, he wondered, had he missed in Swope's bedroom. Maybe he had better return for a second look. He rose, knocked the dottle from his pipe and got into his car. The trip to the Swope house would be brief.

Centerville

Mrs. Swope was less than courteous when she answered the door. "What do you want now? Haven't you seen enough?"

"I want to look at Fred's room again."

"Isn't once enough? How do I know you aren't going to plant something so you can 'find' it?"

"Mrs. Swope, I told you before this isn't television and I'm not a TV cop. That doesn't happen in real life. I'm more like Joe Friday. I just want the facts. The search warrant is still valid. I can bring in someone from the sheriff's office to act as a witness."

"Oh come in and get it over with." She grumbled as she wheeled back from the door. "But don't make a mess."

"I won't" he said rather gruffly over his shoulder as he headed for the stairs. He paused in the doorway of Fred's room. He scanned everything he could see before entering the room. 'What didn't I look at closely?' He asked himself.

He started with the desk. On the top were still the coins, pocket knife and all the rest. Nothing stood out. One by one he opened the drawers. There were comic books, a hunting magazine and in the wide pencil drawer a few arrowheads, but nothing interesting.

The top of the bureau was almost empty, a couple of buttons, a safety pin and not much else. Stuck into the edge of the mirror was nothing worth collecting. The drawers contained typical underwear, socks, tee shirts and the like. He felt his way through them but found nothing. He began to wonder why he bothered to return.

Again he lifted the mattress and retrieved the girly magazine. This time, however, he shook it out over the bed. A piece of stiff paper fluttered out and landed face up on the blanket. The face of Patsy Marks stared up at him. Even though he didn't recognize the face Moyer knew he had the smoking gun. He photographed the school picture and carefully bagged it for evidence.

He grimly smiled as he pulled away from the Swope house. He decided that an unprecedented call to the DA's home was in order.

An hour later, Howard Moyer and DA Ralph Clark were sitting face to face over Clark's desk. "Well, Hard, what have you got?" He asked.

"I think I've got enough to charge Fred Swope with the murder of Betsy Smith, the murder of Patsy Marks, the attempted rape of Judith Mecklenburg and strong circumstantial evidence of the murder of Jimmy Harris."

"Patsy Marks? How do you figure that?"

"I went back and searched Swope's bedroom again. Inside a girly magazine I found this." He placed the photo on the DA's desk. "It's the Marks boys school photo. I just compared it to the report in the sheriff's office and the photo they have attached to the report is the exact same one! Now, with the evidence of the backwards pants." He paused. "I think they were into some kind of sexual play, instigated by Fred Swope, of course. They both, or at least Marks, had their pants pulled down or off when Swope clobbered Marks with a rock. That's an easy murder weapon to dispose of.

"Swope riffled the Marks boy's pockets and found the school photo. He likes souvenirs and so he kept it, hidden in that magazine. In his excitement he put Patsy Mark's pants on backwards. May not even have noticed it. Fred's a big boy. He probably carried Marks to the well, pulled the cover and dumped what he thought was a dead body into the well and put the cover back. The boy landed in the water, unconscious and drowned."

"All that because you found a photo?"

"All that because I found a photo and because too many other things happened in that little town this summer. It all adds up. Besides, the well was covered when the body was found."

"The judge isn't going to like being called on a weekend. But I'll draw up the paperwork to charge Fred

Swope with the murders of Smith and Marks and Harris and the attempted rape of Mecklenburg. What about the drunk, Bart Tuttle?"

"To be honest I haven't even looked into that. All I know for sure is that Jimmy Harris and Ben Snyder saw some watermelons that were smashed by some large rocks there by the stream near where Tuttle was killed. That's pretty thin evidence."

"True enough but I may throw it in just to see if I can scare him into a confession."

Centerville

Chapter 15
Judge Spicer's Court

The judge's gavel dropped and court was in session.

"This hearing is the arraignment of the people of Pennsylvania versus Mr. Fred Henry Swope. Is Mr. Swope present?" the court clerk called.

Fred and Bill Rankin rose. "Mr. Swope is present. I am William Rankin, Mr. Swope's attorney."

"Is the DA present?"

"I am." Said Ralph Clark as he too rose.

"You may be seated." Said the clerk as all sat.

"Mr. Swope, you are here today to be read the charges filed against you by the district Attorney and to make a plea. Do you understand?"

"Yes sir," Fred managed to croak.

"Very well. Mr. Swope, You are charged with the following crimes. First I shall list those crimes and then the details of the District Attorneys charges.

1. On or about May 30, 1955 you did willfully murder Master Patrick Marks.
2. On or about July 13, 1955 you did attack and attempt to rape Miss Judith Mecklenburg."
3. On or about the evening of July 17, 1955 you did willfully murder Miss Betsy Smith.
4. On or about August 14, 1955 you did willfully murder Master James Harris

The whispered background noise in the courtroom came to a complete standstill. Then Fred's mother, sitting in the gallery, cried out and slumped in her wheelchair. Someone behind her called for a doctor and attempted to help the stricken woman.

Fred, himself, became completely numb. His blood froze in his veins. His mind stopped working in the shock

331

of what he had heard. The words of the judge faded as he continued to read the details of the charges. Fred sat that way until his attorney, Bill Rankin, nudged him rather hard in the ribs.

"Huh?" Fred grunted.

"Stand up!" Rankin fiercely whispered as he pulled Fred to his feet.

"I said, 'How do you plead to these charges?'" The judge asked again.

"Say, 'not guilty.'"

"N Not Gu gu Guilty." Fred stuttered.

"The defendant has pleaded not guilty. You may be seated.

"Mr. Clark, Do you wish to present any testimony or evidence?"

"No, your honor, not at this time."

"In that case, because of the severity of the charges I will remand you directly to the county jail until the commencement of your trial. There is no bail. You are dismissed. Take him away" He banged his gavel and the courtroom rapidly emptied. The one reporter rushed from the room to find a telephone.

Two deputies immediately hustled Fred back to his cell as Rankin strode to Fred's now conscious mother.

"What happens now?" she asked.

"He's got two choices as I see it. He can throw himself on the mercy of the court and make a plea, or we go to trial. If we go to trial I'm going to need the help of another lawyer and an investigator. It won't be cheap."

"Will they hang him?"

"Not if I can help it." He replied, 'But I'd do it myself if I could.' He thought. "We'll have to have him tried as a youthful offender. If he's tried as an adult all bets are off."

"Oh god, what have I done to deserve this," she moaned.

Centerville

"You! What about your son? This isn't going to be easy on him you know." His opinion of her was diminishing by the minute. "Jesus" he muttered, "I have to go back to the jail and talk to Fred. Right now." He walked off with long strides.

Rankin found Fred in his cell, sitting on his bed and holding his head. Dry eyed he looked up at the attorney, "Now what?" he asked.

Rankin sat at the end of the bed and shook his head. "You are in so much trouble it may never end. Now tell me the truth, how much are you really guilty of?"

"None of it. I didn't do any of it, I promise."

"That's bullshit and we both know it. They had to find evidence, pretty good and damning, evidence to prepare those charges. They didn't just make them up. So I'll ask you again, How many?"

Fred shook his head. Against his better judgment Rankin slapped Fred on the face. "How many?"

Fred was shocked into the total reality of not only what had just happened to him but why it had happened. And if anyone had asked him why he had done all those things he wouldn't be able to answer. He had no conscious idea. In the enormity of it all he finally began to sob. "Oh god. All of them," he whispered. "And Bart Tuttle too." His voice began to rise. "And I burned the tabernacle." He wailed.

"Jesus Christ! Keep your voice down and don't say another thing – to anybody. I'm your best and only hope to keep your neck out of a noose. God knows you deserve it. Dear god, what were you thinking?"

Fred, sobbing, shook his head. He began to shake as the terror took over him.

"I have to go see the DA now. Like I said, keep your mouth shut."

Wondering what he had gotten himself into he left the jail and walked to the District Attorney's office. He wasn't looking forward to the meeting but he was the attorney of record and the constitution guaranteed Fred representation and a fair trial. 'I don't even know if I'll get paid for this,' He thought.

He entered the DA's office and was ushered directly into Clark's office.

"Bill you look like you could use a drink. Sit down." Clark took two small glasses from his desk and a bottle of whiskey. "I don't usually do this but in these circumstances it is my duty.

"I'm sorry. I know you were shocked at the charges. Things happened so quickly this weekend and not in the way I expected either." He passed one of the glasses to Rankin.

"What happened, Ralph. I knew the kid was in trouble but this?" He took a sip. "I'm stunned. What do you have? I have the right to know."

"You'll get it all. We executed a search warrant on your client's home and found some damning evidence. You know I can't and won't give you any more until you have filed but I will tell you that we have enough to put him away for life."

"He's only fourteen. You have to charge him as a youth, not an adult."

"That's for us to decide, Bill."

"How about a plea deal?"

"Has he confessed to you?"

"You know I'm not going to answer that." He put his empty glass on the desk and Clark obligingly filled it. "Either way, he's too young to spend the next fifty or sixty years in jail."

"We could hang him."

"Don't joke with me."

"I'm not." Said Clark flatly. "We're pretty sure he killed four people, why not more? We suspect that he also killed Bart Tuttle and that he burned the tabernacle and who knows what else."

Centerville

"How about an institution?"

"If you change your plea and win." Clark sipped his whiskey. "I'll tell you Bill. I don't envy you and I don't blame you for trying to do whatever you can for your client. You're a good lawyer, I know you. File for discovery and we'll give you everything we have."

As Rankin left he fumed. He *was* a good lawyer but he knew when he was beat. Their best chance would be to come to a plea agreement. Now if he could convince Fred of that. In the meantime he would file for discovery. And have a long talk with Fred. Maybe there was something there to provide some mitigating circumstances.

But Bill Rankin wasn't too confident.

Chapter 16
Fred Makes a Decision

Fred was in a daze. He still was mostly numb at what had happened in the court room. He never expected that they would charge him with anything but killing Jimmy. With that alone maybe he could have had a better chance but now he knew for sure that he was doomed. He didn't know if they would hang him or strap him in the chair but one of the two would happen.

He knew that he should have said nothing about the others but he was too scared to think. They would ask him why and he didn't have an answer. Saying that he got a hard on when he did it and that he jerked off after each one and that it felt good wouldn't do – and he couldn't say anything like that anyway. You don't admit to things like that. It wasn't that he enjoyed killing them - well maybe with Bart he did - but that he was compelled to do it. Once he started he couldn't stop. Maybe he *was* crazy. Couldn't they put him into the loony bin for a couple of years until he was cured and then let him out? Maybe that was his best option; if they thought he was crazy.

That's what he would do. He'd tell his lawyer that voices in his head made him do those things and once he started he couldn't stop. He'd say it was the devil and that they should look in the attic of the church where the devil told him what to do. If they saw his hideout there they'd believe it. He would have to make up something about the hideout though. He was just messing around up there and wanted to make something scary in case he ever brought another kid up to see it. That's all it really was.

But if he went to the insane asylum over at Franklin maybe they would never let him out and if they did maybe he *would* be crazy. What if they gave him a lobotomy? He'd been hearing a lot about that lately.

Centerville

Or should he plead guilty? If he did he would never see the light of day, he would die in prison. But he was only a kid. If they had a trial maybe the jury would go easy on him, being so young and all. Maybe they'd let him off. But probably not.

The more he thought the more he liked the idea of being crazy. That would be his best chance. He would tell Mr. Rankin when he came back. That's what he'd do.

While Fred was planning his insanity defense, District Attorney Clark was planning on ensuring that that very defense would be thwarted. At first, he thought that Fred had to have been crazy, maybe filled with raging hormones, to do what he did but he decided that if that were the case there would have been all female victims. If Fred Swope had killed Bart Tuttle as Clark was becoming more and more sure of, that blew an insanity defense out of the water, it was too well planned

Killing Betsy Smith and attacking Judith Mecklenburg may have been hormone based spur-of-the-moment actions but not Jimmy Harris or Patrick Marks. They might even claim the Harris killing to be self-defense, except Clark was sure that Fred had no idea that Jimmy had a gun in his knapsack.

He didn't have a large legal team for his office, three assistant DA's and a secretary, not to mention Hard Moyer. He would pull in Tom Pendergast as the lead attorney. Let him and Moyer run with the ball. He reached for his phone.

A few moments later Tom Pendergast answered his phone.

"Tom," Ralph Clark said, "I want you to come over to my office now. I've got a job for you."

"Be right there, Boss."

"If you see Hard Moyer, grab him. He's probably in his office."

About five minutes later Tom Pendergast and Howard Moyer stepped into the DA's office.

337

"Have a seat, gentlemen," Clark said. They sat.

"Tom, I'm sure you have heard all the fuss about the Harris murder. Well, things happened so fast over the weekend that we went from knowing next to nothing about Harris to charging the defendant, Fred Swope, with three counts of murder and one of attempted rape. Hard, here, probably knows more than I do. He did more investigating in the last three days than he did last year." He grinned.

"I want you to take the case and get a conviction. You're the best man for the job and Hard will get you what you need. Won't you Hard?" He looked at Moyer who nodded affirmatively. "What's on your plate Hard?"

Howard Moyer said, "The next thing I want to do is to interview the Snyder boy Ben; He gave John Shambach a whole lot but I need to hear it from him myself. The same goes for Ned Harris. I don't think there is anything more we can discover through search warrants." He turned to Pendergast, "Tom, I'll get copies of everything I have over to you right away. We can go over it together and make our plans."

Tom nodded, "That sounds good. It looks like I have a lot of work to get caught up on, so I'll get right at it."

"The defendant's attorney is Bill Rankin. You know him don't you?"

Again Tom Pendergast gave a nod. "Yes, I've known him for a few years. I've even played golf with him a few times."

"Is he any good?"

"Not bad. He shoots mostly in the low 90s. With my poor putting he's hard to beat but once in a while..." He grinned.

"You'll be hearing from him as soon as he files his motion for discovery."

"What should I give him, boss?"

Centerville

"Probably most of what he asks for, within reason. He and I talked about what we have and it won't help his client one damn bit." DA Clark said as he shook his head. "Not one damn bit."

Tom Pendergast stood, "Hard, let's go to my office and look at what you have."

"Here's all the paperwork I have. It's yours now, Tom." Ralph Clark passed a sheaf of papers to his assistant. As the two men left, Clark thought of the bottle in his desk and sighed.

A few doors down the street Bill Rankin was finishing up his discovery motion. He hoped that there would be something in there that would help his case but he wasn't hopeful. His biggest fear was that the evidence was so overwhelming that a conviction was a foregone conclusion. If it came to that he had no choice but to go for a plea deal. Get Fred to confess to killing the Harris kid and hope for the best. No matter how he looked at it he knew that his client was going to prison for a long time. Of course he didn't yet know about the evidence found in Fred's room or on the window sill in the garage. He didn't know the extent of Howard Moyer's investigation or the testimony that Ben had given to the sheriff. In fact the one thing he did know was that the DA didn't know everything. He didn't know that Fred had already confessed. He had to convince Fred to make a deal. Maybe if he pled on the Harris murder they'd drop the rest.

When he finished the motion he again left his office and walked to the court house. 'Sometimes I think I should have an office there. I practically live in the place.' As he stepped out of his office the August heat hit him like a blast. He would be glad when the weather broke.

A few minutes later he entered the court clerk's office. Marian McClure, the assistant clerk was attending the counter. "What can I do for you Mr. Rankin?"

Centerville

"I'm here to file this motion for discovery in the Swope case. How soon can you get it on Judge Spicer's calendar?"

She paged through her desk calendar and said, "Probably on Wednesday. He has a trial tomorrow and he's tied up this afternoon but his calendar is clear on Wednesday."

"Thanks. If he can get to it any sooner, I'll be available." He passed her the motion. She took it and stamped it and logged it.

"I'll let him know it's here."

Rankin nodded, turned and left. It had been a long day and it was still short of three pm. He decided to go home for the rest of the day. The last thing he wanted to do was to go back to the jail to see Fred. He'd go tomorrow.

Centerville

Chapter 17
Let's Make a Deal

On Tuesday afternoon the court clerk issued a notice to Rankin and the DA's office to be in Judge Spicer's courtroom at nine am Wednesday morning for the brief hearing on the defense motion for discovery. All were present and within a few minutes the judge issued the order to turn over the evidence they had and anything relevant in the future. Court was adjourned.

"Come up to my office, Bill. We'll go over the evidence with you. As you know you can photograph the hard evidence, or make copies of it but can't have the originals." Tom Pendergast spoke.

Rankin nodded and the two climbed the stairs to Pendergast's office. Once inside they sat.

"We don't have a lot of physical evidence. But don't get your hopes up. What we have we think is pretty strong.

"For a start we have a bracelet which has been directly linked to Betsy Smith; her mother identified it. And it's engraved with Betsy's name. It was found on your client's desk. We found this photo of Judith Mecklenburg in the mirror in his room. And this, a photo of Patrick Marks, was hidden in a magazine under his mattress. We contend that all are souvenirs of his activities. We also discovered the words, 'Jimmy knows' written in dust in Swope's garage. Here's a photograph, you can have it The state police have a cotton candy paper cone that was found near Betsy's body. We expect to find your client's finger prints on it. And that's just the hard evidence."

"We also found places where he would go to do - whatever. In each of those places he built a kind of nest and left animal skulls and other things in them. He even had one in the attic of the Reformed Church. We have a psychiatrist evaluating that as we speak. We haven't decided if it's evidence yet.

Bill Rankin was not pleased with these revelations. Not only did his idiot client admit to the killings but he took souvenirs too!

"That's pretty strong evidence, Tom. But it doesn't prove anything. Mr. Swope could have found the bracelet while he was playing in the woods. The Mecklenburg girl is very pretty. He may have just liked her and managed to get her picture and the same goes for the Marks boy. It doesn't prove a thing."

"You can say that, Bill," Pendergast said, "but that doesn't make it so. And what about the writing in the dust. Your client didn't just write it for the fun of it. He must have been thinking pretty hard about the fact that Jimmy Harris appeared to know a whole lot, if not everything.

"Oh yes, we're investigating the Bart Tuttle murder as well."

"You can't pin that on my client," Rankin raised his voice in protest. "You have no evidence that Fred Swope did that. It could have been anyone. Why I understand that everyone in the town knew that that old drunk always slept on the stream bank right there."

"Maybe so, but not everyone wanted to kill him for doing so. We also think that your client burned the tabernacle to the ground."

"You can't prove that either," Rankin complained. Inwardly he cringed. That stupid Swope had confessed to everything including Tuttle and the fire. What else was there? He was beginning to be positive that his best bet was a plea on Harris and hope – no pray - for the best.

"We have some interviews that have been done and there are more to come. We'll give you what's appropriate when they're done. Are we good?"

Grimly Rankin nodded. "Yes, I'd like to take photos of everything you have."

Centerville

"Help yourself," Tom Pendergast said.

Half an hour later Bill Rankin was back in the hot street, heading for his office. 'I guess,' he thought, 'I had better see Sarah Swope.' That would be very distasteful but it had to be done. He had to discuss with her all he knew and what was best for her son. He was afraid it would kill her.

He had a lot to think about on the short drive to Centerville. He parked on the street in front of the Swope house and knocked on the door. Sarah Swope let him in.

He stood in the kitchen. The house had a dry kind of smell to it, not unpleasant though. It reminded him of long gone baking of good things like sugar cookies, cherry or apple pie and maybe a cake. But nothing had been baked in this kitchen in quite a while.

"Have a seat," Sarah Swope loudly said. Her voice was always loud, as though to compensate for being in a wheelchair.

Rankin sat. "I'm here to bring you up to date on what has been going on the past couple of days."

She nodded, "Ok, tell me the worst. I'm ready for it."

"What makes you think I have bad news?"

"I know my son and I know if you had good things to tell me you'd be smiling – and you aren't"

"I just left the DAs office. I saw all the physical evidence they have so far. It isn't much but it paints a grim picture for Fred. They found in his bedroom," He ticked off on his fingers. "One: a bracelet with the name 'Betsy' engraved on it. It was positively identified by Betsy Smith's mother. Two: they found a photo of Judith Mecklenburg. Three: they found a photo of Patrick Marks. Four: They found the words 'Jimmy Knows' written in the dust of the window sill in your garage." As he ticked his fingers he could see her face go paler and paler.

She put her hand to her mouth. "What else?"

343

"We could argue the evidence in trial but there isn't going to be any trial."

"Why not?"

"Because your son is going to plead guilty."

"I thought you were his lawyer. Why would you let him do that?"

He pointed his finger at her and said sternly. "Because your son confessed to me, over in his jail cell. He confessed to every charge and then some. He told me he killed Bart Tuttle and set fire to the tabernacle." He almost shouted. "That's why!

"I think that his best and only chance is to plead guilty to the murder of Jimmy Harris and throw himself on the mercy of the court. If we go to trial he'll probably get the chair, no matter how young he is."

Sarah Swope sat in her wheelchair like a statue and for what appeared to be a long time she did not move. Finally she leaned forward and tapped her finger on the lawyer's knee. "You've got to do what you've got to do. He should'na said anything to you but he did." She leaned back. "Go and do it." She said in resignation. "It's got to be done. You better go now."

She rolled away while Rankin stood and left the house.

'Shit,' he thought. 'Now back to the jail. I'll be glad when this is all over.'

Half an hour later he entered Fred's cell. But he didn't sit. Fred looked like he was waiting for him and spoke up immediately.

"Mr. Rankin, there's something I didn't tell you." He paused, "I didn't tell you that I hear voices in my head. They, they tell me to, uh, do," he paused, "things. I think it must be the devil. He made me do those things. I didn't want to but he made me do it."

"The devil, eh?" Rankin asked.

"Yes sir."

"That's a nice try but I don't think so."

Centerville

"Why not?"

"Because the evidence that the DA has against you is enough to hang you. That's why. A jury will never buy 'voices' in your head. I just spoke with your mother and there's really only one choice for you and one choice only. You need to plead guilty to killing Jimmy Harris and hope to god the judge takes it easy on you. If we go to trial they will convict you of everything and I mean everything. They pretty much know you did in Bart Tuttle and they suspect you in the tabernacle fire as well. If you go to trial they'll either hang you or put you away for the next five hundred years. That's why!"

Fred was taken aback.

"You think about all of this. I'll be back tomorrow morning."

"No, you don't have to," Fred said. "I give up. Just tell me what I have to do."

"You just sit tight. Let me talk with the DA. We'll make a deal."

Rankin left the jail and climbed the stairs, again, to Tom Pendergast's office. Pendergast was in. 'I'm getting too old for this,' he thought.

"Tom. I want to talk with you and Ralph as soon as possible. Right now would be good."

The assistant DA raised his eyebrows as he dialed Ralph Clark's phone number. "Bill Rankin is here in my office. He wants to talk with both of us ASAP." He listened for a moment and nodded his head. He hung up the receiver and said, "Let's go."

Just minutes later the three men were gathered is Clark's small conference room.

"What have you got, Bill?" Clark asked.

Rankin looked at the table and traced a circle with his finger. Then he looked up and said, "Suppose Fred Swope pleaded guilty to killing Jimmy Harris? Would that satisfy you? It would save the time and expense of a trial."

"Is your client willing to do that?"

"Yes, he is. I just spoke with him. But you have to drop the other charges."

"Well, I don't know about that. I'll have to take that into advisement," Pendergast said. The other families will want justice too."

"Won't Fred Swope going to jail for a long time be enough?"

"Well, it might if we phrase it such that a sentence for one is a sentence for all. I won't guarantee it but let our office talk it over. Will you give us a day or two?"

Bill Rankin nodded. "Yes we can wait. How about Friday?"

Pendergast looked at DA Clark who said, "Give us until Monday to talk it over." He stood up. They shook hands and Rankin left.

"I don't know about you, Tom but I'm all for it. We get him on the original charge and throw him in jail. It'll save us a trial all right. Let him stew until next week and then we'll discuss sentencing options."

Tom Pendergast grinned as they went back to their respective offices.

Centerville

Chapter 18
Fred's Day in Court

Monday came and the three found themselves once again in the DA's conference room.

"We made a decision and we'll play ball. I'll put the ball in your court, Bill. What do you think is fair?"

Rankin cleared his throat. "Ten but no more than fifteen years with time off for good behavior. I don't want him coming out an old man."

"Ten is pretty lenient." Clark looked at Pendergast. "How do you two feel about fifteen? I think we can get the judge to agree that if we recommend it."

"No more than fifteen and make the prison the Hillman Juvenile House."

"That's up to the judge. He will probably want Rockville."

"The kids only fourteen! He's not a hardened criminal." Rankin protested.

"Tell that to Betsy Smith's mother."

"If it has to be Rockville, at least it's close enough that his crippled mother can travel to visit him."

'Crippled mother. I like that.' Clark snorted to himself. But he didn't care where Fred Swope went as long as he went somewhere hard and for a long time.

He nodded, "I think we can make the recommendation to the judge but he *does* have the final say."

"If he does go to Rockville at least they can put him in the juvenile wing." Rankin suggested.

"We'll see what happens." Clark said. "We'll see the clerk and get this on the judges calendar."

In those slow dog days of August justice moved awfully swiftly. Little more than a week later they were before Judge Spicer.

347

Centerville

"All rise." The clerk intoned as the judge entered the courtroom.

"Be seated," he said as he took his seat at the bench. He studied the papers before him. "It says here that you gentlemen want to discuss a plea."

Tom Pendergast rose and said, "Yes, your honor. We have conferenced with the defense and have come to an agreement."

"And what's that?" the judge asked.

"The defendant Fred Henry Swope will plead guilty to one count of manslaughter in the death of James Harris."

"Are you in agreement with that Mr. Rankin?"

Bill Rankin said, "Yes, we are."

"How about you Mr. Swope?"

"Yes, your honor." Fred said with a scratchy voice.

"What terms have you agreed to, Mr. Pendergast?"

Tom Pendergast rose again and spoke. "Your honor. As I said we negotiated with the defense and have come to the agreement that a sentence of no more than fifteen years in the juvenile detention center at Hillman would be appropriate, considering the age of the defendant."

The judge turned to Fred, "How old are you, son?"

"Fourteen," Fred answered.

The judge hmmmed. "Continue Mr. Pendergast."

"As I said, considering his age we believe that this will be an appropriate sentence."

"What about the other charges. Are you going to just drop them?"

"Yes, your honor."

"Ok. I'll take this under advisement and render a decision in two weeks from today. At that time Mr. Swope will make a plea and I will pass sentence. Good day gentlemen." He banged his gavel, rose and left the courtroom.

Centerville

Fred turned to his attorney, "Now what?" he asked.

"Now we wait" said Bill Rankin, "We wait."

* * *

The final Tuesday in August dawned hot and dry. There wasn't even a cooling breeze or cloud in the sky to provide the least amount of shade. At nine o'clock that morning the courtroom began to fill in the overwhelming heat. The ceiling fans did little to help as they circulated the hot air through the room. Ben and his father were there as were the Harris family, the Smiths, the Marks and all the rest. Centerville was well represented. People fanned themselves with paper funeral home advertising fans that littered the pews.

Fred and his attorney, Bill Rankin, entered the room and took seats at the defendant's table. Tom Pendergast took his seat at the prosecution's table. The room murmured as they all waited for Judge Spicer. Promptly at nine thirty the judge's chamber door opened.

"All rise," called the clerk. A shuffle went through the room as everyone stood.

The judge walked to his seat and said, "You may be seated," as he seated himself.

"We have before us this morning, the case of the Commonwealth versus Swope. We are informed that the defendant has chosen to waive a jury trial and, instead, enter a plea. Is this correct Mr. Rankin?"

Bill Rankin rose and said, "Yes, your honor."

"The charge is manslaughter. Is this also correct?"

"Yes, your honor."

"Will the defendant please rise?"

Fred stood on trembling legs. He held the table edge with a deathlike grip. His mouth was dry and his heart was pounding so hard he thought everyone in the

349

room could hear it. There was a strange buzzing in his ears and he sweated in his only good wool suit.

"Mr. Swope. You are charged with manslaughter in the death of James Harris." The judge intoned.

"How do you plea?" he asked as he took off his glasses, leaned forward and looked directly at Fred.

"Guilty." Fred croaked.

"How's that? I can't hear you." The judge said.

Nearly choking with fear Fred managed to say, "guilty" loud enough for the judge to easily hear.

"Does the commonwealth have any recommendations for the court?"

Tom Pendergast rose and said, "Yes, your honor. Considering the age of the defendant we recommend that a sentence of fifteen years with the time to be served in the Hillman Juvenile House"

"Very well. Mr. Fred Henry Swope, you have pleaded guilty to the charge and it is now my duty to sentence you.

"I have taken into account the recommendations of the prosecuting attorney and I find them too lenient. You did evil things and did them for no apparent reason that this court could possibly understand. You killed James Harris in cold blood. And you knew that what you did was wrong for you hid in a cave while the authorities looked for you. It is my opinion that you are not a good person and that serving time in a juvenile facility will not be justice served. In fifteen years you will still be a young man.

"With great deliberation I have come to what I believe is a fair sentence for what you have done. I therefore sentence you to twenty years at hard labor at the Rockville State Prison. May god help you find forgiveness from your fellow man. You won't get it from this court."

With that he banged his gavel and left the courtroom. For a moment the silence was complete. Even the funeral fans were still in the hot air. Then the sheriff's deputies put Fred in handcuffs and led him from the room.

Two days later he was inducted into the state prison at Rockville. There he would spend the next twenty years.

Book IV
Twenty Years Later

Centerville

Chapter 19
Just Another Day

Ben Snyder was rooting though his desk. Somewhere he had put the paperwork for the Appleton case. He needed to review his notes so that he would sound fresh tomorrow at the hearing. It wasn't a very important case, Stuart Appleton had beaten his wife and had been thrown in jail to cool off but now she wanted to press charges. 'Probably filing for divorce too,' he thought. Finally he found the folder and opened it. He lit a cigarette as he reviewed the case.

It was an early, sunny June Monday. He looked out of the window to the street below. Traffic was lazily moving though the town square. The thermometer on the bank registered 83 degrees. Hot already. If this kept up the summer would be a scorcher.

He looked back down at the folder before him. He thumbed through the few pages. It really wasn't much of a case at all. But he was the investigating detective so it was he who had to testify tomorrow. 'I certainly could use something more interesting than drunks and wife beaters.' He thought.

In three more weeks he would mark his fifth anniversary with the sheriff's office as a deputy detective. He was up for a small promotion and that meant a raise. He could use that. In another few weeks he would also take his annual vacation. He would go to the northeastern part of the state to fish in the deep and cold lakes, out in the wilds of the Poconos. He owned a small cabin on the shores of Lake Wallenpaupack. The only way to get to the cabin was by canoe. He loved getting away like that. There nobody could bother him.

He loved to fish and had done so all his life. When he was young he and his friend Jimmy would fish all summer long. Back then they had lived in the village of

Centerville, about five miles from where he now sat. But Jimmy was dead. And Ben still thought about being a kid and fishing all summer; once in a while.

Jimmy had been his best friend. They did everything together. Then one summer Jimmy was killed; murdered by an older kid who bullied everyone. The kid, Fred Swope, was caught and thrown into jail. He was still there as far as Ben knew. He really didn't care about Fred Swope, not at all.

It was funny. When they were kids Jimmy was the smart one, always figuring out mysteries. He observed everything. He should have been the one to grow up to be a detective. He'd be good at this job. Ben felt that he himself was just average.

Ben hadn't planned on entering law enforcement when he was a kid. It just kind of happened. When he had turned eighteen he enlisted in the Army. He knew that with the Communist threat in Southeast Asia, especially in Vietnam, that he would probably be drafted, so he enlisted back in '64, hoping he would have a better chance of avoiding Vietnam. But he didn't. Before he knew what was happening he was assigned, right after basic, to Fort McClellan for Military Police training. Upon graduation he was sent off to Vietnam. After two tours he mustered out and came back home.

While in Vietnam he joined the 8th MP Group (Criminal Investigation) in Long Binh. He stayed with them until 1972 then he left the Army as a Sergeant First Class. After coming out of the Army he came home and applied for the position of Deputy Sheriff. He was hired immediately and was now coming up on his fifth anniversary. Because he was in CID in the Army it didn't take him long to rise through the ranks to achieve the rank of Sergeant Detective. If old Ramey ever retired Ben should be promoted to lieutenant and become Chief of Detectives. But being second in command wasn't bad, except that there were only four men in the squad. He sighed, stubbed out his cigarette and got back to his work.

And, of course, his phone rang. "Snyder." He said into the handset.

"Ben, come on up to my office, I have something for you," said Sheriff Faulkville. Ben said that he was on his way and hung up. A few moments later he stepped into the sheriff's office.

Eva Faulkville looked up from her desk and pointed to a chair. Ben sat. "Let me finish this," the she said. Ben watched her as she worked. The sheriff was a stocky woman whose very presence could strike fear in the strongest man. She had strong broad shoulders and it was said that she could easily bench press over two hundred pounds. Ben believed it. She had a light, soft moustache that she kept well groomed. Her face was chiseled and her features well defined.

She looked up at Ben and smiled. When she did that it entirely changed her face and the look of sternness was gone in an instant. "How are things going?" she asked.

"Little slow today, not that I mind."

"Well I have a little something that may perk up your afternoon. Then again it probably isn't anything. I have a job for you over in Centerville." She looked down at the pad on her desk. "You know a Sarah Swope?"

He nodded. "Yes, I've known her most of my life. She's a crippled woman and uses a wheelchair. When I was little they say she fell down the cellar stairs and broke her back."

"Well, she's dead."

Ben nodded and asked, "What happened?"

"That's why you are going over there, to find out. It looks like she fell down the cellar steps again and this time broke her neck. It's probably just an accident but *someone* insisted on calling us. Since you're the only one in the squad today, I guess you got it. Just go over there and look around before they cart the body off."

"Roger that, I'm on my way." Ben rose and left the room. Soon he was in his cruiser and on his way to Centerville.

Sarah Swope was the mother of the kid who killed Ben's friend Jimmy Harris about twenty years ago. He thought it was quite a coincidence that she would fall down the same set of stairs again. But stranger things had happened. The five mile drive was brief and soon he pulled up behind the ambulance at the Swope house. He shouldered his way through the small group of paramedics and onlookers until he stood in the kitchen.

"Who's in charge here?"

"I guess I am," said one of the paramedics.

"Where's the body?" the paramedic pointed to the open cellar door. Ben went to the door and peered down into the dim cellar. "Anybody have a flashlight?" he asked.

One of the paramedics gave him one and said, "Doc. Purnell is down there." Ben nodded and started down the narrow and dark stairs. At the base of the stairs he could see the crumpled body and a wheelchair nearby. Kneeling next to the body was the doctor.

"What have you got, Doc?"

Purnell looked up, "Oh hi Ben. Seems to me that she simply fell down the steps and broke her neck. Not much to it. Don't know why you were even called."

"Me neither but since I'm here; have you moved anything?" he asked as he played the flashlight beam over the dead body.

"Yes, the wheelchair was on top of her when I got here, so I moved it over there, out of the way. But that's all I moved."

Ben nodded. "How long has she been dead?"

"It must have happened yesterday. The cleaning girl come over today and found the body. I'd say it's close to twenty-four hours, give or take."

"Any marks?"

"Nothing that I can see in this light. When I get her upstairs or to the funeral home I may be able to see more, but I doubt it."

Ben turned to look at the wheelchair. It was slightly folded but he could see that it would be wider when someone was sitting in it.

"Did you fold it, the chair?" he asked Doc. Purnell.

The doctor nodded, "Yeah, when I lifted it off the body and laid it down over there it kind of folded itself."

Ben shone the light on the chair and looked at the stairs. Then he climbed them to the door at the top. Examining the door frame he thought it looked narrower than the fully extended width of the wheelchair. He shook his head and went back to the dirt floored cellar.

"Doc, I want the body taken to the county morgue."

"How come?"

"I don't know but something doesn't feel right. Don't move anything, I'm going to go and get my camera." He left and returned a little later, camera in hand. He proceeded to take a number of photographs of the body, the stairs and the wheelchair.

"You can move the body now." He said as he climbed the stairs once again.

He went to his cruiser and thumbed the microphone on his radio. "Dispatch." The radio said.

"This is Deputy Snyder. I'm sending a body to the morgue. Call the coroner and have him meet me there?"

"10-4"

"Roger. Out." He tossed the microphone to the car seat and went back into the house.

He waited while the paramedics struggled with the body up the narrow stairs and around the tight corner into the kitchen and through the door and outside to the street and to the ambulance. The doctor followed and closed the cellar door.

"Thanks Doc, appreciate you coming over."

"I'm on call today, so I had to." He smiled.

"As you know I'm sending the body to the county morgue, and the coroner will meet it when it arrives. I don't know if you need to see him or not."

"I don't think so. He'll get my report."

"Ok, thanks again."

He turned to a young woman. She was dressed in conservative clothes and wore a bonnet. Ben guessed that she was either Mennonite or Amish. "Are you the one who found the body?"

She nodded.

"Ok, please stay right there while I get everyone else out of here." He raised his voice to the other three other people in the room. "I want you all to leave now and nobody to enter this house until I say so." Talking among themselves they turned and shuffled through the door.

He turned back to the girl. "What is your name?"

"Mary Yoder."

"Can you tell me what happened? Start from when you got here until the ambulance arrived. And take your time."

The girl thought for a moment and then said, "I arrived here at about ten o'clock as I usually do. I saw right away that the cellar door was open. So I called Mrs. Swope but nobody answered."

"Then what did you do," Ben asked.

"I went to the cellar door and looked down. The light was on and I could see Mrs. Swope lying at the bottom of the steps. I went down to help her but when I got there I could see that she was dead. I touched her and she was cold.

"Then I came back up and used the telephone to call the ambulance." She finished.

"Anything else?"

She shook her head in the negative.

"Ok Miss Yoder. It is Miss, isn't it?"

She nodded.

"I need your address and, if you have one, your telephone number, or a number where you can be reached."

"We're not Amish. We have a telephone. We even have a car," she smiled.

"Thank you for your help. I may want to speak with you again. But for now you can go." Ben nodded and gestured towards the door. The girl quickly left.

Ben returned to the cellar and folded the wheelchair flat and carried it back to the first floor. There he unfolded it and wheeled it to the open cellar door. But the chair would not roll through no matter how hard he tried.

'That's not right,' He thought as he shook his head. 'Well I'll leave the chair here for now and seal the door.' He pushed the wheelchair into the darkened parlor and left the house. He sealed the front door and posted a trespass notice on it. He walked around to the sun room door and did the same and the slanted cellar doors at the back of the house as well. After that he got back into his cruiser and returned to his office.

Sheriff Fauklville's door was open so he tapped on the doorframe and entered. The sheriff looked up and said, "What do you have, Ben?"

"I'm not sure at the moment," he said as he took a seat. "But something doesn't sit right with me. Doc Purnell was there and he said that she fell and broke her neck. He said he couldn't see any other marks on the body but that cellar is dark. So I had the body sent to the morgue and called the coroner. I'm going over there next."

"So what's up?"

"Well," he scratched his head. "Her wheelchair was in the cellar too. Problem is that it's too wide to fit through the cellar door unless it's folded. I don't see how she could have gone through the door if she was sitting in the chair. She couldn't use her legs at all, so she couldn't have gotten out of the chair and folded it up before falling. And there's almost nothing down there. Why would she go there in the first place?"

"So you think she wasn't an accident?"

"I don't know but I just don't feel right about it. I sealed the house, mostly to keep the curious out. I don't think there is much there to look at or for. I did leave the wheelchair in the parlor."

"Go see the coroner and write up a report and we'll see what happens."

Ben nodded and left the office. The morgue was a short drive away and Ben was there within ten minutes. He found the coroner in the examination room.

"How you doin', Ben?"

"Pretty good, Roy. Have you had much of a chance to look at Mrs. Swope yet?"

"Not really. I just got here. I did notice this, though." He pointed to the woman's cheeks. "See that?"

"Aaah no?" Ben said.

"They aren't livid but look close." He shone a light on the pale cheeks of the dead woman. "See those darker marks? They go from right below the eye orbits down to the jaw bone?" He traced them with his finger.

"Yeah, I kind of see them now."

"I think they're hand prints. I think Mrs. Swope here had her neck broken and was then thrown down the stairs. I'll know a whole lot more after the autopsy. But if you ask me, I think you have a homicide on your hands. Yes I do."

Ben left and walked back to his car. 'Well that's better than dealing with drunks and wife beaters,' he thought. It was definitely time to go back to talk with the sheriff. He would have to take a trip back to Centerville with a lab tech to examine what was now a crime scene.

Centerville

Centerville

Chapter 20
Free At Last

Twenty years is a long time. No matter how you look at it, it's a long time. But the day that Fred Swope had been looking for, had been counting down for until its final arrival, was finally here. His out-processing was almost complete. In another hour he would be a free man. And that would be *good!*

He had gone into this place a green kid, convicted of murder by his own mouth. He had confessed to killing Jimmy Harris and had paid the price. He knew, however, that if he had been tried on all of the charges he would still be in this place, probably forever; if they hadn't given him the chair instead. In his bitterness he still considered himself lucky.

All he wanted now was to get away from this place and start all over. He was now thirty-four years old. He never did graduate from high school but then he might not have done so on the outside either. But he was a lot smarter than when he had gone in. He had learned things he would have never learned in school. Things that would help a lot more than a piece of paper. But, he supposed, the GED that he had earned would help in finding work.

And he had even learned a skill. He was a pretty good mechanic and could work on just about anything. He also had learned to be a machinist. He could make almost anything and in the past few years he had. More than one friend on the inside had requested and received custom made weapons. Fred was really good making knives and shivs.

Yes, he had learned a lot. How to keep his mouth shut and how not to see anything. How to hide things so they would never be found. One cellmate had taught him the value of not leaving, or taking, any evidence; a lesson he had wished he had learned much earlier. From another he had learned the importance of being almost invisible in a crowd. That lesson had come in handy when he witnessed a killing in the yard and had managed to convince the authorities that he had been elsewhere.

"Swope?" the clerk behind the property fence called out.

Fred got up from his bench and approached the window.

"Sign here." Fred signed and a small package of belongings that had been confiscated twenty years earlier was returned to him. He also received an envelope with fifty dollars and a Greyhound ticket to State College.

"Good luck." The clerk said.

Twenty minutes later the other three men had been processed and they were all led to a waiting dark blue prison bus for the short drive to Jersey Shore, the nearest town with a Greyhound station. A light snow was falling in the early March coldness. As the bus pulled away Fred looked back through the snow at the austere grey stone walls of the main building with its square tower that overlooked the interior courtyards and barracks of the prison. The snow covered, but well-tended lawns, trees and the parklike surroundings belied the bleak interior. Fred inaudibly sighed and turned away from the wintery day.

Then for the next hour he simply stared through the bus window and the world that had changed so much outside while it remained static on the inside. He hoped that he could cope.

In State College the prison system had arranged a job for him as a mechanic at an auto dealership. He had been promised $2.30 for each hour he worked and was told he would work at least forty hours each week. That came to over ninety dollars a week. He would be rich!

But, of course, it didn't work out that way. On his first day he was told that he would only receive two dollars an hour with the balance to pay for the tools he used. But, he was told, if he worked real good he might get a raise in six months.

Finding a place to stay was another matter. He needed a room within walking distance until he could get a driver's license and a car, assuming he could learn how to drive. He got lucky with that. Fred found a room only a mile from the dealership. It was a room with board for only twenty dollars a week.

Of course he also needed clothes for work and something nicer than his prison garb if he wanted to socialize. Not having been trained in outside economics he soon learned that eighty dollars a week didn't go very far. But he tried. And by the middle of March he was settled into his job and new lifestyle.

But he wasn't very adept at picking friends. On the inside he had known only one kind of person. For the most part that was the kind of person he gravitated to on the outside. For example there was John. John also worked at the dealership and he had a car to boot. He was willing to drive Fred around on occasion, as long as Fred paid for the gas. And, of course, Fred paid more than necessary.

John also took Fred out at night to bars and then ribbed Fred unmercifully because Fred would not drink, not even a beer. John would often get drunk and Fred learned how to drive by trial and error when John was so soused that he couldn't see straight and even Fred knew that John should not be behind the wheel. So Fred learned to drive.

John had other skills as well. He took Fred shopping and taught him how to steal clothing. In the changing room John put on a pair of pants and then pulled his own pants on over that. He returned three pairs of pants to the rack and hid the empty hanger in the changing room. No one was the wiser. John was also good at floating bad checks. Fred knew that he, himself,

Centerville

wasn't slick enough to try that. So, for the most part, he remained honest.

As Fred gradually settled into his new routine the strangeness of the new world slowly became common. He did well in his job and was given more responsibility and a small raise. He saved his money and by May he was able to rent a cheap room and the car dealership sold him an old Chevy on payments taken directly from his pay check.

He still needed to get a driver's license. But that didn't stop him from driving and exploring the surrounding countryside. He quickly became familiar with the back roads and small villages that cluttered central Pennsylvania.

Fred made more friends; some were of a better class than John but still not high society. But for the most part they were honest folks, not crooks like John. He learned how to go to the movies and to enjoy the local entertainment. He was satisfied with his new life.

But.

Thoughts and desires, buried for years, occasionally came back to him. He still had urges, urges that never went away not even in prison. Sometimes he caught himself looking at younger women and girls and wanting... something. Most of the time he was able to shrug it off and make himself busy doing other things but not always.

He also thought about Centerville and his mother. She had never visited him when he was in prison and rarely had she sent him a letter. He assumed that she was still alive because nobody had ever told him otherwise. He wanted to see her, to ask her why she hadn't contacted him, hadn't visited him.

He also wanted to see how the old town had changed because surely it had. He really didn't have many friends there – in fact he probably had no friends in the village. He had few friends when he was young. He had acquaintances and playmates but few real friends. He had been larger than most kids his age and he knew that they considered him a bully. He liked being a bully, being able to intimidate and command.

He remembered the summer firemen's carnivals and how he had enjoyed them. He also enjoyed remembering what he had done with the little girl. He still got hard thinking about it. He sometimes thought he would like to find someone like that again and the older girl, Judith, as well. That last summer was good, too bad that it had to end. It was all Jimmy Harris' fault. And Ben Snyder's as well.

But he wouldn't dwell on that. Jimmy was dead and surely Ben was long gone. Ben had probably moved far away. Anyway, Fred wouldn't think of them when he went back. He just wanted to look around the town and to see his mother. One of these weekends he would go back to see her. He would go back to Middlebury as well, just to snoop around. He'd probably never even get out of the car.

He was tempted to visit the Reformed Church attic and see if McMaster's barn was still there, two of his favorite hangouts when he was a kid. He wasn't interested in visiting the lime kiln, though he did fish there often enough as a kid. Ultimately he realized that he wasn't so much interested in places as in the village itself. He wanted to drive or walk down the alleys just to see what was there or what had changed. He supposed that they had rebuilt the tabernacle and he wouldn't mind seeing that. But he wouldn't take matches this time. He grinned as he thought of the fire, even though he had been burned. It was fun watching the firemen trying to get water on the fire.

Fred's childhood memories, such as they were, were all that he had that were worth having. Memories of prison weren't worth anything. Though he had learned important things.

366

Centerville

Memorial Day was approaching. Maybe he would take a drive down that way. He would have at least two days off that weekend.

Centerville

Chapter 21
Home Coming

In twenty years the village hadn't changed very much at all and at the same time it had changed a lot. Spruce Street was new and above the Upper Street, which was now called Cherry Street. The Lower Street had been renamed Chestnut Street and Center Street had become Maple Avenue. Even the alleys had names.

The lime kiln had become a muddy spot in the Dry Run; not even worth fishing any more. Few people even remembered that it had once been there. McMaster's field was quickly growing into a weed and scrub infested opening that would one day become a new woods.

Chestnut Street was now more run down that it had ever been and some considered it the "slum" of Centerville. The poorest people lived there in houses and apartments that were owned by landlords living in other towns. Miller's store had closed a good ten years back and the other grocery store barely hung onto its existence. In a couple of years it would be probably be gone as well.

Fred drove slowly down what he knew as Center Street. It was late on a Sunday afternoon and the streets were quiet. He barely recognized the town. There, for example, next to the Reformed Church was a gas station where there used to be an empty field that the fire department flooded in the winter for ice skating. And where the gas station had been, down by the Methodist church, was now a weedy vacant lot.

He slowly drove all the streets, soaking up the new sights that twenty years had made. And yet many things remained the same. The houses certainly had not changed; for the most part. He still recognized the houses of people he had known and he figured that they were still occupied by the same families that had lived there when Fred had been fourteen.

Centerville

As he drove down the Lower Street, now Chestnut, he could see the old familiar row houses but how they had changed, aged and somehow were even more rundown than he remembered them. He was surprised that Miller's store was now apartments, The fire department, across the street was no more. That building too had become apartments.

Harvey Miller's burnt house was, of course, replaced. But even though the house on the lot was less than twenty years old it too had a look of decrepitude as though it had stood on that spot many more years. His old house, across the street, still looked neat and trim and he wasn't surprised. From that spot on down to where the post office used to be, on that side of the street, the houses were better kept and maintained.

No house on this street had a front yard. Some had side yards and all had yards in the rear, leading to the alley. The sidewalks, still large slabs of slate in some places, were heaved and angular due to the large maple and chestnut tree roots skewing them. On the west end of the street no sidewalk was level. On the east there was no room for trees between the houses and the street, only concrete sidewalks, frequently pitted and cracked but level.

After a leisurely tour of the town he turned into the alley behind his mother's house. There he pulled into the parking space next to the barn and stopped. After turning off the motor he sat there and thought.

He wanted to see his mother but didn't know quite why. She had never once in all those twenty years come to visit him. He had only received three letters from her. All three mentioned how much his lawyer had cost her and how her life had become a burden because of him. The letters talked about how the village had shunned her as though she were the confessed murderer. There was never a word of love or encouragement from her.

Centerville

He didn't know why he wanted to see his mother; because he hated her.

After about twenty minutes he left the car and approached the back of the house. He climbed the ageing and unpainted wooden steps of the sunporch and opened the door. As he quietly crossed the porch he looked through the kitchen window and saw her sitting, back to him, at the table. He quietly opened the kitchen door and stepped in.

"Hello, Mother," he calmly said.

Sarah Swope nearly jumped from her wheel chair in the shock and surprise of hearing his voice. As she turned the chair Fred walked around and sat at the table across from her.

"How have you been, mother? I haven't heard from you in a long time. A very long time."

She stammered, "Wh wh when did you get out? Why didn't you call me?"

"Oh," he rubbed his jaw. "I got out back in March and I live in State College now. Moved there just after I got out. I got a job at a car dealership. They taught me a trade there in prison, you know.

"I missed you mom. Why didn't you ever come to visit me? Why in all those years?"

Sarah Swope sat there, stunned. She had never expected to see her son again and now, there he was sitting across from her at her *own* kitchen table.

Speaking softly Fred said, "The town sure has changed a lot. And yet it is still the same, except where it's different. Have you changed mother?"

"Yes, the town has changed. Things change as time passes. You've changed. You're a man now."

"Yes, I'm a man and I have paid my debt to society. And now I'm free. I can do what I want, when I want and there's nobody to tell me I can't. That's the nice thing about being out of jail. Nobody can tell me what to do.

370

Centerville

"But tell me, mom, why didn't you come to *see* me?"

"Fred, it's such a long way and you know I can't drive a car. And there was nobody to take me and I didn't know when visiting hours were held."

"Mother," Fred sighed, "You could have asked. The prison authorities would have told you when you could come to visit. And I'm sure someone would have taken you if you had asked. You did ask, didn't you? You did ask for a ride."

Sarah shook her head and said nothing. Her heart was beginning to pound in her chest and she knew that this was not going to end well.

"And why didn't you write? Only three times in the first couple of years and then nothing. And when you did write all you did was complain. You never even asked how *I* was doing. Do you know how that made me feel?" His voice changed from plaintive to sound chastising as if bringing a child to task.

Nearly numb Sarah sat there. Finally she asked, "Are you hungry? Would you like something to eat?"

"Hungry? Mother, I've been hungry for twenty years and more. Hungry for your love. Hungry for your approval. But you never gave me that."

He rose and walked around the table. Standing behind his mother he put his hands on her shoulders. "You were always a good cook, mom, and I liked your food but I learned at church in prison that a man lives on more than just food. They made me go to church, you know."

He put his hands on her cheeks and gently kissed the top of her head. He could smell the shampoo that she had used that morning when she had washed her hair. Then he violently twisted her head and heard the satisfying sound of the snapping of her neck. He felt a sudden rush of pleasure and was sexually aroused.

It felt good and he savored the moment. Then he dropped his hands to his side as his mother's head slumped to her chest at an odd angle. Fred moved to the kitchen sink and leaned on the counter for a few moments as he gazed through the kitchen window to the still sunny back yard.

'How peaceful,' he thought.

As he gazed through the window he drifted in memory to the time he was a child. He had been playing with his trucks and had deliberately put one on the top step of the cellar stairs, pointing out into the darkness. Later in that day his mother went to the cellar to get some canned peaches for their supper. In the darkness she stepped on the unseen toy and it flew out from in under her. She fell down the stairs and broke her back. Paralyzed, she was confined to a wheelchair for the rest of her life.

Fred turned from the window, looked at his dead mother's body and inaudibly sighed. Finally he opened the cellar door and turned on the light. He lifted his mother's dead body from the chair and threw it down the stairs to the dirt floor below. He wheeled the chair to the cellar door but couldn't get it through the door because it was too wide. He folded the chair and carried it down into the cellar. There he unfolded it and dropped it upside down on top of his mother's body.

Feeling hungry he searched the refrigerator. He found lunch meat and cheese and so made a sandwich. When he finished eating he carefully cleaned up the crumbs, washed the knife and dish, dried them and put them away. He remembered his lessons well about not leaving any evidence. He even went so far as to wipe every surface he might have touched to remove his fingerprints.

Out of curiosity he climbed the stairs to the second floor. There he opened the door to his old bedroom. If anything he expected to find an empty room. Instead he discovered his room exactly as he had last seen it. Nothing had changed except that there was a deep layer

Centerville

of dust over everything and spider webs in the corners. It was obvious that the room had not been entered in twenty years. He stepped into the room, then changed his mind, backed out and closed the door. There was nothing in the room that he wanted.

Slowly he went back down to the kitchen. He left the house as he had entered and took a leisurely drive back to his apartment in State College. He slept deeply and peacefully that night.

Chapter 22
The Investigation

Centerville was a dying village but it wasn't dead yet. And soon, when the word leaked out, which it surely would, the streets would once again be filled with the twitter of front porch gossip. The rumor mill at the post office would be in full swing. Everyone would be talking about the murder of Sarah Swope.

The pastor of the Reformed church, Art Davis, was the one who let it out. He was Sarah Swope's pastor and it would be he who officiated at the funeral and burial. He had heard from the undertaker that Sarah Swope's death had been a homicide but he had not heard the cause of death. Rev. Davis told the part time secretary of the church, Mary Klinger that Sarah has been murdered and Mary, being a good Christian *and* Centervillian, told Mrs. Wetzel and from there the entire town knew that an evil deed had been done.

As the word spread the biggest question, of course, was who had done it. Stories of strangers passing through town began to spread, especially the one about a black man who had stopped for gas and had asked questions about the town. It didn't matter that he was working on a history of the area as a part of a Penn State grant so much as he was black. Though they would swear that they were not prejudiced, the people of Centerville were suspicious of anyone different and there had always been distrust of black people. They should stay across the Susquehanna River where they belonged.

The rumor mill whirled and the names of numerous unsavory characters were bandied about. There was even talk of an escapee from the insane colony only fifteen miles from the village. But nothing had come of it. Interestingly enough the town's most famous, or infamous individual never came to mind. As far as anyone knew Fred Swope was still in prison. Stories of rape rose from nothingness, as did the motive of robbery, though the investigation had shown no signs of that. Interestingly enough the cause of death was widely known to be strangulation, though the sheriff's office had not released the mode of death. No one seemed to consider the fact that she had been found at the foot of the cellar stairs. She had still been strangled. But of course in reality her neck had been broken. But no one in the village knew that.

"Musta taken a might strong man to do that," exclaimed Mildred Spangler to Betty Wetzel, the woman who had started all the rumors.

"Yes, indeed," Said Mrs. Wetzel in a high and reedy voice. "Like a farm worker. I seen migrants coming through looking for farm work. Could'a been one of those."

Mrs. Spangler sagely nodded, "Suppose you're right."

Migrant workers had always been a problem. They came through, usually around Memorial Day to pick strawberries and other early fruit. Some stayed around; field workers for local farmers, until late September. They drove dilapidated cars or pickup trucks and, if they had trucks, seemed to have all of their personal belongings in the truck beds. They wore scruffy clothes and were unwashed. Their children always needed haircuts. Most of the locals called them Gypsies. And everyone knew that gypsies would rob you blind as soon as look at you. Other people called them white trash. Most, however, were simply the down on their luck poor with no place to call home. And, ultimately, they did work that no self-respecting villager would do.

While the rumors made their rounds in Centerville, Fred Swope was contemplating his permanent return to the area. It was a mighty long drive from State College. So he started looking for work a bit closer to home.

In the meantime, on Wednesday afternoon, Ben Snyder was meeting with Sheriff Faulkville. "What have you got?" she asked.

"Not very much. The full coroner's report isn't in but the evidence is there. Someone broke her neck. No doubt about that. There are clear hand prints on both sides of her face and her neck sure is broke. I got the house sealed and will take Nard Boyer over to look for evidence tomorrow. He'll check for finger prints and whatever else he can find. I'll go over the place with a fine toothed comb. I'll get hold of the cleaning girl," he looked at his notebook, "a Mary Yoder and get here over to see if anything is missing."

Sheriff Faulkville nodded and said, "Looks like you got it covered."

Ben nodded back and left.

Later that afternoon Ben contacted Mary Yoder as well as Nard Boyer to make arrangements to meet at the Swope home in Centerville the following day. There were no reports of any strangers in the village and he could not imagine who would kill a crippled woman. There was no evidence of rape and the house was not disturbed so he had the feeling that robbery was not the motive. Could an intruder have come looking for a handout and things got out of hand? It seemed unlikely. Did she have any enemies? That was worth looking into but he doubted that was the case.

Sarah Swope wasn't old. Records indicated that she was only fifty-three; though to Ben she did look older. Maybe she had a boyfriend and they got into an argument. Of course to Ben there were many more questions than answers. All he had to do was to eliminate the questions. That's what he wanted, nothing but answers. Tomorrow, he decided, after he interviewed Miss. Yoder he would canvass the neighborhood. Maybe someone would know something. Ben had a fear that this was going to be a long drawn out investigation. He was afraid that he might not even solve it.

The next morning he met Nard Boyer and Mary Yoder at the Swope house. Ben opened the front door and admitted Nard. Ben motioned Mary Yoder to have a seat on one of the porch chairs.

"I'm afraid that we'll have to sit out here until my partner finishes his work inside. He's taking fingerprints and looking for other evidence." As he spoke he tapped a cigarette from his pack and lit it.

Mary Yoder nodded

Exhaling, Ben said, "when he gives us the OK, I'd like to take you inside and would like you to look around to see if there is anything missing or out of place. Can you do that?"

"Yes, officer, I can do that."

Ben smiled, "You don't have to call me officer. My name's Ben Snyder and I grew up here in Centerville. I lived on the lower street. You can call me Ben, if you like. Do you mind if I ask you a few questions while we wait for Nard?"

"Nard?"

"His name is really Leonard but they started calling him Nard when he was a kid and I guess it just stuck. He doesn't seem to mind. *May* I ask you some questions?"

"Yes, you can ask whatever you want."

"How long have you worked for Mrs. Swope?"

The girl thought for a moment and said, "It's been about two and a half years. My older sister worked for her before that but Margaret got married, so I took over. They got married in November."

Ben nodded. "How often were you in the Swope house in a week's time?"

"I came in every Monday, Wednesday and Friday. I had the weekends off."

"What did you do?"

"On Mondays I did the laundry and hung it up out back on the line. The rest of the time I would clean, make the bed, dust and the like. If she needed me to, I would wash the dishes.

"On Wednesdays I would usually take her shopping. We would drive to the A&P in Middlebury and get whatever she needed for the week. Sometimes I would help her get upstairs so she could take a bath."

"Did you do that often?" Ben asked.

"No, only once in a while. I know that she could get up and down the stairs herself. She would sit on a step and lift herself up or down with her arms. She was a lot stronger than she looked." Mary Yoder smiled.

"Do you know if she had a boyfriend?"

Mary Yoder shook her head and chuckled. "No, she didn't have a boyfriend. I don't think she had many friends at all. She was kind of loud and sometimes she was demanding."

Ben thought for a few moments and then asked, "Did she ever get physical with you; hit you or anything like that?"

"No, she wasn't like that. I think if you live in a wheelchair all alone you might get a little demanding too! It wasn't that bad and I was used to it. And she could be nice as well. She wasn't demanding all the time and she was never mean."

"Ever go to the cellar?"

"No, I never had a reason to. There was nothing down there. She kept canned goods and the like in the pantry back of the kitchen."

As they talked Nard Boyer came through the front door and joined them on the porch.

"I didn't find very much. I got a few prints and that's about it. You can go in now," he said.

Centerville

Ben nodded. "Miss Yoder. Will you let us take your fingerprints? Just so we can eliminate you from the prints Nard got?"

Mary Yoder nodded as Ben led her into the house. As they stood in the kitchen Ben said, "I'd like you to look around the house to see if there is anything missing or out of pace. Take your time."

The young lady walked slowly through the kitchen, touching things and shaking her head here and nodding there as she looked around. She did the same in the pantry and the sunporch. She turned to the dark living room. The room was sparse, a color television stood in the corner and there was an overstuffed chair and a sofa of the same style. There was an empty space in the corner across from the TV. It appeared to Ben that this was where Sarah sat in her wheelchair to watch television.

Next they went through a second door in the living room into an equally dark bedroom. There was a toilet in the corner next to the large four poster bed. There was a bureau with a mirror against the outside wall. Mary Yoder looked carefully at the contents of the bureau and shook her head."

"I can't see anything missing. She kept things in certain places and everything is where she would have put it."

"What about upstairs?" Ben Asked. "Do we need to go up there?"

"No, I only went up there maybe three times a year to dust, all but one room. She told me not to enter that room, so I didn't. Once in a while I also would help her to get up and down the steps and to take a bath."

Ben's detective's antenna went up. "Why the one room? Why is that?"

"I really don't know for sure. But I think it might have been her son's bedroom."

'Fred,' Ben thought. 'But he can't figure into this. He's in prison.'

"Well then, I guess we're through, unless you think of something else. We still need your prints. If you can come to the sheriff's office one day soon and ask for me, Ben Snyder, we'll get it taken care of." He gave her his card.

"I appreciate your coming over and helping me out. You may not have found anything but you were definitely a help. Thank you." He smiled as they left the house. Mary Yoder almost curtsied as she turned and stepped off the porch.

Ben turned back to the house to take one more look. He went upstairs first. Across the hall from the stairway was a closed door. He stepped to it and opened it. The hinges squeaked a little as it swung open. Ben's eyes widened as he looked into the room. It looked like a typical fourteen year old boy's room except everything was covered with a deep layer of dust.

As he explored the rest of the second floor he mused at the condition of the bedroom. One would have thought that Sarah Swope would have cleaned everything out, leaving no signs of Fred's existence; not to make a mausoleum out of it.

He never saw the lone footprint in the dust.

Centerville

Chapter 23
Closer to Home and Into the Woods

Fred was restless. Even though he was now familiar with State College it still was too much of a town for him. It was too noisy, it smelled and was simply not where he wanted to live. In some ways it reminded him of prison; noise and smells and all the rest. He had no desire to live in Centerville but still there was a pull, like iron to a magnet that he constantly felt. He needed to be closer to home. But Middlebury was too close as was Port Mifflin. Maybe Beaverton or Zieglerville would be good, if he could find work. They were small farming communities, much like Centerville and not much more than twenty miles away from the village.

He bought local papers and began studying the want ads. Surely there would be someone who needed a mechanic or machinist. He got lucky. A silk mill in Beaverton needed a mechanic. Calling in sick Fred took a day off and drove to the mill to apply for the job. The interviewer never asked if he had ever been arrested. When Fred said that he would have to move from State College the man even suggested a nearby boarding house. He offered Fred the job on the spot and they agreed that Fred would start the following week.

He found a room at the boarding house and felt satisfied with himself. He would be earning more money and would be closer to his old haunts. It was just perfect. Not being one for protocol he nevertheless gave notice to his boss and to his apartment manager in State College. And in no time he was a resident of Beaverton and working at the Penn-Mills Silk and Knitting Mill.

The work was pretty simple for Fred and he soon mastered the intricacies of the knitting machines, which were now his responsibility. It was a hot and noisy place and quite a few pretty girls worked there. That alone was worth the change of scene. But soon certain thoughts and urges began to sneak up on him. They had been coming for months, even before he had been released from prison. But now they were getting stronger.

He was tempted all day and the feelings haunted him at night. He lay sweating in his bed thinking of all those pretty girls and what he would like to do with them. He was especially attracted to the Mennonite girls. They were always well groomed and dressed modestly – which gave him more to imagine. In the morning at the start of the shift every hair was in place and they smelled of Ivory soap. To Fred nothing smelled better than that.

One girl, in particular, attracted his attention. He didn't know her name yet but her dark hair, folded up and pinned neatly under her bonnet was somehow tremendously erotic. She ran a knitting machine and occasionally Fred was required to make some small adjustment or repair to it. When he did so the girl would watch him work, fanning herself in the heat. Though he could see sweat beaded on her forehead she always looked somehow cool. No matter the time of day or the intensity of the work, her clothing were always in place. When he finished the repair she would smile and thank him. Her smile turned her pretty face into a thing of beauty.

He watched her every day. And he knew that he wanted her.

Soon he learned that her name was Mary Weaver. A day or two later he discovered that she was going to a dinner at the local volunteer fire hall. It was a community affair and she had been invited by one of the other girls in the mill. This would be on Thursday evening and the fire hall was close to where Fred lived. He decided to go, and then to follow her home.

When Thursday evening came Fred stationed himself near the fire hall and simply watched. It wasn't

Centerville

long before he saw Mary Weaver and the other girl arrive and enter the building. Though it was open to the public Fred did not enter. He stayed sitting in his car in the shadow of a large maple tree not far from the gathering. He figured that he would have a long wait. And he was right.

Mary had arrived around six and it was shortly after eight that she finally left. Her friend was with her and they walked a few blocks together before Mary Weaver turned on her own path home. Fred slowly followed, keeping a good distance back and even parking once in a while to let her get some distance ahead.

The farm on which she lived was about three miles from the village and she walked in the twilight all the way to her home. This time Fred simply watched from a distance and observed the girl as she meandered down the road and onto the lane leading to the farm house in which she lived. As she approached the house a collie ran out to greet her. It jumped and ran joyfully around the girl all the way to the house.

Fred smiled.

That night he began to make his plan. The silk mill wasn't very far from the fire hall and so Mary Weaver would probably walk home every day. Maybe one day he would offer her a ride, or not.

Fred studied her route. At one point on her path there was a small wood that the road ran through. It was bound on one side by a creek and on the other by fields and the road ran through it for about a quarter mile. A small stream cut through the landscape and steep banks rose on either side of the stream and the road which hugged the bank. Even on sunny days the wood was shrouded in deep shade and was dimly lit. At one point an ancient trail led away from the road and deep into the woods.

Fred soon knew what he needed to do and where he would do it. Now it was only a matter of time.

Centerville

Every day his desire grew stronger. A long week passed until it was Friday. Each passing day brought his plans into sharper detail. And then Fred put his plan into action. He left the mill early and made his way on foot to the woods which he knew Mary would be passing through. He turned to the side path and hid himself behind a copse of elderberry bushes and waited.

About twenty minutes later she came down the road – alone as he expected. As she passed the trail and Fred's hiding place he sprang out behind her and grabbed her around her slender waist. He put his other hand over her mouth as he lifted her off her feet and turned back to the trail leading deep into the woods. Her bonnet flew from her head in the violence of his attack.

She struggled and beat against him as best she could. Fred was surprised at how strong she was as he hissed into her ear to stop struggling and everything would be ok. For a moment she went limp and when she thought that Fred was relaxing she renewed her struggles. But Fred was stronger.

He carried her into the woods and over the damp and spongey earth. The erection that had begun when he hid in the bushes was almost painful in its intensity. He knew that she must feel it herself. But all the while she was kicking at his shins as best she could. She tried twisting in his grasp so that she could attack his head but he held her too strongly.

After about a hundred yards he flung her to the ground with such force that the collision with the earth nearly knocked the wind out of the girl. As she struggled to get up Fred kicked her in the stomach and said, "Stay where you are and you won't get hurt. Just don't move."

In pain Mary Weaver held her stomach with both hands and looked incredulously at Fred. "You," she gasped. "Why is it you? I thought you were such a nice man at work."

"Well, I'm not such a nice man."

Centerville

"Maybe if you were," she paused, hoping, "things could be different."

"I seriously doubt that. I may look stupid but I'm not. You wouldn't go with me. I'm sure you have a nice boyfriend out on the farm. But we've talked enough."

"Are... are you going to kill me?"

"No, Mary," Fred softly lied. "I'm not going to kill you. But I'm going to get what I want."

Her back to the ground she crabbed away from him on her hands and feet. But Fred was fast and in seconds had pinned her to the ground. She began to struggle even harder than before. Fred struck her on the side of her head – a ringing blow. Mary Weaver went limp. Not knowing whether she was faking or not Fred struck her again and he knew she was out.

In frenzy he flung her black apron and flowered pink dress up over her head and tore her plain white panties from her and threw them into the bushes. Dropping his own pants he struggled to enter her body and finally in pure rage and frustration was successful. In mere seconds he wasted himself inside her.

No longer was either of them a virgin. Sated Fred picked up her body and carried it deeper into the woods and finding a likely spot flung the girl to the ground. Not knowing whether she was dead he found a rock and struck her on the head several times until he heard the satisfying crack of her skull fracturing.

He had an immediate erection and finally assuaging his rage he masturbated over her body. Then he pulled her skirt down as well as her apron and left her face up on the path, the dappled sunlight playing on her bloody face.

Fred walked back to his rooming house satisfied with a good day's work.

Centerville

Chapter 245
The Search

When Mary failed to arrive home at the usual time her mother, Martha, as all good mothers do, began to worry. When her husband, Levi came into the kitchen an hour later her worry had deepened into fear. Mary was a good daughter. She always came promptly home or called if she would be late. On Fridays, after supper, Mary corralled the younger children while Martha spent a couple of free hours with the neighborhood lady's guild.

"It's almost six, Levi, and Mary is not home from work. She didn't call either. Something must be wrong."

"I don't think so; maybe she stumbled on the road and sprained an ankle or something. I'll drive out to find her. I'll be right back."

Levi left the house and climbed into his black Pontiac LeMans and started for Beaverton. He drove all the way to the mill and saw nothing of his daughter. The building was locked and dark so he knew that she could not be inside. Not knowing where to look next he slowly cruised the few streets. Finally he decided to return home in hopes that he had somehow missed her along the way.

But she was not there when he arrived back home. She was nearly three hours late by now and Levi himself was getting worried.

"I called all the neighbors," Martha told him. "But none of them have seen her. I even called her friend she works with, Charlene, in town and she said that when she last saw Mary she was walking home from work. I think we should call the sheriff."

"Let's wait a little longer, until dark. If we haven't heard from her by then I'll call." Finally when Mary had not arrived by dark Levi called the sheriff's emergency number. Relaying the information Levi was assured that a deputy would be dispatched immediately.

Centerville

Half an hour later Deputy Bill Martin pulled into the Weaver's driveway. It was dark by then and fireflies were winking in the darkness. Levi Weaver answered the door. Martin took off his hat as he entered the kitchen of the farmhouse.

"What can I do for you folks?"

"Our daughter Mary has not come home from work." As he spoke Levi motioned for the deputy to take a seat at the kitchen table.

As he sat Bill Martin pulled a notebook and pencil from his shirt pocket.

"What's her name?" he asked.

"Mary Louise Weaver."

And so the interview began. The deputy obtained all the important details and description of Mary and her clothing.

"Mr. Weaver, do you have a photograph of your daughter?"

"No sir, we do not. Graven images are not a part of our way of life, so we don't allow photographs either."

"I understand and assumed that but I did have to ask."

"That's all right." Martha Weaver said. All the while through the interview she had sat at the table wringing her hands. "We've told you everything we can."

"I understand that too mam. Unfortunately it's too dark to start a search party now but we'll organize one first thing in the morning. On my way back into town I'll follow her path and use my search light. Maybe..." he trailed off shrugging.

"I'll gather some of my neighbors in the morning and we'll search too." Levi told the deputy.

"I'm sure we'll find her safe and sound with a perfectly reasonable explanation."

"We hope you're right," Levi Weaver said as he and Martha rose from the table. Deputy Martin turned from the couple and walked the short distance to his car.

While he slowly drove to Beaverton along the route Mary would have taken he scanned the roadside and fields with his search light but all he saw were the glowing eyes of deer in the darkness.

When he got back to the sheriff's office he called Sheriff Faulkville to relay the information he had on the missing girl.

"Notify Ben Snyder and the state police," she told him. "Have dispatch call in everyone for a search at six o'clock tomorrow morning. Meet me at the office and we'll go out from there."

Next Bill Martin called his immediate supervisor, Ben Snyder.

"Ben, this is Bill. We've got a missing Mennonite girl. She left the silk mill in Beaverton at three thirty this afternoon and never got home. I was out to speak with her parents and got as much information as I could. The sheriff wants us all here at the office at six o'clock tomorrow morning to set up a search party. The girl's father said he would get his neighbors to help."

"What's her name?"

"Mary Weaver. She's nineteen."

"I don't like the sound of this. She either ran off or was abducted. Nineteen year old Mennonite girls just don't up and go missing without a reason. What was the demeanor of her parents?"

"They were worried, of course. Her mother was kind of strung out, if you know what I mean. He father was level headed but you could tell that he was scared stiff with worry. What with the news getting out that the Swope woman was murdered, I can understand why."

"I hate to think that Bill. I don't want a serial killer on the loose. We had that happen when I was a kid and it scared hell out everyone within twenty miles. Don't say anything about the Swope case to anyone. We don't want to start anything. For all we know she might have run off with her boyfriend."

Centerville

"Roger that. I gotta call the staties. See you in the morning."

As he hung up his phone Ben's thoughts went back to the time some twenty years ago, when Fred Swope had gone on a killing spree. It was a time he would never forget.

'Thank God he's still in jail.' He thought as he stubbed a cigarette out in the ashtray which was filling up. 'I gotta cut back,' he thought.

The next morning as she combed her soft mustache, Eva Faulkville thought, 'I'll bet she's dead. Girls like that just don't go missing. I just know that this isn't going to turn out well. Maybe she got hit by a car and is lying in a ditch somewhere'.

At her office she met with her three deputies and Nard Boyer. Five of them weren't very many but it was better than nothing. While they were discussing the search plans three state police officers arrived to help with the search.

Then she got a call from Levi Weaver.

"Sheriff, I've got seven other men and boys who can help with the search. Where do you want to start and how do you want to proceed?"

'He sounds awfully calm,' she thought.

"We'll meet at the silk mill and then make a decision. Be there within half an hour."

"Ok, men," she said. "Let's go. We're going to the silk mill in Beaverton. That's where she was last seen. The girl's family had raised a team of eight, so that should be enough to start. Let's go!"

The three car caravan pulled out onto the street in a column. It was only seven miles to Beaverton. Fifteen minutes later they were gathered in the parking lot of the silk mill with Levi Weaver and his searchers. Somehow the mill's manager had received word as he was there to meet the sheriff, as were a few curious neighbors.

"Ok gather round," Sheriff Faulkville shouted.

389

Centerville

"A few ground rules here. We're going to gather into two groups. In each group will be a state police officer, a couple of deputies and four of you civilians. We'll start at opposite ends of the road leading from the mill to the Weaver home. We'll meet in the middle.

"The person we are looking for is Mary Louise Weaver. She is nineteen and was last seen walking down that road." She pointed. "She was wearing a blue blouse with a pink flowered dress and a black apron. She has dark hair and was wearing a white bonnet.

"If you find anything, anything at all, do not touch it! I repeat, do not touch. We'll photograph it, just in case, and properly handle it as evidence. This is just a precaution. We aren't assuming that a crime has been committed. There could be any number of reasons why Miss Weaver is missing but because we do not know what has happened to her we will take precautions and do this right. Civilians; please obey the officers and your team lead. I will lead one team and Deputy Snyder," she pointed to Ben, "will lead the other. Remember, watch where you step, and keep your eyes and ears open."

She then divided the group into two teams. She assigned Ben's team to search from the mill while her team would start at the Weaver property.

As the sheriff's team drove off Ben said, "All right. Remember what Sheriff Faulkville said. Eyes and ears open and pay attention to what you see. I want two groups of four to spread out on either side of the road. Where the land is open and you can see your feet, in other words short grass, spread apart a reasonable distance. Where it gets weedy then close in. If necessary we will make multiple passes over large open areas. Pay special attention to the areas closest to the road. She could have been hit and thrown into the weeds or a ditch. But I also want to cover as much ground as we can. It's only three miles to the Weavers, so we only have about a mile and half to cover. Now let's get going."

Centerville

He split them into two groups and they took their positions on either side of the road and began the search. The temperature rose as the sun climbed higher into the sky. The fields on either side of the road were open for two to three hundred yards so the men were spread out in a wide pattern. But as the terrain changed they came closer together. Moving slowly they took in the ground, pausing once in a while to examine a tuft of weeds or a brightly colored patch of wild flowers.

After an hour and rounding a curve Ben could see the fields ending and woods begin. He called a rest break and gathered the men around. "Do any of you know those woods?"

One man nodded, "I hunt squirrel in it."

"What can we expect?"

"Well," the man took off his hat and mopped his bald head with a handkerchief. "On this side of the road," he indicated to the left side where they were gathered. "Is a little run. Not much water now but it has steep banks that goes about four foot down. Then the hill goes up pretty steep and turns into a clift. On the far side of the road the bank goes up pretty good too. And about fifty yards in on the other side there's an old tractor path that goes up back of the woods to some fields. Squirrel huntin's pretty good back there."

"How steep are the cliffs?"

"Well, I wouldn't climb 'em. They're pretty steep."

"Can we get on top?"

"It'll be a mighty hike. Best bet would be to get in from the other side of the woods. That side is farmed and you could walk in from the fields on top of the ridge."

"Ok, we'll decide that when we get there. But I think it's unlikely that a girl would try to climb those cliffs. Let's get back to work and when we get to the woods we'll stop and regroup. Back at it."

After their brief rest the sun seemed even hotter as the men once again spread out into the fields and fruitlessly continued their search. The woods loomed closer and most of the men thought about the coolness of the air and all that shade.

Centerville

Chapter 25
Searches' End

An hour later they paused again at the edge of the woods. Ben walked ahead in to the shaded woods and surveyed the surroundings. The area was flat for a ways into the woods but they would have to keep close. Then he could see the cliffs rise on either side. He returned to the group of men.

"Ok, here's what we'll do. It looks like it is relatively flat for the first fifty yards on the right side. But it's only half that on the left. You can see undergrowth going back from the road and looks kind of thick. Keep close to each other. If you have trouble seeing your feet, because of the scrub then get closer together. Move slowly and carefully." Ben dropped the stub if the cigarette he was smoking and ground it out on the side of the road.

Again the men moved out but this time keeping almost within arm's length. The stream on Ben's side made walking difficult and more than once he had to watch his footing carefully. It wasn't long before he and his group had to retreat to the road as the land became impassible.

The going for the other group was a bit easier, there was underbrush but it wasn't as thick. In fact they had moved far ahead of Ben's team. As they approached, Ben could see a kind of widening of the road just in front of the other team. This, he assumed, must be the old tractor path that had been mentioned.

"Let's get up there to help them. That tractor path may be worth investigating."

They moved ahead and arrived as the others were spreading out down the path. Almost immediately the state police officer in that team shouted, "Halt!"

Centerville

Ben moved quickly to the man's side. The officer simply pointed. There lying beneath the thicket was a patch of white. Kneeling Ben could see that it was a white cloth bonnet; the very kind that a Mennonite woman might wear.

"Nard, get over here." Ben shouted. "Everyone else, get back to the road." He turned to the officer, "But not you."

Nard quickly arrived.

"Photograph that," Ben pointed, "and bag it for evidence."

Nard quickly got out his camera and took a number of photographs of the bonnet from various angles. Then he got a paper bag, wrote the time, date and location on it then carefully put the bonnet into it.

"Nard, stay here unless I call you. Woody," he waved at his other deputy, "Come over here."

Deputy Benfer walked to where Ben and the others were standing. "We just found a bonnet like the girl was wearing. I want you to keep those men on the road and out of the way. Got it?"

Woody nodded and went back to the road.

Turning to the state police officer he said, "Corporal, come with me. You know the drill."

The two men carefully walked the side of the path in order not to disturb any possible evidence. It wasn't long before they could see signs of a struggle. The earth was scuffed. Ben called Nard to photograph the area as he and the statie moved on. Deeper down the path they saw a clear footprint in the soft earth. They marked the spot and continued deeper into the woods along the path.

When Ben saw a bright patch of blue and pink he stopped and turned to the other. "This doesn't look good."

They carefully approached the splash of color in the dark green of the weeds. There, lying on her back, eyes open, was Mary Weaver. Flies crawled over her bloody face. Her skirt pulled demurely to her ankles.

394

Centerville

"You might as well use your walkie-talkie to call the sheriff's group. We'll need an ambulance and the coroner.

"Nard," he shouted. "Meet me." To the trooper he said "I'm going back to the footprint. I think it's vital evidence now. Take a look around."

He carefully hurried back to the footprint just as Nard arrived. Gesturing to the footprint he said, "Take pictures and if you have plaster, make a cast. If not protect it."

"You know me, Ben. I have what I need to make a cast in my pack. I'll get right on it."

Ben walked back to the road. "Woody," he quietly said, "We found the body of the girl. There's good evidence up the path, so I want you to do crowd control. Keep these men here, no matter what. When her father gets here you have to restrain him. He doesn't need to see her and I don't want anyone on the path except the sheriff and Coroner Parker when he gets here. You and the other officers keep everyone out. Got it?"

"Yes sir! Don't worry."

Already Ben could hear an approaching car from the other end of the woods. He waited and soon saw the sheriff's car followed by a state police cruiser and a black Pontiac. Sheriff Faulkville got from her car and came straight to Ben.

"What do you have?"

"We found the girl. We also found at least one footprint, definitely a big man's by its size. We also found her bonnet. The body's about a hundred yards down this path. Nard's making a cast of the footprint and the corporal is watching the body."

"Let's go," she said.

As they started down the path they could hear the agonized cry of Levi Weaver as he heard the news. Looking back they could see a scuffle as the officers held the grief stricken man back.

The sheriff shook her head, "That's what I hate about this job."

They soon reached Nard who was guarding his now plaster covered footprint. He waved them on. Not long after that they approached the body of the girl.

"Jesus Christ, what a waste," the sheriff swore. It was something she rarely did. "Ben you had better find the bastard that did this."

The state police officer approached and said, "I found what looks like her underwear laying over there," he pointed. "And what looks like a bloody rock over there." He pointed to a different place.

Ben shook his head. "Nard will be busy. I'm going back to get him. I hope the coroner gets here soon." He turned back down the trail to Nard. When he arrived he asked, "Is your cast ready yet? I have more evidence to be photographed and gathered."

"Can you give me another five minutes?"

"You go. I'll watch the print. The statie will show you what he found and you can photograph the body. I won't touch your print till you get back."

Nard gathered his camera and pack and headed down the path. Ben squatted and looked at the nearly hardened plaster. Nard's initials, the date and time were neatly etched into the surface. 'He misses nothing! This may be the most important clue we can find.' He thought.

A few minutes later Ben could hear the siren of the ambulance. He didn't think the siren was necessary but at least he knew the ambulance was almost here. He would let the coroner go back to the body but nobody else until he had secured the scene. There may be other evidence that he didn't want disturbed, especially the plaster cast.

After about five minutes the coroner carefully came down the path. "What have you got Ben?"

Ben pointed. "There's a dead girl down the path. Nard's there taking photos and gathering evidence.

Centerville

There's also the sheriff and a state policeman. It looks like the girl was murdered; struck in the head."

"I assume it's the missing Mennonite girl."

Ben nodded, "Unfortunately it is."

"Do you think it's connected to the Swope woman?"

"I don't think so. The only similarity as of now is that they were both female."

Coroner Parker turned to go. "When will you let the ambulance crew through?"

"As soon as I've secured all the evidence. I got a footprint right here that may be vital. Nard would kill me if I let anything happen to it."

Roy Parker carefully continued down the path and Ben was left alone with his thoughts. He now had two investigations on his hands. Two murders; he'd seen only two others since he joined the force. After his initial excitement his calming mind told him that it could be very well a jealous boyfriend. He didn't want to jump to conclusions.

Soon Nard came back down the path and approached Ben. "How's my print?"

"Should be perfect. What did you get back there?"

"Mostly photos," Nard replied. "I did bag her panties and the rock definitely looks like it has dried blood on it. I'll know for sure when I get it back to my lab but I'd bet my left foot on it." He stooped and gently pried the plaster cast from the earth and turned it over. Brushing off the dirt he revealed a perfect copy of the sole of a man's left boot.

"They don't get much better than that." He proudly said. "Look at that. It's a Vibram soled boot, all right. And look there." He pointed at one of the lobes in the sole's waffle pattern. "There's a dead giveaway if we ever find the actual boot. That lobe is broken clean off. We locate the man wearing the boot and we'll have the man that did this. This is good stuff." He enthused.

Centerville

"I have all I can get. I'm heading back to the road. I'll put all this stuff into the sheriff's cruiser.

"Send the ambulance crew in with a stretcher and tell them to keep to the side of the path. Insist on a stretcher. I don't want wheel and drag marks. There may be more prints to find." Ben thought he might be overly cautious but better safe than sorry. He made his way back down the path to where the growing crowd was gathered about the body of Mary Weaver. As he arrived Coroner Parker stood up.

"Blunt force trauma. And she was raped. It looks like there's also traces of semen on her pubes. I'll know more when I get her back to the morgue. My guess is that he hit her with a rock at least twice."

A few minutes later the ambulance crew came carrying a litter and a body bag. They efficiently put the girl into the bag and onto the litter. Sheriff Faulkville turned to Ben, "Once we're all out of here take another good hard look. Just to be sure. I'll have someone get your car back here for you." She turned away and in a few seconds Ben was alone.

He covered the area thoroughly but there was no more evidence that he could find. Unfortunately the ground had already been too scuffed by all those who had been on the scene. Still he lingered, thinking of the girl; all of life before her and so brutally murdered. He vowed that he would catch the man who had done this, be it a boyfriend or a fiend from hell. Justice would be served. He would see to it.

Centerville

Chapter 26
Investigations

Later that afternoon Ben visited Coroner Parker at the morgue. 'I'm getting too familiar with this place,' he thought.

Roy Parker brought him up to date.

"You can see there," he pointed to the girls left temple. "She was struck at least twice. The attacker probably used a rock. I hear that Nard has a bloody rock. I'd like to see it."

"I'll talk to Nard and have him bring it over."

Next Parker pointed to her now cleanly washed face. "You can see bruises here where he hit her with his fist. Also he probably hit her more than once."

"His fist?"

"Yes," the coroner nodded. "If he had used his open hand the bruise would be larger. If he had used a rock the skin would be broken, there would be cuts and abrasions, also bones would be chipped or broken"

He then moved down her body and put his hand over her stomach. "Couple of things here. He kicked her pretty hard, you can tell by more bruising on her stomach. And there is dried semen on her pubic hair. There was also semen in her vagina. My guess is that he raped her and probably masturbated over her. Sick bastard."

"What was the time of death?"

"I'd say it was four, four thirty yesterday afternoon. Not much later."

"Anything else you can tell me?"

"Only that she was a virgin before this happened."

Ben shook his head and cursed under his breath. "Let me know if you find anything else." He turned and left.

Centerville

On Sunday he drove to Beaverton and the silk mill to search the parking lot. Maybe there would be something there that could be useful. He had no such luck. He drove back down the road to the woods. Parking his personal vehicle he walked into the woods. He could immediately see that the ground was trampled and that there would be no more evidence to be found. Either family or gawkers – or both had done a number on the area. His time was wasted. Disgusted by the day he drove back through Beaverton on his way home. As he passed he didn't notice Fred Swope walking down the sidewalk in front of the A&P grocery store.

The next day he drove back to Beaverton to interview the silk mill manager. Maybe he could shed some light on Mary Weaver. As he entered the building Fred Swope saw him in his uniform and immediately ducked into a maintenance closet. He didn't recognize Ben – this time.

The manager, Jim Fleming, led Ben into his office and offered the deputy a seat. "I can guess why you are here. You want to know about poor Mary."

Ben nodded, "Yes, I *would* like to ask a few questions."

"Go ahead," Fleming said as he filled his pipe. "I'll tell you as much as I can."

"What kind of worker was she? Did she have many friends here in the mill?"

Fleming thought as he put a match to his pipe and drew the flame into the bowl. When the tobacco was smoldering properly he took a puff and said. "She was one of the best I had. She was always on time and worked her full shift. She rarely called in sick. I don't think she had many friends, though I do know she was friends with one girl, Charlene Snook. She's not a Mennonite like Mary but they seemed to be good friends. They often took lunch together. In fact I'm giving her the afternoon off to attend Mary's funeral."

Centerville

"How about boyfriends?"

"None that I'm aware of. She kept pretty much to herself. She was a good worker."

"Did any of the men in the mill show any interest?"

"There aren't too many men, Fred, Bob and Paul. They don't have time to socialize with the girls and they're all at least twice her age."

'So much for that idea.' Ben thought. He decided that he wouldn't get anything more out of the manager so he asked to speak with Charlene Snook.

"I'll have her come in to the office," Fleming said.

A few minutes later Charlene Snook entered the office. Been signaled her to a chair. She sat, fidgeting, showing that the was nervous.

"Thank you for agreeing to talk with me. I won't keep you long and you have nothing to worry about. I just want to ask you a few questions. Are you OK with that?" Ben asked.

The girl visibly relaxed and nodded.

"Mr. Fleming told me that you were friends with Mary Weaver."

The girl shook her head.

"*Were* you friends with her?"

"Yes, we were good friends. I even went to her place a couple of times. Last week we went together to a dinner at the fire hall."

"Did she drive a car?"

"In bad weather her father would drive her to work but most of the time she walked. I have a car and more than once offered to take her home but she always said that she preferred to walk."

"How about boyfriends? Did she go with anybody?"

"No," Charlene shook her head, "She didn't have a boyfriend. I think she was sweet on a Mennonite neighbor but she rarely mentioned even him."

"How about the men in the mill? Did any of them pay special attention to her?"

She shook her head. "*No!*" she exclaimed. "They're old enough to be her father."

Ben smiled briefly then he asked "Are you going to her funeral this afternoon?"

"Yes, I'm going."

"Thank you. I don't think I have anything else but you have been very helpful" Ben said. "I'm sorry for the loss of your friend. You can go back to work."

Ben left the mill and returned to his office. He would be attending the funeral in the afternoon; to watch for anyone who looked suspicious. He returned to his office and added a few notes to his case file and then went to talk with Sheriff Faulkville.

As he sat she asked, "What's up Ben?"

He shook his head. "There's nothing there. No boyfriend that I'm aware of. She was a good worker and had one friend at the mill. I'm going to her funeral this afternoon. Maybe I'll be able to sniff up something there."

"It's still early."

"Yeah, I guess. I went back to the scene but it looks like everyone in the county was there as well. The ground was totally trampled. Any trace of evidence is totally gone. I just don't like the looks of it. The only real clue we have is that plaster footprint. The rocky ground certainly won't hold footprints or the rocks fingerprints. It may not even have been anybody local, a salesman passing by. It could have been a crime of opportunity."

The sheriff shook her head, "It was someone local, all right. I'll bet on it. How many passersby would be on that road on a Friday afternoon? It had to be someone who knew the area. I'd look for a spurned boyfriend or maybe a horny old man."

Centerville

"You're probably right. There are some men who work at the mill. They tell me that they are old enough to be her father. Maybe I'll take a look at them. I don't know; for some reason this one bothers me more than it should. Things like this aren't supposed to happen."

"No, they're not." Sheriff Faulkville shook her head. "No, they're not - but they do."

At two o'clock that afternoon Ben was among the large crowd of mostly Mennonites, crammed into a small hot country church. Many of the women were fanning themselves with the paper fans found in the pews. The men just sweated in their dark clothing. The solemn service was relatively brief with preaching, scripture reading, prayer and a hymn or two. Afterwards they processed to the cemetery for the graveside service. It was there that Ben paid especial attention to those attending and, more importantly, to those who kept to the edges.

Though he watched and looked carefully he could see nothing out of the ordinary. He remained at the cemetery after the graveside service and watched everyone leave. No one lingered, no one stood out. Unusually depressed he went home.

The next morning as he arrived at the office he was met by the sheriff who waved him into her office.

"Have you seen this?" she pointed to the local newspaper's front page that was lying on her desk. There clearly printed in bold text, though a secondary front page story was the headline, '**Murder Evidence Includes Clear Footprint**'.

"Oh shit," he said. "How did that get out?"

"That is the question but it's probably not too hard to answer. Yes, it was our secret weapon but too many people either saw the plaster cast or heard talk of it last Saturday, so there should be no surprise."

Ben shook his head, "No, I guess not but I never expected to see this in the paper. If the killer sees this

403

he'll ditch the boots as fast as he can. We can't search all the trash bins in the county and if we could we'd never link them back."

"Don't waste too much time worrying about it. It may be a clear print but there are thousands of boots like that out there. We can't search all the people's feet either. We just have to live with it and move on."

Ben nodded and headed for his desk.

Centerville

Chapter 27
The Boot

Fred Swope did, indeed, see the headline. He did not regularly read the papers even though the rooming house where he lived always had the current edition of the **Daily Post** on the coffee table in the living room. He was planning on watching television until it was time to eat but the headline caught his eye. He picked up the paper and read.

> *The Daily Post has learned that there was a significant clue found at the scene of the murdered Mennonite girl, Mary Weaver. Apparently, we are told, a single footprint was found in the soft earth near the body. It is of a Vibram soled boot. We learned that the print was distinctive in that there was a significant cut into the rubber cleats, damaging one of them in a manner that it would be recognized if seen again.*

Fred stopped at that point and looked down at his boots. He turned first the right and then the left, looking at the soles. Sure enough the left sole was damaged. One of the lobes was clearly broken off. He immediately went to his room and took the boots off and turned both sole up. The damage to the left sole was clear and unmistakable. Fred knew that if any suspicion led to him, any at all, and they found the boot, it would be the end. It would be proof positive that he was guilty of the murder of Mary Weaver.

He put on a pair of shoes and wrapped the boots in the paper bag that lined the waste basket. Leaving the house he looked for a safe place to dump the boots. He threw the bag onto the front seat of his car and drove aimlessly around looking for a safe and permanent place. He happened by the rear of the A&P grocery store which was lined with dumpsters. He saw no one as he put the bag into one of the dumpsters, one that was nearly full. He drove away satisfied that the boot would never be discovered, or linked to him. Emboldened he returned to the rooming house and a supper of ham and string beans.

After supper he realized that he needed footwear for work. His casual "good" shoes would not do in the rough and dirty work at the mill. They would be destroyed in a day. He needed boots but couldn't buy them locally. What if someone remembered selling work boots the same day the newspaper had an article about the footprint found at the murder scene. He ended up driving all the way to Lewistown. There he found an Army and Navy store and bought a good pair of slightly used combat boots. They fit well and looked properly worn. Nobody would ever know. Arriving back at the rooming house at nearly nine pm he went to bed satisfied.

What Fred didn't know was that at the time he was disposing of the boots a local tramp was resting in the shade of a line of shrubs and trees across a narrow alley only a few feet from the rear of the A&P store. He watched Fred as he got out of his car and threw the bag into the dumpster. After the car drove off the man rummaged through the trash in the dumpster and quickly found the bag with the boots inside. Looking inside the bag he liked what he saw.

Old Jack, for that is what he was called ambled back to his shaded spot and looked closely at the boots. Then he removed his own much worn and tattered shoes and tried on the boots. They fit like gloves for his feet. Very satisfied he put his own shoes into the bag and once again walked to the dumpster. This time he threw the bag of shoes into it. There, resting on top of the rubbish, he saw a watermelon that didn't look too badly bruised. Fishing it out he wiped it on his shirt and satisfied he walked away heading for the abandoned farmhouse on the edge of town, where he stayed, to enjoy his new boots and the watermelon for his supper.

Centerville

The next day Old Jack went on his rounds, looking for odd jobs or handouts. His route took him all over the small town. Not far from the silk mill he crossed a patch of damp ground on the infield of a makeshift baseball diamond. Local boys played ball here all summer long. Finally in the early afternoon, he found a task of clearing some brush from a back yard fencerow that earned him five dollars. When he was finished and was paid he left feeling very satisfied. He thought he might go fishing later in the afternoon. After all he had nothing better to do.

Jimmy Struthers was bored. It was a lazy hot July morning and he had nothing to do. But maybe he could round up enough guys to have a ball game. They hadn't played in a few days and he thought that his friends were just as bored as he was. So he set out on his bicycle to see who he could rustle up. It wasn't long before he managed to meet up with a few friends and they all headed home for equipment and then to the field.

Jimmy got there first. As he put his bat, ball and glove down near home plate he noticed a footprint in the now dry earth. At first he didn't think much of it but then as he looked closer he saw that it looked something like the boot print described in the newspaper. He didn't read the papers, of course, but had heard his dad describing it to his mother and murder was always a juicy topic that all of the kids followed.

And he wasn't alone. He showed the print to Joe Davis when he arrived and he agreed that it looked like the one in the paper, especially the Vibram pattern and the broken lug.

"I think we better call the cops. That's what I think," Said Joe.

By then others had arrived and they all gathered around the site to see what was going on. Calls of "what is it?" and "What are they looking at?" filled the air as the boys jostled for position.

407

"Don't let anybody disturb the evidence," said Jimmy. "I'll go over to the store and call the sheriff." He raced away on his bike while the rest of the boys crowded around.

"Keep back!" shouted Joe, taking charge of the situation. "Just wait 'till the cops get here.

"Think they'll make a cast of it?" someone asked.

"Probably," another replied.

"Just think, the killer walked right through our ball field!" someone else chimed in. and the chatter went on, the baseball game completely forgotten.

Meanwhile Jimmy Struthers pedaled up to the store and leapt for the payphone. Pulling the receiver to his ear he dialed the operator. When he heard the familiar "Operator" he shouted, "Please connect me to the sheriff's office. We found evidence of the murder!"

"Calm down, young man," the operator replied.

Jimmy took a breath and said as calmly as he could, "I found a footprint in the ground at my ball field that looks just like the footprint found at the murder scene a couple of days ago and I need to tell the sheriff. I don't have any money."

"Ok. I'll connect you."

Moments later a voice said, "Sheriff's office. How may I help you?"

"My name is Jimmy Struthers and I'm calling from Beaverton. I was at the ball field here and found a footprint in the ground that looks exactly like the one described in the paper. *The one that the murderer left at the scene of the crime.* We think someone should come and take a look at it."

"Ok, who is we? You said I then you said we, which one is it?"

"I'm the one that found it," Jimmy said in exasperation, "But there were a bunch of guys who came to play ball. We decided that you should come and look at it. It has the right pattern and there is a cut in it just like the paper said."

"All right, where is it located? We'll send someone over."

Jimmy described the location of the ball field, which was near the silk mill, and hung up the phone. Mounting his bike he returned to the field.

Mariam Yoder, the sheriff's secretary and receptionist ended the call and immediately dialed Ben Snyder's office. When he answered she said, "Ben, it's probably nothing but a bunch of boys found a footprint that they say looks like the one described in the newspaper."

Ben nodded and asked, "How long ago?"

"They just now called. They're over in Beaverton at the ball field near the silk mill."

"There may be something to it then. I'll head right over. Call Nard and have him meet me at my car with his casting kit."

'At last,' he thought. 'We might have something to go on. There may be more prints leading towards the mill, or the back road or who knows. And then – it may be nothing.'

Minutes later he met Nard Boyer at his car. They climbed in and headed for Beaverton. The ride only took fifteen minutes but to the waiting boys it seemed to be hours. As they pulled up one of the boys ran to Ben's cruiser.

Ben and Nard got from the car as Jimmy Struthers approached, running. Ben flicked his cigarette away as the boy skidded to a stop. Ben asked, "Who are you?"

"I'm Jimmy Struthers. I'm the one who found the boot print."

When Ben heard the name Jimmy his mind heard "Jimmy Harris" and his memory immediately leapt back twenty years to the day he found Jimmy Harris' body in the field by the lime kiln in Centerville. For a brief horrifying moment his memory superimposed Jimmy Harris' face over that of the boy's standing in front of him. And then in an instant it was gone.

Ben shook his head, "Show us what you found." Then he and Nard followed the boy across the lot to the group of boys clustered around a spot on the earth. They moved away as the deputy approached.

"Right there it is," Jimmy pointed.

Ben knelt by the boot print and could immediately see that it was very similar to the one in the woods. Nard knelt with him and gingerly brushed the print with a soft brush. As he did so the imprint became clearer.

"Look at that," Nard pointed. "See where the lobe is cut off? It's the same boot, all right. Let me get a picture of it." He opened his ever present pack and removed the Nikon that he had been using for years. He took photographs from all sides and angles of the print.

"Do you think we need a cast?" he asked.

Ben thought for a few seconds and replied. "Yes, I think so. If it is a perfect match we will know that it is definitely someone local. If it doesn't match – well..."

Nard gathered his plaster and other materials and started in. First he took cardboard strips and formed a dam around the print. The boys watched, fascinated. Next Nard mixed plaster and water in a plastic tub until the plaster was thick as cream. Then he poured it over the print until it almost filled the cardboard dam. The boys crowded close, forming a circle around Nard.

"You boys spread out. Tell you what. Keep your eyes peeled and see if you can find any more prints. They might lead somewhere." The single print pointed towards the southwest, away from the silk mill, and the boys immediately spread out and began to search the ground.

"That ought to keep them away and busy," Ben grunted.

Centerville

It wasn't more than a few minutes before he heard a cry of "over here" and saw one of the boys waving. "Give me your brush and I'll take a look." Nard handed him the soft bristled brush and Ben waked to the boy. Sure enough, there was another print in the earth but Ben could immediately see that it was the wrong foot. This was of a right foot and the print found at the murder site and here in the field, had been of a left foot.

He shook his head, "Nice try but it's the wrong foot. It needs to be the left foot. But keep looking that way." He pointed in the direction of travel that the two prints made, southwest towards a small copse of trees. The boy turned and was followed by most of the others. Jimmy Struthers followed Ben back to where Nard knelt by the rapidly setting cast.

"How did you find the print?" Ben turned to the boy and asked.

"I don't know. I was just waiting for the rest of the guys to get here and was just looking down, I guess."

"Well you did an excellent job not only recognizing it but in calling it in and keeping the other boys from damaging it. Good job." He shook Jimmy's hand which filled the boy with pride. "Now if we can only find the man wearing the boot that made the print."

Nard looked up and said, "It's ready." He carefully lifted the plaster cast from the footprint and flipped it over. He retrieved his brush from Ben who was still holding it and brushed the few patches of dirt clinging to the cast.

"It's a perfect match. Couldn't be better. Yeah, now let's find the feet that are inside the boots and we got our man."

Meanwhile Old Jack was tromping all over the town with his new boots.

Chapter 28
These Boots Are Made For Walking

Ben and Nard returned to the sheriff's office where Ben showed Sheriff Faulkville the new print. "It's a perfect match to the first one. I was thinking that maybe we should release this information, maybe even one of Nard's photos, to the paper. Maybe it will flush out our man."

Eva Faulkville thought for a moment and nodding said, "That might work. The print is no secret so we might as well build on it. But I think you should call the paper and have them come here to interview us and take their own photos of both the plaster casts. We might as well get some good publicity on this. Yes, call the paper and invite them over."

Ben returned to his office and lifted the handset of his phone. Dialing the **Daily Post** he considered what he would say. When the paper's receptionist answered Ben asked for the reporter who had written the original article about the footprint.

"Wilheits," came the one-word introduction into Ben's ear.

Confused Ben said, "Is this the reporter who wrote the article about the footprint?"

"Yeah, that's me, Jason Wilheits."

"I'm detective deputy Ben Snyder of the sheriff's office. Would you be interested in seeing another cast of the same boot print we found at a different place? We can also give you more information about the investigation."

Wilheits who had his feet up on his desk sat bolt upright and grabbed a pencil. "I'm sorry; would you repeat your name?" Ben did so as the reporter began to take notes.

Centerville

"What did you find and where and when did you find it"

"We found it today but if you want to see it you can come over to our office. I'll show it to you personally and you can photograph it if you wish."

"I'll be there in half an hour." Jason Wilheits said and hung up the phone.

At the same time Old Jack was back at the A&P to look through the dumpsters. He did this regularly and often times found good fruit like apples and oranges. He had found a couple of potatoes the other day as well as that watermelon. When he was lucky he could subsidize this diet with food he could purchase when he picked up a few dollars from his odd jobs. Today he was lucky. He found two oranges, an open bag of carrots, a small damaged block of cheese and a loaf of bread that had been torn open. He stuffed the oranges and carrots into the copious pockets of his coat which he wore even on the hottest of days and carried the bread. He headed for what he called his house.

Old Jack's place was an abandoned farm house on the edge of town. The windows were broken out and the doors were mostly gone but he had created an almost cozy place to sleep in an inner room, away from the drafts. It must have been a pantry at one time because there were shelves still in place in the small room and the door actually closed. Jack had an old kerosene lantern and had cobbled together a small cook stove from bricks, cinder blocks and a sheet of steel that he had scavenged from behind a nearby factory. Using some old chimney pipes he had salvaged from the local dump he had made an effective chimney that he vented up through a hole in the ceiling. It wasn't much but he called it home.

After stashing his food he continued on his rounds. He was a regular around town and some people even nodded to him in the streets. But none of them would shake his hand or touch him. They kept their distance and some swore they could smell him coming. But he was considered harmless by everybody. The younger boys would talk with him or tease him but even they knew that he was harmless.

Old Jack's biggest problem in life was finding alcohol. He liked a drink now and again, mostly now and was always looking for whiskey. The nearest State Store was miles away, so he depended on the kindness of local bar owners who might give him a sip out the back door. None of them would allow him to actually enter their establishments but would provide him a little whiskey, sometimes as much as a pint, for doing odd jobs outside their joints, like hauling trash, doing a little painting or the like. Today Jack was looking for that kind of work. So he and his boots walked all over Beaverton.

He knocked on the back door of Rick & Rachel's Bar and Grill. Rachel opened the back kitchen door.

"Do you have anything I can do today?" Old Jack asked.

Rachel, who was always a soft touch, thought for a second and said, "I have a bunch of empty beer kegs over there." She pointed to a number of aluminum kegs that were lying scattered nearby. "The distributer will be over later today to collect them and leave full ones. He won't want to run all over the place to gather the empties. So if you stack them up real nice and neat I'll give you a sandwich and a beer."

Jack immediately set to work and in a few minutes he had accomplished the task. Not long after that Rachel returned with a ham and cheese sandwich in a plastic bag and an unopened can of Budweiser. She nodded towards the stack of kegs and smiled. "Good job, Jack, thanks. Here's your reward."

The old man nodded in thanks and walked off with the rest of his supper. He went back to his room and feasted. It wasn't many days that he was able to eat this well.

Centerville

It only took Jason Wilheits twenty minutes to arrive at Ben's office. The receptionist showed him in as Ben rose from his desk.

"Jason Wilheits?" he asked.

The reporter nodded, "Are you Detective Snyder? What have got for me?"

"Take a look." Ben gestured to the table along the wall that had the two plaster casts on it. The reporter walked to the table and looked long and hard at the casts.

"How can you tell them apart?"

Carefully Ben turned them over to reveal the top sides of the casts. Each had a date and time that Nard had written in the wet plaster with a stick along with his initials so that they could be positively identified.

"This one," Ben pointed, "is the one we took at the murder scene. This other one we made this morning in Beaverton at a makeshift ball field that the kids use. It's near the Penn-Mills silk mill." He turned them back over to reveal the Vibram prints. "As you can see here," he pointed to the damaged lug, "both prints have the exact same damage to the sole of the boot in the exact same place. There is no doubt in our minds that these two prints were made by the same boot. We find the boot, we find the person wearing the boot, we find the killer."

"That easy?" Wilheits asked. "If we print this don't you think the killer will see the article and get rid of the boots?"

"That's a possibility," Ben said, "But it may also flush him out if he goes somewhere to buy a new pair of boots."

"I suppose so. Mind of I take a couple of pictures?" the reporter asked as he removed his camera from its bag. For the next few minutes he took photos of Ben pointing to the damage, of the casts side by side and of the individual casts. Afterwards he interviewed Ben.

"When and where did you find the second footprint?"

"We got a phone call this morning from a boy who found it at their ball field in Beaverton; out near the silk mill. We went right over and saw that it did look like the same print so we made the cast. After that we decided to call you because we thought you might like to print it I your paper."

After a few more questions the reporter left with the assurance that the article would be in the morning's paper.

And it was.

The next afternoon as Fred was sitting down to his supper his landlady chattered on about a number of topics. Fred barely listened to her. She spouted the same trivial news every day at mealtime.

"And then did you see what was in the paper? Why the killer must still be around here somewhere. They found his boot print near the mill, in a ball field, and the sheriff is sure it's the same boot. Why they even had pictures of it in the paper. Front page, no less, why…"

Fred stopped listening and tried to finish his meal as quickly as possible without appearing to rush. When he finished he went to the living room and found the paper in its usual place on the coffee table. There on the front page was a photo of Ben Snyder pointing to the damaged Vibram lug in both casts. The caption read, *"Deputy Ben Snyder points to the identical damage in both prints. More photos page 8."*

Almost instantly Fred wondered whether there could be any possibility that this was the same Ben Snyder he had grown up with. He quickly turned to page three and saw the photo of Ben holding the plaster casts, one in each hand. Fred's blood ran cold as he recognized his former boyhood friend. 'God,' he thought, 'that's all I need to have him looking for me.'

He quickly scanned the article but learned nothing that he felt was important. He went to the front porch and sat on the swing to think. The afternoon heat

Centerville

was oppressive and a thunder storm was building in the west. Fred thought he had gotten rid of the boots but someone had found them. That someone had probably seen him drive up to the dumpster and ditch the boots. But Fred had seen no one when he had been there. There had been no cars or kids. And whoever had seen him throw them away had dug them back out of the bin and kept them, wearing them around town. Fred believed there was nothing wrong with that; except the person who had found the boots had probably seen him throw them away. Someone knew what he looked like and what kind of car he drove.

'What kind of person would dig through a dumpster like that?' he asked himself. There was only one person that he knew of. Yes, by now even Fred knew who Old Jack was and only Fred knew that Old Jack was wearing his old boots and that Old Jack was the only person who could identify Fred.

Fred knew what he had to do. Old Jack's days were numbered.

Centerville

Chapter 29
Old Jack Speaks

The next morning Old Jack ambled down the sidewalk near the center of town. The day was bright and clear. A thunder storm had washed everything clean overnight. Even Jack had a spring in his step this day. As he passed the barber shop he saw a newspaper on the bench by the front door. Jack didn't normally read the newspapers, or much else, but as he passed one word caught his attention. One word in the headline. That word – "**Boot**"

Old Jack turned and slowly and picked up the paper and walked around the corner of the building to rest in the shade. There he read the entire article and then read it again. Finally he looked at his left boot, knowing what he was going to find. Sure enough there was damage to the tread that was exactly like the photos in the paper. "Holy fuck," he muttered. "I don't need this shit." He decided to get rid of the boots but then thought of how good they fit and decided, instead, to call the sheriff. They wouldn't arrest him for having the boots. He never thought that they might take them from him.

There was a pay phone at the gas station down the street so Jack made his way down the alley, peering into various trash cans as he traveled. Some habits just die hard. When he reached the gas station he fumbled through his many pockets and came up with a dime. He fed the telephone and dialed 0.

When the operator answered Old Jack said, "Get me the sheriff's office please."

"One moment" the female voice said.

Jack waited while the phone rang at the other end. Finally a woman answered, "Sheriff's office."

"Hello. I think I have some information about the boots that you have prints of."

Centerville

After a pause, "Hold one moment please."

Mariam Yoder put Jack on hold and dialed Ben's number. When he answered she said, "Ben, I got a guy on the other line who wants to talk about the boot prints. He's on line two."

Ben switched to line two and said, "Detective Snyder here. I understand you have information about the boot prints that were mentioned in the paper."

"Yeah," Jack said. "I have 'em on my feet."

For a moment Ben's heart stopped. Cautiously he said, "Would you please explain?"

"I have the boots on my feet. Been wearing them for about a week. I got them at the A&P."

'But the A&P doesn't sell shoes or boots,' Ben thought. 'Is this some kind of joke?'

"Who is this?" He asked out loud.

"My name's Jack Showalter. I live in Beaverton. They call me Old Jack. Anyway I found 'em in the dumpster back of the A&P. I saw the man that threw them in there too."

Ben immediately came to attention. "Where are you right now?"

"I'm at the Arco station in Beaverton, the one *in* town."

"Stay right there. I'm coming to pick you up."

"Are you going to arrest me?"

"No, don't worry about that. But I want to know more about how you found the boots. Don't move. I'll be there in a few minutes."

Old Jack hung up the phone and sat on the bench beside the Arco station, and he waited.

Ben immediately called Nard, "I have a good lead on the boots. A guy just called and said he is actually wearing them! Let's go pick him up."

In minutes Ben and Nard were on the road to Beaverton. The day was getting hot. There was not a cloud in the sky nor a breeze in the trees. They wound

419

down the windows to help keep themselves cool on the short ride. When they arrived at the Arco station they found Old Jack nodding on the bench by the phone.

Ben prodded him and as Old Jack looked up Ben asked, "Are you Jack Showalter?"

Jack nodded, "That's me."

"Will you get into the car please? We want to take you back to Middlebury to talk about the boots and the man who threw them away. But first, can we see the bottom of the boots?"

Old Jack obligingly raised his feet to show them the souls of his boots. Ben and Nard could clearly see the broken lobe on the left soul. They ushered Old Jack into the back seat and returned to the sheriff's office. There they led the old man into an empty office and had him sit.

"Would you please take off the boots?" Ben asked.

"You're not gonna keep 'em aren't ya?"

"If they match the plaster casts that we have, I'm afraid so."

"But what am *I* gonna do? I need something to wear."

"Tell you what. If these *are* the boots we're looking for and you help us out as much as you can we'll buy you a new pair of boots when we take you back to Beaverton."

Mollified Old Jack took off the boots. As he did so both Ben and Nard backed away to try to avoid the smell of the old man's feet. 'We need to clean him up a bit too. Maybe take him over to the jail and give him a shower. Surely we have some old but clean clothes around we can give him. That is if these are the boots.' Ben thought. He lit a cigarette to help cover the odor and offered one to Jack. "Don't touch the filthy things," Jack declared.

Nard got the plaster casts and brought them into the room. He turned the left boot over and matched it to the cast. It fit perfectly. He nodded, "It's a match, all right."

420

Centerville

Ben called Miriam Yoder, who also acted as a stenographer, into the room.

"Well Mr. Showalter, tell me exactly how you got these boots. Take your time. Mrs. Yoder, there," he gestured, "will write down what you tell us."

"I'm not under arrest, am I?" Jack almost pleaded.

"No, no, no. We simply want to know all about how you got the boots. As I said, just relax and take your time."

Old Jack took a deep breath and then began.

"Well, it was a few days back. I live in an old farm house at the end of Royer Road and I go to the A&P pretty regular, you know, to see if there is anything good to eat in the dumpster." As she took notes Miriam wrinkled her nose. "Don't make fun of me. Besides there is usually good and clean food back there.

"Anyway a few days back, maybe a week, don't exactly know, I was sittin' in the shade behind the store waiting for them to come out with the produce. They usually do that around five or six in the afternoon. Anyway, like I said, I was resting in the shade when I saw this old, kind of beat up car, pull up and this guy got out.

"He took a paper bag from the front seat and carried it over to the dumpster and threw it in. Then he drove away."

"What kind of car was it?"

"I think it was a Chevy; it was dark green – I think."

"How about the driver?" Ben asked.

Old Jack thought for a few moments, "Well, best I recollect, he looked like he was about 35 or 40. Kind of a big feller. I'd say close to six feet and maybe two hundred pounds. I seem to remember that he had short brown hair and big hands. Strong hands.

"Any way, after he left I kind of walked over to look in the dumpster. To see what he threw away, you

421

know. And I found this paper bag and inside it were these boots. I tried them on and they fit perfectly."

"Anything else you can think of?"

Old Jack shook his head. "That's about all I can remember." After a pause he said, "Oh yes, he was kind of stoop shouldered and he swung his arms more than most when he walked, not that he walked very far. Yep, that's it."

"Do you think you would recognize him if you saw him again?"

"I don't know, mebbe I would."

Ben thanked Mrs. Yoder as she left to transcribe her notes. Nard followed with the boots. To Old Jack Ben said, "Well I guess we owe you a new pair of boots. Tell you what. How would you like a shower and get a clean set of clothes as well?. I'm pretty sure we can dig up some dungarees and a shirt and underwear from the jail. We'll go over there and see what we can do for you. After all the information you've given us is pretty good stuff."

Old Jack thought for a moment, "You're not going to throw me in jail are you?"

Ben laughed, "No, I promise. Surely you would like to have a good shower and clean clothes, wouldn't you?"

"Well I guess that would be all right at that. Haven't had a bath in a while and I guess I could probably use one. And some new jeans would be nice, but don't you forget about the boots! I need boots."

"I won't forget. We'll get you brand new boots over at Breeland's hardware store; they sell good boots there. We'll stop before I take you back to Beaverton. That's a promise." With that Ben took Old Jack off to the jail to get cleaned up. Afterward, when Jack had his shower and even a shave, as well as new clothes he looked like a different man. The jailer found an old pair of sneakers for Old Jack to wear until they got to Breeland's.

Centerville

Old Jack was almost comical as he picked through the work boots at the hardware store. He tried a number of boots until he finally settled on a pair that he thought would last him a good long time.

Watching Old Jack clomp around in his new clothes and boots Ben thought that no one would recognize him in the streets of Beaverton. But, he supposed, like Pig Pen in the Snoopy comics, Old Jack would revert to character pretty quickly. Ben paid for the new boots and then took the old man back to his dilapidated abandoned house in Beaverton.

He would never see him alive again.

Chapter 30
Fred Makes a Mistake

Fred fumed all night. He knew that he had to do something and that something was to find whoever stole his boots from the dumpster. Someone who had seen him and who might talk to the cops. Fred didn't need that.

Obviously he had been seen by someone at the A&P. It hadn't been an employee and it hadn't been the average citizen who would go shopping in the dumpsters behind the store. So it had to be a local drunk or bum who dug in the garbage.

Fred was getting close but he didn't know about Jack just – yet.

He knew that he would have to wait until after work today to take a good look behind the A&P. Then he could decide what he would do next. Of course the day at work was long. He wasn't very busy and so the time dragged. And as it dragged he got angrier and angrier. Not so much at his own stupidity but that some idiot found and actually *wore* his boots and made a footprint.

Fred feared that if he had been seen that he could be identified to the police and he certainly didn't want that. With his list of suspects narrowed down and knowing one of that person's haunts Fred knew that he just had to be patient and he would finally spot the person. Then he would take care of things.

The work day finally ended Fred drove to the store and parked across the alley behind the A&P in a lot reserved for the boutique next door. There he sat and watched. After a long two hours and missing his supper he finally gave up for the day. There was no activity behind the store at all but he would be back every day until he saw the person he was looking for. Quietly fuming Fred returned to his rooming house. Hungry he rustled through the refrigerator and made himself a sandwich which he ate at the kitchen table and sipped the accompanying glass of milk. He was constantly thinking of what he would do with the man when he caught him.

The following day after work he was there again, parked in the same spot, watching the rear of the A&P in hopes of seeing the man. His interest was roused when a store employee opened the back door and carried what looked like produce and dumped it into the one dumpster. But it was just a teenager and Fred knew it couldn't be a store employee that he was looking for. He sat for over two hours and saw no one else and so finally gave up for the day. The next day would be Saturday and he would watch all day, if he had to.

Saturday afternoon was always a good day at the store. Old Jack knew that around two o'clock in the afternoon they almost always threw away good stuff that didn't look right or was a little wilted or bruised. Today he was hoping for a small watermelon. Sometimes they got dropped and were cracked. They couldn't sell cracked watermelons, so they would toss them as a matter of course. And, as a matter of course, Jack would watch to see what they disposed of. Then he would dig through the trash and see what he could find that was good. Today he was especially lucky because he found a plastic shopping bag lying next to the dumpster – as though waiting for him.

Fred, almost in a stupor in the heat of his car, jerked to attention as he saw a man approach the rear of the store. The man picked up something that was lying beside the dumpster and then he looked inside the dumpster itself. Apparently seeing nothing worth rooting for he turned and walked to the row of trees and bushes that lined the other side of the alley. There he sat in the shade of a tree and almost blended in to the scenery.

Fred watched with almost animal alertness. Barely breathing he waited to see what would happen next. He didn't have long to wait for the rear door of the A&P opened and an employee came out pushing a shopping cart half filled with what looked like produce.

Jack's eyes lit up when he saw the cart. 'They must have had a bad batch of something,' he thought. He almost never saw them bring out stuff they were going to throw away in a shopping cart. He hoped there would be a watermelon. The teenager went to the bin where food stuffs were normally thrown. The other bin was used for cardboard, broken jars and bottles and other things that might be recycled. He threw the contents of his cart into the bin and returned to the store.

As soon as he was gone Jack rose from his resting place and scampered over to the dumpster. As he went Fred noticed that the man was wearing what looked like new boots and that they were of a much lighter color than Fred's old boots. He wasn't sure of what that meant but he was sure this was the man he was looking for.

Jack hit the jackpot this day. He did find the watermelon he was hoping for. He also found a securely wrapped piece of steak that had passed its date, as well as other good things. He still had two potatoes at home and a little cheese from his last foray. He should have a good meal today. Now if only he had a beer. He quickly stuffed his plastic shopping bag and headed for home.

Fred carefully followed at a distance as Jack made his way to the farmhouse he called home. Once inside Jack put the watermelon and the meat into the Coleman cooler he had scrounged at the dump. It still worked, if only he had ice. But he kept it kind of cool with bottles of spring water he filled in what was left of the farm's spring house not far from the house. The spring house also supplied his drinking and cooking water.

By now it was after three in the afternoon and clouds were gathering in the west. It looked like a thunderstorm might form in the afternoon heat. For Fred that would be ideal as he sat in his car and watched the

Centerville

dilapidated farm house where his quarry had gone. He watched for another hour and saw no activity. By then the wind was beginning to whip the trees and the sky was darkening. For Fred it was time to act.

He left the car and walked around the house looking through windows to see if he could tell where the man was. Most rooms were dark. Then Fred smelled burning wood and, while looking around, saw the smoke came from a makeshift chimney pipe protruding from a broken window on the second floor. Rounding to the back of the house he carefully opened a door and entered.

It started to rain.

The house smelled musty and as he walked Fred had to be careful of the rotting floor boards in the hallway he had entered. Stopping he listened for any sounds coming from the interior of the darkening house. Hearing nothing but the wind in the trees he ventured carefully into the interior. He stopped frequently to listen but now all he could hear was thunder rumbling as the storm approached. His senses were heightened to almost supernatural level. Now, even over the wind and sudden rain he could hear Jack talking to himself in the room to his right. Fred crept down the hall to the door that led through the kitchen and into the pantry. As he peered carefully around the door frame he could see the man squatting over a frying pan which was cooking on a makeshift stove made of cinder blocks and bricks. Wood was merrily burning in the stove.

'Perfect,' Fred thought.

Quickly Fred entered the room. Jack saw him from the corner of his eye and quickly stood. In doing so he tipped the pan of frying potatoes and steak onto the floor. He muttered under his breath and stopped to pick up the pan. Fred moved faster and kicked the pan away into a corner of the tiny room.

"What do you want?" Jack shouted over the roar of now pounding rain.

"I want you," Fred calmly replied.

"What do you want me fore?" Jack asked. "I don't even know you."

"Ah, but I know who *you* are," Fred replied.

Lightening flashed in the clouds and brightly lit the room for an instant. Jack thought, 'Oh shit.'

"Now I know who you are too. I saw you throw them boots away down at the A&P."

"Yes you did," Fred acknowledged. "And now you are going to pay for it!" In an instant Fred lunged and overpowered the much smaller man. He took Jack by the neck and shook him like a rag doll. He threw him across the small room and then picked him up again, by the neck, pressing his thumbs against Jack's throat. He lifted Jack as Jack futilely kicked at Fred's legs. Thunder rolled as Fred squeezed the life out of Jack Showalter. When his victim stopped moving Fred threw him across the room again, as though he weighed nothing. Then Fred pushed over the bricks and cinder blocks from the homemade stove opening the wooden floor to the flaming wood. Fred then piled more wood onto the fire and left, secure in the knowledge that the house would burn.

The fire spread. But Old Jack hadn't quite given up the ghost, as Fred had assumed. He painfully and slowly crawled to the doorway and then into the hall. There he lay across the threshold as the fire spread. He died of smoke inhalation.

The fire continued to spread but the damp and rotten wood did not burn as Fred had expected but smoldered for the most part as some flames reached the outside wall and greedily began to climb the drier wood. The smoke grew thicker as the fire spread to the second floor. A passerby saw the smoke and flames pouring from the broken windows and immediately went to the nearest house to call the fire department. In short order the firemen arrived and there in the wind, thunder and rain they quickly quenched the flames.

Centerville

Entering the house a firefighter discovered the body of Jack Showalter and relayed the information out to the captain. It was he who called for the coroner who came and took Jack's remains away.

The next day the fire marshal went to inspect the damage. His immediate conclusion was that the fire may not have been accidental because of the strewed remains of the makeshift stove and the scattered wood. He wouldn't declare it arson but did believe that some outside force had acted on the stove in order to scatter its fiery brands around the room.

The sheriff's office was duly notified and Ben found himself visiting the coroner on the following Monday morning. As he entered the room Roy Parker looked up from the dead naked body of Old Jack. "Hi Ben, It's not what it looked like on Saturday."

"What do you mean?"

"On Saturday I set the cause of death as smoke inhalation, which it indeed was. But it wasn't the causing factor."

Again Ben asked, "What do you mean?"

"Well it looks like this man was roughed up and then strangled."

One more time Ben asked, "What do you mean." He realized that he himself was beginning to sound like a broken record. "I mean, what do you have, Roy, that brings you to this conclusion?" There, that sounded better.

"Come and take a look at this." Ben crossed from the door and looked down at the body.

"My god, that's the man who had the boots!" He exclaimed.

"Boots? What boots?"

Ben quickly explained interviewing Jack Showalter and taking the boots from him. Ben pointed to the body. "He said that he would recognize the man who threw the boots away," he finished.

429

"Yep, that's his name. At least that's what the firemen told me. They said that he lived in that old farm house."

"So," Ben asked, "What is it that you wanted to show me?"

"As I said this man, Mr. Showalter did die of smoke inhalation. He has some burns on his back where a door frame collapsed and pinned him to the floor but that isn't what broke his hyoid bone. That takes a strong grip; and thumbs. This man was strangled. He would have died from that anyway. I'm really surprised he lasted long enough to crawl any distance at all. He also has bruises on his body, not from falling debris but because someone beat him. I think you have another murder on your hands."

Ben's mind swirled as he gathered this information. Now he had three murders to deal with. But this one was directly connected to the murder of the girl Mary Louise Weaver, because Jack Showalter was wearing the boots of the murderer. And now the murderer had killed, again, this time the only witness who could have identified him.

Enervated, Ben made his way back to the sheriff's office. It was only Monday morning and already he wished that the day was ending. He made his way to Sheriff Faulkville's office. He knocked on the door frame and entered.

"What's up Ben? You look beat. Are you ok?" The sheriff asked.

"I'm fine, just a little down. We have another murder on our hands; this one is Jack Showalter, the man who had the boots."

"What happened?" She asked.

Ben sat in the empty chair and said, "Apparently our suspect figured out who found the boots. Perhaps he staked out the A&P back lot. Anyway, it looks like he followed Showalter to the old farm house where he lived and then strangled him. Then he must have scattered a cooking fire there in hopes the house would burn down and take our man with it. But Showalter survived and was trapped, instead, by fallen burning debris. He died of smoke inhalation. But the coroner says that he was strangled first. So now we're back to square one."

"Well, it sounds like you ought to go over to Beaverton and look around. Maybe something will come up."

Ben nodded, rose from his chair and left.

He drove to Beaverton and parked by the Post Office, thinking of nothing as he idly watched the street. He knew he should visit the burned farm house but he didn't want to move. Across the way was a Speedy Market, open all day and night. Ben watched a man walk into the store. Something about the man grabbed his attention but he couldn't figure out what it was.

He waited and in a few minutes the man came back out of the store. He looked to be about Ben's age and had a familiar humped shoulder look and a long, swinging arms, gait. A car horn sounded and the man turned to look over his shoulder, right in Ben's direction.

"Holy fucking mother of god," Ben gasped out loud. "It can't be." He shook his head as the man turned a corner. For a moment he would have sworn that he was looking at a grown up Fred Swope. But it couldn't be. Could it?

And then it all suddenly made sense. Ben left his car and hurried down a side alley to get ahead of the man so that he could see his face again and know for sure. He stood in the shadows of a building on the corner and watched. Soon the man approached on the other side of the street and Ben was able to see his face clearly. He was right, there was Fred Swope. Older for sure but it was the same person he knew when he was a kid!

Ben returned to his office, lit a cigarette, and called the State Bureau of Prisons and asked for the status of one Fred Henry Swope. Ben was stunned to learn that Fred had been released four months ago, in March. As he hung up the telephone Ben's mouth was dry.

He rose and walked down the short hall to Sheriff Fauklville's office. Without knocking he entered and took a seat.

"What's going on Ben? You look like you've seen a ghost."

"I did. Just now."

The sheriff raised her eyebrows but said nothing.

"I was up to Beaverton looking around and I swear that I saw Fred Swope."

"Who?"

"I thought he was still in prison up in Rockville but he was released in March. Fred Swope killed four people back in '55 over in Centerville. One of the victims was my best friend Jimmy Harris. They put Fred away for twenty years. Well I guess his time has been served."

"I kind of remember that. I was in high school then. Tell me, is he related to Sarah Swope?"

Ben nodded, "She was his mother."

"Is it possible?"

"I think it must be. But I have to be sure. I have to track him down. I'm going to have to go back over to Centerville too. I want to make sure that his mother's house hasn't been disturbed."

The sheriff nodded, "Good idea. Go back and begin where it all started."

Ben rose and left her office, his thoughts swirling and he was again energized. 'I'll get that bastard,' he thought. 'I'll get him for sure!'

Centerville

Chapter 31
The Investigation Narrows

Ben returned to his office and immediately called Nard. They agreed to meet in fifteen minutes with Nard's full kit. As they drove to Centerville Ben brought Nard up to date.

"I don't know if you heard but Jack Showalter, the boot man, was murdered on Saturday. He was strangled. The other, maybe even bigger part is that Fred Swope, the son of Sarah Swope, has been out of prison since March. I believe it was his boot prints we found.

"Fred Swope killed four people back in Centerville when I was a kid. They sent him to Rockville for twenty years. He got out last March.

"We probably won't find anything in Centerville but I want to go through the house one more time just to be sure. I guess there is a slim possibility that we might have missed something."

Nard nodded, "We should take a close look at the cellar. Who knows, there might be a footprint there."

"There might be but I kind of doubt it. The floor down there has been pretty scuffed. I'm hoping that we might find a fingerprint or two on the handles of the wheel chair. What do you think?"

Nard frowned, "Well, I already dusted it once and didn't find anything. I doubt there will be anything new since then. But if you want I'll dust it again, just to be sure."

"Good," Ben said. He flicked the remains of his cigarette out of the car's window.

The house had been empty for six weeks and the air had a stale, almost dry, odor about it. It wasn't strong but it was there. Ben and Nard examined the cellar thoroughly. As expected there was nothing to be found. There were many old footprints and scuffed places where people had walked on the packed dirt floor. Ben found some old shelves, once used to hold canned goods but now empty save for cobwebs. There was a short stair leading to the outside entrance. But that was all.

Nard attempted to raise finger prints from the handles of the wheel chair but as he surmised, there were no new prints to be found. The same was true for the arm rests.

They combed the kitchen once again as well as the parlor and the bedroom. There was nothing out of place in either room. The men looked briefly through the pantry and the sun porch that led away from it at the back of the house. The place was empty.

"Let's go upstairs and take a look." They climbed the stairs that led off the kitchen. At the top Ben immediately went to Fred's old bedroom and opened the door. Nard was right behind. As Ben was about to step into the room Nard grabbed his arm and said, "Not so fast, Ben. Look down where you're going, look down!"

Ben looked down at the floor but didn't see anything but thick dust covering everything.

"What do you mean, Nard? All I see is dust."

"Some kind of detective you are," said Nard. "Look at that." He pointed at a spot on the floor. "Look closely."

Ben peered at the floor and then saw a faint footprint. 'No way,' he thought. He knelt and looked closely.

"Give me your flashlight. I left mine down in the kitchen."

Nard obligingly handed Ben his five cell flashlight. Ben hit the button and shone the light at the footprint at a shallow angle. Suddenly the lobes of a Vibram sole were clearly highlighted. It was a left footprint and one of the lobes was damaged in a way that was very familiar to both men.

Ben rocked back on his heels and looked at Nard. "Holy fuck, will you look at that? We got it! All these footprints lead only to Fred Swope. Nard, get as many clear photos of this print as you can. It's a shame we can't make a cast of it."

"We may be able to get the state police crime lab to take a look. They may have a way to lift the print. I know I don't have the skill or equipment to do it. But I'll get the best damn pictures I can."

Ben backed away while Nard removed his camera from his pack. He also pulled out a small tripod and opened its legs. Then he mounted the camera on it and began to take photos from as many angles and lighting as he could.

"That should do it," he said after taking a number of pictures.

"I'm going to seal this room and the house, once again. It's still an active crime scene. Let's get back; I want to see those photographs as soon as you've developed them."

A couple of hours later Nard brought to Ben the still slightly damp photographs he had taken. They spread them out on Ben's desk and the looked at them all.

"I like this one. It's nice and sharp and it really shows the damaged lug. Now I'm going to see the boss."

Ben took the photo and walked down the short hall to the sheriff's office. He knocked on the door frame because she was talking on the telephone. She waved him into her office. He took his accustomed seat and lit a cigarette while she talked. In a few moments she finished the call and looked at Ben and asked, "You look like the cat that ate the canary. What have you got?"

Ben slid the photo across her desk. She peered at it and asked, "What am I looking at."

"A hangman's noose, if we can find the man. Look carefully at this footprint. It's the print of a left boot with a Vibram sole. And note that one lug is busted just like those on the casts we have."

"Where did you get this?"

"In Centerville, in Fred Swope's childhood bedroom." Ben then explained the search of the house in Centerville and the fact that Fred's bedroom had apparently not been cleaned or even entered in twenty years. But Fred must have stepped into the room sometime in the last six weeks. It didn't matter when, and they couldn't prove that anyway, but the fact remained that Fred had been in that house and in that room. Furthermore the house had been sealed ever since the murder. The seals were unbroken when Ben and Nard entered the house that morning. To Ben that indicated that Fred had been in the house and that particular room on or before the time his mother was killed.

"He killed her and then explored his childhood home. Interestingly there was only one footprint in the dust. It's like he stepped in, then changed his mind and backed out. But he left a pristine print. I'm going to contact the state police to see if they have a way to lift the print itself."

"Good work, Ben. Now you just have to find your man. Do you have any idea where he might be?"

"Well I'll certainly start in Beaverton. There's too much evidence that points to him being in that area, especially since I saw him myself."

"Just remember that all you have is circumstantial evidence. It's good and hard evidence that puts him in those boots. But you still have to prove it. Don't move too quickly – take your time." The sheriff admonished.

Ben nodded in agreement and left her office. Sitting at his own desk he lit a cigarette and pulled his legal pad to the center of the blotter and picked up a pencil. He began by drawing a vertical line down the center of the page. On the left he wrote the heading, "what I know" on the right he wrote, "what I don't know."

Centerville

In the left column he quickly wrote:

What I Know	What I Don't Know
Sarah Swope – murdered	That Fred Swope killed anyone
Mary Louise Weaver – murdered	Exactly where Fred Swope lives
Jack Showalter – murdered	Where Fred Swope works
Footprints found at 1 & 2	That those were Fred Swope's boots
Jack Showalter had the boots	How long Fred Swope has been in the area
Fred Swope out of prison in March	Who actually killed those three people
Fred Swope in or around Beaverton	
Fred Swope drives an older dark green Chevy	

He flipped the page and continued.

"I suspect that Fred Swope is the perpetrator of these crimes but I cannot prove it. Evidence points to Fred Swope but it is all circumstantial. The footprint of a Vibram soled boot has been found at two of the crime scene sites, Sarah Swope and Mary Louise Weaver. I must assume that the same person who was wearing the boot committed the murders or was present at the time, at both locations.

"I know that Jack Showalter found the same pair of boots that left prints at the crime scenes, in the dumpster at the A&P in Beaverton. I know that Jack Showalter was murdered soon after he was interviewed in this office.

"I know that I saw Fred Swope in Beaverton three days after Jack Showalter was killed."

In frustration he tore the pages from the tablet, crumpled them and threw them in the trash. All of that information was in the files he was keeping. Lighting a cigarette he dialed the state police. The forensics lab told him that they believed that they could possibly lift the boot print but that if Ben had good photographs that would be sufficient as evidence.

"But if you wish, we'll send a team over. They are located in State College so it may take a day or two for them to schedule something."

Ben thanked them for offering to lift the print and asked them to schedule a time. Next he dialed the state correctional offices. He wanted to learn more about Fred Swope's release. From the Bureau of Prisons Ben learned that Fred Swope had been released on March 18th, 1975 to the town of State College. There it had been arranged for him to work for a local auto dealer, L&M Auto. That was all they had. They did agree to fax Fred's release papers and a photo. Again Ben thanked them for their help and hung up the phone.

Ben decided that once he received the release information and photo he would go to State College and try to back track Fred's movements. He notified the sheriff that he would be going to State College the next day to begin his search. She agreed that it was a good place to start.

Just then the fax arrived. Ben watched Fred Swope's face come out of the fax machine. Twenty years had hardened it and Fred looked older than his thirty-four years. Ben took the faxed material and went home. He would study what little there was of it tonight and get an early start in the morning.

Centerville

Chapter 32
A Bit of Clarity

The drive to State College was pleasant. The sun shone in a cloudless sky and the temperature was not oppressive, for a change. Traffic was almost nonexistent and Ben felt an unusual lightness. The fifty-five mile drive took about an hour and a half. He finally arrived at L&M Auto, which was near the center of town. He entered and asked for the manager. Soon he was talking with Jerome Showers.

"I'm looking for this man. His name is Fred Swope and I understand that he worked here last March. Do you recognize him?"

Ben showed the man the photo of Fred. Showers nodded his head and said, "Yep! That's Fred, all right. He was actually a pretty good mechanic and seemed like a nice guy."

"Did he ever get into trouble here?" Ben asked.

"Nope," Showers shook his head. "He was here on time every day, worked his shift and never complained."

Ben thought for a moment, "When did he leave your employ? Did he quit?"

"Yeah. I hated to see him go."

"Did he say why he was leaving?"

"No, just gave notice and took off. He's a good guy though. Every month I get an envelope in the mail with a cash payment on his car."

"What kind of car was that?"

"I sold him a 1965 Chevy Bel Air. It was kind of beat up but it ran and he worked on it himself. As I recall it was a two tone green. Dark body and lighter green top. Not my favorite color. Yeah, sold it to him for twelve hundred."

"Do you know where the mail came from?"

"As a matter of fact, I have his last payment on my desk in its envelope. I got it last week and I haven't deposited the cash yet." He led Ben to his office and rummaged through the detritus on his desk for a few moments before locating the envelope. He handed it to Ben.

Ben examined the envelope and could easily see the Beaverton post mark and the date of July 13, 1977. The address of L&M auto was clearly written and the return address was clear as well. Inside the envelope were two twenties and a ten dollar bill.

"May I have this envelope?"

"Sure. May I ask why?"

Ben shook his head. Thinking carefully he said, "This man is only a person of interest is something I'm working on. That's all. By the way, do you know where he lived?"

"Let me look that up." Showers went to a battered filing cabinet and rummaged through the drawers. "Ah, here it is." He pulled out a file folder and handed it to Ben.

Ben examined the few pages in the folder. There was really nothing outstanding or of interest. He read a few entries showing that Fred was a good worker and little more than that. There was a note, near the end of his employment where he called in sick. The most interesting and important bit of information was the address of the apartment house that Fred called home. There was also another address that had been crossed out. Ben asked about it and was told that it was a rooming house that Fred had stayed at when he first came to town. Ben wrote both of these addresses in his notebook and put it back into his pocket. He thanked Jerome Showers and left. Once in his car he carefully placed the envelope that had contained the money into a manila envelope. Then he studied the local map to find the two addresses he wanted.

Centerville

He went to the rooming house first because it was the closest. He spoke to the woman there but she gave him little information. Just that Fred kept to himself, paid on time and was never a bother.

Ben drove next to the apartment house. The brick building was three stories high but not in the better part of town. The apartment manager was not much better. His response to Ben's questions was almost like a litany on every roomer but he had nothing significant about Fred. All in all Ben learned nothing.

Never the less he drove back to Middlebury with a greater anticipation of finding Fred. After all he had concrete proof that Fred was living in Beaverton. Not only had he seen him there but he had a confirming address on the envelope. Now if he could only find him.

Returning to his office he placed the envelope and copies of his notes into his evidence file and reported back to the sheriff. All in all it had been a good day.

* * *

Fred's day was pretty good as well. He got off work early and drove to a local garage where they let him work on his own car. Fred paid only rent on the tools and for any parts he used. He wanted to adjust the carburetor and check the timing. He also checked the plugs, cleaning them and adjusting their gaps. The car had a little roughness to the engine at idle and that bothered him. He enjoyed working on cars and was considering looking for a job as an auto mechanic. Surely he could find a job paying more than the mill.

After an hour of work he started the car and it ran smoothly, Satisfied he paid for the use of the tools and drove away. Having time on his hands he decided to drive to Centerville, just to look around again. The place drew him like a magnet.

441

Centerville

As he came down route 140 into the village he saw a sign advertising the Firemen's Carnival on August 10 through 14. Fred thought it would be fun to go to the carnival and remember the good old days. He figured that nobody would recognize him after all these years.

He cruised down Center Street and when he got to the end of town he turned right and drove back down the Lower Street, now Chestnut but Fred couldn't make the change in his head. He parked a block from his old house and walked. As he passed the cross street that led down to McMaster's field he took that street to its end. McMaster's field was overgrown and the growing row of trees down by the run did not look at all inviting. He walked down the alley past where Harvey Miller's burned out house had stood. The house that replaced it, a ranch house incongruent in a row of two and three story houses, many bordering on a hundred years old, looked rundown and completely out of place. A rusted swing set stood crookedly in the unkempt back yard.

Fred continued down the alley to the next cross street. There he turned right and came back to the Lower Street. There he turned right again and began to walk back towards his old home. He cut diagonally across the street and came to the front door of the house. There he was police tape and a notice that the place was an active crime scene and it was illegal to cross. There was a seal over the door lock and in a moment of realization Fred turned from the house and continued his journey down the street.

Back in his car he drove to the Upper Street, up past the old Holiness Grove. It was still there and a new open concrete tabernacle stood where the older one had burned down back when he was a kid. He rubbed his arm as he remembered the burn he had received as he had set the tabernacle on fire. What a glorious site it was. He laughed as he recalled how the village fire department, all volunteers more interested in drinking at the fire hall rather than learning how to use their equipment, couldn't get the pumper to work. Mostly they watched as the neighboring town's fire trucks and teams tried in vain to fight a fire that was from the very beginning a losing proposition. By the time the village firemen got water to flow from their pumper the tabernacle was nothing but a pile of fire and ash.

Oh but it was fun!

He continued past the school and then on impulse drove the dirt road back of town, past the water tank, and down to where the dump was still used. When he got back to the valley road he decided to take the "back" way to Beaverton. The ride was a bit longer but had nicer scenery. He passed an Amish farmer pulling a horse drawn wagon loaded with bales of hay. Also Fred had seen a couple of farmers bailing Alfalfa that had been drying in the fields in the summer sun for a few days.

The wheat would soon be harvested and then they would rake and bail the straw. All this brought back memories of the good times he had when he was young. He missed some of those days, especially playing in McMaster's barn, building forts in the hay and straw bales. He remembered how he had built a circular fort from bales in the top floor of the barn where he could look out over the field and see everything going on there and at the lime kiln.

Unbeknownst to him he shivered slightly as he remembered watching the sheriff discovering Jimmy Harris' body there in the field. Jimmy was freshly dead – dead at Fred's hands. Fred recalled everything that had happened to him from that moment on until he was sent to Rockville State Prison.

Those memories made him shiver but also brought to fore the urges, and they were getting stronger. With a bit of clarity he knew that he would have to soon do something about them. His loins tingled with anticipation.

Centerville

Centerville

Chapter 33
Nightmares and Wet Dreams

Thunder muttered in the hills as Ben cooked his supper. Today he was having spaghetti, one of his favorite meals. As the pasta boiled he warmed the sauce, a rich meaty sauce that he liked. He wished that he had some garlic bread. But he did have a bottle of red wine, a good Merlot.

The thunder continued to rumble as he ate his meal. An hour later the storm hit town and the wind and rain lashed at the trees behind his house. It was Saturday but he had no plans to go out this particular evening. Instead he went over everything he knew. And tried to decide what he would do. Ben had a number of options. One was, of course, the address that was on Fred's envelope. He also wanted to check the service stations and garages in the Beaverton area to see if Fred was working there.

It never crossed his mind to go back to the silk mill to inquire about Fred. Why should he? It wasn't like they employed auto mechanics there.

That night he watched a movie on TV while the storms continued to rumble their way down the valley. In the night he dreamed.

This recurring dream was pretty much the same every time it came. It involved his tour in Vietnam. In the dream he and his partner, through an interpreter, were interrogating a captured North Vietnamese Army soldier. The NVA would not talk and began biting his tongue. Ben's partner hit the prisoner on the side of the head. The prisoner spat blood and the tip of his tongue. His partner pulled his side arm and placed the muzzle against the prisoner's temple.

"Tell him he's a dead man." He shouted at the interpreter.

Centerville

The interpreter said something to the prisoner, who turned to Ben's partner and said through his bloody mouth, "Fuck you!"

Ben's partner shot the man and as he fell to the floor the dream segued to Ben and his partner patrolling the streets of the city where they were stationed. The streets were crowded with Vietnamese and Ben realized that they didn't even know who or what they were looking for.

His partner said, "Let's pick up that girl. Maybe we can get her to do more than talk." With an evil grin he called out to the girl to come to the Jeep. She came and his partner still grinning turned to Ben. Shocked Ben realized that his partner had turned into Fred Swope as he reached for the girl who was suddenly the girl from the silk mill, Mary Louise Weaver!

Ben woke with a start and sweating sat upright in his bed.

'Shit, he thought, I know Fred killed her. But I have to prove it. The boot print is not enough. And why her? What was the connection between Fred and the girl? Did they know each other or was she just a random victim? Picked out of the crowd at a social gathering?'

For the rest of the night his sleep was restless and he woke in the morning tired. Sunday was not much better. The temperature rose to the low nineties and made the lawn mowing, that he had put off from the day before, almost unbearable. When he finished he sat on his front porch drenched in sweat and panting. He was too beat to even get a cold beer from the refrigerator.

As he sat on the porch his thoughts went back to the dreams in the night. He was positive that Fred was responsible but how would he prove it. If he found Fred and was able to talk with him maybe he would give something away. But he knew that Fred was cagy and it would be hard to get anything out of him at all. Well, with a little luck he would have the opportunity to talk with

Centerville

Fred tomorrow. He would go to the address on the envelope around six in the evening. During the day he would find every garage that had mechanic services. Either way he would get to Fred in person.

* * *

Fred's weekend wasn't bad at all. On these hot summer weekends Fred just wanted to explore the area. When he was a kid he never got out of Centerville but now with his long awaited freedom and a good car he could look around, maybe find some secluded places or simply enjoy driving the mountain roads. There were definitely secluded spots up there. Just the kinds of places he thought he might be needing in the next couple of weeks. He wouldn't be stupid again. Anything he left would be well hidden and far from the road.

There were plenty of short roads leading off the named road. All of them dirt or gravel at best. One side road led, after a quarter mile, to a dilapidated saw mill. Fred explored the crumbling structure. There was nothing there but a few rough cut boards. There was no equipment. It would be a nice place to visit after dark.

On one road near the base of the mountain, bordering a small river, he discovered a cave. It wasn't much of one from the looks of the entrance. Not having a flashlight he didn't attempt to enter but it made him think of the cave he had discovered and had used as a hiding place many, many years ago.

Fred was pleased with this Saturday. He was learning the geography of the area, finding interesting places to visit in the future. He especially liked the saw mill. He thought it was one of those places that would be visited seldom, if ever. It might take a long time to find anything hidden up there. A long time.

In the early hours of Sunday Fred had dreams too. They weren't nightmares but he remembered some of them. In one he dreamed of a girl he had seen in town. In the dream she turned in the street and smiled at him in a very seductive manner. When he woke in the morning he could not get her out of his mind. As he lay in bed he caressed is throbbing penis, thinking of her. Was she real? He hoped so.

He decided to go out looking – just to see what he could find. He knew he wasn't going to act, he wasn't ready yet, but he could look. He left his room and walked the streets, wondering here and there with no goal in mind. It was Sunday and he passed a few churches and saw some very attractive girls entering and leaving the sanctuaries. He strolled past the elementary school and paused to watch a girls' softball game. They were hot with their shapely legs flashing in their shorts.

Dreamily he walked on, still no goal in mind. He stopped at the A&P and bought a cold can of Coke from a machine and sat outside while he drank it. He watched people as they entered and left the store. Then his attention was captured by a girl, perhaps eighteen years old, leaving the store with a small plastic bag swinging by her legs. She was wearing a short skirt that really enhanced her well-formed and tanned legs. Putting his empty Coke can in the trash can next to the bench on which he was sitting, he rose and began to follow her. Maybe she would turn and smile at him, like in the dream, even though it wasn't the same girl.

She casually walked down the street, looking into shop windows, brushing her shoulder length auburn hair from her face, the better to see. Fred kept a good distance as he didn't want to alarm the girl. At one point she crossed the street. Fred followed on the opposite side until she turned a corner. He crossed at the same corner and continued to follow.

She soon came to the Historical Society museum and park. It wasn't much of a park, if you asked Fred, but it did sport a couple of pine trees and a shaded picnic table. There, as though waiting for the girl, was a young man about her own age. She joined him at the table and flashed a smile that lit Fred's heavens. For a brief moment he was in ecstasy until they kissed and sat at the table. Reality came crashing down around Fred as he kept his pace and eventually he returned to his rooming house.

He knew he would look for that girl again and hoped that one day he would meet her. What then, he didn't know.

Chapter 34
Ben Meets Fred

The next day Ben began the task of finding Fred. Surely he would be working at a garage. And so he searched. But every garage had the same answer when he showed his photo of Fred. No one recognized him, or heard of him.

Going down his list Ben stopped at Riches Arco station. It was on a back street and had a two bay garage that opened into an alley. Going through his usual routine Ben asked the manager if he recognized the man in the photo.

"Yeah, I seen him a few times."

"Does he work here?" asked Ben.

"No, he doesn't work here but he comes in once in a while to work on his car. It's an old Chevy Bel Air. He tinkers with it and pays for the use of the tools and any parts he needs. In fact I think he was in a few days back, said it was idling rough. He worked for about an hour and left."

"Do you know where he works?" Ben asked.

"No idea. All I know is his name is Fred and he pays for what he uses or needs."

Leaving the garage Ben knew he had hit a dead end. After all if Fred worked at a service station he wouldn't have to go to another in order to work on his own car. Not knowing what to do Ben drove aimlessly through the streets of Beaverton. Somehow his path led him past the silk mill. There, in the parking lot, he spied an older Bel Air; two toned green at that.

'No! Why didn't I think of that?' But he knew that Fred wasn't in his sights when he first began his investigation of Mary Weaver's death. Ben thought he was still in jail. With excitement in his heart he parked in the lot and, taking the photos of Fred and the boots, he entered the mill's office. Jim Fleming, the mills manager greeted Ben and offered him a seat in his office.

"Have you had any luck?" He asked.

"I don't know, maybe I have. Does this man work here?" He showed the photo of Fred to Fleming.

The man's eye brows immediately rose, so quickly and sharply that Ben thought they might fly off his head. At the same time the manager nodded and said, "Yeah, that's Fred Swope. He's one of our best mechanics."

"Could I see him – here?" Ben asked.

"Of course. Sally," he called to his receptionist, "can you find Fred and have him come to my office."

Sally nodded and turned to the PA system. "Fred, please come to the office." She said into the microphone - twice.

Ben could hear the announcement echo through the large building. He waited only a few minutes when he heard a man say to Sally, "Here I am."

"Go into Mr. Fleming's office, he wants to see you."

Seconds later there was a knock on the door. Ben rose as the manager told Fred to come in. The door opened and Fred Swope faced Ben Snyder for the first time in twenty years.

'Holy shit,' he thought. 'It's the law and Ben Snyder to boot! I'm dead meat.' For a moment he considered running but he didn't, not knowing for sure that he was in any kind of trouble. But he thought he was in big trouble.

"Fred, this is Deputy Ben Snyder. He would like to talk with you." At that Fleming left the office. Fred was stunned when he heard Ben's name. He did his best to conceal his surprise.

"Hello Fred. It's been a long time." Ben said.

"Yes it has, a very long time. So you became a cop?"

"Yes, I was in military police in Nam and got a job as a deputy in the Stone County Sheriff's office when I got out. I wish we weren't meeting this way but I have to ask you some questions." He pointed at a chair and Fred sat.

"What kind of questions?"

Ben showed Fred a photo of the boots and the damaged sole. "Ever own a pair of boots like this?"

Calmly Fred shook his head. He pointed to his feet, "These are the only boots I have. I got 'em when I got out of prison." He lied.

"Did you ever know Mary Louise Weaver?"

"The girl that got killed? Yeah, I knew her. She worked here and I did maintenance on her machine. She was a nice young lady."

"Fred, did you ever see her, in any way, outside of work?"

"No! I only ever saw her here at the mill. Nothing more!"

Ben thought Fred's answer was a bit stronger than the question deserved. He thought for a few moments deciding whether to ask Fred about his mother. If he asked, then Fred would know that the game was on. If he didn't, then he could keep Fred in his sights and maybe Fred would make a mistake. He didn't want Fred to run so he decided not to ask.

"It *has* been a long time." Ben said in a friendly voice. "So how you been since you got out?"

Calmer now Fred answered, "Not bad. It was a shock how much things changed when I got out but I got used to it. I learned to be a mechanic at Rockville and I got a good job here and I'm doing OK."

"Good, I just had to ask you about the boots so I can tie up some loose ends."

"But how did you find me here?" Fred asked.

"Like I said, just tying to some loose ends. In my investigation your name came up, so I looked you up and found out that you work here. That's one hell of a coincidence that I couldn't let pass." He shrugged his shoulders, "So I stopped here to ask. And here you are."

Fred wasn't being fooled for a minute. His mind was racing. What should he do? If he ran they would be on him like lightning. Best to stay really cool and maybe the heat would go away.

"Yes, here I am. I hope you are satisfied. They aren't my boots."

"But they are your size," Ben smiled and stood. "Thanks for talking with me. I'll let you get back to work."

At that Fred turned and left. As the door closed Fleming entered the office through the door he had left, one that led to the mill's floor.

'That was a fast entrance,' Ben thought. 'Wonder if he was listening through the door?' Aloud he said, "Thanks for letting me talk with Fred. He helped a lot in my investigation."

"Is he the man you are looking for?"

Ben shook his head, "No" he sighed, "but he was a person of interest." Ben turned and left the building. Sitting in his car his hands shook as he tried to light a cigarette.

'Holy shit!' he thought. 'The mother fucker has been here all along. Why didn't I look here first? If I had asked to interview the men who worked in the silk mill I would have hit on Fred immediately.'

He got his cigarette lighted and drove back to his office. There he went immediately to Sheriff Eva Faulkville's office. Without knocking he entered and immediately sat. He was still shaking.

"I got him!" he said.

"Who?"

"I found Fred Swope and even talked with him. He works at the same silk mill that Mary Weaver worked."

"No wonder you look so excited. So what happened?"

"Well," Ben said as he leaned back into the chair. "Of course he denied that owned the boots and said only that he worked on Mary Weaver's machine a few times and he never saw her outside of work. But he looked like he was thinking hard and answering my questions very carefully. But one time he nearly shouted when I asked him about seeing her outside of work. The way he said it didn't ring true."

"Did you ask him about his mother?" The sheriff asked.

"I thought about it but decided that he might start running if I asked and I didn't want that. I'm sure he doesn't know about the footprint in his boyhood bedroom. But I'll get him. I know where he lives, where he works and what kind of car he drives."

"So what are you going to do next?"

"Wait and watch. I still have to put those boots on his feet. If only we had a fingerprint that we could tie to Fred. But we don't" Ben sighed.

Centerville

Chapter 35
Should I Stay or Should I Go

Fred's immediate thought was to flee the area as fast as he could and go as far as possible. But then he realized that they would have every cop in the state looking for him. They didn't have any proof, only a photo of a pair of boots. Of course they had been Fred's but there was no way they could prove it.

'What will I do?' he asked himself over and over. But no clear answer came. He simply did not know what to do.

'I guess my best bet is to stay here and act normal. If they had anything on me they would have arrested me in a heartbeat. Maybe Ben was telling the truth about tying up loose ends. Maybe that's all I am, a loose end.'

He finished his work day, maintaining the machinery at the mill. The work, for the most part, was boring but now he couldn't look for another job. If he changed jobs they would want to know why. The cops would just think he was trying to get away from them. All he could do is keep doing what he had been doing for months. But now he had to keep his head down.

Fred left the mill and drove to his rooming house. The quietness of his room simply amplified his thoughts; caging him in so he could do nothing. 'Well, we'll see about that,' he thought.

And think he did. He rolled over in his mind every possibility. If he left the area, how long would it take them to find him, if they could in the first place? It was an option but he didn't think it was the best one.

And, he wondered, how would this affect his plans? When the urges came he couldn't control them – it was like he was compelled to do those things. Like there was an evil monster in his brain that took total control. He felt as though he was simply a passenger in some kind of homicidal robot that took over everything. It was if he was watching a movie, strapped into his seat, from the camera's point of view.

'If I stay what do I do? Without a doubt I know that if I find the girl something will happen. I don't want to do it but when the switch is flipped I have no control.'

Fred wrestled with all of these thoughts through the night. His sleep was interrupted with dreams of things he had done in the past. The dreams were horrifying but yet he felt a deep sense of satisfaction; contradictory feelings he was incapable of dealing with in any meaningful way.

In one dream he was helpless as he watched himself from a third person point of view as he strangled Mary Louise Weaver. He saw her every struggle and he saw himself hit her on the head with a rock and then rape her dead body. He awoke with a start and found he had a raging erection that would not go away until he satisfied himself and whatever daemon lived inside him.

That's what it was, he decided, a daemon that lived within him and took control to get what *it* wanted. And when it finished the act it would flood Fred with a total sense of satisfaction and pleasure, perhaps as a way of saying thank you for letting the daemon use Fred's body. A pleasant reward for a job well done.

It was a revelation to Fred. He understood now that had no control over these things, that he was a helpless passenger, along for the ride, but it wasn't he. He wasn't at fault. If he could he would remove the daemon but he had no idea how that was even possible.

And, of course, it wasn't.

And so Fred struggled with himself. It was something that he had never done as a youth and in prison there was no temptation because, big as he was, there were bigger men and he knew they could kill him, and would for a pack of cigarettes. Not once over the past twenty years had Fred had any kind of inner reflection about what he really was. Now that he faced it he blamed it, not on himself, but on a daemon living inside his body. When these things happened he was simply along for the ride, an observer.

But as he struggled, the urge was getting stronger.

At the same time Ben was struggling too. But his struggles were centered on putting those damn boots on Fred's feet. Ben knew full well that no jury would convict Fred just because he wore the same size as the boots, no matter that there were footprints in Fred's own mother's house and where they found Mary Louise Weaver's dead body.

Maybe he should have asked Fred about his mother. Perhaps if he had Fred reaction would have revealed something. Maybe revealing the fact that they had boot prints from his mother's house and the murder scene would compel Fred to act.

Ben wondered whether he should have brought up Old Jack. Ben was certain that Fred was involved in the death of the tramp. It was just too coincidental that Jack's house was burned down and Jack himself was beaten severely shortly after the newspaper printed the story of the boot print found in the ball field in Beaverton.

Ben re-created in his mind Fred's actions. He probably waited near the rear of the A&P, perhaps watching the dumpsters for days, until finally Old Jack came to scrounge. Fred followed him home and killed him because Jack could identify Fred. Jack was the only person who could identify him. With Jack's death the whole case was lost.

'There *has* to be something else, something I missed' Ben thought.

But there wasn't and Ben knew it. The only way he would get Fred was to get the man to admit to one of the killings. That was a challenge that was beating Ben over the head as Fred had beaten Jack.

Centerville

'I'm as positive that Fred killed these as he killed four back in 1955. I can't prove it in court but I am certain. Somehow I have to trick Fred into talking. I guess I'll go and talk with the boss.'

Ben left his office and entered the sheriff's. "So how's it going? You don't have your usual glow." She smiled.

"I am so positive that Fred killed his mother, Mary Weaver and Jack Showalter that I would stake everything I own on it. I wish to god that I could put those damn boots on his feet. I just don't know what to do."

The sheriff thought for a moment and then said, "Why don't you pull him in for an interview. Work him good and tell him about the footprint in his mother's house. Tell him what you got from Showalter and tell him that if he won't cooperate you'll arrest him for the three murders. That may get his attention. But wait a few days, let him stew, knowing that you are looking at him."

"Maybe I'll let him see me in my cruiser for a few days, at the mill, his rooming house and maybe shadow him on the street." Ben said. "Maybe that'll rattle him a little first, and then I'll pull him in."

"That might do the trick," the sheriff said.

Beginning to put a plan together Ben left her office and went back to his own.

'I'll get the bastard. I'll get him if it's the last thing I ever do!'

In the following days Ben made sure that Fred saw him everywhere. Ben would park his cruiser at the mill and shadow Fred back to his rooming house. He would watch him at the A&P or the Speedy Market.

And Fred was totally aware of it. And he didn't like it one bit. After about a week Fred walked up to Ben's cruiser at the end of his work day.

"What the hell are you doing, following me all over the place?" He shouted at Ben.

"Just doing my job." Ben replied.

"Your job is to follow me?"

"Yep."

"Why don't I just phone in every day and tell you what I'm going to be doing?"

"That's an excellent idea, Fred. Good idea but I'd still have to make sure that you're giving it straight."

Furious Fred stalked off. Ben smiled and followed Fred as he drove home. But nobody followed Fred at night. And that's when he made his next move.

The daemon, or whatever it was that occupied him, filled Fred with the urge to get a big knife. A hunting knife. But Fred couldn't buy one locally, he had to drive to Lewistown to the Army Navy store. He had seen a display case full of all kinds of knives. They would have what he needed.

Fred waited until Saturday night. He remembered the **OPEN** sign at the store showing business hours and on Saturday they were open until ten pm. Lewistown was a good forty-five minute drive. He would watch for the deputy's cruiser and when it was gone he would leave himself.

Saturday came and after lunch he didn't see the cruiser at all. He didn't know that Ben had been called to investigate a three car pileup and would be tied up for hours. Not seeing the cruiser was enough for Fred. He got into his car and drove to Lewistown.

Once at the Army Navy store he looked around at everything before focusing on the knife case. An employee asked him if he was interested in anything in the case.

Fred pointed at a large Bowie knife with a sheath. The clerk retrieved the knife and held it out for Fred to examine.

"Careful," she said, "it's sharp."

Fred balanced the knife in his hand and carefully touched the blade. It was sharp as a razor. He then ran it down his arm and saw the hairs cut cleanly off.

"It's sharp, all right. How much is it?" Fred asked.

Centerville

The clerk looked at a card and told Fred the price. It was higher than he expected but he had the cash so he bought it. He took it to his car and hid it in the wheel well in the trunk. He drove home and went to bed.

Over the next two weeks he was followed everywhere and then it suddenly stopped. That was good for the daemon was beginning to take over Fred's body and he knew why he bought the knife. He would take it to the Firemen's Carnival in Centerville. And that was next weekend.

Centerville

Chapter 36
The Carnival

The traveling carnival arrived in Centerville on the ninth of August. It always took a day to set up the rides. The local kids would watch and get shoed away when they got too close. The women of the village would bake cakes and pies for the cake wheel and pie pitch. The ladies auxiliary cooked gallons of chicken corn soup for their booth.

The firemen set up the high striker, a bell ring game that required strength to hit the pad on the striker enough to get the weight to rise up the tower to ring the bell. Most contestants didn't know that the game operator could rig the game with a hidden foot peddle so that it was all but impossible to ring the bell. Local farm hands would spend a fortune in quarters to impress their girlfriends before finally being allowed to ring the bell. Of course the game operator had a helper, a skinny guy who could ring the bell with ease. After all if he could do it, any strong man certainly could as well.

The BINGO stand had been refurbished for this year. It was freshly painted and some of the sagging seating boards had been replaced. Prizes donated by local businesses ranged from stuffed animals to canned goods to rotating fans donated by the local furniture store to the big prize, a one hundred dollar bill in a frame. It would be displayed right below a sign pointing to it. This particular bill hadn't been won in five years.

The penny pitch was also set up. It was a very popular game. It was set on a low platform inside a waist high railing which surrounded the board at more than an arm's length distance. The board itself was about three feet square. Printed on it were rows of squares, each containing a single number from 3 to 5. The numbers signified how much would be paid back in pennies if the

461

thrown penny was legally inside the square. The squares were barely large enough to hold a penny without touching the edges. The rows were arranged concentrically eight rows deep. In the corners of the board were three larger black squares with a circle in them. If a penny entered the circle without touching the sides it paid back twenty-five cents. In the center of the board was a large circle. It also had four twenty-five cent payouts. In the very center of the board was a small circle, barely larger than a penny that paid out one dollar. The rails were always crowded by kids and adults. When the board got too full the manager would use a long handled squeegee to clear the board. The pennies would fall into an apron around the board. Of course there would be players who claimed that they had a winning coin that had been squeegeed off. They never recovered their alleged winnings. After the carnival, kids would scrounge the area around the spot in hopes of finding a few pennies. The early risers found the few pennies that had been missed. The late arrivals found nothing.

The bandstand was also freshened up this year. The walls were painted, the lights all rewired and the loud speakers and jack board were all replaced as well. This year they had snared some pretty popular groups. There would be three shows every night. The music would range from country to rock and roll; something for everybody.

On Wednesday at six pm they would have the parade. The streets would be lined the whole length of the village. Local fire departments would bring a truck or two. Farm equipment dealers would drive a few tractors pulling flatbed trailers with pretty girls sitting on bales of straw. They would wave at the crowd but wouldn't throw anything. There was always a hardware store that threw fly swatters. The kids gobbled those up too. Many a house in the town had plastic fly swatters from this store.

Centerville

The National Guard would send a squad to march. As they passed the crowds could hear the sergeant quietly calling the cadence. "Hup, hup, hup", forever. And if everyone was lucky they would bring a tank. The local high school would send the marching band. They would either play only one tune for the entire length of the parade or simply a drum cadence. Everyone watching always remembered that the band didn't play when they passed – always the drums.

Girls with pompoms or batons twirling and tossing would march. Local businesses would ride by in cars and throw candy to the children who scampered after every tiny Tootsie Roll or Double Bubble. After the parade had passed there was not a single piece of candy to be found in the street.

Ambulances would sound the sirens and the fire trucks would follow suite. Older folks might remember the elephant from years past.

Back in the mid-1950s a circus was in Middlebury at the same time as the Firemen's Carnival. They brought an elephant to march in the parade and advertise the circus. When the firemen started the siren on the ancient firetruck which was right behind the elephant it went crazy and nearly stampeded the small crowd. Of course the guys from the local National Guard unit, who were in the parade, had to chase the elephant with their tank and jeep. Ben remembered that. He and his best friend Jimmy thought they were going to shoot the beast but thankfully they didn't have any ammunition for the tank's big gun. The tusker ended up down in McMaster's field near the lime kiln. There the local "mad" bull took it upon itself to protect his turf and attacked the elephant. Of course the bull lost. The elephant charged back and swatted the bull with his trunk, hard enough to toss the bull into the run. The bull was unhurt but was also a lot tamer after that. It must have taken a hundred people to corner the elephant and calm it down. Finally it was led to a circus truck and hauled back to Middlebury. But the boys thought it was great fun!

After the parade ended, the carnival opened and it was immediately crowded. Entry was free and even parking was only fifty cents. Local fire police would direct traffic and the sheriff's office always sent a deputy or two as backup and law enforcement. Mostly the deputies watched for drunks. There were always a few of them. Often someone would bring a pickup with tubs of ice. Men would put their six packs into the ice and tend the truck's bar through the night.

Once in a while a man would get riled because he didn't win at a game and the deputies would have to calm him down. And, of course, there was the obligatory fight. Usually over a girl and the deputies had to contend with that as well. All in all it was an easy shift and the carnival food was good. Not only that, but the entertainment was pretty good as well. The deputies would stroll past the games and through the crowd. Occasionally they might place a dime bet at the cake wheel or try their luck at the dump tank but mostly they kept to business.

Ben drew Saturday night. Saturday was always the busiest. Saturday's climax to the carnival was a fireworks display and the crowds came out for that.

At night the BINGO caller could be heard all over the village and many a night children would hear the caller and the sounds of the carnival as they lay in bed, listening through the open windows.

On Thursday night Fred went to the carnival just to look around. He strolled the lanes and looked. He had the best chicken corn soup at the ladies aid. He watched the cake wheel but didn't bet. He had no idea what he would do with a cake if he won it. Fred did see a very pretty woman working the game. She looked slightly familiar but he couldn't place her after twenty years. The daemon told him he should come back and look for her.

Centerville

He listened to the music and generally blended in. Nobody came close to recognizing him. Now he knew that he would come back on Saturday.

Ben visited the carnival on Friday; mostly to get the lay of the land, which was already familiar to him growing up in Centerville. The midway was like home. On the north were lines of booths ranging from the Pick-A-Duck game and other games for the little kids. Ben pitied the parents of any kid winning a goldfish. Then there were the food stands, mostly sweet things like cotton candy, caramel corn and the like. Down near the end were the pie pitch where you pitched ping pong balls at paper cups in hopes of winning a pie. Next to that was the cake wheel. At the end of the midway were the dunking booth and the high striker.

On the south were the ladies aid soup kitchen, a hamburger and hot dog grill next to the French fry stand. Picnic tables were arranged between the ladies aid and the hamburger stand. Behind these stands one could buy a cold soda. A few games, bottle toss, basketball throw and the ever favorite penny pitch finished out this side. Ben marveled that all these stands had probably not changed their position by an inch in the past twenty or more years.

And then there were the rides. The Ferris wheel dominated the end of the midway. Next in line was the Tilt-A-Whirl, a carousel, the Booster ride and assorted kiddie rides. The Booster ride was the most feared and paradoxically the most ridden. Some called it the vomit ride. Two cars on the end of long beams rotated so the rider was always upright to a degree while the supporting beam spun around the central hub, raising the cars to a height of about forty feet and then back to ground level. The ride lasted for about three minutes of pure gut wrenching force – or terror. More than once the ride operator had to hose out one of the cars after a ride

465

because a brave rider lost more than his dignity. Loose change was often found around this ride.

Out of uniform that night Ben blended in but the locals all knew him and greeted him. He too had chicken corn soup and a slice of cherry pie at the ladies aid. He only stayed an hour or so because he knew he would be back the next day. But it was entertaining.

Centerville

Chapter 37
Saturday Night's All Right for Fighting

Fred was edgy. He felt tense and anxious. He felt the way he always did in those times when the daemon took over, when he felt compelled to do something. He paced his room and stropped his new knife until he was almost afraid to touch the blade for fear it would take a finger off. It would slice anything and he knew that tonight it would and that it would taste blood.

The woman he had seen at the cake wheel the other night was constantly on his mind. She was his target. He wanted her. He wanted to cut her clothes off her body. He wanted to feel her tits, to squeeze them and bite them. He wanted to fuck her. His heart pounded as though it would break from his chest in his desire. And the compulsion was getting almost too strong. But he knew that he had to wait until the evening.

In the meantime he planned. He would grab her from behind and stuff a bandanna he had into her mouth so she could not scream. He would take her into the woods behind the last row of concession stands. And then, deep in the woods, he would cut off her clothes and rape her. Then he would cut her throat.

His loins ached in anticipation. He thought he would explode. But then a sudden calm came upon him. He didn't know what it was but he welcomed it. It would help him get through the rest of the day.

For Ben it was just another Saturday. He had to mow the lawn and do other chores around the house. In the afternoon he would go into his office and ponder, as he did daily, how to put those damn boots on Fred Swope's feet. There had to be a way. He knew that Fred understood quite well that the boots were key. He knew as well that Fred knew there was no way that Ben could prove anything. He regretted that he had not brought up Fred's mother and her death when he had the chance. If he could put Fred in the house he had him dead to rights because *then* he could put the boots on Fred's feet. Maybe he would bring him into the office on Monday and hit Fred with his mother's murder and then arrest him on the spot. Who knew, maybe Fred would make a confession. But somehow Ben didn't think that would happen.

Judy Stansell, nee Mecklenburg, spent the day keeping the kids in line, getting the clothing washed and hung on the line. She had a dryer but she preferred the feel and smell of clothes freshly off the line. She had to work the cake wheel tonight at the carnival. She was glad that it was the last night. Oh working the cake wheel wasn't bad. It was easy and she got to talk with just about everybody in town. But it was the long nights. She was up at five every morning to get the family off and then get to work herself and so was used to going to bed early. Well, tomorrow she could sleep in. This afternoon she had to bake a couple of cakes. She would have to be at the carnival grounds by five.

And so the day passed.

It was nearly five and Judy was the first to arrive at the cake wheel booth. She put the two cakes she had baked; a chocolate layer and an angel food cake on the display stand. She tied her auburn hair into a pony tail revealing fully her pretty face. She looked to be in her twenties but was, indeed, nearer thirty-six. Her trim figure was all due to the busy days she spent at the only chain grocery store in Port Mifflin. Not long after she arrived Sue Canfield came in with her two cakes. She also had the cashbox and they were ready for business. But things would be slow for a couple of hours. Things didn't really pick up, even on Saturday, until the farmers finished milking and got cleaned up for the carnival.

Centerville

Then they would be busy until the fireworks began. That's when all business stopped.

As the two women prepared their stand the other concessions and games began to come alive. Older local children, within walking distance, started filtering in, a number of boys heading for the penny pitch. It was a magnet to the ten to twelve age group.

Ben pulled up and parked near the large generator. It belonged to the traveling carnival and powered all their rides. Standard electricity was supplied for the rest of the carnival by the town. But it wasn't up to running the rides. He glanced around as he ground his cigarette butt under his foot. He hitched his belt and began to walk around the grounds. After his circuit he would stop for soup at the ladies aid and a coke from the Boy Scout troop's soda stand.

It was quiet this early but in two hours the place would be hopping. There could be close to a thousand people here by ten when the fireworks would start. After that the place would quickly empty and by midnight everyone would be gone except the carnies. They would work most of the night to disassemble the rides, collect the electrical cables and get everything back on trucks so they could head for the next town to do it all again.

He had his supper after his first circuit. While he was eating he saw that Bill Martin, his partner for the night had arrived and was looking around. He saw Ben and joined him at the picnic table. "Looks like it will get crowded later. It's a perfect night, clear and warm. I just hope it's peaceful."

"So do I. I suspect that we'll have a drunk and a fight of some kind, we always do." Ben said.

Bill nodded, "Yeah. Let's hope for the best. How do you want to work it?"

"Oh, nothing special. Just be seen and enjoy yourself. Centerville's pretty laid back. It ought to be an easy night, drunk or no and I prefer no." Ben finished his meal and rose. "Let's make a circuit." The two deputies walked up the midway, such as it was and down the other side long the rides.

The BINGO stand was opening up. They could hear the announcer, calling for players and women began to sit and collect cards for the first game. Attendants put small piles of dried field corn on the tables at regular intervals, near enough so that the players could keep themselves well supplied. If they had the called number on their card a kernel went on the number. Things always got tense after ten or twelve numbers had been called.

As Ben and Bill Martin passed the penny pitch Ben told him how he and his boyhood friend Jimmy would play the game. How they had strategies and methods. He remembered how Jimmy would put everything he won in one pocket and not spend it. The pennies in his other pocket were to be played. When the one pocket was empty he would quit. Ben never had that much commitment. The carnival always brought back memories. Most of them were good.

Ben and Bill kept walking their beat. Occasionally they would stop to talk to someone they knew who was working a concession or game; people from the town or firemen that they knew.

Fred came to town at six. He didn't want to get there early because he was afraid he would stand out. He assumed that by six o'clock people would start showing up and that the place would get busier and busier the later it got. He wore dark clothes and did his best to blend in. He wouldn't stop too long at any one place but kept moving.

His target, the cake wheel was always in site. He could see the pretty woman that had attracted him the other night. She was there, smiling at everyone and talking with most. Once, as Fred passed, he heard someone call her Judy. She would spin the wheel and when it stopped she smiled as she raked in all the dimes

Centerville

that had been bet and lost. Once in a while someone would win. Then she would award the selected cake. For each game that was played, a cake would be selected as the winning cake, if the wheel stopped on the winning number the player got that cake.

Fred watched the wheel spin and his head spun with it. He could hear the click-clack-click of the wheel's pointer every time the wheel was spun. The sound dove into his head and would not go away. He could feel the compulsion, the daemon begin to push forward. He could feel the tenseness in his loins and a tightness in his chest. His head was filled, stuffed, with whirling thoughts and sounds. The clang of the high striker blended with the Pennsylvania Polka played by the group on the stage.

He walked in a fog round and round the carnival, passing rides, games, food stands and all the rest. Not seeing any of them except the cake wheel. The wheel loomed larger and larger in his head. He wanted to hold his head and scream. There was only one thing that would relieve the pressure – but not yet.

Ben and Bill split up, each taking a different path around the carnival, stopping to watch and listen. Relaxed but ready for anything that might break out. Neither expected much to take place this Saturday evening.

As they followed their rounds they would meet at some point to compare notes. All in all it was a particularly quiet night for a Saturday. One time, when they met, they sat for a few moments and simply enjoyed the evening.

"I hope it stays this way," said Ben. Bill agreed as Ben crushed his cigarette with the toe of his shoe. "Well, back to work." The two deputies rose and continued their separate rounds.

It was about eight thirty that Ben first saw Fred. He didn't know that Fred had seen him first and was keeping an eye on him. Ben did not react when he saw

Fred. Instead he kept on walking. 'Not surprised to see him here.' He thought. 'Just as long as he behaves himself. But I'll keep an eye on him as much as I can. I'll know where he is.'

And so the game began. Each keeping an eye on the other without trying to let the other know. Fred kept close to the cake wheel. At one point he sat on a bench, his back to the game while he watched the band.

Ben stopped beside the high striker, watching Fred. He smoked a cigarette and while the young bucks paid their quarters and tried to ring the bell. "Don't shill them too hard, Pete." He said to the fireman running the game.

"Don't worry, Ben. I'll let 'em win – eventually." Pete grinned.

Ben smiled and continued his rounds. Time passed and the carnival grounds became more crowded. It was full dark and a half moon hung low in the sky. The night was clear and the moonlight bathed the carnival grounds in pale light.

A few boys out beyond the high striker lit off a string of firecrackers. The rapid explosions reminded Ben of Chinese New Year in Saigon; fireworks constantly going off in the night. Ben recalled witnessing a fight in the street and chasing one of the men involved. He was led into the narrow side streets, seemingly surrounded by fireworks and explosions. Then at what appeared to be a dead end he faced the man. He had a knife and lunged at Ben. Ben dived to the side and pulled his club. Swinging he waded into the man and soon had him lying in the street. Ben chose not to arrest the man because he had no backup. Kicking the prone man he walked away. Ben made his way back to the main thoroughfare, shaking. He could have killed the man. It would have been justified but never the less it was horrifying.

When he looked up he couldn't see Fred – anywhere. He turned completely around, gazing at the crowd but Fred was nowhere to be seen. Fred had taken the opportunity to slip behind the concession stands and into the edge of the woods which was only a few feet away. And there he waited, patient and now calm, like a lion stalking his prey.

Judy continued to work the cake wheel, unaware that she was the center of Fred's attention. In fact she was the only thing that he was aware of. He sat in the darkness of the woods and yet was only ten feet from the cake wheel. He felt the knife concealed in his waistband, hidden by his shirt. He fingered the bandanna tucked into his hip pocket. The pressure rose in his head. Every time the wheel spun it got louder and louder. Soon it seemed to match his heartbeat. His loins hurt, he had an erection, the air in his lungs felt as though he was in very deep water and he breathed in only short bursts.

Fred sweated and it ran down his back and between his legs. His arms grew taut and his thoughts slowed as the daemon compulsion began to take control of his body. His vision narrowed until all he could see through the leaves was the bright glow of the cake wheel, clattering deeper and deeper into his head.

Ben continued his rounds. It was nearly ten o'clock now and soon the fireworks would start. The country western band began to play and the song they played made Ben laugh. They were performing Homer and Jethro's, *The Billboard Song."* A song about the messages on a tattered billboard. Ben remembered laughing and howling when he first heard it sung at this very place when he and Jimmy were kids. Now the only line he could remember was, *"Simonize your baby with a Hershey's candy bar,"* The song made Ben laugh but he wondered how many of the current generation even know of many of the now long gone products mentioned in the song. Ben smiled as he continued his round. Fred was completely forgotten.

Centerville

The band finished and the lights went down. It was time for the fireworks. Most of the concessions and games had stopped in anticipation and people gathered in the lawn in front of the bandstand to get the best view. Blankets were spread and people sat. Children couldn't it still in anticipation.

Ben continued his tour and soon found himself near the high striker once again. Only about ten feet away he saw one of the women working the cake wheel duck under the boards and disappear behind the stand, near the woods. He saw a brief flash of flame and then the glow of a cigarette.

A bright flash and a thunderous boom announced the beginning of the fireworks display. In an instant the sky was filled with the brightness of the fireworks and the cracks and booms echoed off the mountain. Children and adults cheered as showers, blossoms and bright bangs filled the air. Smoke hung in the still air and began to sink a little. Soon Ben could smell the burned acrid gunpowder smoke of the spent fireworks.

Judy watched the fireworks from behind the cake wheel as she smoked her cigarette. She wrapped her arms around her waist and enjoyed the show. She had always liked fireworks, ever since she was a little girl and tonight was no exception. It was a good display and she was mesmerized.

Fred saw his target, so close and so absorbed in the fireworks that she would never hear him approach. Carefully he drew his knife and the bandanna and stood. Moonlight dappled him and the ground as he silently moved from the woods. Smoothly he moved to a point directly behind her. Bandanna in his right hand, crumpled he jumped. He swung his arm around Judy's neck and pulled her back against his body. She dropped her cigarette. Stifling her scream Fred violently shoved the bandanna into her mouth. She bit and fought. Kicking him she was transported to her youth, when she was sixteen. Then she had been attacked at the carnival and had been dragged into the woods. She had been lucky then and was unhurt. But now the nightmare came rushing back as she kicked and clawed at the man trying to control her.

Ben heard Judy's short, almost muffled, scream and turned to see what was happening. He couldn't see much except her white blouse in the moonlight. She looked like she was dancing but Ben had never seen a dance like that. He started toward where she was in order to see what was going on.

Fred dragged her into the woods and threw her to the ground. She hit hard enough that the wind was knocked out of her. She was helpless and that's what the daemon in Fred wanted. He knelt over her and savagely and cut her white blouse from her body and threw it behind him. He slit her bra in front and pulled it off as well. Judy began to struggle to a sitting position when Fred slapped her hard enough to knock her flat to the ground. Dazed she lay on the leaves, unable to fight. Fred fumbled with her skirt, trying to pull it down and off. But then he pushed it up to her waist and ripped her off panties. He clumsily climbed on top of her, pulling his engorged penis from his pants. He held the knife at her throat.

"Move and you're dead!" Fred hissed.

Ben came around the back of the high striker; fireworks and moonlight eerily lit the scene. He could see the woman on the ground and Fred on top of her.

'Fuck,' He thought. 'But I finally got him.' Ben drew his gun and aimed at Fred.

"Don't do it Fred!"

In a rage Fred turned and saw Ben, with gun drawn. Moonlight glinted off Fred's knife blade as he rose and lunged.

The single shot was not heard among the fireworks finale.

Centerville

Huntsville, AL
August, 2019 – January, 2022
Revised Edition November 2024

www.ingramcontent.com/pod-product-compliance
Lightning Source LLC
Chambersburg PA
CBHW030847030726
47495CB00005B/1412